KISSING

"Are you crying, Gill[...] soft amazement.

"Don't be ridiculous. As if I would cry over [...] stupid as this." As if she would cry over the mistaken assumption that he liked her, when apparently he did not.

"Then what is this I see on your cheek?" He gently brushed a gloved finger over her face. "Yes, there is a tear, sparkling like a jewel. How extraordinary."

"Don't you dare make fun of me." She glared up at him, rather a tricky feat when one was trying not to bawl.

He barked out a laugh. "Believe me, I find this situation anything but amusing. Painful would be a more apt description."

That dried her tears. "If you don't let me go this instant, I will make you very sorry. And I don't give a damn if you are a bloody duke." He wouldn't be the first man she'd kneed in the bollocks, and she didn't suppose he'd be the last.

"Right now, I don't give a damn either."

And with that, Leverton hauled Gillian up on her toes and covered her mouth in a fierce, smoldering kiss . . .

Books by Vanessa Kelly

MASTERING THE MARQUESS

SEX AND THE SINGLE EARL

MY FAVORITE COUNTESS

HIS MISTLETOE BRIDE

The Renegade Rogues
SECRETS FOR SEDUCING A ROYAL BODYGUARD
CONFESSIONS OF A ROYAL BRIDEGROOM
HOW TO PLAN A WEDDING FOR A ROYAL SPY
HOW TO MARRY A ROYAL HIGHLANDER

The Improper Princesses
MY FAIR PRINCESS

AN INVITATION TO SIN
(with Jo Beverley, Sally MacKenzie, and Kaitlin O'Riley)

Published by Kensington Publishing Corporation

My FAIR PRINCESS

VANESSA KELLY

ZEBRA BOOKS
KENSINGTON PUBLISHING CORP.
http://www.kensingtonbooks.com

ZEBRA BOOKS are published by

Kensington Publishing Corp.
119 West 40th Street
New York, NY 10018

All Kensington titles, imprints, and distributed lines are available at special quantity discounts for bulk purchases for sales promotion, premiums, fund-raising, educational, or institutional use.

Special book excerpts or customized printings can also be created to fit specific needs. For details, write or phone the office of the Kensington Sales Manager: Attn.: Sales Department. Kensington Publishing Corp., 119 West 40th Street, New York, NY 10018. Phone: 1-800-221-2647.

Zebra and the Z logo Reg. U.S. Pat. & TM Off.

First Printing: September 2016
ISBN-13: 978-1-4201-4109-2
ISBN-10: 1-4201-4109-0

eISBN-13: 978-1-4201-4110-8
eISBN-10: 1-4201-4110-4

10 9 8 7 6 5 4 3 2

Printed in the United States of America

Chapter One

Sicily
February 1816

The man who'd murdered her stepfather was finally in her sights.

Unfortunately, he was still beyond her rifle's range. Gillian Dryden breathed out a curse that would have had her grandmother boxing her ears. They would need to get much closer to the bandits before taking a shot.

"You didn't learn that dainty expression in the salons of Palermo's distinguished nobles, I'll wager," her brother murmured. Like her own, Griffin Steele's gaze was locked on the small cluster of men in the gorge below them.

"Indeed not. Their language is a great deal more shocking."

When Griffin huffed out a laugh, Gillian's heart warmed with wonder and gratitude. Strictly speaking, he was her half brother, which didn't make him any less of a marvel. She'd only met him a few weeks ago, and yet there he was lying next to her on a limestone outcropping in the hardscrabble Sicilian hills. As was hers, Griffin's rifle was aimed with deadly intent. If that didn't constitute true familial affection, she couldn't think what did. Particularly since he didn't entirely approve of her actions.

"You do realize I'm here under duress," he said, echoing her thoughts. That was another thing she'd discovered about him. He had a precise ability to read people.

Gillian peered at their target, a hulking man who'd just swung off his horse and handed the reins to one of his men. His gang of cutthroats had stopped to rest and to water their animals. One of the bandits quickly built a fire, while another retrieved a brace of rabbits hanging from a saddle and began skinning them. By all appearances they would be loitering for some time in the pleasant meadow. That suited Gillian perfectly. It was easier to kill a man taking a leisurely smoke under a tree than to pick him off the back of a cantering horse.

"I'm aware you don't wish to be here," she said quietly. "I'm very grateful for your company."

"Your dear mother will roast me over the coals if she finds out about this little escapade. As will my wife," he muttered.

One only had to look into Griffin Steele's cool, dark gaze to realize how dangerous he was, but he turned into a puppy dog in the presence of his wife, Justine. With everyone else, a genial wolfhound was a better description for him, but one with a lethal bite.

"They won't have anything on Grandmamma," Gillian said. "You can't imagine what she'd say about this."

Not that it mattered what her mother or grandmother thought. Not when she was so close to achieving the goal she'd pursued these past five long years. And now that Antonio Falcone was in her sights, Gillian would allow nothing to stop her from exacting justice.

Griffin shifted, as if trying to get comfortable on the unforgiving rock surface beneath them. "Actually, I've heard quite a lot on the subject from Lady Marbury. She's extremely concerned about your impetuous behavior."

Gillian twisted to look at him, narrowing her gaze on his tanned, clever face. His eyes were shadowed under the brim of his slouched hat, and his features were devoid of expression. The long black hair clubbed back over his shoulders and the thin scar running down the side of his face made him look more like the bandits below than a wealthy, educated man who had royal blood running through his veins.

"They want you to get me in hand, don't they?" she asked. "I assure you, it's pointless."

"So I told Lady Marbury. She found my reply less than satisfactory, I'm sorry to say."

"If you don't approve of what I'm doing, then why are you here? This isn't your fight. And it's not like I don't have help."

He snorted. "An old man and a boy."

"Stefano taught me everything I know, and his grandson is coming along quite nicely."

Griffin glanced over his shoulder to a rocky alcove where the man and the boy held the horses. "Stefano looks to be at least eighty, and his grandson is barely big enough to mount a horse."

Gillian switched her attention back to the bandits. "So that's why you came with me today. You promised my family you'd protect me. It's entirely unnecessary, I assure you." She had been patiently working toward this moment for years. If she didn't have the strength, the skill, and the brains to take down Falcone now, she didn't deserve another moment's peace.

I won't fail you, dear Step-papa.

"I told Lady Marbury that you're more than capable of defending yourself," he said. "I just thought I'd come along and lend a hand."

She was so grateful that Griffin never talked to her as if

she were some silly miss. Or worse, treated her like a lunatic for seeking vengeance for her stepfather's brutal murder. She was fine with not being like other girls, but it wasn't always easy to be an outsider, living half in the shadows with her name—her very existence—marked by scandal. The fact that her half brother and his wife had come to Sicily to seek her out warmed Gillian down to her toes.

They studied the men below in the meadow. Dappled sunlight fell along the banks of the nearby stream, and the trees partly obscured a clear shot. The best firing position would be down and to the right, on a rutted path that ran along the cliffs.

Gillian had received word only a few hours ago from a local villager that Falcone was on the move. She'd had to scramble, but fortunately it had been early enough that no one had seen her race to the stables of her grandmother's villa—no one except Griffin. She'd been stunned when, instead of trying to stop her, he'd simply rolled his eyes and saddled another horse.

"You don't need to do this, you know," Griffin murmured. "I can take care of it for you."

She peered at him, squinting in the strong morning sunlight. From the look on his face, he was entirely serious. That unfamiliar sense of gratitude once more curled its warmth around her heart.

"No one's ever offered to do that before," she said softly.

He flashed a grin. "Most people aren't in the habit of offering to shoot people for young ladies."

"Except for you, of course."

"You wouldn't be the first."

For a fleeting moment she was tempted to let him kill Falcone for her. After all, it wasn't as if she relished killing. The first time she'd taken down one of the bandit's men, she'd barely escaped before having to drop to her knees and retch up the contents of her stomach. The second and third time, the same thing had happened. It might even be the same with Falcone himself, despite the fact that he'd been the one to put the pistol to her stepfather's head and pull the trigger. Seeking justice—or vengeance, some would call it— did tend to wear on one's soul. More than once, she'd almost given the whole thing up. But for too long Falcone and his men had been allowed to roam free, committing murder and mayhem. Gillian would hold fast to her purpose, and to the vow she'd made to her stepfather the day they'd entombed him in cold marble.

"I'm touched, Griffin, but I need to see this through."

He blew out a frustrated breath. "You do realize the bastard's death will never truly bring you peace."

"I don't seek peace; I seek justice."

"Revenge, more like it. The authorities in Palermo should handle this."

A derisive snort was her only reply. Her grandmother, the Countess of Marbury, had spent years seeking justice from the authorities. They weren't interested, and neither was her stepfather's heir, the current Count Paterini. As long as Falcone continued to fill their coffers with bribes, the authorities and the local noblemen were content to let the bandit lord wreak havoc on the Sicilian countryside.

Griffin studied her. "You needn't soil your hands with their blood, my dear girl."

"They're soiled already, Griffin."

He shot her a puzzled look before understanding dawned. "Good God. How many men have you killed over this?" He sounded thunderstruck.

"A few," she hedged.

"Oh, is that all?"

"They deserved it."

The bandit scum had killed Step-papa, his two body-guards, and the young groom accompanying him on that fateful trip through the Gorges of Tiberio. It was fitting that

Gillian would deliver justice in almost the same spot where those innocents had breathed out their last moments of existence.

Her brother cursed under his breath. "Gillian, this should not be your life."

"Do I look like a proper young lady to you?"

He cast a sardonic glance at her attire—sheepskin coat, buckskin breeches, and riding boots. "You could be. You're an attractive, respectable-looking girl when you're not disguised as a bloodthirsty ruffian."

"I thought you, of all people, would understand," she said, exasperated.

"I do, but if you continue along this course, it will take its toll. Killing always does."

She managed not to flinch. "I don't have a choice."

"There is always a choice, Gillian."

She flicked her gaze back to Falcone, who was sitting on a rock as he smoked a pipe. He was also splendidly out in the open, but she had to get closer.

"There's no point in discussing this. I'm doing it," she said.

"No, I will—"

"It was my fault," she hissed. "That's why *I* have to do it. No one else."

He frowned. "I don't understand."

She had to swallow before she could answer. "It's my fault that my stepfather was murdered. I sent him straight into Falcone's line of fire."

"So . . . it's guilt that motivates you. Killing Falcone will likely be nothing more than an empty victory, if such is the case." Griffin squeezed her arm. "As long as you continue to blame yourself, you will never find peace."

She hoped to God he was wrong. He had to be wrong. "You are the most irritating man I have ever met."

"So my wife informs me on a regular basis."

Below them, Falcone knocked the tobacco out of his pipe and then hauled his formidable bulk to his feet. Gillian mentally cursed as he began to stroll over to join his men under the trees.

She turned and signaled to Stefano and his grandson. The old man pulled his pistol from the brace on his saddle, ready to cover her back.

"Griffin, help me or not, but I'm doing this now." Before he could answer, she slung her rifle across her back and slithered away from the edge. As quickly as she dared, she crawled down the narrow, rutted path that ran along the rim of the gorge. If she stood, it was unlikely the men below would notice her, but she was taking no chances. Falcone had evaded her too many times over the years.

Her brother followed her. She could practically feel him seething with frustration, but he made not a sound. She had to give him credit—he was awfully good.

A few feet short of her goal, Gillian held up a hand to halt her brother's advance. She stole a quick glance over her shoulder. Just behind them Stefano crouched, his tanned, leathery features cast into shade by his broad-brimmed hat. Griffin's expression registered shock at the sight of the old man so close, pistols at the ready. Stefano might be getting on in years, but he was still vital and strong. He could move like a ghost, silent and lethal, at her command.

After crooking a finger to signal Griffin to follow, Gillian wriggled up to the edge of the cliff. She cautiously peered over the rocks and saw the bandits under a stand of beech trees, their attention on their flasks of wine as they waited for the rabbits to cook over the open flame. Unfortunately, Falcone was half obscured by one of his men and was partly in shade. She would have to stand up if she wanted a clear shot.

She came up in a crouch and pulled the rifle from her back. She'd already checked it three times, but did so once more. The Baker was a fine weapon. It had belonged to a

Hussar, and had a light, short carbine, which made it easier
to handle. But it was less accurate than rifles used by sharp-
shooters. Although she could reload quickly if she missed
her shot, she'd make an inviting target while she did.

So get it right the first time.

Griffin came up beside her. He gave her a terse nod as he
brought his rifle to bear on the men below. But he then
sucked in a harsh breath when Gillian rose swiftly to her
feet, taking aim at Falcone.

As bad luck would have it, an eagle soared right over-
head, screeching out a cry. The men below automatically
glanced up, directly at her and Griffin.

Gillian fired. The shot echoed through the gorge in a
deafening report. Another boom followed as Griffin fired a
second later. Falcone stumbled against a low rock, roaring
as he clutched his shoulder. Another bandit went down like
a sack of grain tossed from a cart.

The other bandits scrambled for their weapons.

"Get down, you daft woman," Griffin barked, reaching to
pull her away from the edge.

Gillian evaded his grasp, sliding on the rocky scree and
almost losing her footing. Still, she managed to recover and
reload. Griffin did the same as he let loose a string of hair-
raising curses. She yanked up her rifle, took aim, and fired
again.

A moment later, a bullet slammed into her shoulder,
throwing her to the ground. The back of her head connected
with rock, and pain exploded through her skull. Gillian lay
there stunned, staring up at a sky that shimmered with a
milky haze. Her ears rang with the sound of a thousand
church bells.

Move, you idiot.

She couldn't—not even one blessed finger.

Griffin's face suddenly swam above her, only slightly less
hazy than the sky. Gillian forced the words out past the pain.
"Did I get him?" she whispered.

"For Christ's sake, not now," Griffin spat.

He pressed something into her shoulder, so hard that bile rose in her throat and black dots swam across her vision. She forced back the encroaching darkness.

"Is Falcone dead?" she ground out.

Griffin glanced over his shoulder and barked something to Stefano. Then he turned back to her.

"Yes," he said.

Relief swamped her, momentarily driving out the fire consuming her body.

"We did it, Griffin." If she had to die in the effort, thank God she'd been successful.

"Indeed." Griffin yanked something tight around her shoulder and upper arm. She had to bite back a shriek. "But trust me, dear sister, your killing days are over."

When he lifted her onto his shoulder, the blackness rushed in, pulling her away from the heat, the light, and the pain.

From everything.

Chapter Two

London
May 1816

Charles Valentine Penley, Sixth Duke of Leverton, hastily stepped off the curb and into the street, narrowly avoiding collision with three little boys barreling down the pavement on their way home from the park. As much as he could appreciate their high spirits, they were covered in mud, and one generally didn't make social calls looking as if one had been rolling around in the stables.

"Slow down, you little hellions," Kates yelled from the seat of the curricle. "You almost knocked His Grace flat on his arse." Kates, an excellent groom, occasionally forgot himself as his rather disreputable origins in the London stews bubbled to the surface.

"No need to shout," Charles said.

"They might have spooked the horses. And you all but scared the wits out of the poor things, jumpin' off the curb like that," Kates added in an accusatory tone. In his world, nothing was worse than ruffling the high-strung nerves of the animals under his care.

"How dreadful of me," Charles said. "Do you think I should apologize to them?"

When Kates was upset, his resemblance to a sad-eyed basset hound verged on the remarkable. "Now, no need to make a jest out of it, Yer Grace. You know this pair hates goin' out in all this wind. It's well-nigh a gale, I tell you."

As if to underscore the point, a stiff breeze swirled down Brook Street, kicking up both dust and the skirts of the three nursemaids hurrying after their ill-behaved charges. Two were young and pretty and smiled flirtatiously as they passed, murmuring apologies for any inconvenience the boys might have caused.

Charles gave them a polite smile before turning back to Kates. "Very well, you may return to Grosvenor Square now I'm not sure how long I'll be staying, and God forbid I should keep the horses out in a hurricane."

It was merely a blustery day, an unseasonably cool one in an unseasonably cool spring. Still, it felt good to be outside. Only recently returned from his estate in Lincolnshire, Charles had spent the last several days buried up to his eyeballs in paperwork in his parliamentary offices. He already missed the long rides, the crisp, clean air, and the quieter, more ordered way of life in the country.

Kates cast an assessing glance at the slate-gray sky. "Are you sure, sir? It looks as if it might be comin' on rain. You don't want to be gettin' them boots wet. Jobbins will be pitchin' a fit if you do."

"Let me explain something, Kates. I'm the duke, and Jobbins is the valet. I pay his wages. I do not pay him to pitch a fit."

The groom eyed him uncertainly. "If you say so, Yer Grace."

The staff at Leverton House lived in terror of Jobbins, who'd been around since Noah's Flood and who had a knack for reducing even the butler to grudging compliance.

Jobbins had acquired his intimidating manner from his previous master, the Fifth Duke of Leverton. Unlike that duke, however, Jobbins had a heart. Charles had always found it rather amazing that his valet treated him with more genuine affection than his own father had.

Charles took pity on his clearly worried groom. "Would you rather the horses get wet or me?"

Kates darted another alarmed glance at the sky, then at the patiently waiting pair. "Right you are, sir. I'd best be getting these two safely home."

While Kates set a brisk trot down Brook Street, Charles turned to mount the steps of the building in front of him. The handsome brick and stucco townhouse had belonged to the Marburys for as long as he could recall, although it had been rented until Lady Marbury and her family's recent return to England after many years abroad.

They were his family too, as he had to remind himself. He and Lady Marbury were cousins a few times removed on his father's side, and Lady Marbury's daughter, now the widow of an Italian aristocrat, had been married at a young age to one of Charles's maternal uncles. That union had only lasted a few years before his uncle died of a heart attack in the bed of a notorious courtesan. The young dowager duchess had then gone on to scandalous escapades of her own—so scandalous, in fact, that the Marburys had taken their errant daughter and decamped to the Continent, settling first in Naples and then Sicily.

They had remained there for well over twenty years, even after the death of Lord Marbury. Why they had returned now—and why Charles had been so peremptorily summoned by Lady Marbury—was a mystery that instilled a certain caution. But they *were* family, and Penleys always put family first. That lesson had been drummed into his head from an early age and wasn't one he was likely to forget.

A liveried footman ushered him in with a quiet greeting,

taking his hat and gloves. A moment later, an extremely correct butler appeared from the back of the house to escort him to Lady Marbury. The surroundings exuded an atmosphere of quiet, familiar elegance. Charles had visited the house often as a child, and he could almost imagine nothing had changed since those long-ago days, before the family's ignominious fall from grace and social exile from England.

The butler led him to the back of the house, to what he vaguely recalled was Lady Marbury's private sitting room. That was interesting, since he'd been expecting to make a formal call. After all, the last time he'd seen her had been when he was a callow youth of eighteen, on the Grand Tour with his tutor. Much had changed since then, including the fact that Charles was now Duke of Leverton.

After a quick tap on the door, the butler announced him.

Charles entered the small room and came to a halt, feeling as if he'd stepped back in time. The furnishings hadn't altered a jot. Even the yellow swags draping the windows looked the same, albeit rather faded. He remembered the ornate French bracket clock on the mantel and the portrait of a previous earl of Marbury, painted by Romney, hung over the fireplace.

It made him feel like a child again, not a sensation he relished.

A soft laugh jerked him out of his reverie. "It's uncanny, isn't it? I almost felt like a young woman when I walked into this room. We have been away for much too long."

Lady Marbury stood there, elegantly attired in a style more French than English. Her clear blue eyes regarded him with amusement, and a welcoming smile lit up her handsome, barely lined face. Only the white hair under a dainty lace cap gave testament to her age of more than seventy years. Her life had not always been easy, but she had certainly retained much of her beauty and quiet grace.

Her smile slid into a grin. "Charles, it's very good to see

you again. I do hope, however, that my appearance has not struck you dumb. Have I aged so much that you no longer recognize me?"

"Please forgive me," he said, taking her hand. "I truly was struck dumb by your youthful appearance. You've hardly aged a day."

"What nonsense." She stretched up and pressed a fleeting kiss to his cheek. "You too have changed a great deal. You've grown into a handsome man, which is hardly surprising since you were a good-looking and charming boy."

He mentally blinked at her affectionate compliment. The Lady Marbury he remembered was not a woman prone to such high praise and flattery.

And no one would have ever labeled him charming— awkward and tongue-tied was more like it. True, he'd acquired social polish over the years. But since Lady Marbury wouldn't know that, her words made him even more suspicious. He knew her to be a brilliant woman and the true force behind her husband's political career before their exile to Sicily. Lady Marbury had always been the canny one, a fact he must not forget.

"Please sit, Charles," she said, waving him to an armchair covered in gently faded but still beautiful embroidery. She took the claw-footed settee across from him. "I hope you'll forgive our rather shabby appearance. We've not yet had the chance to redecorate."

"There's nothing shabby about it, my lady. It's charming and very . . . homey."

"That's one way of putting it," she said in a dry tone that sounded more like her. "And, please, there is no need for such formality between us. If you keep referring to me as 'my lady,' I shall be obliged to refer to you as Your Grace. You used to call me Aunt Lucy, after all."

He refrained from expressing polite incredulity. Charles had sometimes called her Aunt Lucy when he was a boy, more to annoy his elders than anything else. Neither the Marburys nor his parents had encouraged such informalities.

"As you wish, Aunt Lucy," he said. "Now, how may I be of assistance to you?"

Her eyebrows lifted a tick. "Why would you assume I'm in want of assistance? Perhaps I simply wished to see one of my nearest relations after so many years away from home."

"Are we such near relations? I will have to check the family Bible." He pretended to ruminate for a few seconds. "Although I suppose you must be referring to your daughter's marriage to my uncle which, as I recall, was extremely short-lived."

She blinked, but then her eyes warmed with laughter. "How wretched of you to point that out. Are you suggesting that I'm doing it rather too brown?"

He gave her a half smile. No point in letting Aunt Lucy think she could push him about for her own purposes. Once, he had been very easy to manipulate, but those days were long gone.

"Perish the thought," he said. "Your missive, however, seemed to carry a rather urgent undertone. Forgive me if I assumed incorrectly."

Warmth lingered in her gaze. "You would be wrong, you know. I am happy to see you. But you are correct—I do need your help. I was simply trying to figure out the most successful line of approach."

"Directly, I would think. There's no need to beat around the bush with me."

"I'd forgotten how blunt and honest you were as a boy."

"I believe you mean clumsy."

"No, that was your father's assessment, not mine. I did not agree with him."

He nodded his thanks, not wishing to encourage that discussion. Charles was well aware of his late father's opinion of him.

"Besides," she continued, "I understand that you are now a paragon of courtesy and good taste. Peerless Penley, is that not what people call you?"

They did, and he hated it. But like many things in life, he'd learned to turn it to his advantage. "Also Perfect Penley and Impeccable Penley. You have your pick."

She nodded. "Yes, I've heard those as well. Your reputation as a leader of the *ton* is quite formidable."

Now they were getting to it. "And is that why you seek my help?"

"Let me ring for tea before I explain."

He held up a hand. "Perhaps we can dispense with the social formalities just this once, despite my fearsome reputation. Please, Aunt, speak freely." As much as he'd learned to value the social niceties, he sometimes found them irksome and time-consuming.

She eyed him dubiously. "Very well. Perhaps it's best if we have tea once my granddaughter joins us."

Surely she didn't mean . . . "Are you referring to Miss Gillian Dryden?"

"I am." Her answer held a touch of defiance.

"You brought her back to England with you?" He couldn't keep an incredulous note from his voice.

His aunt starched up, looking every bit the imperious aristocrat he remembered. "Is there some reason why my daughter and I shouldn't bring Gillian home?"

Besides the fact that she was the bastard daughter of the Duke of Cumberland, the Prince Regent's brother? But, of course, he would never be so rude as to state it so bluntly. "Forgive me. I simply assumed her to be married and living in Sicily. She's . . . twenty-two by now?"

"Twenty-one. And I think you can guess why she's not married."

"I'm sorry. I had no desire to offend." He offered her a

wry smile. "Clearly, my reputation is not so well deserved after all."

She drummed her fingers on her knee. "That is certainly not what I was given to understand."

Now they were going around in circles, an even bigger waste of time. "Is it Miss Dryden you wish to speak to me about?"

She let out a sigh that sounded both weary and worried. "Forgive me for biting off your head. It's been a long two months."

"I have no doubt your travels were taxing. Nor could it have been easy to return home after so many years abroad." Although decades had passed since the Marburys left England, the scandal that had forced them away was still not forgotten.

Aunt Lucy's gaze softened. "Yes, England is still home, for all that. Despite the difficulties, I am happy to be back here in my declining years."

"Good Lord. I had no idea you were verging on such decrepitude."

She let out a reluctant laugh. "That, my dear Charles, was anything but polite."

"No, but I needed to point out that you are anything but in decline. Your remarks suggest, however, that not everyone is happy that you've returned. Meaning your granddaughter, I presume?"

"How disgustingly perceptive of you. I shall have to remember that. Yes, Gillian is not taking the transition well. And I won't pretend that we're not having problems because of that."

"Because of her, er, status, or because she's not terribly familiar with English manners and customs?"

Aunt Lucy sighed again, but this time it was the sound of exasperation. "Both, although her behavior is the more vexing of the two at this point."

"I wouldn't have thought that possible." In a woman of the upper classes, the stain of illegitimacy was an almost insurmountable obstacle.

"Anything is possible with Gillian," she said, shaking her head. "What do you remember of her?"

He thought back to his visit to Sicily over twelve years ago. Although he'd stayed with the Marburys at their charming villa on the outskirts of Palermo, he'd seen Gillian Dryden only a few times. She'd only been nine at the time, so there would have been little reason for her to be out in company. He'd also had the sense that Lord Marbury had objected to his granddaughter's presence in their household. As a result, she'd been kept out of sight as much as possible.

"I remember that she was very quiet, like a little ghost hovering around the edges of the room."

For a moment, Aunt Lucy looked stricken. "That is a very apt description. My husband did not approve of Gillian's presence, although I'm happy to say that her stepfather was a great deal more accepting."

Charles nodded. "Lady Julia married a member of the Italian nobility, as I recall. Count Paterini, I believe?"

"Yes. He was a wonderful man who treated Gillian like his own daughter. We were all devastated when he died so tragically. It was as hard on Gillian as it was on her mother."

"I'm sorry to hear of your loss," he said.

"Thank you. But I suppose there is little to be served by rehashing our family's sad history. I should get to the point instead of wasting your valuable time."

"I cannot help you until you do," he said with a smile.

"Very well, then. I would like your help in teaching my granddaughter how to be a proper English lady instead of a wild, impetuous baggage who offends every person she meets."

Chapter Three

Charles eyed his aunt. She seemed dead serious. "I beg your pardon," he said. "I could not have heard you correctly."

"There is nothing wrong with your hearing. You are the only person in this family who can provide Gillian with the necessary social skills to survive in the *ton*."

Good God. She wanted him to introduce her scandal of a granddaughter into British society. It was an insane idea. "Leaving aside the unusual nature of the request, what would be the end goal of such a project?"

"The usual end for genteel young ladies—marriage."

It would be false modesty to deny that he had considerable social and political influence, but even he couldn't perform miracles. "Pardon my plain speaking, but do I look like a matchmaker to you?" He didn't bother to mask his incredulity.

"Don't be such a ninny, Charles. As if any man would be up to the task," she said with a dismissive wave. "Her mother and I will manage that element. But Gillian is, for lack of a better term, a gem in the rough. Your assistance is needed for one purpose only—to smooth out the rough edges and make her a suitable marriage prospect for a respectable gentleman."

Mystified that his aunt would even consider so outrageous a project, he glanced around the handsomely appointed room, then ran a quick, practiced eye over her gown and first-rate jewels.

She laughed, clearly reading his mind. "We're not out to catch a rich husband for her, Charles. Nor do we stand in need of financial support from you or anyone else. Gillian has a very generous dowry, bestowed on her by her step-father. What we do require is your social capital and your support as the head of the family."

So the girl was wealthy. That would certainly help—or at least encourage eligible suitors to overlook her unfortunate background. "That part shouldn't be a problem, as long as she is presentable."

"And therein lies the rub," Aunt Lucy said dryly.

"Why? Her mother is a most charming, accomplished woman. Can she not take her own daughter in hand? With the help of the appropriate tutors and a dancing master, of course."

"Unfortunately, Julia suffers from uncertain health. I do not wish to tax her anymore than I have to. And Gillian can be *quite* taxing."

"What about a governess?"

"My granddaughter doesn't want a governess. Never did," Aunt Lucy said tersely.

"Most girls don't. That doesn't mean they don't need one."

"Regardless, it was next to impossible to find an accept-able English candidate willing to move to Sicily. The point is moot."

"Aunt Lucy, forgive me, but this sounds like a mad scheme destined to fail."

"It cannot fail," she said in a tight voice. "You know

Gillian's difficult situation. Her security and happiness depend upon finding a good, respectable man who can look out for her. Protect her from . . . from all the pitfalls that lie in wait for a girl like her."

God, what a thickhead he was. Of course that was the problem.

The *ton* had its share of roués, rakes, and others who engaged in less than respectable activities. Most of those men made a point of steering clear of gently bred girls, knowing there would be hell to pay if they dallied with them. But to a woman in Gillian Dryden's position, they would be merciless. Every rake in London would try to drag her down into his sordid world, where she would be forever lost to her family and friends.

To such men, it would be a delicious challenge to ensnare a girl like Gillian—innocent, but by their foul standards, still fair game.

"Aunt Lucy, why in God's name did you bring the poor girl back to England in the first place? Surely you understood what would happen."

She chewed that over like a piece of moldy old bread. "We didn't have a choice."

Obviously, his aunt was holding something back, but Charles decided to let it go for now. If he did decide to help Miss Dryden—and that was a big *if*—he'd demand a full accounting of what he was up against. He hated surprises, and this little interview had already exceeded his tolerance for them.

"All right, perhaps we should be approaching this problem from a different angle," he said. "Why don't you tell me exactly which accomplishments and skills Miss Dryden does possess? Then I might be able to deduce how I can assist you."

"Assist Gillian," his aunt said stubbornly.

Though tutoring a grubby girl would hardly rate high on any man's list of preferred activities, he gave her an encouraging nod.

"Well, she speaks three foreign languages and is quite adept in Latin, too."

One generally didn't need to parse verb tenses in a ballroom, but it was a start. "Is one of those languages French?"

"Of course. Gillian's accent is excellent, I might add. She also speaks very good Spanish."

"Splendid. What else?"

"She's well versed in history and good at mathematics and the natural sciences. Her knowledge of animal husbandry is remarkable, in fact. That comes from spending most of her life on her stepfather's country estate."

Unless she intended to pursue a first at Oxford—or marry a farmer—those skills were more a hindrance than a help. But it sounded as if the girl had a good mind, which was nothing to sniff at. After all, there were men who had no desire to marry an ignorant woman, no matter how pretty she might be.

Charles was one of them. He had learned long ago how dangerous pretty could be.

"And what about feminine accomplishments? Does she play an instrument or sing?"

Aunt Lucy shook her head.

"Not an insurmountable problem," he said. "Does she draw or paint?"

"No."

"How is her needlework?"

Aunt Lucy was beginning to look morose. "Gillian would rather stab herself in the eye with the needle than spend even a minute butchering an innocent piece of cloth."

"A direct quote, I assume. Well, then, can she at least comport herself with grace on the dance floor?" He feared he already knew the answer.

"We hired a dancing master for the voyage back from

Sicily, but it didn't go well. Gillian insisted we dismiss him before we reached England or . . ."

"Or?" he prompted.

Aunt Lucy's expression suggested she'd just swallowed a nasty dose of physic. "Or she'd run him through."

"You cannot be serious."

"She wasn't feeling well at the time, so it wasn't entirely her fault. The lessons aggravated her shoulder injury."

"What happened to her shoulder?"

Aunt Lucy's gaze skittered off to the side. Then she took a deep breath and looked him directly in the eye. "She was shot. In a fight."

He couldn't repress a laugh. It couldn't possibly be true.

"It is no joking matter," Aunt Lucy said stiffly. "Gillian almost died."

Charles was almost afraid to ask for details, but he'd gone too far to pull back now. And he had to admit to a morbid fascination at this point. "Who shot her?"

"Sicilian bandits. Very dangerous men, and exceedingly dangerous for Gillian."

Before he could muster another question, the door opened, and a man strolled in—a man who resembled a bandit himself. But for his white shirt and cravat, he was dressed entirely in black, even down to his waistcoat. The look was completed by long black hair tied back over his shoulders and a faint scar that scored the side of his face.

He was a man who'd made his fortune running some of the most notorious gaming hells in London, one whose reputation as a scoundrel of the first order had only recently been mitigated by the sale of those hells and his marriage to the niece of a well-regarded viscount. Griffin Steele, bastard son of the Duke of Cumberland. Which made him the half brother of Gillian Dryden.

Good God. The situation was even worse than he thought.

"Ah, there you are, Griffin," Aunt Lucy said with an affectionate smile. "Please come in and meet our guest."

Charles sighed and came to his feet. "Now I know why you need my help," he muttered.

Gillian Dryden was a walking scandal just by virtue of her existence. With Griffin Steele in the mix, the gossips would be delirious with joy. It was a social powder keg in the making, waiting for a spark.

"What did you say, Charles?" Aunt Lucy asked.

"Nothing, ma'am."

"Then allow me to introduce Griffin Steele. I'm quite sure you've deduced his relationship to Gillian."

"With thundering clarity," Charles said. Steele, the rotter, simply flashed him what could only be described as an evil grin.

Aunt Lucy ignored the comment. "Griffin, allow me to introduce you to His Grace, the Duke of Leverton. Your Grace, Mr. Griffin Steele."

If a bow could be described as ironic, the flourishing one that Steele put on display fit the bill. Charles returned him a brief bow, fully aware that the man's blood was bluer than his.

Aunt Lucy stood and took Charles's hand in a firm clasp. "Leverton is going to help us with Gillian. I can't think of anyone better able to do so."

Steele gave him a slow, insolent perusal. While Charles was taller, Steele was whipcord lean with the air of someone who would just as soon cut your throat as shake your hand. Having been raised by a man who'd mastered the fine art of intimidation, Charles found Steele's glare nothing more than annoying.

"His Grace doesn't look too enthusiastic about the notion, if you ask me," Griffin finally drawled.

Charles gave him a polite smile. "Funny, I don't recall asking."

Aunt Lucy's scowl suggested they were acting like ill-behaved schoolboys.

"Griffin, would you fetch Charles a brandy, and yourself as well?" she asked. "I'm sure you could both use one."

"Your guest seems quite at home," Charles said, watching Steele stroll over to the drinks cabinet and select two glasses.

Aunt Lucy raised a haughty brow. "I count Griffin as a member of the family. As does Gillian."

"I would assume so, since they are brother and sister," Charles calmly replied. "But you certainly aren't making things easier on yourself."

"Because Gillian and I are both bastards?" Steele said, returning with the brandies. "That's not an insurmountable obstacle. I'm living proof of that."

"It's much more difficult for a woman to overcome that particular impediment," Charles said. "And since we're speaking so frankly—"

"I always speak frankly," Steele interrupted with a cold smile. "That way my intent is perfectly clear."

"Then in the interest of being perfectly clear," Charles said, "let me point out that your close relationship with Miss Dryden is unlikely to be of advantage to her. Rather the opposite, in fact."

"Agreed," Aunt Lucy said. "But since there is nothing to be done about that, we must simply work around it."

"I hate to be the bearer of bad tidings," Charles said. "But I believe it well-nigh impossible for you to achieve your goals in London. You might have more luck in one of the smaller spa towns, where standards are less exacting. Tunbridge Wells, perhaps."

"That is not acceptable to me or to Gillian's mother," his aunt replied in a frosty tone.

"Or to me," Steele added.

Charles allowed himself an exasperated sigh. "Aunt Lucy—"

"Charles, please listen. If we had another choice, we

would take it. But we must find my granddaughter a suitable husband, one who is strong and powerful enough to protect her. Her position in life, the type of girl she is . . ." She paused, her lips thinning into a distressed line.

"Yes?" Charles asked gently.

"Gillian is very vulnerable," she said. "More than I like to admit, and certainly more than she will admit. For all her strength and courage, she has craved male affection and approval ever since her beloved stepfather passed away. I don't need to tell you where such a vulnerability could lead."

"I understand."

"I will not have my granddaughter sliding into the demi-monde, either through her reckless behavior or because some wretched man takes advantage of her."

Charles frowned. "Has anyone tried?"

Aunt Lucy nodded. "I have dealt with threats of that nature in the past, but I'm getting old. I will not be around forever."

"I would never allow it to happen to Gillian," Griffin said in a hard voice.

"The problem is that you would do such a splendid job of protecting her," Aunt Lucy said, "that no man would have the nerve to come near her."

"Well, the girl needs someone to look out for her," Griffin said. "She's too bloody reckless. It's only a matter of time before she triggers a full-blown scandal that will sink her reputation for good."

"Charles, if you don't come to our aid, I don't know what we'll do," Aunt Lucy said, sounding rather desperate.

He wanted to say no, but . . .

A Penley always does the right thing.

His father's voice echoed in his head. Charles felt sure, however, that the old man had not envisioned this particular situation. Still, Aunt Lucy and even the mysterious Gillian were family.

"Perhaps you'd better tell me everything," he said.

As Aunt Lucy talked, Charles experienced a growing consternation. To say that Miss Dryden was a catalogue of social disasters was a massive understatement. In addition to threatening the dancing master, she'd gone riding by herself in Green Park, strolled past White's in the middle of the afternoon—again, by herself—and inadvertently insulted an ancient and very distinguished marquess at the one small party her family had dared take her to.

Apparently, that was just the beginning.

"For God's sake, Aunt Lucy," he broke in, "even I cannot groom a savage. What were you thinking to bring her here in the first place?"

Steele leaned forward, his gaze turning flat and cold. "Careful, Your Grace, or you're likely to end up with my blade between your ribs."

"Oh, please," Charles said in a dismissive voice.

"I brought her to England to save her life," Aunt Lucy said. "She may not be up to your exacting standards, Charles, but I could not let her die at the hands of ruthless brigands. That would surely have been her fate if we'd stayed in Sicily."

"Ah, yes," he said. "About those bandits. Why the devil—"

His aunt shook her head and came to her feet. Charles and Steele quickly rose in response.

"Forgive me for wasting your time, Your Grace," she said with a resigned dignity. "I see now it was too much to ask of you. I only ask that you keep these matters private for Gillian's sake."

Mentally sighing, Charles took her hand. "No, Aunt, it is I who must ask your forgiveness. My manners indeed went begging, and I am sorry for it. Let us just say that I was surprised into forgetting myself."

She eyed him, looking doubtful, troubled, and weary.

"But there's one thing I still don't understand," he said.

"Why is Miss Dryden so resistant to learning conventional behavior?"

His aunt shrugged. "She seems to equate conforming to acceptable standards with training a monkey to perform tricks. Pointless was how she described it."

"There is nothing pointless about civilized behavior," Charles said. "Or in treating our fellow creatures with appropriate dignity."

God, that sounded priggish even for him. Steele's derisive snort signaled he thought so too.

"I've told her that a thousand times," Aunt Lucy said. "But only her stepfather could get her to see reason, I'm sorry to say. Gillian had a great regard for him, both as her adopted parent and as patriarch of the family."

"How boringly traditional of her," Griffin commented.

"Well, she was raised in Sicily," Aunt Lucy replied. "They're sticklers for that sort of thing. Which is another reason why I thought of you, Charles. You are indisputably the head of *our* family, as well as a duke. I'm hoping the combination will generate at least a modicum of compliance on Gillian's part."

As Charles looked into his aunt's pleading gaze, he found it impossible to say no. "I suppose it wouldn't hurt to meet her. See if she would be amenable to taking some, ah, guidance from me."

"Good luck with that," Steele said in a sardonic tone.

Aunt Lucy flashed Charles a relieved smile. "She's really a very nice girl, despite her rough edges. I'm sure you'll like her."

Charles kept his considerable doubts to himself.

"Griffin, will you ring for the footman?" Aunt Lucy asked. "He can fetch Gillian."

"I know exactly where she is," Griffin said, striding to the door. When he pulled it open, a woman tumbled into the room, landing on her knees.

"Confound it," she muttered. She hopped to her feet in a swift, contained movement and flicked the skirts of her gown back in place over her slim figure. She gazed directly at Charles with big, sherry-colored eyes, apparently not the least bit embarrassed by her outrageous entrance.

"So, you're the one who's going to tame the savage," she said in a crisp voice that carried the hint of an exotic accent. "What fun for both of us."

Chapter Four

Tumbling down at the feet of the high and mighty Duke of Leverton was not how Gillian had planned their first meeting. Lately, however, most of her plans had displayed an irritating tendency to go awry.

Her grandmother glared at her. "I see you've been eavesdropping again. I do hope none of the servants saw you in such an inelegant position."

"Parsons did," Gillian said. "He looked appropriately appalled."

Actually, the butler had simply looked resigned, evidently getting used to her.

"Really, my dear, I wish you would stop skulking about, listening in on people's private conversations," Grandmamma said. "It's in such poor taste."

"How else am I supposed to know what people are saying when I'm obviously the topic under discussion?" Gillian asked.

"Perhaps you might try asking them," Leverton said in a deep, cultured voice perfectly calibrated with sarcasm.

Gillian crossed her arms over her chest and gave him a slow perusal. "I don't recall asking for your opinion on the subject. Then again, I'm a savage, so what do I know?"

Irritation tightened his aristocratic features, but then a polite mask dropped in place. Gillian had to give him credit. She'd wager he was unused to young ladies falling at his feet and compounding the awkward situation by insulting him. Then again, perhaps he *was* used to women falling at his feet. He was certainly both rich and handsome enough to elicit that sort of swooning.

Insulting him, though? From what she'd heard, people went to extraordinary lengths to court his favor.

"Since you were listening at the door, Miss Dryden, you must know that I also apologized for my rude behavior," the duke said.

"Not to me. Not that I care one blasted bit if you do one way or the other."

Her grandmother let out a heavy sigh, and even Griffin shook his head. The duke, however, simply regarded her with a perfectly unruffled manner, as if she were some recently discovered species, only vaguely interesting. Gillian began to get quite a bad feeling that she'd finally met her match.

She'd been hearing for weeks how Leverton was the key to solving *Gillian's little problem,* as her family called it. According to them, he was *perfectly* suited to guide her into society's good graces, and *perfectly* capable of managing away even the most troublesome elements of her background.

He must be a bloody perfect miracle worker, if that was the case.

As she cautiously eyed him, she couldn't help concluding that he did seem rather perfect in some respects. He was certainly prettier than she was, with thick, tawny-colored hair, striking blue eyes, and a face straight off a Greek statue. And he was certainly a good deal more stylish than she was, although that was true of almost anyone. But even she could appreciate the way his beautifully tailored coat showcased his broad shoulders, and how his breeches clung to his muscled legs with nary a wrinkle. As for his cravat, it was practically a work of art.

In fact, he was so damn perfect it made her stomach hurt. She'd been drawn in by perfection before, and it had almost ruined her.

"Stop trying to shock us, Gillian," her grandmother said. "You know quite well it won't work."

"*Au contraire,* Lady Marbury," Griffin said. "I find myself quite riven with horror."

He flashed Gillian the conspiratorial smile that always made her feel someone truly did understand her. And, more important, Griffin didn't find her wanting, unlike apparently everyone else in London. She couldn't wait to shake the dirt of England from her boots and return to Sicily—the sooner, the better.

"Miss Dryden is quite right," Leverton said.

Gillian frowned. "I am? About what, exactly?"

He slowly crossed the room to her. He didn't prowl, precisely, but something in the way he moved made her think of . . . a wolf, perhaps. Slipping silently through the night as he hunted in silence.

An exceedingly clever wolf, she guessed. One with very sharp teeth well suited for ripping apart a person's carefully ordered life.

Leverton's height forced her to tilt back her head to meet his gaze, and she found herself staring into eyes a beautiful shade of cobalt. She had to admit they were really quite amazing.

"Please believe me, Miss Dryden, when I say I meant no insult. I was merely surprised by a few details regarding your situation. It caused me to forget my manners." A glint of amusement lurked in his gaze.

Her stomach twisted at the notion that he might be

laughing at her. But when he smiled, her stomach seemed to untwist and start dancing with butterflies.

"Come, my dear girl," he said in his beautifully cultured voice. "I beg you to forgive me before I'm compelled to do something drastic—like throw myself at your feet. That would be embarrassing for both of us."

"Bloody coxcomb," Griffin muttered.

Leverton ignored the aside, keeping his attention on Gillian. Her heart began to thump and heat crawled up her neck. "Oh, very well," she grumbled. "I forgive you."

"You are most gracious," Leverton said. "Now, perhaps we can start over and leave all this awkwardness behind."

"What a splendid idea," Grandmamma said. "Your Grace, my granddaughter, Miss Gillian Dryden."

The duke bowed as if she hadn't just tumbled through the door, and as if they hadn't just spent the last few minutes insulting each other.

"Gillian, I have the pleasure of introducing you to the Duke of Leverton," Grandmamma added.

"Good Lord. I know who he is," Gillian replied, not hiding her exasperation.

"Then make him a curtsey, my dear. A proper one."

Repressing the urge to roll her eyes—one curtsey was as good as another, as far as she was concerned—Gillian dipped down and quickly came up.

Leverton's eyebrows ticked up. On him, she rather expected it was the equivalent of a horrified gasp.

Well, nobody ever said she was graceful, at least when it came to that sort of silliness.

"Hmm," he said. "We'll have to work on that."

"It's all nonsense, if you ask me," Gillian said. "All this bowing and scraping like a peasant before his master. Perhaps you'd like me to polish your boots while I'm at it."

His disapproving gaze made her blink, and she almost

took a step back. This was a man who did not like being crossed.

"Gillian Dryden, you will cease acting like a heathen," her grandmother rapped out.

"I had no idea you had revolutionary tendencies, Miss Dryden," the duke said. "How very interesting. And no, I would not like you to polish my boots. My valet would not approve."

Now he sounded bored. And if he was bored, he would be more likely to go away and leave her alone. Splendid.

Still, she couldn't help feeling irked by his dismissive tone and demeanor. The Duke of Leverton was certainly a snob and probably a fop. She didn't know which was worse.

"Why would you think I have revolutionary tendencies, sir?" she added in a sugary-sweet voice. "Is it because I think I'm as good as anyone else, despite my unfortunate social status?"

Gillian braced herself for the expected put-down. She'd grown used to being labeled a prince's by-blow, or worse. It was best to simply accept it and then do her best to avoid anyone who looked down on her because of her parentage. She'd learned that hard lesson a long time ago.

The duke studied her for a few moments before replying. "Of course you are."

"Of course I am what?" she asked.

"As good as anyone else. Any sensible person must think so," he said.

"That eliminates most of the *ton*," Griffin said.

Leverton seemed to weigh her brother's droll comment. "I believe your assessment is too pessimistic, Steele. Shall we say, perhaps fifty percent?"

The exchange was so silly that Gillian had to laugh. Leverton's eyebrows ticked up again, but not, she thought, with disapproval. Then he flashed her another dazzling smile that made her feel like the floor had just tipped sideways.

"That's much better," he said.

She shook her head, exasperated. "I don't understand any of this."

"Never mind." Leverton glanced at Gillian's grand-mother. "Madam, would you be averse to my asking Miss Dryden a few questions? To get the lay of the land, as it were."

"You mean to figure out how hopeless I truly am," Gillian said.

Griffin took her arm and steered her to sit with her grandmother. "Might as well get it over with, old girl."

"Easy enough for you to say," she retorted. "No one cares if you're a royal by-blow. No one *ever* cares about that sort of thing when it comes to men."

"Not exactly true," Griffin said. "I had my problems, although I admit the situation is trickier for you than it was for me."

"But not insurmountable, as I think we all agreed a few minutes ago," the duke said, resuming his seat.

"I was not in the room at the time of that discussion," Gillian said.

"But you were listening in," the duke responded. "I will, therefore, assume you to be in agreement with the rest of us."

Confound it. The man was all but unflappable. "That remains to be seen."

His glance shifted to her grandmother before returning to her. "Miss Dryden, am I to understand that you do not wish to be accepted into polite society? Surely that cannot be correct."

"Of course not." Grandmamma pinned Gillian with a look that all but dared her to disagree. "Is it, my child?"

Drat. She was caught in her own trap.

Her mother and grandmother had already made it clear that her introduction into British society was happening regardless of her wishes. Refusing to cooperate would hardly achieve the desired outcome—her family's agreement to let her return to Sicily. They genuinely believed she could make a go of things here in England, despite all the evidence to the contrary.

They also believed that to send her home was tantamount to a death sentence. Gillian didn't agree. Things might be a little sticky for a while, but she'd find a way to manage the situation. She always did.

"Of course I wish to be accepted into polite society." She adopted an earnest expression as she gazed at the duke. "Is that not the wish of any right-thinking English girl?"

"I'm not interested in other girls," he said bluntly. "I want to know what *you* think about it."

Gillian waved an airy hand. "No need to worry about me, Your Grace. I am all compliance."

Her grandmother made a small, choking sound.

"I'm thrilled to hear it," Leverton replied. "Then shall we proceed?"

"Of course."

"I understand that you speak several languages, and your English is excellent. That will certainly help smooth the way."

Gillian's brief episode of compliance evaporated. "I'm not a moron, sir. In fact, I suspect I'm much better educated than the average English girl. From what I can see, most of them are complete ninnies."

"Gillian," her grandmother warned.

"Sorry, Grandmamma, but you know it's true. Ten minutes with the likes of Lady Allister's daughters is enough to prove that point."

Lady Allister was an old friend of Gillian's mother's, and Gillian had been forced to endure two gruesome outings with her ladyship and her daughters. The girls had twittered endlessly like a pair of demented sparrows, interested in nothing but clothes, men, and the latest gossip.

They'd also made little effort to conceal the fact that they found Gillian beneath their notice, treating her with disdain whenever Mamma and Lady Allister weren't looking. It had taken every ounce of discipline she possessed not to box their ears. Only her mother's anxious desire for Gillian to make friends had held her back.

"I take your point about Lady Allister's unfortunate daughters," Leverton said. "They are a remarkably dreary pair of girls."

"Oh, um, thank you," Gillian said, momentarily flummoxed. "I did try to give them the benefit of the doubt, as I told Grandmamma."

"You called them twits and told them to stop screeching like banshees," her grandmother said. "In public."

"Well, they kicked up the most ridiculous fuss," Gillian said, "simply because a spider crawled up the younger Miss Allister's sleeve. You'd think the French had launched a full-scale invasion of London."

"You didn't help matters by taking off your hat and striking her with it," her grandmother replied.

"I was simply trying to knock the blasted spider off her dress. For all the good it did me," Gillian muttered.

"So, that's what happened," Griffin said.

"Oh, dear," sighed Grandmamma. "You heard about that incident?"

"I expect half of London did," Griffin said with a grin. "It isn't every day that young ladies attack each other in Gunter's."

"I did not attack her," Gillian protested. "I was trying to help her. It's not my fault she toppled over and sent the table flying."

All the ices and drinks had been dumped onto Lady

Allister's ample lap. The resulting shrieks had been so loud that Gillian's ears had rung for hours.

"Since you didn't hear about the incident, Charles, perhaps it's not as bad as we initially thought," Grandmamma said, looking hopeful.

The duke had been staring at Gillian with what looked like horrified fascination, but he quickly pulled himself together. "I only returned to London a few days ago. I've been locked up in my offices since and am not yet privy to the latest gossip."

"Oh, dear," her grandmother said with a sigh.

The duke gave her a sympathetic grimace. "Never mind, Aunt Lucy. Most everyone agrees with Miss Dryden's trenchant assessment of the Allister girls, so I don't think the damage will be acute." He shot Gillian a stern look. "As long as you refrain from similar incidents."

"I promise," she said in a pious voice. Unfortunately, her vow was undercut by the look exchanged by Griffin and her grandmother.

"You might as well tell me," the duke said in a resigned voice.

"There was that incident in Hyde Park the other day, when she went for an early morning ride," Grandmamma said.

"Not by herself, I hope," the duke said.

"Of course not," Gillian said. "I had a groom with me." Her grandmother had seen to that. The servants barely let Gillian out of their sight.

"Then what was the problem?"

"She wore breeches," her grandmother said.

Leverton blinked slowly.

"It's the only way I can ride astride. I hate sidesaddle," Gillian explained.

"Did anyone see you?" Leverton asked.

"Not so as to recognize me," she said. "So I don't see what the problem is."

His gaze went cool again. "I'm sure you know exactly what the problem is, so please don't insult my intelligence, Miss Dryden."

She felt her cheeks flush. Of course she'd known what the problem was, which was why she'd gone out riding early in the morning. She truly didn't want to embarrass her family, but that didn't mean she didn't chafe against the restrictions placed on her—or circumvent them, on occasion.

Griffin stirred. "Speaking of insults, I'd advise you to address my sister in a more respectful tone. An offense to her is an offense to me. Believe me, you don't want that."

Leverton didn't seem the slightest bit discomposed by her brother's threat. In fact, the two men commenced staring at each other in a way that raised the hairs on the back of Gillian's neck.

"It's fine," she hastily said. "I'm sure the duke didn't mean to insult me. Did you, sir?"

He held Griffin's gaze for a moment longer, then looked at her. "Of course not, Miss Dryden."

"Good, then let's continue." The sooner this appalling interview came to an end, the better.

"Lady Marbury has given me a fairly good understanding of your education," he said. "It sounded, however, as if you've lacked sufficient tutoring in the traditional female accomplishments."

"You mean like drawing and needlework? Sorry, I never saw the point of it."

She could stitch a shirt and cook a stew with the best of them. Those were useful tasks that served a purpose. But wasting one's time on producing decorative samplers or boring landscapes? She'd always had better things to do with her time.

"And what about music? Do you play an instrument or sing, or did you not see the point in those activities, either?"

Gillian liked music, especially opera, but she'd never had the patience to learn how to play. And the less said about her singing voice, the better. She gave a shrug.

"My dear girl," Leverton said, sounding exasperated. "Do you have no hobbies or leisurely pastimes at all?"

"Actually, yes," she said. "I'm quite good at hunting bandits."

She could barely hear the duke grinding his teeth over her grandmother's groan.

Chapter Five

Standing in the middle of the path, Gillian studied Charles with a bemused expression, as if he were speaking Hindi.

"Why the devil—" She stopped, pressing her lips together when he raised his eyebrows. "Why in heaven's name would you take us to see an ornamental dairy in the middle of London?" She punctuated her marginally more polite comment by rolling her eyes.

Aunt Lucy had been correct—Gillian Dryden was a social catastrophe in the making. Charles wondered again why he'd agreed to tutor her in the fine art of polite behavior.

After Gillian's quip yesterday about hunting bandits, the discussion had gone rapidly downhill, only ending when Aunt Lucy ordered them to stop behaving like children. That had been an accurate assessment of them, especially Griffin Steele. He'd threatened to run Charles through with a blade if Charles made one more insulting comment about his sister. Steele's threat had come when Charles suggested that Gillian's lowbrow behavior was more suited to a tavern brawl than a polite discussion. Gillian had retorted that she'd find a brawl a great deal more entertaining than talking to him.

When Aunt Lucy had finally reduced them to grumbling acquiescence, she'd looked at Charles with a woeful expression and released him from any obligation to Gillian or the family.

"You mustn't stay a moment longer and subject yourself to this unfortunate scene," she'd said, fluttering her lace hankie at him as if waving a flag of surrender. She'd ended on a little quaver that Charles suspected was entirely feigned.

Clearly affected by her grandmother's artful performance, Gillian had blushed pink and bitten her lower lip. Still, she held her tongue, neither apologizing nor contradicting her grandmother. Steele obviously didn't want Charles there by that point either, so they'd given him the perfect out.

Though he'd had every intention of taking the opportunity to escape from the Marbury Madhouse, he'd found himself settling back in his chair, thinking for a minute or two. Then he'd made some inane comment about growing pains and how he knew they'd all get along just fine. His about-face had stunned Gillian and Steele, but not, he suspected, his aunt.

Aunt Lucy had exploited his weak point—his infernal pride. If there was one thing Charles hated, it was the notion that there was someone he couldn't bend to his will. He came from a long line of warriors and politicians, stretching back to William the Conqueror. Nobody ever told a Penley what he could or couldn't do. It was like waving a flag in front of a bull, and yesterday it had worked like a charm on Charles.

He touched Gillian's elbow and got her walking again. "Many visitors to London come to see the ornamental dairy. And I thought you might enjoy seeing Green Park and its various attractions."

"You obviously don't know me very well." She glared at the pretty little farm building as if its very presence was an offense against nature. "The whole thing is ridiculous, but I suppose nothing should surprise me about Londoners."

"Miss Dryden, it's usually not the done thing to berate a

gentleman when he's kind enough to take a young lady on an outing. Instead, she displays a becoming gratitude by showing her enthusiasm for the activity, even if such enthusiasm is partly feigned."

"Lie, in other words." She crossed her arms over her chest, ignoring the large feather muff that dangled from one wrist. It hung down like some strange animal, making Charles wonder why she'd carted it along in the first place. Fortunately, it was the only flaw in her otherwise elegant ensemble. A dark green, close-fitting pelisse displayed her tall and naturally graceful figure to excellent advantage, and was matched by a dashing grenadier-style hat that sat at a rakish angle on her glossy, dark curls.

There was no doubt Gillian was a lovely girl, though not in the usual style. She had high, sharp cheekbones and a determined chin, countered by a surprisingly lush mouth and big, sherry-colored eyes that dominated her face. It was an enticing combination that would attract a fair amount of masculine attention, if she didn't scare off every potential suitor.

He steered her off the Broad Walk onto one of the paths to the dairy, throwing a glance over his shoulder to check on the progress of the Contessa Paterini and her maid. They lagged behind, strolling at a pace that was little more than a crawl. Gillian's mother was serving as chaperone on this most harmless of outings. Given the rumors that were already beginning to swirl about Gillian, Charles wasn't taking any chances. For the next several weeks he would do all he could to ensure that not a shred of scandal could attach to either Gillian or himself.

Good luck with that, old son.

The contessa gave them a cheery little wave. "Don't worry about us, my dears. Maria and I will meet you at the dairy."

Gillian turned around. "Are you all right, Mamma? Would you like to stop and rest for a few minutes?"

"We're fine, darling. We'll just toddle along at our own pace, won't we?" She smiled at her companion, a stout Italian woman who regarded London in general and Green Park in particular with morose disapproval. The poor woman seemed to have only a few words of English, so the move to England must have been particularly difficult for her.

"Well, if you're sure," Gillian said.

"Perfectly. You must stop worrying about me and enjoy yourself."

It was clear, however, that Gillian worried about her mother a great deal.

The contessa was a faded beauty with a gentle, fragile manner that spoke to both her kind nature and poor health. She was much changed since the last time Charles had seen her, years ago in Sicily. Then, she'd been a vivacious young matron, basking in the love of a devoted husband and enjoying a gay life in Palermo. Her spirit had vanished after her husband's murder. As far as Charles could tell, the contessa now drifted through life, content to let Lady Marbury or Gillian make all the decisions. The contessa clearly had no influence over her daughter's behavior, only clucking ineffectually with distress when Gillian said or did something outrageous.

Their relationship was entirely upended, as far as Charles could tell. When he'd arrived this morning to escort them to the park, Gillian had fussed over her mother like a cat with a lone kitten. He'd finally gotten them moving by promising to bring them straight home if the contessa displayed any sign of fatigue. Even then, Gillian only agreed to venture forth into the wilds of Mayfair after standing outside on the steps for a good three minutes to make sure that the air was neither too damp nor too cold for her mamma.

"Come, Miss Dryden, your mother is in good hands. The weather today is quite mild, and I'm sure the fresh air will do her good."

"I doubt it," Gillian said. "The weather's been positively beastly since we arrived. I always knew England was cold and damp, but this is ridiculous. It's May already, and we're all freezing our ar—" She cut herself off with an adorable grimace. "Sorry. What I meant to say is that it's already May, and it seems unseasonably cool."

"That was a commendably dull comment on the weather. Well done. One would think you a born Londoner."

She flashed him a smile that transformed her face from pretty to entrancing. "I'm not a complete dolt. In fact, I have it on good authority that I'm actually quite teachable."

"On whose good authority?"

"My own," she said in a droll voice.

Charles had to laugh. She clearly could be charming when she chose to be. She also possessed a surprising degree of fortitude for one so young. That was another reason he hadn't been able to say no to her tutoring. Simply by being born, she'd been forced to share her mother's shame, and it would trail behind her like a noxious cloud for the rest of her life.

Not if I can help it.

"The English prattle on about the weather all the time," Gillian said, "and not simply because it's a safe topic. If you ask me, you're all obsessed with it."

"Spoken like a woman who has spent her life basking in a sunny clime. If you had to live in a damp, drafty house with a chimney that invariably smoked, you'd be obsessed too."

When she smiled up at him and took his arm, he almost jerked from the shock. It was the first time she'd willingly touched him. It somehow felt . . . important.

"Actually, we think about the weather quite a lot in Sicily," she said as they strolled. "It's bloody hot in the summer, and if we don't get enough rain, it can be disastrous for the farmers."

"Substitute ghastly for bloody, and you've made another

unexceptionable comment. I'm quite amazed at our ability to carry on a rational conversation, as if we were two ordinary civilized people."

"I did promise Grandmamma I would try. However, a disgustingly wealthy duke strolling about Green Park with the illegitimate daughter of a prince doesn't strike me as very ordinary."

"Perhaps not, but I would suggest you refer to neither my wealth nor your parentage in polite company. Or any company, for that matter."

"Yes, I suppose it would be horribly vulgar to acknowledge my natural father in any way."

"Almost as vulgar as referring to the state of a man's purse."

She laughed, a full-throated, delightful sound, warm and infectious. Charles had no doubt it would draw men to her in a snap. His duty was to make sure they were the right kind of men.

"No one seemed to have such delicate compunctions in Sicily," she said. "All the aristocrats I knew talked about wealth a great deal, especially the women. That isn't surprising, I suppose, since they're usually dependent on male largesse." She shook her head. "I'm so glad I'm not."

"Did you know many aristocrats in Sicily?" He'd formed the impression that she'd been kept very much out of the way by her family, especially when Lord Marbury was alive.

"Enough to know what I'm talking about," she said in a defensive tone.

He would lay bets there was a story behind that comment. But she obviously had no desire to talk about it, and he really wasn't interested in knowing.

Or so he told himself.

"I assure you that the average English aristocrat is as obsessed with money as his counterparts in other countries," he said. "We just have the odd notion that one doesn't talk about money. We'd rather just spend it."

"Most everyone worries about money, now that I think about it."

"Especially if you don't have it," he said dryly.

"There are a lot of people in Sicily who don't," she said with a frown. "The poverty in the countryside is appalling."

"It's the same here. Now that the soldiers are returning home from the war, it's difficult for them to find work." Even on his own prosperous estates, he'd had trouble absorbing the men who'd returned to their villages and tenant farms after the long conflict.

"You seem to be doing all right. But I imagine disgustingly wealthy dukes generally do make out rather well." She flashed him a quick smile that took the sting out of the comment.

He held up a finger. "Vulgar, remember?"

"I stand corrected. What topics may I properly engage in, Your Grace?"

Charles glanced over his shoulder. Contessa Paterini and her woman had fallen even farther behind.

"We'll get to that in a minute." He steered her to a small enclosure next to the dairy, where a few cows ambled about and grazed. "There's something I need to ask you first."

Gillian lounged gracefully against the fence, negligently swinging the muff that dangled from her wrist. Charles made a mental note to work on her posture at another time.

"Fire away," she said.

He repressed a sigh. *One problem at a time.*

"It's not an easy topic to discuss," he said, "and I have no wish to embarrass you. But since we're already talking about dukes, I thought I'd better ask you about . . ." He hesitated, searching for a delicate way to phrase it.

"My esteemed father, His Royal Highness the Duke of Cumberland? Is that what you want to ask me about?" She still leaned casually against the fence, still swinging her purse. But the air around her now seemed charged with tension.

"I know it's awkward," he said. "But I need to know how things stand with him."

"It's not awkward for me at all," she said in a cool voice. "Surely you know that I've never met the bastard."

"Miss Dryden . . ."

"Oh, wait," she said in a musing tone. "I forgot. Technically, I'm the bastard, not my natural father. I suppose I shouldn't confuse the point."

Charles resisted the impulse to rub his temples. He could sympathize with her feelings about her father, but her near-fatal inability to guard her speech would surely be her undoing. Though Cumberland was not a popular man, he was a royal duke. The sins of the father would be visited upon the child if she didn't learn to hold her tongue.

"I readily understand your feelings, but might I suggest that you refrain from using such terms to describe him?"

"How about poltroon, then? Or loose fish? Oh, I know—complete bounder. Will any of those do?" She smiled brightly at him, as if she were trying to be helpful.

"I would suggest *Your Highness,* or perhaps *sir,* if you are forced to address him or refer to him. I'm hopeful that you won't be placed in such a position, but we must be prepared for it. While it's unlikely that you'll ever be introduced to him, you may one day find yourself at a ball or social event where he's present."

Gillian stood up straight. Anxiety darkened her big eyes as she glanced down the path toward her mother. The contessa had paused to speak with two little girls on an outing with their nursemaids. "You're worried about what people might say to me about him, aren't you? That if they make mean-spirited remarks, it will set me off."

He nodded.

"People can say whatever they want about him—or me, for that matter. I'm used to it." Gillian gave him a rueful smile. "And despite what you may think, I do know when to hold my tongue. My grandfather saw to my tutoring in that regard."

Charles could believe it. From what he'd known of Lord Marbury, those lessons would not have been easy on her. It had been no secret that he'd vehemently objected to his daughter's decision to keep her illegitimate child, and that the earl had been furious that the resulting scandal had forced them to leave England. Even though he'd subsequently gone on to have a distinguished career as a British diplomat in the Kingdom of Naples and Sicily, Marbury had never forgiven either his daughter or his granddaughter for subjecting the family to such humiliation.

"It's a useful skill, even if the learning of it is often painful," Charles said quietly. "I, too, had to learn how to curb my tongue. I won't pretend it was easy."

She threw him a sharp look, as if weighing his statement for truth. Then she nodded. "I didn't like it much either. And I have to admit that I sometimes forget the lessons." She huffed out a quiet laugh. "With predictable results, I'm sorry to say."

His sympathy stirred. Gillian could be brash, but she also had a sweet, self-deprecating manner he found enormously appealing.

"The best way to handle gossip or ill-mannered remarks is to feign ignorance," he said. "Simply give a vague smile and excuse yourself from the discussion."

"You mean I shouldn't plant them a facer or threaten to shoot them?" she asked, opening her eyes wide.

"I know it's hard to fathom, but Englishwomen don't generally engage in fisticuffs or duels."

"How boring of them. I suppose I'll have to find other ways to avenge myself on the gossips of London." She lifted an eyebrow. "What do you think of poison?"

He was tempted to laugh. "Miss Dryden, it's fine for you to engage in this sort of raillery with me or with intimate family, but—"

She waved a dismissive hand to interrupt. "I know, I know. If the situation should ever arise, I promise to be a paragon of good manners and stupidity. All of London can insult me until the cows come home, and I won't say a word. I'll simply smile and commence speaking of the weather."

"Why does that promise fill me with more alarm than reassurance?"

She chuckled, then glanced past him. Her smile faded. "I do mean it when I say I don't care if the gossips prattle on about me. But I worry about Mamma. She's very sensitive, you know."

Gillian tapped her chest, right over her heart. The gesture had the unfortunate effect of bringing his attention to the gentle swell of her breasts under her close-fitting garment. She wasn't a buxom girl by any means, but she had more than enough curves to attract any man's attention. They'd gotten *his* attention.

He jerked his gaze upward. Fortunately, she didn't seem to notice his inappropriate regard.

"It upsets Mamma when people say something nasty about me," Gillian said. "I won't pick fights on my own behalf, but if they insult her, I won't be held accountable for my actions."

Her loyalty was commendable, but hardly helpful.

"Then I suggest you let me handle any problems that may arise." When she started to object, he held up a restraining hand. "I'm quite capable of doing so, and a good deal more effectively than you could. Your grandmother and I should be able to keep any gossip to a whisper that will fade away once you've been out for a few weeks. Your task is to exercise self-restraint. If you do, eventually the *ton* will become bored with you and move on."

She started to cross her arms over her chest, but got caught up in the ribbons of her muff. Blowing out an impatient breath, she tugged it off her wrist and looped it on the fence post behind her. When Charles raised his eyebrows with polite incredulity, she either didn't get the point or chose to ignore it.

Subtlety was not her strong point.

"Do you also have power over the weather?" she asked. "Perhaps you can arrange for a sunny day, for once."

He smiled. "I'll see what I can do. Miss Dryden, please trust that I can handle any gossip about you or your mother, as I trust that you will have the good sense to allow me to do so. You have already told me that you are quite capable of keeping the peace when necessary. I expect nothing less of you."

"Do you think you have the right to order me about because you're a duke? I don't care a fig about that."

"As head of our family, I have your mother's and your grandmother's support in this matter. I'm sure they wish you to accord me the same level of trust."

It seemed a bit risky to play the head of the family card this early in the game, but, somewhat to his surprise, it seemed to work. Gillian fumed for a few moments and then gave a grudging nod. "Oh, very well. But never assume I'll sit quietly by while people insult my mother." She reached out and poked him in the chest. "I expect you to deal with any such episodes in a decisive fashion. If you don't, I will."

"You have my word. And may I point out that young ladies are not encouraged to go around jabbing men in the cravat. They might take it amiss."

"No doubt. You poor dears spend so much time on the blasted things, you'd probably burst into tears if I disturbed the folds." She gave him a look of mock concern. "I do hope you're not going to go into hysterics now."

"My dear Miss Dryden, may I just say that you are an exceedingly annoying young lady?"

She laughed, her good humor restored. "So I understand. But here's Mamma now. Perhaps we can finish this conversation another time."

"We can agree that this particular conversation is closed."

He ignored her muttered comment about having the last word as he turned to greet her mother.

"Gillian," the contessa said, "do you not find Green Park simply delightful? It's quite changed from my youth, when men often met here to fight duels. And you could never be sure a cutpurse wouldn't leap out from behind a tree and rob you."

"Goodness," Gillian said, slipping a hand through her mother's arm, "that does sound rather exciting."

"Only to you, my love," her mother said with rueful affection. "Shall we stroll back to the carriage? I think I've had enough fresh air for one day. Now don't leave your muff dangling on the fence, Gillian. You don't want to lose another one."

With a sheepish smile, Gillian fetched her muff. She took her mother's arm, fussing over her as they slowly made their way back to Piccadilly. Though the contessa gently protested that she was fine, it was obvious she was happy with her daughter's attentions. Gillian's devotion was commendable and touching, but Charles couldn't help noting the imbalance in the relationship. Did anyone fuss over Gillian? Did anyone let her be what she should be—a pretty girl whose only care was which book to read next or what gown to wear at a ball?

Charles bent to retrieve the handkerchief the contessa had

accidently dropped, when a voice he hadn't heard in months came from behind him. It jerked him upright, as if someone had prodded him in the backside with a sharp stick.

"Well, look who it is," the woman said with an amused lilt that was all too familiar. "Who would think to find His Grace, the Duke of Leverton, in Green Park at this hour? How splendid that you would descend from Mount Olympus to join us mortals in so pedestrian an activity."

Charles swallowed a curse and adopted a perfectly bland, perfectly polite expression before he turned to confront the woman who'd once ruined his life.

Chapter Six

Leverton jerked upright, dismay marking his features. The lapse in his impressive self-discipline surprised Gillian. She'd been needling him all morning, and not once had he lost his temper. He'd clearly gotten her measure, which she found both annoying and deserving of respect.

She was beginning to realize that he was also a very nice man. It was quite a refreshing change, since in her experience a wealthy and handsome man was usually very careless toward the people in his life.

The duke's expression smoothed out, then he turned to greet the woman who'd accosted them. She was exquisitely garbed, as was the man who escorted her. In fact, they were the most fashionable couple Gillian had ever seen.

The lady was a petite beauty, with hair almost as pale as moonlight. That ethereal appearance, however, was offset by a curvaceous bosom and hips, which were displayed to great advantage by her beautifully tailored walking gown. She looked both dainty and seductive, a tricky combination to pull off. Next to a woman like that, Gillian must seem like a stick, with approximately the same level of sexual allure.

Not that she cared. She never cared what other women looked like.

The lady's companion, although cast a bit in her shade, was what most women would consider a handsome fellow. He had a pleasing face, artfully arranged brown curls, and a charming smile that could coax the songbirds from the trees. Currently he was leveling that engaging smile at Leverton, who didn't appear charmed in the least.

In fact, the duke's expression was a virtual blank. If Gillian hadn't already heard the woman address him by name, she would have assumed that Leverton considered them strangers.

"Come now, Charles," the woman said in a light, pretty voice that held a great deal of amusement. "Surely you knew that Gerry and I were back in town. There's no need to act like you've just spotted an apparition." The woman laid her elegantly gloved hand on his arm. "Have you no words of greeting for your oldest friends?"

Leverton stared down at her for a second, then his lips curved up in a faint smile, one that stopped miles below his eyes. "Forgive me. I was merely surprised, madam. I have just returned to London myself after some weeks away."

"At Oakdale Hall? Or, perhaps, your estate in Yorkshire?" she said. "You did always prefer the country, which was something I could never understand."

"No, you never could." Leverton briskly removed the woman's hand from his arm and turned to Gillian's mother with a sincere smile as he handed over her kerchief. "Your handkerchief, madam. I do hope it's not too dirty."

Gillian blinked. His snub was so obvious that even she'd been able to catch it. That the lady had caught it too was evidenced by the flash of fire in her azure-blue eyes.

Her escort hastily moved forward and took her arm. "Now, my love, you're awfully good at teasing, but you mustn't do it to Charles. We fellows don't stand a chance once you start in on us." Though his manner was easy, his tone carried a subtle warning.

The woman affected a pretty pout. "I always used to tease our dear Charles. He never minded it before."

Leverton's eyebrows went up in an incredulous lift that made Gillian even more curious. Who were these people, and why did the duke find them so annoying? Vastly more annoying than her, she'd wager, and that was saying something.

In fact, His Grace was now regarding the man with an appraisal so cold that it confirmed her suspicions. The Duke of Leverton was not a man to cross. He might dress almost as exquisitely as the gentleman standing before him, but Gillian had little doubt Leverton could lift him right off his feet and shake him like a terrier shaking a rat.

The other gentleman barely managed to hold on to his smile. "Well, my love, no one likes to be reminded of their youthful follies. Leverton is no different from the rest of us, despite his exalted status," he finished in a jesting tone.

Leverton had succumbed to youthful follies? Gillian could hardly begin to imagine.

The little joke fell flat, and an uncomfortable silence fell over their small group. The duke was now beginning to look bored by the encounter.

Mamma, who'd stood quietly by with a slight frown, finally cast a worried look in Gillian's direction and then sighed, as if coming to a decision. "Your Grace, perhaps you could introduce us to your . . . friends," she prompted.

He was obviously reluctant, but what choice did he have? They couldn't stand around all day like addlepated dimwits.

"Contessa, may I introduce the Honorable Gerald Stratton and his wife, Lady Letitia Stratton. Stratton, Lady Letitia, the Contessa di Paterini and . . ."

He hesitated a moment, his glance flickering to Gillian. She gave him a tiny shrug. She had to start meeting people outside their small circle sooner or later, whether she was ready for it or not. And whether the rest of her family was ready for it or not, including the duke.

"And her daughter, Miss Gillian Dryden," he finished.

"Mr. Stratton, Lady Letitia," Mamma said with an easy nod of acknowledgment. "How nice to meet you."

The Strattons seemed stunned for a few seconds. Then Lady Letitia's mouth curled up in a smile that looked rather gleeful. Mr. Stratton, however, regarded Gillian with avid curiosity, which struck her as rather rude. Since Gillian was used to rudeness, she simply stared back at him.

Finally, Stratton made a precise bow in Mamma's direction. "Contessa, Miss Dryden, it is exceedingly pleasant to make your acquaintance."

"Oh, yes. This is simply delightful." Lady Letitia trilled to Mamma in a voice so cloying that Gillian's teeth began to hurt. That level of false sweetness usually meant that the veiled insults and sly comments would commence sooner rather than later.

"We had heard of your return, madam," Lady Letitia continued, "and have been eager to meet you. You are quite the talk of the town, as you must know. Everyone has been absolutely dying to welcome you back to your rightful home. And to meet your lovely daughter, of course."

Gillian was hard-pressed not to roll her eyes. The bloody woman was practically quivering with excitement. She must be thrilled to have run smash into the Duke of Cumberland's notorious bastard daughter as she strolled in the park with the exceedingly proper Duke of Leverton.

"Gillian, what do you say to Mr. Stratton and Lady Letitia?" her mother gently prompted.

Gillian considered responding by tugging on the brim of her bonnet, like a street urchin, but decided against it. She never liked to waste a good insult, and this lot clearly wasn't worth the effort. Nor did she wish to distress her mother.

Directing her best smile at Stratton, she dipped into a

proper curtsey that was a vast improvement on the one she'd tossed off yesterday at Leverton. "Mr. Stratton, Lady Letitia, it's a pleasure to meet you."

Stratton blinked at her like an owl before smiling back. The slow curve of his mouth made him look like he held a particularly delicious secret. He took her hand, giving her a flourishing bow. "Indeed, the pleasure is all mine. Little did I know when I left the house this morning that I would meet so charming a young lady and her equally charming mother. A fellow doesn't stumble upon such bounties every day, you know."

Good God. When Gillian tugged her hand away, Mr. Stratton put on quite a little show of reluctance.

"Gerry, it's much too early in the day to be making a cake of yourself," his wife said in that coolly amused tone of hers. "Miss Dryden, please don't be disconcerted by my husband's fulsome compliments. He flirts with all the girls, although I'm sure in your case his assessment is entirely well deserved."

Gillian was sure there was an insult in there somewhere. She supposed she really couldn't blame the woman. While the men of the *ton* ladled out sweet nothings to the ladies like they were slopping gravy over a joint of beef, it seemed wrong for Stratton to do it so blatantly in front of his wife. Gillian almost preferred dealing with Sicilian bandits. At least one knew where one stood.

Stratton let out a good-natured laugh. "One could hardly blame me, my dear, given the delightful provocation. I'm sure Charles would agree with me completely."

Leverton finally pried his lips apart. "I'm afraid I agree with your wife. You're making a complete cake of yourself, and not for the first time, either." He punctuated his comment by lifting his lips in a smile that looked remarkably like the snarl Gillian had once seen on a wolf she'd encountered on a Sicilian hillside.

Even Stratton's good humor couldn't survive so direct an insult. The man's eyes flashed with anger, and he took a short step forward. Leverton raised an imperious, challenging eyebrow.

Lady Letitia wrapped a firm hand around her husband's arm. "Now who's being a tease," she said in an arch tone. "I know you men love to engage in that sort of jesting behavior, but it's vastly boring for the ladies. Don't you agree, Countess?" She turned a prettily imploring gaze on Gillian's mother.

Mamma gave her a gentle smile. "Goodness, I'm the worst person to ask. Jests simply go over my head. Gillian, shall we start back?" She directed an apologetic glance at the Strattons. "Do forgive me, but I am not used to the British climate. I find myself growing chill."

"Forgive me, madam," Leverton said, looking rueful. "I am a brute to keep you standing around in this damp weather. Let me take you and Miss Dryden back to the carriage."

"I say, is your carriage up on Piccadilly?" Stratton exclaimed, apparently over his fit of pique. "If so, why don't we all walk together? Countess, may I lend you my arm?"

"How kind of you," Mamma said. "But it's entirely unnecessary."

"Oh, please do let us walk with you," Lady Letitia said so sweetly that it made Gillian's teeth hurt again. Everything about the woman made her teeth hurt, mostly because she seemed so . . . perfect.

And Gillian was getting perfectly sick of perfect.

Lady Letitia slipped her arm through Leverton's. "I haven't seen the duke in an age, and I am simply *dying* to find out how he came to be acquainted with you, my dear countess. And your lovely daughter, of course," she said graciously.

At least Gillian thought she was being gracious, but it was a little hard to tell. Clearly, her ladyship was a dab hand both at navigating the rocky shoals of polite conversation and at the art of the subtle insult. Sadly, Gillian was adept at neither.

"There's not much of a story to tell," Leverton said in a blighting tone.

Though he didn't seem happy to have Lady Letitia hanging off his arm, there was obviously nothing he could do about it.

When Stratton stepped forward to take Mamma's arm, she waved him away. "Thank you, but no. You young people always bustle along too fast for me. I'll walk with my maid, if you don't mind." She turned and nodded to Maria, who'd been standing quietly behind her mistress during the entire exchange. Maria's lack of English meant that most of the conversation had sailed over her head. If she had understood it, she'd probably have boxed Stratton's ears for being so forward with her beloved lady's daughter.

"Mr. Stratton, perhaps you could give my daughter your arm," Mamma said, smiling at Gillian as if she were offering up a splendid treat. "Maria and I will catch up with you at the carriage."

Stratton clapped a hand to his chest. "Countess, I should be *de*lighted to escort your daughter. In fact, you have just made my day."

This time Gillian did roll her eyes. "Obviously doesn't take much," she muttered.

He peered at her. "I'm sorry. What did you say, Miss Dryden?"

"Nothing of any import," she replied, taking his arm. She had no desire to stroll with the man, but Mamma obviously thought it would be a good opportunity for Gillian to practice polite conversation.

Leverton glared at Stratton, as if about to object to the arrangement. Lady Letitia, however, dragged him in the direction of the Broad Walk, already chatting away like a magpie. Gillian had to repress the impulse to laugh, if for no other reason than to see the Duke of Leverton so expertly rolled up. She felt a bit sorry for him, but it was good for a man to be managed every now and again. As nice as Leverton was, he could be a tad arrogant. It wouldn't kill him to be taken down a peg, and Lady Letitia certainly appeared capable of doing it.

That there was some sort of history between the two was obvious. Leverton's reaction suggested that it hadn't been all sweetness and fairy tales but Lady Letitia seemed to think otherwise. In fact, she looked almost possessive of him.

And he now looked as if he'd finally climbed off his high horse. Leverton even dipped down a bit to listen to her, their fair heads coming together in a glory of burnished sunlight.

Gillian frowned, startled that the sight bothered her.

"They make a handsome couple, don't they?" Stratton said as he and Gillian followed. His voice held a tinge of bitterness, as if echoing her thoughts. "Two paragons of perfection." His pleasant expression seemed at odds with his voice.

"Then it's lucky for us that we don't have to walk alongside them, isn't it?" Gillian said. "I don't know about you, but I find perfection to be an extremely irritating trait." When he threw her a startled glance, she smiled. "I expect it's because I'm anything but perfect myself. Then again, think of how tiring it must be to have to live up to such a standard, day in and day out."

He laughed. "Quite right, Miss Dryden. Let us indeed count ourselves lucky that we can simply plod along like ordinary people."

"It must be terribly hard to have one's nose up in the air all the time. One is likely to get a crick in the neck."

"Oh, my Letitia is quite down to earth, though one can't say the same about Leverton. There's a reason they call him 'Perfect Penley.'"

Gillian mentally blinked at the venomous undertone in Stratton's voice. It seemed at odds with his kind manner toward her and Mamma, and she didn't like it.

They strolled in silence. Gillian kept her gaze fastened on Leverton and Lady Letitia, while Stratton seemed more interested in studying Gillian. Like most of the Londoners she'd met thus far, he seemed to regard her as if she were some exotic species that might, if given the chance, do something alarming.

Or at least entertaining.

Stratton finally spoke up again. "Might I be so impertinent as to enquire how you and your mother happen to know the duke?"

"I don't think I could stop you from inquiring even if I wanted to, could I?"

He burst into laughter. "Oh, I say, I do like you. So refreshing to have such unvarnished speech from a young lady."

"I'm rather known for it. And I'm told it's not always to my advantage."

He gave her hand a little squeeze. "Then we shall get along famously. I must say I find you to be entirely delightful, Miss Dryden. Anyone who thinks otherwise needs his or her head examined."

She cast him a doubting glance, but he simply smiled. Most men were put off by her manner, at least the type of men her grandmother deemed proper. Stratton's manners might be a bit too informal, but she was the last person who could hold that against him.

"Thank you," she said. "You're very kind."

"And you are kind not to scold me for my forward behavior. Now, since you clearly don't mind my impertinence, perhaps you'll tell me how you know Leverton."

"He's a near relation of my grandmother, Lady Marbury."

Stratton flashed her another charming smile. "It's deuced

difficult to keep straight all the connections among the great families, don't you think?"

"I do indeed," Gillian said dryly, thinking of her own complicated family history. Everyone knew who her father was, and they held it against her, as if it were her fault. While she loathed how unfair that was, there was nothing she could do but shrug it off. Her parentage, however, didn't seem to bother Stratton, which was rather decent of him. "If you don't mind *my* asking, what is your relationship to the Duke of Leverton? You seem to know each other quite well."

"You can ask me anything," Stratton said, settling her hand more snuggly in the crook of his elbow. Gillian had the impulse to put a little more daylight between them, but resisted, not wanting to be rude. Stratton was one of the few people she'd met who seemed to genuinely like her. "I have a feeling we're going to be great friends," he added.

At that exact moment, Leverton glanced back at them, and his eyebrows snapped together in a heavy scowl. Gillian wondered what she'd done to annoy him now.

"Charles and I have known each other forever," Stratton said. "We were the best of friends at Oxford. Thick as thieves, actually."

That surprised her. "What happened? You're obviously not friends anymore. At least not *best* ones."

"We drifted apart after I married and he became duke." He let out a little laugh. "The responsibilities of life, I imagine."

It was hardly an adequate explanation. She let it drop, however, since they were approaching Piccadilly. Leverton was impatiently waiting for them by the carriage, while Lady Letitia appeared to have not a care in the world.

"Miss Dryden, may I be honest with you?" Stratton said in a low voice. He slowed his pace, forcing her to slow as well.

In her experience, that particular question usually preceded a remark that was anything but honest. "I think we've already ascertained that you needn't mince words with me, sir."

"Splendid. It is simply this. If you ever stand in need of a friend, or someone to confide in, I'm your man." He pressed a hand to his chest, looking soulful. Gillian couldn't help noticing that he was careful to avoid squishing his cravat. "Believe me," he continued, "I know how vicious the *ton* can be toward anyone who carries even the slightest hint of notoriety. One often needs a friend in those circumstances, and I stand ready to be yours."

"Thank you," she said cautiously. "I'll be sure to remember that."

"Perhaps you'll honor me with a walk in the park sometime soon, or even a drive." He winked at her. "Just the two of us."

Gillian mentally sighed. Now she understood. "I doubt my grandmother would approve, sir, but thank you for the offer, regardless."

"Well, you wouldn't need to tell Lady Marbury, would you?"

"What exactly are you suggesting that Miss Dryden withhold from her grandmother, Stratton?" the duke asked in a loud voice.

Gillian jerked in surprise, since she and her escort were still some distance away from the carriage, and Stratton had been speaking in low tones. Leverton must have the hearing of a bat. She made a mental note to remember that. But for now, she had to deal with Stratton's impertinent suggestion.

"Nothing of any importance, Your Grace," she said brightly. "I was simply telling Mr. Stratton how very close I am to my grandmother. She is, indeed, my greatest confidant." She gave her escort her sweetest smile. "I tell Grandmamma *everything*. In fact, I can't wait to tell her all about meeting you today. I'm sure she'll be vastly pleased to hear I've made a new friend."

He winced, but quickly recovered. "Quite," he said, joining his wife. "Nothing like making new friends, eh, my love?"

When Lady Letitia took her husband's arm, Gillian fancied he winced under a grip that looked rather painful. "Indeed." Lady Letitia directed a sly smile at the duke. "Almost as delightful as reviving cherished relationships with old friends, wouldn't you say, Charles?"

"I suppose it depends on the circumstances," Leverton replied. "And the friends."

"Well, we must be off," Lady Letitia said, obviously taking the hint. Gillian had to give her ladyship credit—her smile never faltered. "Miss Dryden, please convey my best regards to your mother. I'm sure we'll be seeing you again very soon."

"I look forward to it, Miss Dryden," Stratton said. "And I hope to meet your grandmother soon, as well. She sounds delightful." Then he winked at her. Clearly, he was not a man to be easily discouraged.

Gillian glanced at Leverton, but he'd half turned away to talk to his coachman. Stratton might be a cad, but he had the brains to conceal his pathetic attempts at flirtation from the duke. He obviously didn't feel the need to modify his inappropriate behavior in front of his wife, however, which was rather odd.

Then again, nothing about aristocratic bad behavior shocked Gillian anymore.

With a final smile and wave, the Strattons set off along Piccadilly. Leverton returned to scowling at Gillian again. She was beginning to wonder if he deserved his reputation as the politest man in London, but whatever he was going to say was forestalled when Mamma joined them.

"Well, that was a delightful outing, was it not?" Mamma said. "Gillian, did you enjoy your stroll with Mr. Stratton?"

Gillian shrugged. "He was all right. A little too chatty, if you ask me."

"I certainly hope you didn't tell him so," her mother said.

"No, Mamma. I was very polite."

"Cousin Julia, would you object if your daughter and I walked home?" Leverton said abruptly. "It's such a fine day, and I'm sure Miss Dryden would enjoy a little more time outdoors."

Her mother cast a worried glance at the cloud-riven sky. It was anything but a fine day, but Gillian didn't mind walking a bit more. It was very nice of the duke to make the offer, since she was sure he had better things to do.

Then again, perhaps he intended to deliver another lecture or scold.

"It's fine, Mamma," she said. "I'd much rather be out than cooped up indoors."

"Very well, but don't linger. It looks like rain." As if to underline her point, a gust of wind swirled around them, kicking up their skirts.

The duke helped Mamma and Maria into the carriage, then turned to Gillian and took her hand, settling her beside him. She noticed how much taller he was than Stratton, and how muscular his arm was under her fingertips. She supposed she couldn't blame Lady Letitia for giving the duke sheep's eyes since Leverton was such a handsome, well-built man.

"Miss Dryden, I have something I must ask you," he said.

A scold it is. Only a dolt would have missed his disapproving tone.

"Go ahead," she said, resigned.

"What the devil did Stratton want you to keep secret?"

Chapter Seven

"Even more to the point," Leverton said, "what did you say to him that encouraged such liberties?"

Gillian jerked her hand away and came to an abrupt halt. "For someone with your vaunted reputation, I find such an unjust accusation quite rude. You're not exactly living up to your nickname."

Anger turned his gaze to a cold blue flame. Gillian tried to cross her arms over her chest as she glared back at him, but got tangled up with her dratted muff.

"I asked you a question, Miss Dryden," he said. "I expect an answer."

She was tempted to storm past him and make her own way home, but he blocked her way like a brick wall. Besides, she wouldn't put it past him to grab her if she did try to stalk by, and wouldn't that be a nice little display? They were already attracting the attention of fashionable young ladies out for a stroll and shoppers hurrying about their business. Gillian didn't truly care, but her grandmother would be displeased if her troublesome granddaughter called yet more gossip down on her head.

She gave him a wolfish smile instead. "Are you in the

habit of demanding accounts of other people's private conversations, sir? Then let me give you a bit of advice—just eavesdrop. It's much more efficient."

He ignored her taunt. "May I point out that it's highly improper for a young lady to be engaging in private conversations with a man she's just met?"

She widened her eyes at him. "At what point is a young lady allowed to have a private conversation with a man, especially when her own mother is nearby? And at the risk of being overly punctilious, are *we* not having a private discussion?" She made a great show of looking about. "And I no longer see Mamma."

When he stared at her in disbelief, Gillian simply smiled. It was rather entertaining to poke fun at the infernally proper Leverton, trying to ruffle his imposing demeanor. Grandmamma always said that poking the hornet's nest was Gillian's fatal flaw, but the duke posed an irresistible temptation.

Besides, it was beastly for him to assume it was she who'd misbehaved, not Stratton. Men generally liked to assume the worst about women, often dodging responsibility for their own bad behavior.

Leverton reached for her, clearly intending to take her arm, when a stout woman, loaded down with packages, almost ploughed into him. He caught a small box that tumbled from the stack in her arms and handed it back with a polite smile. "Forgive me, madam, the fault is mine for not paying attention," he said.

"Bloody right it is." The woman resettled the packages in her arms and stalked off, muttering something about *bleedin' toffs*.

To Gillian's surprise, Leverton simply shook his head. "It would seem I owe more than one person an apology. Miss

Dryden, forgive me. I had no business biting off your nose like that."

She eyed him warily. In her experience, men didn't generally apologize to a woman unless they wanted something. But Leverton appeared to be genuinely contrite.

"Apology accepted, sir," she finally said.

When he continued to study her with a thoughtful expression, Gillian had to resist the urge to shuffle her feet or swing her muff. She almost preferred to have him annoyed with her. At least then she felt on equal footing.

Then his mouth curved into that dazzling smile of his, and Gillian forgot about feeling awkward.

"I think we've provided quite enough entertainment for the locals, don't you?" he said. "If you don't mind, I'd like to continue our stroll."

When he held out his arm, she took it. "Very well. I do need to find my way home sooner or later. But no more lectures in the middle of the street. I don't think Grandmamma would like it."

"I will try to refrain," he said dryly.

He guided her across the busy thoroughfare, briefly pausing on the other side to give a coin to the grubby little boy who'd swept vigorously in front of them. The urchin's eyes went round as plates, and he stuttered out his thanks before darting back into traffic to return to the other pavement.

"I hate to see children forced to earn their living in such a dangerous way," Gillian said, glancing back after the boy. "It's a wonder some carriage hasn't run over him already."

"One probably will at some point," Leverton said, sounding grim. "Unless he can find better employment, which doesn't seem likely."

"There are so many children like him in London. It's heartbreaking. I just wish something could be done for them."

"Some of us in Parliament try to alleviate the worst of the conditions, but the situation seems intractable."

They turned onto Carrington Place, leaving the bustle of the shopping district behind as they moved into the quieter streets of Mayfair. He glanced down at her. "You saw such poverty in Sicily, did you not?"

"Yes, Palermo has more than its share of beggars. It's not always as evident in the country, though, and certainly not on my stepfather's estates. He was very attentive to the welfare of those under his care."

"A most estimable gentleman," Leverton said. "I'm sure you and your mother miss him a great deal."

Gillian was unable to speak around the sudden constriction in her throat, so she nodded instead.

"You must have been very sorry to leave Italy," he said, "since it has always been your home."

"Yes, but I suppose it was time." Her heart rebelled against the painful admission.

"What with ruthless brigands trying to kill you, and such."

Gillian waved her ridiculous muff, setting the feathers fluttering. "My mother and grandmother exaggerate the dangers. But that's not what I meant."

"What did you mean?"

"It's just not the same since Step-papa died." She realized how inadequate that sounded. "I mean, of course it's the same in many respects, and his heir was very kind to us, but . . ." She trailed off, finding it difficult to explain.

Her stepfather's title and estates had passed to his nephew, a decent enough fellow who had the grace to treat Gillian and Mamma with respect and generosity. Still, Mamma had insisted they pack up their belongings and move into the elegant Marbury villa in Palermo. It was a wrenching good-bye not only to the only home Gillian had ever known, but also to the loyal Paterini servants who'd all but raised her from infancy. Only Stefano and Maria had gone with them. Stefano had been Gillian's bodyguard and mentor since she'd been a little girl. He'd taught her how to fight, shoot, and take care of herself, and he'd steadfastly refused to leave her side.

Eventually she'd been forced to say good-bye to Stefano, too. To be virtually exiled from his own country would have been too much for the old man. Gillian would never forget their leave-taking on the docks of Palermo. She'd wept so many tears then, knowing she might never see her old friend again.

"I think I understand," Leverton said. "When your stepfather died, you lost both your loving parent and your protector. His death made your situation more precarious."

She glanced up, startled not so much by his acumen but by his willingness to discuss her position in society.

"Although you did have Lord Marbury's protection, at least," he added.

"Yes. Though Grandfather never really approved of me, he was frightening enough that no one dared be impertinent. But he passed only a year after my stepfather, and then . . ." She tried to think of a way to put it without sounding vulgar.

"People dared to be impertinent with you?" Leverton gently suggested.

"That's one way of putting it." It had actually been much worse than that, but Gillian would die before she ever shared that with anyone.

The duke paused to draw her aside as two elderly matrons, dressed like crows in black bombazine, passed by. They all exchanged nods, the ladies murmuring polite *Your Grace*s while staring curiously at Gillian. With her deeply tanned skin and lanky figure, she supposed she looked rather odd and anything but fashionable compared to most English girls.

Leverton picked up where they'd left off. "I thought as

much. That brings me back to our original discussion. I promise not to bark at you again, but I do need to know what Stratton was quizzing you about."

When she hesitated, he sighed. "Miss Dryden, surely you realize that your grandmother would never ask for my assistance unless she felt sure I would never betray or embarrass you. You *can* trust me."

She didn't bother to hide her skepticism. He was right to say that Grandmamma trusted him, and that Gillian could as well. But deep inside it felt impossible to let down her guard. After all, she'd spent years building it up, precisely because of men like him.

They stood on the quiet street, locked in a silent contest of wills. Gillian half expected him to begin lecturing her again. Yet his gaze warmed with understanding—and sympathy.

"I am not the first man to ask you to trust him, am I?" he asked.

She winced. "Blast. Is it that obvious?"

He started her forward again, for which Gillian was grateful. It would be easier to discuss such an embarrassing topic if he wasn't looking at her.

"I put two and two together," he said. "And, as a reminder, I would suggest you refrain from using terms like *blast* when in polite company."

"All right, but only on the understanding that I can say whatever I want to immediate family."

"I suppose I can't really stop you, can I?"

"I doubt it. Some things are just bloody difficult to change."

"You can't shock me, you know. Although I think I must drop a word in your brother's ear, all the same."

"Ha. That's not much of a threat. I was using bad language long before I ever met Griffin."

"No doubt."

Gillian pretended to ponder for a moment. "Perhaps if you write down all the words I'm not supposed to say, I can commit them to memory."

"I'm quite sure you know exactly what you should and shouldn't say," he said.

Gillian couldn't help giving him a little smirk.

"Very well," he said. "We'll leave the language lessons for some future date. We have again been diverted from our main topic, which is—"

"Mr. Stratton." The duke clearly wasn't going to let it go, so she might as well get it over with. "From your reaction, I imagine you already have a good idea of what he said."

"Did he insult you or importune you?" he asked in a hard voice.

"Mr. Stratton would be walking with a limp right now if he had. Or not walking at all, depending on my aim."

Leverton made a slight, choking noise, then cleared his throat. "Then what did he say, exactly?"

"He asked me to meet him for a walk or a drive in the park."

"By yourself? And without telling your grandmother?"

"Yes."

"Bastard," Leverton muttered.

She couldn't resist. "Language, Your Grace. But don't worry. Why would I want to go driving in the park with a married man? I'm supposed to be finding a husband, not larking about with ineligible men."

"You're not to be engaging in such behavior with an unmarried man, either. Not unless you have the express permission of your mother or grandmother, and only after they've met your escort."

"I'm not a half-wit, nor am I naïve. I know exactly what men like Stratton are after. I'm quite familiar with the type."

That silenced him for half a block. "I'm sorry you even have to worry about that," he finally said.

"Grandmamma warned me some years ago what to expect." After Pietro. Because of that gentleman, Gillian would never be naïve again. "I have no intention of allowing myself to become a member of the demimonde. I would not enjoy such a life."

"I should bloody well hope not," Leverton said.

Gillian feigned astonishment. "Sir, I am truly shocked. Perhaps I should draw up a list of words for you."

"I would ask for your apology, but I doubt very much that I offended you."

"Of course not. I'm as tough as old boots."

"No, you're not. And you're as deserving of respect as any young woman. I regret that we even need to have this unfortunate discussion."

She couldn't help smiling. "I know you're trying to help. And I don't mind at all. Truly."

"You should mind," he said. "But back to Stratton."

Gillian groaned. "Must we?"

"I need you to understand that he might well not be the only cad who tries to take advantage. I want you to be well armored against that possibility."

"Of course. But Mr. Stratton is harmless, you know."

He shook his head. "He's exactly the type you have to worry about."

Gillian heard something in his voice that gave her pause—an undertone of bitterness. This was more than a well-intentioned warning. It sounded personal to Leverton. "I'll be careful, Your Grace."

"You're to come to me or to your grandmother if you have any concerns of this nature at all."

"Yes, I promise."

He let out a reluctant laugh. "Now you're patronizing me. Or behaving as if I'm a fussy old maid who sees a rake lurking behind every tree."

"No, you're behaving like someone who cares. But why are you doing this?"

"Warning you about bounders like Stratton?"

She tugged on his arm. "Now you're being deliberately obtuse."

"Perhaps just slightly evasive," he said with a wry smile. "But now let me ask you a question. Do you want this little experiment your grandmother cooked up to actually work?"

"You mean teaching me not to swear, and how to curtsey without falling on my ear?" she asked in as innocent a voice as she could muster. Sadly, Gillian didn't do innocent very well.

"Those things are simply a means to an end, and you know it. Your family wishes you to find a suitable husband, and I'd like to know if you want that too."

Confound it. "What girl doesn't?"

He snorted. "You, I suspect."

"And I suspect that you are quite wrong." Dodgy, but at least it wasn't an outright lie.

He stopped her again. Reluctantly, she looked up to meet his searching gaze. "Miss Dryden, what is it that you fear? Do you think you will be laughed at, or somehow punished for trying to make a respectable marriage?"

She scoffed, giving that question the response it deserved. "Most already do laugh at me, and will continue to do so. I don't really care about that."

"Everyone wishes to be accepted by his or her peers."

"I don't." It would never happen anyway, she knew.

"Well, your family wishes it. Since I'm a member of your family, I share that desire on your behalf. Besides, people won't laugh at you if you don't give them any fodder."

She studied him. Again, he seemed perfectly sincere. "Why do you even care whether I succeed or fail?"

When he started to say something about family and responsibility, she cut him off with an irritable wave. "Please, that's ridiculous. You can lend my family support without playing governess to me. I want to know why you care about *me*, one way or the other."

Gillian had learned long ago that most people had a motive for helping others. She'd only met a few who didn't. Her stepfather had been one.

And look how that had turned out for him.

Leverton shrugged. "For now, just accept that I do, and that I sincerely wish you to succeed."

She had no choice but to accept. From everything she'd heard about the duke—and everything she'd observed—he was a man who kept his word. According to her grandmother, Leverton was as trustworthy as he was powerful.

There was just one problem: she wished him to fail. She wished the entire scheme to reform her to fail. Unfortunately, that put her in the position of using a man who was apparently willing to inconvenience himself to a considerable extent in order to help her. There was more than a degree of irony in the situation, since she was the one with the ulterior motive, not Leverton.

She toyed with the idea of telling him the truth. But as nice as the duke was, he'd made his position clear—the family desired her to remain in England, and he supported that. If she truly wished to return to Sicily, Gillian had to give the impression that she was trying to learn to be a proper lady. That meant accepting Leverton's help, at least for now. Once everyone saw how pointless the venture was, then perhaps they would begin to listen to her.

"All right, I'm willing to give your plan a go," she said, forcing herself to ignore an inconvenient sense of guilt. "Shall we shake on it?"

He took her hand and shook it with appropriate gravity. With that business concluded, they resumed their walk and soon reached Brook Street.

Leverton was about to escort her up the steps of her

grandmother's townhouse when Gillian stopped him. "I know I'm not very good at reading social signals, but it's obvious you weren't happy to see Mr. Stratton. As for Lady Letitia, however . . ." She shook her head. What was it about the woman, and Leverton's response to her, that she found so troublesome?

"Is there a question in there somewhere, Miss Dryden?"

She heard the warning note in his voice, but decided to ignore it. Curiosity was another of her besetting sins. "It was obvious even to me that Lady Letitia was . . . well, she called it teasing, but it seemed more like flirting to me. Why would she flirt with you, especially in front of her husband?"

The duke's scowl suggested he was about to haul thunderbolts down from the heights. "Miss Dryden, I am not a fan of gossip. You shouldn't be, either."

She waved a dismissive hand. "Everyone in London gossips. Besides, I'm simply trying to distinguish what sort of behavior is appropriate between men and women with a certain degree of, er, familiarity. And Lady Letitia does seem very familiar with you." She lifted an eyebrow. "Am I wrong about that?"

He looked disgusted. "No."

She waited for several long seconds for more detail. He remained tight-lipped.

"Well," she prompted. "How familiar are you and Lady Letitia?"

When Leverton finally answered, he gave the impression that he had to pry his jaws apart. "She was almost my wife."

Chapter Eight

"It wasn't necessary for you to come with me to pick them up," Charles said to his sister as he handed her down from the town coach. "In fact, I think you'll be in the way."

Lady Elizabeth Church, Countess of Filby and his younger sister by four years, poked him with her fan. "Charles, it is beyond me how people regard you as such a paragon of courtesy."

"Anyone who knows *you* would almost certainly forgive my lapse in manners."

She laughed. "Sadly true, I'm afraid. I am entirely nosy, and I wanted to meet Miss Dryden before the ball. You know Lady Barrington's affairs are always such a crush. I wouldn't have a hope of speaking to the girl with any degree of privacy."

"Trust me, you'll wish you hadn't. Gillian's behavior would send the proverbial saint into a frenzy." He led her up the steps of the Brook Street townhouse and gave the knocker a few good raps.

"Gillian, is it? I didn't realize you two were on such intimate terms."

"Elizabeth, you are quite off the mark if you—" The door opened, choking off his reprimand.

She gave his arm an affectionate squeeze as the butler ushered them into the entrance hall. "I'm teasing, dear brother. I think it's splendid you're trying to help them."

He cut her a rueful grin. "We'll see how splendid after tonight. Our odds of success are no better than fifty per cent."

"You're to be commended for even trying," she said stoutly. "Very few men would bother."

His sister's praise warmed him, as always. Warmth had been sadly lacking in his family, mostly due to his father's discomfort with *odiously sentimental* displays of familial affection. Charles and his older sister, Eugenia, had been schooled to conduct themselves with dignity and restraint. Though their mother was not nearly as intimidating as their father, the duchess had expected her two eldest children to act with a decorum befitting the Penley name.

Elizabeth had always been different. She'd been a happy child, possessing an open and winning personality that had charmed even their father off his high horse. Then she'd become a beautiful girl who'd grown into a lovely woman. Elizabeth had always been the heart and soul of their family, building bridges and tearing down walls. It was exhausting work, given how pigheaded they all were, but she never seemed to begrudge the effort. Still, even she hadn't been able to throw a span over that last, fatal breach between Charles and his father.

"Will your husband be joining us at the ball?" Charles asked as they followed the butler up to the drawing room.

"You know how much he hates crowds. He's just as happy to stay home with the children." She let out a dramatic sigh. "He prefers the company of toddlers to that of sensible adults. I simply don't know what to do with him."

Charles wasn't fooled. Elizabeth adored her husband, a kind-hearted man who preferred a quiet life in the country to the whirlwind of the beau monde. But he loved his wife, so he dutifully brought her to town for the Season. In London, he focused on his duties in Parliament and left the socializing to his fashionable wife.

"I doubt there will be many sensible adults at Lady Barrington's ball," Charles said. "The woman is a bird-wit if there ever was one, as are most of her guests. I expect to find little in the way of intelligent conversation."

"Goodness, me. I'm not used to such plain speaking from Perfect Penley. Is this refreshing change in your personality due to the influence of Miss Dryden?"

"Elizabeth, don't be impertinent. It's not becoming."

She let out a delighted chuckle. "That's the brother I know and love."

He refused to take the bait—or acknowledge that she'd scored a hit. The truth was, Gillian was a trial. The girl was quick and whip smart, but she was also as stubborn as a donkey. Every lesson invariably dissolved into a disagreement or an interrogation into the whys and wherefores of social rules that had been taken for granted for decades, if not centuries.

Determined to be fair, he'd occasionally admitted to seeing her point. But she was the last person who should test the outer boundaries of social decorum. It had been a lesson he'd been trying to impress on her for ten days.

When the butler quietly announced them, Aunt Lucy, elegantly dressed in a dark green gown shot through with gold embroidery, rose to her feet with a welcoming smile. "Good evening, Charles. And this must be your sister, Lady Filby. What a perfectly lovely young woman. I am enchanted to meet you."

Elizabeth sank into a formal curtsey. "It's an honor to meet you, my lady."

The older woman took her hand. "No need to stand on ceremony, dear child. You are family, and you have graciously stepped forward to help in our time of need. I cannot thank you enough."

"No thanks are necessary, ma'am. My brother has told me all about your granddaughter. I must confess that I'm dying to meet her. She sounds utterly charming."

"That's one way of looking at it," Charles said in a dry voice.

Elizabeth shook her head. "Really, Charles, what is Lady Marbury to make of such jests?"

"That I agree with him. That is why I'm pleased I can speak with you before Gillian comes down." Lady Marbury took her seat and waved them to the sofa opposite. "And please do call me Aunt Lucy, as your brother does."

Elizabeth darted a glance his way, clearly startled. Charles shrugged.

"Very well. But you must call me Elizabeth," his sister replied after a moment's hesitation.

"I shall be delighted," Aunt Lucy said.

Charles had discovered that the Countess of Marbury was a fine tactician. The more allies she brought to her side, the easier would be the path for Gillian. It was, he thought, one of the reasons his aunt was so determined to stress their family bonds. Elizabeth would be another feather in the older woman's bonnet. His sister was a popular and well-regarded young matron in the *ton*. To have the support of both the Duke of Leverton and the Countess of Filby would be a coup for the Marburys in general and for Gillian in particular.

"Shall we wait for the Contessa di Paterini to join us before we begin to plot Gillian's conquest of the *ton*?" Charles asked.

Aunt Lucy let out a barely audible sigh. "My daughter is feeling a bit poorly tonight. I'm afraid the crush at Lady Barrington's might be too much for her."

More likely she didn't feel up to dealing with either the

gossip or her daughter's behavior. Gillian's mamma tended to wilt under stress. Charles couldn't blame her, though he'd hoped she would find it in herself to support her daughter's first major foray into society.

"I'm sorry to hear that," Elizabeth said. "I was looking forward to meeting her."

"Yes, it's unfortunate that she won't be with us to support Gillian at her first ball," Aunt Lucy said. "It's quite a shame that Griffin and Justine cannot join us, either. Griffin's presence always gives Gillian a boost. He's very protective of her."

Charles mentally grimaced. It irritated him that Gillian was so comfortable with her half brother. As far as Charles was concerned, Steele brought out the worst in the girl. Steele had even more contempt for polite society than Gillian, which was truly saying something.

"The spectacle of the Duke of Cumberland's by-blows at the same ball would generate precisely the sort of gossip we wish to avoid," he said. "Besides, Steele's idea of protection generally runs to beating a man senseless or even slipping a knife between his ribs."

"Justine said the same thing," Aunt Lucy said.

"Mrs. Steele is a very sensible woman," Charles replied. How the man had managed to find himself such a paragon of a wife was something Charles couldn't fathom. Justine Steele was intelligent, beautiful, and exceedingly kind. She also clearly adored her husband, which was another mystery.

"Griffin Steele sounds very exciting," Elizabeth said. "I'd love to meet him."

"No, you wouldn't," Charles said.

"Spoilsport," his sister murmured.

He ignored her. "Aunt Lucy, do you have a specific concern about tonight?"

"I'm worried that we may be rushing things," she said. "Don't you think an event this large is too much for Gillian's first outing? I'd thought we'd go more slowly, with a few dinner parties and perhaps a musicale."

"In theory, I don't disagree, but in practice it's not only necessary but imperative."

His sister tilted a curious eyebrow. "Why?"

He hesitated.

Elizabeth smiled. "I'm a married woman with children, Charles. You will neither offend nor shock me."

"Very well. Gillian has already been the subject of a considerable amount of gossip, though most of it has been fairly harmless. Recently, though, there have been some rather crude jests about her and a few unfortunate bets."

Elizabeth frowned. "What sort of bets?"

Charles glanced at Gillian's grandmother, reluctant to put the gossip into words. Just thinking about it made his anger flare like a torch.

"Bets on who will be Gillian's first protector and when that will occur," Aunt Lucy said in a cool voice. When Charles raised his eyebrows, she shook her head with disgust. "Yes, I've heard the rumors. A few of my old friends have made a point of telling me."

"That's horrible," Elizabeth exclaimed.

Charles agreed. "I think it's time for you to find some new friends, Aunt Lucy."

"Indeed. Those who dared to raise the issue were shown my front door in no uncertain order."

"Is that the real reason the contessa will not be going to the ball tonight?" he asked.

Aunt Lucy grimaced. "Yes. I wish she could be stronger for Gillian's sake, but I cannot say that I blame her. And perhaps it's for the best. If anyone dared to insult my daughter—especially in front of *her* daughter—the outcome would not be a pretty one."

"Especially if there were a heavy object within reach," Charles said.

The two women gaped at him, then Aunt Lucy let out a reluctant laugh. "Wretch. You said that to pull me out of my foolish gloom, didn't you?"

"Gloom is rather a waste of time, don't you think?" he said. "Instead, we will hit back with a display of force. Show the *ton* that Miss Dryden has not only the support of her grandmother, but of the Duke of Leverton, as well."

"And Lady Filby," his sister piped up. "Now I'm doubly glad I'm going, Charles. Thank you for asking me."

"It is I who owe you thanks. Both of you," Aunt Lucy said, looking rather misty. "And I'm sure Gillian will be appropriately grateful as well."

Charles rather doubted it, but he held his peace.

His aunt glanced at the handsome French ormolu clock on the mantel. "Gillian will be down in a few minutes. I don't want to discuss the more scurrilous rumors in front of her. It's quite upsetting enough as it is."

Charles wouldn't be surprised if Gillian already had a good inkling. He'd learned that she was exceedingly good at ferreting out information, especially from the staff. He had little doubt that she had every servant in Aunt Lucy's employ wrapped around her finger, and that meant she had a direct channel to the best gossip. Too many aristocrats didn't have the brains to keep their mouths shut in front of their household staff, and servants in one household frequently spoke to servants in another.

"I suspect she already knows some of it," he said. "I tried to broach the issue with her in a general way, and she waved me off. Said she didn't give a hang about nonsense bandied about by gossiping fools."

Elizabeth wrinkled her nose. "How wretched that a young woman should even have to worry about something like that."

"It's unpleasant, to say the least," he said. "We must make it quite clear that she is under our joint protection. That is what tonight is about."

His sister nodded. "That makes perfect sense, and it should keep the worst of the wolves away from her door."

"Very well," Aunt Lucy said. "But I am still a tad anxious about introducing Gillian at one of the biggest crushes of the Season."

"I understand, but she is making progress. With a bit of luck, I think we will manage the evening without any disasters."

Aunt Lucy began to fidget with her fan.

"Is there something else?" he gently prompted. "Besides your granddaughter's propensity toward near-fatal honesty?"

"That's the problem. She's not being honest in this case."

"I don't follow."

"Charles, I doubt she has any intention of trying to find a husband," Aunt Lucy said. "In fact, she asked me when we would be returning to Sicily."

That gave him an oddly unpleasant jolt. "I understood you would not be doing so."

"Certainly not in the short term. It would be much too dangerous for Gillian."

"When did she ask you?"

"Shortly after that gruesome incident with the French dancing master."

Charles winced at the memory. He'd employed the most expensive dancing master in London, confident that the man could teach Gillian, a naturally graceful girl, in record time. Unfortunately, teacher and pupil had clashed at first sight. One thing had led to another, ending with some rather rude insults on Monsieur Pepin's part. Gillian had then threatened to run him through with a blade. Charles had quickly relieved Monsieur of his duties, paying him for a full month's work and sending him on his way with a stern admonition not to spread a word of gossip about Gillian.

"Yes, that was unfortunate," he said. "But we've recovered

nicely from that particular crisis. She seems to get along well with the new dancing master."

Aunt Lucy gave him a hesitant smile. "It was a stroke of genius to hire Signor Garibaldi. An Italian dancing master was just the thing to settle her down."

"Has she raised the issue of returning to Sicily again since?"

"No, but I'd already told her it was much too early to even consider such a thing. I said that she must try very hard to make England her home."

Elizabeth, who'd been sitting quietly, leaned forward with an expression of sympathetic concern. "And how did she respond?"

Aunt Lucy gave a helpless shrug. "She seemed to accept it, but she's not happy."

"I can't say as I blame the girl," Elizabeth said. "The marriage mart is a nightmare at the best of times. For a girl in Miss Dryden's position, it must seem particularly daunting."

"Daunting, but not impossible," Charles said. "And let us please not refer to it as a nightmare in Gillian's presence."

Elizabeth scoffed. "I'm not an hen-wit, Charles."

"My dear, I would never think such a thing."

She grinned at him. "Yes, you would."

"Shall we return to the subject at hand?" he suggested. "Specifically, whether Gillian will try to sabotage her chances of attracting appropriate suitors."

"How shocking of her," Elizabeth said. "Imagine a woman not obsessed with finding a husband."

She was referring to Eugenia, of course. Their older sister had never wished for marriage, and had happily turned down all the suitors who'd courted her over the years. She enjoyed her life on Charles's principal estate, taking care of their mother, bossing the servants, and generally doing an excellent job of running things. That Eugenia preferred spinsterhood to marriage was clear to all of them.

"You're not helping," Charles said. "You know Gillian needs the safety and security of a good marriage. She's much too vulnerable otherwise."

"Then I suppose we must help her become invested in that sensible goal," Elizabeth said.

"If she is successful tonight, that will help," he said.

Aunt Lucy sighed. "I just hope she can refrain from saying something outrageous."

"I advised her to listen rather than speak," Charles said. "That way she has at least an even chance of not terrifying her partners."

"Charles, you didn't!" exclaimed his sister, trying not to laugh.

"In my granddaughter's case, that is actually sage advice," Aunt Lucy said in a rueful tone. "But I truly hate that she is unhappy. I wish . . ." She pressed her lips shut.

Charles went to sit by her, taking her hand. "Let's see how it goes, shall we? Gillian is a lovely young woman who is sure to attract admiration. She's also turned out to be a surprisingly good dancer, thanks in part to Signor Garibaldi. Perhaps she'll enjoy herself. After all, it's her first real dance, and that's always an exciting event."

Aunt Lucy eyed him with a dubious expression, but was spared the need to answer when the door opened and Gillian walked in.

Charles glanced over to his protégé, intending to give her a bracing smile. Instead, he stared at the vision before him and promptly forgot how to breathe.

Chapter Nine

The Marquess of Lendale executed a faultless bow as Gillian came up from her curtsey. "Well done, Miss Dryden. You have completed your first set of public dances and with nary a mistake."

"You sound surprised, my lord," she said.

"No such thing. You were grace personified."

"Really? Are we discounting the fact that I stepped on your foot *and* turned the wrong way, not once but twice?"

His dark eyes held laughter. "That could happen to anyone. It is not even worth a mention."

"Then of course you are correct," she said, taking his arm. "My performance was all but perfect."

Gillian had found herself surprisingly nervous when she took her place in the first set of the evening. Fortunately, Lord Lendale was an accomplished dancer. He'd smoothly corrected her mistakes and had completely ignored her tromping on his toes. Her success was mostly attributable to his skills, not hers.

Although she'd been vaguely surprised that Leverton had not stood up with her for the first dance, Gillian had been relieved as well. The more time she spent with him, the more nervous she was in his presence. The epitome of masculine elegance, the duke never set a foot wrong or said anything unintentionally. No slips of the tongue, no unbecoming displays of temper for him. Never had Gillian felt more like a country bumpkin than when she was in his company.

Even worse, he was the most physically spectacular man she'd ever met. More than once, she'd caught herself admiring his broad shoulders or powerful legs showcased by snug breeches. Gillian experienced a funny feeling in the pit of her stomach whenever she looked at those legs, especially when Leverton was garbed for riding. Not even Pietro had made her feel such disconcerting sensations, and she'd been madly in love with him at one time.

Leverton was also incredibly patient with her, and had even taken her side in the humiliating incident with the French dancing master. After he'd coolly dismissed Monsieur Pepin, he'd simply told Gillian that it was bad form to threaten to skewer one's tutors with a rapier. She'd been so surprised by his mild reprimand that she'd bobbed a curtsey and thanked him for his advice.

In fact, she'd been so flustered by the whole episode that she'd asked her grandmother when they could return to Sicily. In doing so, Gillian had stupidly tipped her hand to her family. It was another indication of how out of sorts she felt these days.

"Shall we return to your party, Miss Dryden?" Lendale enquired. "I've spotted them near the top of the room."

"Yes, my lord. I'm sure my grandmother must be on pins and needles to hear the report of my first official dance at my first official ball. With this mob, it's doubtful she saw very much."

"You did very well, my dear," said the middle-aged woman who'd been in the set with them. The lady leaned in close and gave her a wink. "Not that you didn't have an absolutely splendid partner to inspire you. I'd keep an eye on that one, if I were you."

"Yes, madam. Thank you," Gillian said, trying not to laugh.

The lady had been both friendly and forgiving of her mistakes, even whispering a few corrections when Gillian was out of position. The other two women in their set had not been nearly as good-natured, but neither had they snubbed her. That certainly counted as progress.

Leverton's plan was to introduce her into society while attracting as little attention as possible. If she could manage to attend a number of events without causing a scene, people would get used to her and move on to more fruitful subjects of gossip. That suited Gillian perfectly. The sooner she could sink into obscurity, the better her chances of convincing her relatives to let her go home.

She and Lendale made their way back to the top of the room, where they'd left her grandmother chatting with old friends. It was slow going, and more than once the marquess used his elbows to keep Gillian from getting squashed.

When they reached Gillian's party, Grandmamma was deep in conversation with Mrs. Paxton and Lady Merchant, who was some sort of Marbury relation. Her grandmother seemed to have quite a lot of cousins of one degree or another, and a few seemed cautiously willing to help with Gillian's launch into society. Lady Merchant was one of them.

"Ah, my dears," Grandmamma said with a relieved smile. "I was wondering when you'd reappear. Did you enjoy your dance, Gillian? I was only able to catch a few glimpses of you."

"It was very nice. I only stepped on Lord Lendale's feet a few times. Fortunately, he's much too polite to remark on it."

Her grandmother shook her head, but the marquess simply laughed. "Nonsense. Lady Marbury, your grand-daughter did exceedingly well. I would be happy to dance another set, but it wouldn't be right to keep her all to myself."

"And that way you spare yourself from being tragically crippled," Gillian said, smiling up at him.

Her grandmother rolled her eyes, but Lady Merchant and her granddaughters, two pleasant girls a bit younger than Gillian, all laughed.

"No fear of that," the marquess said. "After spending several years in the Peninsula, I'm as tough as a draft horse. Why, I'm certain you could haul off and kick me in the shins, and I'd barely feel a thing."

Gillian found it hard to resist Lendale's easy charm. He was handsome, with dark, almost saturnine looks she suspected left girls swooning in his wake, and he had a friendly manner that wasn't the least bit patronizing. He didn't make her nervous at all.

Grandmamma approved of him, of course, and Gillian had no doubt that her mother would also find him a perfect suitor. After all, he was rich, titled, and a good friend of Leverton's—which meant he passed muster. If Gillian were looking for a suitor, she could do much worse than the Marquess of Lendale.

But she had no intention of allowing herself to become attracted to Lendale or anyone else, not even Leverton.

Attracted to Leverton? Why did that truly demented notion insist on sneaking into her brain? With an effort, Gillian forced her attention back to her companions.

Lady Merchant tapped Lendale with her fan. "My dear sir, how are you finding life since you returned? I believe you haven't been back long."

"No, I was in Paris for some months after the war and only returned to London when my uncle fell ill." Lendale had only recently come into his title and estates, having inherited them from a bachelor uncle. Until that time, he'd been a career officer in the military. Understandably, he was now considered a prime catch on the marriage mart.

While his lordship chatted with the matrons, Gillian joined Lady Merchant's granddaughters, Lady Sarah Rundall and Miss Honoria Cranston. She'd met them when they had come calling with Lady Merchant a few days ago. Gillian knew her grandmother was eager for her to befriend them, so she'd made an extra effort. Fortunately, the task had been an easy one.

Sarah and Honoria were both sweet girls who'd been out for three years. According to Grandmamma, they'd both failed to take, a phrase Gillian despised. While neither was a ravishing beauty, they were perfectly nice, intelligent girls. Yes, Sarah had a few spots and Honoria was a tad plump, but Gillian didn't see why that should be a problem. She'd seen any number of young men with numerous spots, spindly calves, or plump torsos, and nobody held that against them.

"Miss Dryden, you and Lord Lendale looked splendid together," Sarah enthused. "Honoria and I squeezed down the set to watch, and we both thought you did a bang-up job."

Gillian smiled. "You're very kind, but actually I galumphed all over the poor man's feet. He must have been tempted to abandon me completely."

"We saw no such thing," Sarah said. "Besides, you're so slender and graceful it would be hard for you to look clumsy, even if you did trod on his toes."

"Unlike me," Honoria said. "I'm such a dumpling. It's impossible for me to look graceful, no matter how hard I try." She let out a sigh as she directed a longing look at the pairs lined up in their sets. "I suppose I shouldn't be surprised no one ever wants to dance with me."

"What rot," Sarah exclaimed. "You're an accomplished dancer. It's not your fault if men are too stupid to see it."

"No. All they can see is that I lumber about like—" Honoria cut herself off with a grimace.

Her cousin squeezed her arm. "Don't even think about it, pet. It was a horrid thing to say, and you should simply forget about it."

"I'd like to," Honoria replied. "But it was the sort of thing that tends to stick like taffy. Or like a little rabbit running around in your brain."

"Was someone rude to you?" Gillian asked.

Honoria tried for a casual shrug, but she blinked several times, as if holding back tears.

"You don't have to tell me if you don't want to," Gillian said.

"You'll probably hear it by the time the night is out, anyway," Honoria said in a glum voice. "But promise me you won't laugh."

"Believe me, I've been on the receiving end of considerable nastiness," Gillian said. "I would never laugh."

Honoria nodded. "I'd forgotten for a moment how difficult it must be for you. It's awful, isn't it?"

"I do my best to ignore it," Gillian replied.

Sarah cast a quick glance around. Their neighbors were engaged in their own conversations. "It happened last week, at Almack's," she said, leaning in a bit. "One of Honoria's partners said that dancing with her was like dancing with a Guernsey heifer."

Gillian shook her head. "I'm sorry, I don't understand. Why a Guernsey heifer?"

"It's because my family owns estates on the island of Guernsey," Honoria said. She paused for a few seconds. "And because I'm such a cow."

Gillian had to pause as well before she answered. Although in her case, it was to tamp down a surge of fury. When she heard a crack, she realized she'd snapped one of the ribs of her fan.

"Who dared say that to you?" she asked through clenched teeth.

"Lord Andover," Sarah said.

"Is he here tonight?"

"Unfortunately, he is," Honoria said.

Gillian laid a hand on her shoulder. "I want you to point him out to me as soon as you see him."

Honoria nodded. "So you can avoid dancing with him?"

"No, so I can knee him in the bollocks if I do dance with him."

The cousins stared at her, their mouths dropping open in identical, stunned expressions.

Blast. Gillian had again forgotten what hothouse flowers English girls tended to be. She'd started to apologize when the girls exchanged a glance and burst into laughter. Gillian raised her eyebrows before starting to laugh, too.

Honoria struggled to contain herself. "Oh, Miss Dryden, that is the most delicious thing I've ever heard. I would give half my dowry to see such a thing."

"I think I would give my entire dowry," Sarah said. "What a shame you can't do it."

Gillian could and would, but she supposed she'd better not say that.

"You ladies are certainly enjoying yourselves," Lord Lendale said, sidling over to join them. "Care to let a fellow in on the joke?"

The cousins looked at each other again and burst into laughter.

"I'm afraid not," Gillian said.

"Why not?" Lendale asked.

"It wouldn't be proper. At least not according to my grandmother."

"I always miss the good jokes," he said with mock disgust. "Oh, well, I suppose I can at least make myself useful. Would you ladies care for some punch? I'm off to find a footman and secure some refreshments."

Lady Sarah smiled at him. "That would be lovely, my lord. Thank you."

He bowed. "It's my pleasure. Now, Lady Sarah, Miss Honoria, I expect you both to save me a dance. It's the least you can do after cutting me out of the joke."

The two girls smiled shyly as they accepted. With a promise to return quickly, Lendale disappeared into the crowd.

"What a nice man," Honoria said. Then she gave Gillian a sly smile. "You're very lucky. He likes you."

Gillian shrugged. "Perhaps. I like him, too."

"But not in the same way," Lady Sarah shrewdly observed. "I can see why. Lendale's handsome and funny, but the Duke of Leverton is, well, magnificent. I don't blame you in the least."

Gillian's stomach gave a lurch. "I think you have the wrong impression."

"Are you sure?" Honoria said. "I couldn't help noticing that he's spent much of the evening staring at you."

"That's because he's helping with my introduction into society. Almost like a sponsor." Gillian forced out a thin laugh. "He's probably taking mental notes so he can lecture me later on all my trip ups."

"Really? What an odd thing for a duke to do," Honoria said. "Are you sure?"

Gillian repressed a sigh. "Very."

"Oh, I do hope he's not interested in Lady Letitia," Sarah said as she peered out at the dance floor. "She's simply dreadful."

The temptation to follow Sarah's gaze was too great. Gillian turned, and her stomach took another uncomfortable flop. For there were the duke and Lady Letitia. She was clinging to him in the most shocking manner as they concluded a waltz. Gillian was no prude, but she had to resist the urge to storm over there and drag the blasted woman from his arms.

"Don't forget that she's a married woman," Honoria said.

Sarah let out a delicate snort. "As if that ever stopped a man."

The three of them studied Leverton and his partner in silence. Unfortunately, Gillian couldn't deduce what he was thinking from his expression. The man was bloody inscrutable when he wanted to be. Apparently, now was one of those times.

Lady Letitia was speaking to him in an earnest, rapid-fire way, and it appeared that Leverton was listening just as earnestly. He even nodded once or twice, as if giving her encouragement. At least her ladyship seemed to take it as encouragement, because she snuggled even closer, all but rubbing her breasts against him.

Ugh.

Gillian supposed she shouldn't be surprised at the intimacy, since the duke had once been engaged to the woman. That, however, was all she knew. Leverton had refused to impart anything but the fact that they'd been betrothed, and that Lady Letitia had broken it off and married Stratton instead.

Gillian turned her back on the disturbing sight. "I'm sure the duke is just being polite. He's very polite to everyone."

"If you say so," Honoria replied, skeptically.

"Oh, no," Sarah hissed, grabbing her cousin's arm. "Don't look now, but—"

"Well, look who's here," a male voice cut in. "The notorious Miss Dryden and her wallflower friends. What fun for me."

Chapter Ten

Gillian turned to find a gentleman standing before them, in company with Mr. Gerald Stratton. She thought Stratton's smile looked a little strained, but his companion regarded Honoria, who'd gone pale and thin-lipped, with a nasty smile. Sarah, meanwhile, glared at the men with an ill-disguised look of outrage.

Stratton executed a pretty bow. "Miss Dryden, it's a pleasure to see you again, and in such pleasant company. And everyone is looking splendid tonight, I must say."

The other man was a tall, clever-looking fellow with padded shoulders and an exquisitely tied cravat. He quickly inspected Honoria and Sarah through his quizzing glass before turning the glass on Gillian. She was tempted to knock the blasted thing from his grasp and grind it under her heel, and then knock the sneering expression off his face.

"Some of us are," he drawled as he studied Gillian. Through the glass, his eye looked gigantic and bug-like. "But you do love to flatter the ladies, Gerry, and they love to flatter you back."

Stratton let out an uncomfortable laugh. "Don't talk nonsense, Andover. Besides, there's nothing wrong with complimenting the ladies, is there?"

Andover. That explained it. The man who'd insulted Honoria.

"Perhaps Mr. Stratton was merely trying to be polite," Gillian said. "It's a quality often in short supply amongst members of the *ton,* especially the men."

That gave the gentlemen pause.

Andover recovered first. "How delightfully blunt. I had heard so much about you, Miss Dryden, that I had to beg old Stratton here for a formal introduction."

"You'll be sadly disappointed, sir," she replied. "I'm really nothing special."

"Fishing for compliments, are we?" Andover purred. "I'll be happy to oblige." What he no doubt thought was a seductive smile was spoiled by his stained front teeth.

"Don't trouble yourself on my behalf. I assure you it's a waste of time."

His eyebrows shot up. "Ah, I see you're an original. How delightful. Perhaps your modesty is offended because we've yet to be properly introduced?"

Gillian shook her head. "No, I think I'm just generally offended."

Andover's expression turned ugly when Sarah and Honoria choked back startled giggles.

"My fault for not making the proper introductions," Stratton blurted out. "So sorry, ladies, I don't know what I was thinking."

Gillian frowned. Stratton, who'd struck her in their first meeting as a self-possessed man, looked thoroughly uncomfortable. She glanced over her shoulder, looking for her grandmother. Unfortunately, Grandmamma had moved away to speak to a friend, and her back was now turned.

"Yes, Stratton," Andover said. "Do make the appropriate introductions. I would hate for Miss Dryden to be uncomfortable with me. Quite the opposite in fact."

She sighed. There were times when she preferred insults to flattery, and this was one of them.

"Andover, may I introduce you to Miss Gillian Dryden," Stratton said. "Miss Dryden, my friend, the Earl of Andover."

The earl flourished a bow. "Miss Dryden, it's an honor. I've been quite longing to meet you."

She gave him a toothy smile. "You said you've heard about me. Well, I've heard about you, too."

He looked disconcerted for a moment, but then recovered. "All good, I hope."

"Quite the opposite, but I'm not one to gossip."

Honoria let out a startled squeak that brought Andover's attention back to her. The poor girl cringed a bit, but then stiffened her shoulders and stared defiantly back.

"A word of advice, Miss Dryden," Andover said. "It's best not to listen to gossip, especially from resentful little wallflowers jealous of attractive young ladies such as yourself."

Sarah and Honoria gasped at the insult, and Stratton sounded like he was choking. As for Andover, he deserved a swift uppercut to the jaw—or a knee to the bollocks. But Gillian had promised her grandmother that she'd behave. Besides, causing a scene would hardly help her friends.

"I will be sure to take your words under advisement," she said in a polite tone. "Since I'm a wallflower myself, however, I hardly think I'm in any position to judge."

"Come now, Miss Dryden," his lordship said. "No girl with your lovely face and many physical charms could ever be deemed a wallflower. I do wish you would allow me to take you for a turn around the room or honor me with a dance."

The man was a complete bounder. "I'm sure you'd find me utterly boring in no time. Besides, I'm perfectly happy with my present company." She smiled at her friends, who both beamed back at her.

"What a pity," Andover drawled. "And here I thought you were such a goer. At least that's what Stratton said."

Though Gillian was unfamiliar with the term, Honoria's shocked expression and Sarah's outraged huff gave her a clue.

"I never said any such thing," Stratton objected loudly. That had the unfortunate effect of causing several heads to swivel and crane in their direction.

Sarah glared at Andover. "Sir, apologize to Miss Dryden or leave us immediately."

Gillian appreciated her friend's loyalty. Sadly, though, they were drawing more notice by the second. For once, it wasn't her fault—a nice bit of irony that, under the circumstances, meant little. She patted Sarah's arm. "It's nothing I haven't heard before. It's all just silliness, best ignored."

Andover's gaze narrowed with an ugly sneer. Clearly, he wasn't used to rejection. "No doubt you've heard quite a lot. I'm sure that's true for your dear mamma, too. She had quite the reputation in her day, did she not? And you know what they say—like mother, like daughter."

Something incendiary seemed to go off in Gillian's chest, flashing anger throughout her body. Still, she managed a pleasant smile. "I'm not sure I take your meaning, my lord. Italian was my first language, so sometimes my understanding of English lacks subtlety."

"I'm quite sure you understand, my dear," he said, boldly staring at her décolletage.

"You're a monster." Honoria's voice vibrated with fury. "Leave her alone."

"Good God, man, you're clearly in your cups," hissed Stratton, grabbing Andover's arm. He cast a nervous glance at the growing circle of eavesdroppers. "Why don't we go to the card room?"

The earl shook him off and let his gaze sweep slowly and

contemptuously over Honoria's figure. "I'm sorry, did you say something, Miss Cranston? Or was it just a moo I heard?"

As Honoria raised a trembling hand to her mouth, Gillian patted her shoulder. "Don't worry, dear. I'll take care of this."

She gave Andover the same chilling smile that had prompted more than one Sicilian bandit to take to his heels. "My lord, you should have taken your leave when you had the chance."

"Dear Charles, I'd forgotten how well you dance," Letitia purred. "I insist that you save me the second waltz, for old time's sake."

As he led her from the floor, Charles was tempted to remind her that those old times had almost ended in the ruination of her good name. Only his steadfast determination to prevent a scandal—and his father's money—had swept the nasty affair under the carpet. While Gerry and Letitia had escaped more or less unscathed, Charles had not. He would never forget what the ugly episode had done to his father and to their relationship. His father had warned him about Letitia, but Charles had refused to listen.

When he didn't answer, Letitia took his arm and snuggled close, brushing her full breasts against him. Once, the temptation of her lush body would have driven him mad with lust. Now he wanted only to escape.

"Unless, of course, you're promised to dance with someone else," she said as he steered her around a cluster of matrons.

Two old friends of his mother snapped their fans in judgment. The others simply smiled and gave friendly nods. Lady Letitia Stratton might have been considered fast in her salad days, but that didn't mean she wasn't good *ton*. Her father was an earl, after all, and her husband was heir to a respectable estate and title. A beautiful and stylish hostess, Letitia threw lavish and entertaining parties. Only the highest of sticklers disapproved of her anymore, while most explained away any mistakes or faults of the past as flowing from youthful exuberance.

They didn't know what Charles knew.

Letitia was turning out to be damned hard to shake. She'd latched onto him in the same manner at two other social occasions since that unfortunate encounter in the park, and Charles was firmly convinced she was up to something.

Right now, however, his goal was to get back to Gillian. She could get into trouble in endlessly inventive ways, especially in a setting like this one.

"Well, Charles?" Letitia said.

"Well, what?" he absently asked as he gave the crowd a quick scan. He finally spotted Gillian halfway up the room with Lendale and the rest of their group. He allowed himself a small sigh of relief. Jack would keep a weather eye out for her until Charles could make his way over there.

"I asked if you were already engaged to waltz with someone else," Letitia said with asperity. "Goodness, why are you so distracted?" She turned and followed the path of his gaze. "Ah, so you *are* interested in your adorable little protégé. I suspected as much."

Only a fool could miss the venom in her voice.

"If by *interested* you mean I'm concerned for her welfare, then yes." he said coolly. "The Marburys are members of my family, as is Miss Dryden."

"And do you always take such an interest in your family's unmarried young ladies? Half of London is talking about how His Grace, the Duke of Leverton, is lending his august approval to an untutored chit of a girl. It's vastly amusing, you must admit."

"Do I look amused?"

She studied him, as if truly looking at him for the first time that evening. "I must admit that you do not."

"I would think that you, of all people, Letitia, would know better than to listen to half-baked gossip."

"Ah, but gossip can be so instructive, Charles. And a good many people find Miss Dryden to be a very diverting topic of conversation."

"How very dull of them," he said. "Miss Dryden is an unexceptionable young lady, I assure you."

Letitia directed her attention to where Gillian stood with her grandmother and a few friends. Charles got a small jolt when he saw that Jack had suddenly disappeared. Charles had been depending on him to keep the wolves at bay.

"Still, she is lovely," Letitia said. "Miss Dryden is sure to attract many admirers."

Letitia didn't need to point out the type of admirers the girl was most likely to attract, looking as she did. Tonight, she was displaying as a diamond of the first water in a cream and gold-spangled gown that flowed lovingly over her graceful figure. Her dark hair was coiled around her head in a simple braid, with a few tendrils whispering like silky ribbons around her temples and neck. Under the glow of the candlelight, her skin, tanned by the rays of the Sicilian sun, seemed like gold, too. In fact, everything about her shimmered, like a Roman coin polished to a high gleam. Gillian had rendered Charles all but speechless when she'd walked into her grandmother's drawing room tonight, and he was not a man normally at a loss for words. The last woman to strike him dumb with her beauty was, unfortunately, standing right beside him now.

Let that be a warning.

"I have no doubt she will garner a number of respectable suitors," he said.

"Including you?" Letitia taunted. "I wonder how your mother would feel about having a prince's by-blow for a daughter-in-law."

"How vulgar of you, Letitia. But I suppose that shouldn't surprise me."

He had to give her credit when she didn't even flinch. Instead, she trilled a pleasant, entirely artificial laugh. "Ah, but I forgot. No whisper of scandal must ever attach to the Leverton name. Perfect Penley would never lower himself to make so shocking a connection."

She knew he hated that nickname. After all, she'd given it to him and had been delighted when the *ton* took it up as a great joke.

"How could you forget?" he said. "God knows I will always remember the price I had to pay to salvage your good name—and mine."

His tone was hostile enough that she retreated an inch or two. He was about to take his leave, and to hell with good manners, when she surprised him by resting a hand on his arm. "I'm so glad," she murmured. "I was quite worried you might be taken with the girl. I should have known better."

He frowned. "Why the devil should you care one way or another?"

"Can't you guess?" she said, stroking his arm.

Charles removed her hand from his sleeve. "No, I cannot."

When she opened her fan and began to leisurely wave it as she scanned the room, Charles knew she was toying with him. Her very presence was a reminder of what a callow youth he'd been. She'd manipulated him to great effect, and only by chance had he escaped.

But what was her game now, and how much trouble would it cause?

"You were always a handsome boy, Charles. But now you're so much more than that. Sometimes I think I made the wrong choice when I walked away from you."

"Your memory is faulty, ma'am. I walked away from you."

"Alas, so formal," she sighed. "I much prefer when you call me Letitia. You used to do it so easily, remember? Especially when you wanted to kiss me."

"No, I don't remember." Of course he did, though. He remembered every fevered moment from his youth. She'd only allowed him some teasing kisses and a few fumbling caresses of her lush body, but it had kept him dangling from her hook like a besotted fool.

Scowling at the memory, Charles glanced across the room, searching again for Gillian and frowning when he couldn't find her.

"How chilly and proper you are," Letitia said. "You've changed so much from that passionate boy who wore his heart so charmingly on his sleeve." She moved closer again, not touching him but making sure her heat and scent surrounded him. Her heavy perfume was a dagger to his brain.

"For God's sake, Letitia," he said, finally out of patience. "What the hell do you want?"

"Must I spell it out?" she asked in a gently plaintive tone. "Very well. I would like us to rediscover those feelings we once had for each other, Charles. To be close again."

He only just stopped himself from gaping. A quick glance around showed that no one, thank God, was paying them any mind. In fact, all their neighbors were craning their necks to see something on the other side of the dance floor.

"You wish to become my mistress," he said.

Irritation flashed across her features. "And you call *me* vulgar, my dear. But, yes. I would like us to be involved in an intimate relationship."

Now he understood. "You and Gerry in debt again, are you? So you're looking for a wealthy lover." He ran an expert eye over her jewels. "Yes, if I'm not mistaken, that lovely diamond parterre is paste. Apparently, you've had to sacrifice the family jewels to keep afloat."

The skin around her mouth pulled taut and white. "How dare you insult me?"

"Letitia, I'm the one who should be insulted. You rejected me once, and now you're propositioning me in the middle of a ballroom. Did you really believe I would fall for your tricks again?"

She struggled to control her temper and made a credible job of it. "Poor Charles, you always were a fool. That, I see, has not changed."

"Well, now that we've exchanged a sufficient number of insults, I think—"

Before he could finish, Jack materialized from behind a nearby pillar. "Excuse the interruption," he said brusquely, "but I need to borrow Leverton."

Letitia sneered. "You may have him. He's quite as rude as you are, Lendale, which I had not thought possible."

Jack laughed. "Up to the old game again, eh, Letitia?" He looked at Charles. "She tried it on me a few weeks ago, if you can believe it."

Her pale blue gaze brimmed with hatred. "You are no gentleman."

"And you are no lady, so we're even," Jack said in a cheerful voice.

Charles thought she would choke on the spot. And he thought he would choke on the laugh he decided to swallow. "I suppose I should be annoyed that I was her second choice. Again."

"Consider yourself lucky," Jack replied. "But enough of this nonsense, old boy. You need to rejoin your party immediately."

The vague anxiety that had been lurking around the edges of Charles's consciousness sprang into sharp definition.

"Dear me," Letitia said in a catty voice. "There is a commotion on the other side of the dance floor, and I believe I see your protégé, Your Grace. She seems to be engaged in some kind of dispute with my husband and Lord Andover."

When Charles took a hasty step toward the dance floor, Letitia grasped his arm. "Are you sure you want to do that? You know how much you hate scandal, my dear Charles."

"Letitia, what did you do?" he asked.

She shrugged her beautiful white shoulders. She'd almost destroyed him years ago, and now she'd apparently decided to do it to Gillian.

"Why?" he demanded.

"Because she decided she wanted you, old son," Lendale said. "And she clearly thought Miss Dryden was an impediment."

"I don't have time for this," Charles said, disgusted. He stalked away, trying to ignore Letitia's mocking laugh. He wove his way through the crowd, moving as quickly as he could without knocking anyone over.

"Why the hell weren't you keeping an eye on Gillian?" Charles snapped when Lendale caught up with him.

"I'd just gone off to get some refreshments, for God's sake. I'd snagged a footman with a tray of drinks when I saw that Letitia had trapped you in her evil snare."

"You shouldn't have left Gillian on her own, Jack."

"She's your damn responsibility, not mine. Besides, she was with her grandmother the last time I saw her. How the hell was I supposed to know she would get into an argument with one of the greatest morons in London?"

"You have no idea how many ways that blasted girl can get into trouble," Charles said. "And speaking of Lady Marbury, where is she?"

"There she is," Jack said, all but pushing a corpulent earl out of their way. They ignored his protests as they hurried to join her.

"Charles, there you are," she said in a relieved voice. "I stepped away to the retiring room, and I came back to this.

You must make Lord Andover go away before Gillian does something dreadful."

"I intend to," he said in a grim voice. Unfortunately, he was still several feet away when he saw Gillian's lips curve up in a smile that made it clear mayhem was about to occur.

By the time he got clear of a gaggle of excited debutantes, Gillian was practically standing on Andover's toes, saying something that Charles couldn't hear over the din of the crowd. A moment later, she delivered an outstanding right hook that caught Andover under the chin.

Since the earl was well-known at Gentleman Jackson's for having a glass jaw, the effect was both predictable and profound. He toppled like a felled tree, straight into a cluster of bystanders, including a footman carrying a tray of champagne goblets. The poor footman tumbled into a middle-aged matron possessed of a well-padded figure, and both went crashing down to the floor, along with the champagne.

"What a nice, flush hit," Jack said in an admiring voice.

"Do *not* tell her that," Charles growled as he elbowed past a pair of girls who were shrieking and fanning themselves in a dramatic fashion.

Jack shot a sly grin at Charles. "I don't mean to interfere, old boy, but you might want to drop a word in Miss Dryden's ear that boxing isn't usually the done thing in the middle of a ballroom."

"Thank you for that extremely helpful bit of advice, you idiot," Charles said in a blighting tone.

Jack simply laughed.

Charles stalked up to Gillian, who stood over Andover, flexing her hand. When she glanced up at him, she let out a sigh. At least he thought she sighed, since it was hard to hear anything in the growing pandemonium.

Gillian clasped her hands at her waist and patiently waited, a picture of serene beauty in the midst of chaos.

"Well, Miss Dryden," Charles said, "now that you've

provided the main entertainment for the evening, what have you planned for an encore?"

She flicked a glance around the crowded ballroom that seethed with excitement and gossip. Then she looked back at him and shrugged. "I hadn't thought that far ahead, Your Grace. I am, however, entirely open to suggestion."

Chapter Eleven

"You must stop hiding, Miss Dryden," Leverton said as he handed her down the front steps of her grandmother's townhouse. His handsome face was serious, but far kinder than she deserved after the debacle the other night at Lady Barrington's ball.

"I wish you'd stop being so bloody nice," she said. "You're making me feel worse."

His brows went up in a politely incredulous arch. Leverton's eyebrows were always excellent indicators of his mood. Their lift could reduce an impertinent dandy to embarrassed silence or elicit a flustered apology from the most judgmental of society matrons. Gillian wished she could learn the trick. Then she might not have to go around punching people.

"Language, Miss Dryden. Would you rather be locked in your room with only bread and water? I could speak to your grandmother, if you'd like."

She perked up. "I promise I wouldn't complain if you did."

He took her arm and gently urged her forward. "Hiding will only make things worse."

"Not according to Mamma. She thinks it's foolish to go

traipsing about London as if nothing happened. It'll only cause more talk."

The gossip had already spread like wildfire, and a few choice nicknames for Gillian were in circulation. She didn't really care, but the cruel chatter and whisperings hurt her mother. That truly did make Gillian want to hide away in shame.

Or better yet, return to Sicily, since it now might be the best way out of the mess. That hadn't been her intent at the ball, but she could hardly have picked a better way to further her cause. Unfortunately, she'd left quite a bit of debris in her wake.

"We cannot run away from London as if you were the only guilty party," he said. "That would only encourage Andover and those of his ilk in more bad behavior."

"But my mother—"

He silenced her by drawing her hand through his arm. Every time Leverton touched her, Gillian's insides started to jump. It was a disconcerting reaction to say the least, yet also rather lovely.

She had to clamp down on even the thought of tender feelings toward Leverton. It would only lead to the sort of heartache she'd sworn off years ago.

"I know your mother finds the situation very distressing," he said. "But she has a rather fragile spirit. You do not. You are a brave young woman, more than able to stand up to some gossiping old tabbies and Andover's idiotic friends."

His praise soothed her ruffled pride. "Do you really think I'm brave?" No one had called her that since her stepfather died. Foolish, strongheaded, impetuous, yes—but not brave.

"You took on Sicilian bandits, did you not? Although one might deem that foolish as well as brave."

She wrinkled her nose. "Now you've ruined it."

"Forgive me, Miss Dryden. I'm not quite sure of the etiquette involved in hunting vicious brigands."

"One generally just points and shoots."

"Thank you," he said sarcastically. "I'll try to remember that."

She couldn't help grinning at him. "You're really quite a nice man, despite your Perfect Penley manner."

When he stiffened, she cursed her thoughtlessness. "I'm sorry, Your Grace. That was poorly done of me. If there is anyone who deserves my consideration, it is you."

He looked about to respond to her apology when a curricle swung around the corner from Park Street, forcing them to step back from the curb. They waited for the vehicle to pass, and then continued on their way to Hyde Park.

"No thanks are necessary. I am happy to assist in any little way I can," he said.

That was balderdash. Leverton had been incredibly helpful, especially in dealing with all the commotion at Lady Barrington's ball. He'd brought the situation quickly under control after Honoria and Sarah had explained how Andover had insulted them all in the grossest manner. The duke had glared down at the still unconscious earl before plucking a goblet of champagne from the tray of one of the footmen. Much to the delight of the crowd, Leverton had poured the cold beverage onto the earl's face.

After Andover came spluttering to life, Lord Lendale and Mr. Stratton had hauled the earl to his feet and carted him off. Leverton, meanwhile, had herded Gillian and her friends back to their respective grandmothers as if nothing untoward had occurred.

But the damage from Gillian's knockout had been done. Clearly, a young lady was simply expected to stand meekly by while a man insulted her. Well, people who subscribed to that philosophy would continue to be sadly disappointed if they thought she would ever put up with that sort of behavior. That didn't mean, however, that she wasn't embarrassed, mostly for her grandmother's sake. Poor Grandmamma had been mortified, and furious with Gillian for drawing even more attention to the Marbury family with her impulsive behavior. According to her grandmother, Gillian and the girls should have simply excused themselves and walked away from the caddish earl.

Gillian had never been very good at walking away.

"I've not yet properly thanked you for taking my side of things," she said. "I think Grandmamma would have murdered me if you hadn't come to my defense. According to her, no man of sense will ever wish to marry me." In fact, her grandmother had told Gillian that her actions had now made her toxic. And while something like that had been a key component of her plans, it still hurt to be described in those terms.

"The situation is far from hopeless," Leverton said. "But I should have done a better job of looking out for you."

"You didn't exactly drop me in the Mongolian Desert to fend for myself. Lord Lendale didn't leave for long, and Grandmamma was lurking about somewhere."

He looked disgusted with himself. "I didn't expect Lendale to leave you alone at all. I should be apologizing to you for failing to protect you from a cad like Andover."

"Well, you did seem fairly distracted at the time."

He shot her a sharp glance, but didn't answer as he steered her around a group of nursemaids and their charges on their way home from the park.

"It's easy to get distracted at large gatherings," he finally said in a cool voice.

"Ah, I see. You're trying to warn me off this particular topic of conversation."

He gave her a reluctant smile. "Is it working?"

"No," she said. "You already know I have deplorable manners."

"That is rather an understatement."

"Think of it as yet another opportunity for a lesson in my

social schooling. You'd given me the impression the other day that you didn't particularly like Lady Letitia."

Gillian knew she was being shockingly nosy, but she had to ask. She'd been thinking about the intimate scene between Leverton and Lady Letitia ever since the ball—when she wasn't stewing over her own idiotic behavior, that is.

"Is there a question in there, Miss Dryden?"

"Now you're being deliberately dense. Of course there is."

"Then I suggest you cease beating about the bush and just ask it."

"Very well. Not to be too blunt—"

"Which I feel very sure you will be," he interjected.

"As I was saying," she said firmly, "it seemed to me that you and Lady Letitia were, hmm, exceedingly friendly with each other at the ball. Now, I understand that married ladies, married gentlemen, and unmarried gentlemen all engage in affairs with one another quite regularly. It seems rather taken for granted in the *ton*." She frowned. "Now that I think about it, the only people who don't engage in such affairs are unmarried ladies. I understand why, of course. But it doesn't seem all that fair, does it?"

When he didn't answer, she glanced up at him. His expression suggested she'd just started flapping her arms and crowing like a rooster.

"Miss Dryden, are you by any chance a devotee of Mary Wollstonecraft? Because that would be most unfortunate, I assure you. As is the tone of this disturbing conversation."

Gillian waved a hand, banging her reticule into her elbow. "Yes, I know I'm not supposed to talk about things like this, but I have to ask someone if I'm to learn how to get along with all the silly people you're forcing me to meet. Grandmamma certainly won't discuss anything with me."

"Nor will I, except to say that there are many, many people in society who do not engage in illicit behavior."

She eyed him dubiously, but he clearly wasn't going to

budge. "All right. But I would still like to know about you and Lady Letitia."

"There *is* nothing to know about me and Lady Letitia," he said in an austere voice. His face was like a mask.

"You're very good at that," she said.

"What?"

"Hiding your feelings."

"The only feeling I hold toward this particular topic is irritation."

"Hmm," she said. "You don't like to even talk about scandals, do you?"

"No." He lifted an imperious eyebrow. "Do you?"

She shrugged. "I'm rather agnostic on the subject. By definition, I'm a walking scandal, so I've had to get used to it."

"Miss Dryden, you are *not* a walking scandal. You are a young lady with a happy future ahead of you. In order to achieve that future, you simply need to listen to your elders and obey them. That includes me."

"That's no fun," she said.

"Young ladies are not supposed to have fun."

Gillian stopped, forcing him to stop too. "And that attitude is exactly why young ladies get into trouble, sir. You treat us like hothouse flowers and refuse to explain things to us. I assure you, ignorance is *not* bliss. It would be much better to treat us like sensible human beings with the capacity to understand what is in our best interest."

They stood in the middle of the pavement, staring at each other as people passed around them. When an errand boy rushed past, bumping into Gillian, Leverton scowled. "Watch yourself, lad," the duke called after him.

"I don't think he heard you," Gillian said.

Leverton took her arm and set them to walking briskly in the direction of the Stanhope Gate.

"Are you really going to ignore what I said about treating

me like a sensible human being?" she asked after a lengthy silence.

He threw her a wry glance. "All right, I capitulate to your logic, and I am prepared to answer a few questions. Within reason."

"You must admit that my logic is sound."

"Don't push your luck, Miss Dryden."

She had to repress a smile. "Very well. First, I'd like to know why Lady Letitia broke your engagement. I thought that sort of thing was severely frowned on."

He shrugged. "She preferred someone else."

"Mr. Gerald Stratton."

A terse nod was Gillian's only answer. Clearly, he'd been hurt, and quite badly, she suspected. She got a funny pang in her heart at the thought that he might still be in love with the woman who'd spurned him.

"Then she was a fool," she said.

"I appreciate the vote of confidence, but most consider him a bang-up fellow with a friendly, approachable manner."

"He's a fake," she said. "I've seen the type before."

"I imagine you have," he said in a thoughtful tone.

"Besides, people respect you. And listen to you. That's much better than being thought of as a bang-up fellow, if you ask me."

He raised his eyebrows. "Don't you wish to be liked, Miss Dryden?"

"Of course, but to be respected is better. And feared is best of all."

That won her a genuine laugh. "You are the strangest girl."

"So I'm told on a regular basis," she said cheerfully.

He huffed out another laugh and then led her through a gate into Hyde Park. Though it was still a bit early, there were several young ladies of fashion on the stroll and the occasional carriage bowling along.

"Are you and Lady Letitia not even friends?" she asked, wanting to get clear on that important point.

"Definitely not," he said firmly.

"I'm so very glad," Gillian said. Then she practically swallowed her tongue at the dreadful slip.

Leverton's head jerked down, and he peered at her with a frown that looked more perplexed than annoyed. "Miss Dryden, I—"

"Look," she exclaimed. "There are my brother and Justine." *Thank God.* She vigorously waved to catch their attention.

"Cease wind-milling your arms, please," the duke said. "They clearly see us. And how did that confounded brother of yours know we were going to be walking in the park?"

"He sent a note around this morning saying he needed to speak with me, so I suggested we meet here. Since we've had very little decent weather, I thought we should take advantage of it." She took in Leverton's irate expression. "You're the one who suggested a walk, after all."

"Not with your brother."

She pulled her hand from his arm and came to a halt. "Your Grace, might I enquire as to why you dislike my poor brother so much?"

"Referring to Steele as *poor* is ridiculous on a number of counts. And he is only your half brother."

"I prefer not to dwell on that minor distinction. Would you please answer my question?"

He eyed her as if she were a squib about to explode. "Climb off your high horse, Miss Dryden. I like your brother well enough, and Mrs. Steele is a very charming woman."

Taking her elbow, Leverton nudged her forward, unleashing a smile at the two young ladies who'd slowed their steps to a crawl and were watching them. "Keep walking, Miss Dryden," he murmured. "You don't want to draw attention to yourself."

"I thought that's exactly what I was supposed to do. Why else would we go on this bloody, er, silly outing?"

"We wish to attract the right kind of attention. Standing about arguing like fishwives will garner us exactly the opposite."

"You started it by insulting my brother."

"I did no such—never mind," he said in an exasperated tone as Griffin and Justine approached.

"Ah, my dear sister and her faithful English mastiff," Griffin said. "Looking like he wants to bite my head off, as usual."

Gillian sighed. "You're just as bad as he is. I wish the two of you would at least try to get along."

Her brother pressed a dramatic hand to his heart. "I am the most amiable man in London. A veritable fount of charity and goodwill."

"You're nothing of the sort, Griffin Steele," Justine said.

Griffin let out a heavy sigh. "What's the world coming to when a man can't even depend on his wife for support?"

"Please ignore him, Your Grace," Justine said in a good-humored voice as she dipped into a quick curtsey.

"I'll do my best, Mrs. Steele," Leverton replied.

"Men are such a trial," Justine said, before pressing a quick kiss on Gillian's cheek. "How are you, dear girl? You're looking exceptionally pretty today."

Gillian smiled as she gave her sister-in-law a quick hug. Justine was a calm, lovely woman who seemed capable of bringing order to even the most chaotic or upsetting situations. She'd cared for Gillian after she'd been shot, nursing her with a quiet efficiency that had soothed everyone's nerves.

Justine also had a knack for managing her mercurial husband. Of course, it certainly helped that Griffin was madly in love with his wife, and she with him. Gillian could only hope that she would someday find that sort of happiness.

"Leverton, stop scowling at me like I'm a demon from the pits of hell," Griffin said. "I thought we'd reached the point where we could spend at least ten minutes together without coming to blows."

"Normally, I would be delirious with joy to partake of your company," the duke replied. "But today is not the day for Gillian to be seen with a reformed reprobate and former crime lord."

"Your Grace, your truly charitable regard brings a tear to my eye. I am completely unmanned," Griffin said. Justine elbowed him in the ribs. "Ouch," he protested. "That hurt."

"And there's more where that came from if you don't behave," his wife said.

"But Griffin *is* reformed. Isn't that the point?" Gillian asked. "Why should I avoid my own brother?"

"True, but he is hardly what one would call dull and respectable," Leverton said. He gave a slight grimace as he looked at Griffin, as if apologizing. "And despite your reformation and your truly excellent spouse, there are still a great many in the *ton* who give you a wide berth. While you have well-placed friends in society, you also have enemies, as I'm sure you realize."

"Only because they still owe me money," Griffin said.

"They sound like awful people," Gillian said to her brother. "And I don't care to be friendly with people who don't approve of you."

"That's the spirit, pet," Griffin said. "We reprobates must stick together."

"That's not helpful, my dear," his wife said. "And the duke has a good point."

"He does?"

"Guilt by association can still damage one's reputation," Justine replied.

"After that confounded ball I don't have much reputation left to damage," Gillian said.

"Which is to the point," Leverton said. "Your reputation is hanging by a slender thread, Miss Dryden. And spending time in your brother's company won't help, I'm afraid. Notoriety is never a young lady's friend."

"That I know all too well," Justine said with a sigh.

"Turned out pretty damn well in your case," Griffin said. "After all, you married me."

"Yes, but we were lucky, and we had quite a lot of help."

"And I want to help Gillian," Griffin said, suddenly turning serious. "I want her to remain in England, where we can keep an eye on her. Returning to Sicily would be too bloody dangerous."

Blast. Gillian didn't need her brother standing in her way, too.

"Then we're agreed that you should not be seen in public with her for now," the duke said. "I'd like Gillian to keep a low profile over the next few weeks. She can go for strolls or the occasional ride in the park, dinner parties, and musicales in small number, and only in the most select company. If we can do that successfully, the uproar over Andover should soon die down."

When Griffin and Justine exchanged glances, Leverton expelled a sigh. "What now?"

"Gillian seems to have acquired a nickname," Justine said. "Perhaps you've heard?"

"No, I've been attending to parliamentary business the last few days," Leverton said. "Just how bad is it?"

"I actually think it's rather good," Griffin said. "And apt."

"Are you referring to the Pugilistic Princess?" Gillian asked.

The other three gaped at her.

"You already know?" Griffin asked.

"I found out yesterday," she said. "I believe it was coined shortly after we left the ball."

"You poor thing," Justine said. "Why didn't you tell one of us?"

"It doesn't bother me. Trust me, I've heard worse." Like Griffin, she quite liked the name. In fact, she'd burst into laughter when she heard about it.

"Miss Dryden, how did you acquire this knowledge?" Leverton asked.

She waved a vague hand. "You know. Just around."

"I assume it was from the servants," Griffin said. "Always the most reliable source of information."

Yes, she'd heard it from the servants—Roger, her grandmother's coachman, to be precise. Gillian often slipped out at night to visit the stables. She loved spending time with the horses, grooming them or simply keeping company with them. They calmed her when she was feeling too restless to sleep. Roger, who'd served the Marbury family for years, was an old and trusted friend.

Leverton, naturally, would not approve of such low friendships.

Right on point, the duke narrowed his gaze. "I thought I told you to stop pumping the servants for information."

She narrowed her gaze right back. "You're just annoyed because you're the last to know."

Surprisingly, his lips twitched. "Sadly true. I've been much engaged these last few days and haven't visited my clubs. An oversight I will be sure to correct."

Gillian imagined it wasn't very often that anyone stole a march on Leverton.

"Well, the damage is done," Justine said, "so now we must simply determine how best to deal with it."

"The voice of reason, as always, Mrs. Steele." Leverton gave her a rueful smile.

"I don't think it's all that bad," Gillian said. "The Pugilistic Princess has rather a nice ring to it. And it will probably keep the rakes and the bounders at a safe distance."

"As long as it doesn't frighten off the respectable suitors, too," Leverton said. "Still, the name could be worse. At least it's not lewd."

"Speaking of worse," Griffin said. "Look who's coming to speak with us, brazen as day."

Gillian turned to see Gerald Stratton coming toward them with a grim, determined look on his face.

"Bloody hell," Griffin growled. "The man has balls."

"Griffin, behave yourself," his wife hissed.

Gillian was in full agreement with her brother, and part of her was inclined to live up to her nickname right now. But though Stratton had started the whole mess at the ball by introducing her to Andover, he'd seemed first uncomfortable and then horrified when things got ugly. She even thought he might have babbled out an apology on Andover's behalf, although she wasn't quite sure. There'd been such a commotion after the earl had gone crashing to the floor that it had been difficult to hear anything.

"Let me deal with him, Steele," Leverton said in a hard voice. "You'll draw too much unwanted attention."

Gillian glanced around. *Too late.*

The afternoon promenade was now well under way. Phaetons, landaus, and curricles were moving through the park in a fairly steady stream, and many fashionably dressed people were out for a stroll. And many of them were clearly taking note of their presence and no doubt gossiping like magpies.

Griffin moved around to Gillian's side, as if to guard her. When she took his arm and squeezed it, he lifted an enquiring brow.

"Don't cause a fuss," she murmured. "The duke can handle it."

Much to her surprise, her brother smiled. "Of that I have no doubt."

"That's far enough," Leverton said, stepping forward to meet Stratton. "Miss Dryden has no wish to speak to you."

Stratton winced. "Look, old boy, I've not come to make trouble. I'm just back from calling at Upper Brook Street, and I wanted to extend my apology to Miss Dryden." He hesitated. "And also warn her."

"Warn her about what?" Griffin asked in a low, lethal voice. Stratton blanched as white as a corpse.

"It's all right, Mr. Stratton," Gillian said. "You tried to apologize at the ball, did you not?"

He grimaced. "I did, Miss Dryden. I'm exceedingly sorry about that unfortunate scene. I had no idea Andover would be such a lout to you and the other ladies."

"Letitia sent you over to make trouble, did she not?" Leverton asked in a cold voice.

"No, that was her dear friend, Andover. I was simply my darling wife's unwitting pawn," Stratton said bitterly.

Leverton stared at him for a few seconds before nodding. "I think I understand."

"I imagine you do," Stratton said, looking somber. "I'm sorry, Charles. I'd like to explain it, if you'd let me."

The duke's glance flicked to Gillian, then back to Stratton. "Later."

Gillian rolled her eyes. As if they could say anything that would shock her. "What is it you wished to warn me about, sir?"

"You've acquired a nickname, Miss Dryden," he said. "And it's not a very nice one, I'm afraid."

Her companions seemed to breathe a collective sigh of relief.

"The Pugilistic Princess?" Griffin said. "We already know."

"Yes," Stratton said. "But there's another one."

A loud burst of laughter interrupted them, drawing their attention to four men and two ladies strolling nearby. Lady Letitia, along with her companions, stared at Gillian with undisguised glee.

"Blast," Stratton groaned.

"Now I am definitely going to have to murder someone," Griffin said.

Lady Letitia said something else to her friends, provoking another raucous peal of laughter. It was rather daring of them, given that both the Duke of Leverton and Griffin Steele were staring daggers at their little group.

The duke turned and clamped a hand on Stratton's shoulder. "Let's you and I have that talk right now."

Chapter Twelve

Charles stirred when the contessa inched aside the curtain and peered out the window at the desolate landscape of fields and marshes. She was clearly anxious to still be on the road as night approached. Her daughter, however, showed no such discomfort, nor did his sister. The fact that Gillian and Elizabeth were much alike in their practical and cheerful approach to life was a blessing, considering the four of them had been cooped up in a traveling coach for the last five days.

With Gillian's reputation a hair's breadth away from ruination, they'd decided on a quick retreat from town. Temporarily removing her from the eye of the storm was now the only path to restoring her good name—if they even could. Charles was beginning to have some serious doubts on that score, although he kept them to himself.

Even he hadn't thought one little uppercut to the jaw of an earl would cause so much trouble.

"It's getting quite dark," the contessa said. "Perhaps it would have been best to spend the night in Spilsby, after all."

"Good God, Mamma," Gillian said. "That little inn was incredibly dirty and damp, and I shudder to even think of the sheets." She took her mother's hand. "I promise everything will be fine, darling. His Grace won't let anything happen to us."

Gillian was devoted to her mother and endlessly attentive to her comfort on the dreary trip. That the mother seemed unable to care for her own daughter, however, was sadly evident. Although no one could find a sweeter, more gentle-tempered woman, the contessa suffered from a melancholy that rendered her all but useless in dealing with life's travails and managing her own child.

"Indeed not," said Elizabeth. "And I'm sure we'll arrive at Fenfield Manor well before nightfall, won't we, Charles?"

He lifted the curtain on his side of the coach with one finger. Bands of purple and pink shimmered on the horizon, bleeding up into darker bands of blue. Although full night-fall would come within the hour, plenty of light remained for the coachman to see. This far north, the days were long enough for them to push ahead and finally reach the end of this seemingly interminable journey.

"There is no cause for concern," he said. "I know this part of Lincolnshire seems remote, but we are perfectly safe."

"It's just that we've encountered hardly anyone in almost two hours," the contessa said. "Anything could happen to us, and no one would even know it."

"I would never allow anything to happen to you or your daughter, madam."

"What about me?" Elizabeth demanded.

"You? I'd turn you over to the highwaymen in order to give us time to make our escape."

"Wretch," Elizabeth said with a grin. Gillian snickered.

The contessa didn't so much as crack a smile. Charles couldn't blame her, given that bandits had murdered her husband. He'd best remember that before he made any more careless jokes.

"My groom and coachman are well armed and well

trained, my lady," Charles said. "And we will reach my estate within the hour."

"Thank God." Stretching her arms, Gillian arched her back, pulling herself into a slim, beautiful curve that showcased the gentle swell of her breasts under the trim fit of her spencer. "Not that your coach isn't exceedingly comfortable, sir, but my muscles are so bloody stiff that I feel like an old lady."

"My love, you must not swear," her mother admonished with a gentle smile. Charles suspected that Gillian's language had been precisely intended to distract her mamma. He, however, was distracted by some extremely inconvenient images of what Gillian's body might look like without all that clothing.

He forced his gaze from her trim figure up to her face. Unfortunately, it was just as enticing as her body. His attraction to her was becoming quite the problem, since the rumors circulating amongst the *ton* affected him almost as much as Gillian.

"Sorry, Mamma." Gillian shifted to look at Charles. "I suppose you want to scold me, too. Go ahead. I promise I won't say a peep in my defense." She adopted a martyred expression.

"Since your mother has already corrected you, I'll let it pass. Just this once."

"You are kindness itself, sir," she said, clasping her hands over her chest and sounding comically dramatic.

Elizabeth laughed. "You are truly the most ridiculous child."

"Someone has to keep us entertained," Gillian said. "Lord knows the duke has been falling down on the job. He just drones on about the peerage and the proper way to dance a figure or hold a fork. I find it exceedingly unfair, since I'm a captive audience."

"We're *all* a captive audience," Elizabeth said. "I've been tempted to throw myself out of the carriage at least twice a day, especially when he pontificates about appropriate topics of discussion for gently bred ladies." She leaned over to Gillian, as if to confide in her. "He used to do the same to me when I was a young girl. He was always correcting my bad behavior."

"Because there was quite a lot to correct," Charles said.

"Well, if that's what older brothers do, I'm very glad I never had one," said Gillian. "Except for Griffin, of course. He's a notable exception."

Amusement gleamed in her eyes. Once again, Charles was struck by her sanguine, even good-humored attitude. Most girls would have taken to their beds in hysterics in the face of all the nasty rumors. But Gillian didn't seem to care. "Your brother is worse than you are," he said.

"That's why I like him so much."

Elizabeth laughed again, but the contessa looked worried. "Gillian, you shouldn't be teasing. We're very grateful for everything the duke has done for you."

"Of course we are, Mamma. Leverton has been exceedingly kind."

"I've been more than happy to help," he said.

Gillian studied him, her expression turning thoughtful. "I very much doubt that. But, truly, you've been so nice to me and to Mamma. I can't even begin to think how I'll repay you."

Charles could think of several ways, none of them nice. Naughty, in fact, would describe them perfectly. "You could start by paying better attention to me when I'm explaining something. Such as how to behave like a proper young lady at a ball instead of like a hoyden."

"Anything except for that," she said, mischief once more gleaming in her eyes.

Charles had to repress the impulse to laugh. He had, in fact, given up trying to instruct her, at least on the trip.

Gillian had enough trouble sitting still for hours at a time, let alone trying to focus on lessons. Though she did read quite often, at least when the roads were good enough to allow it, her reading primarily consisted of the novels of Mrs. Radcliffe.

Despite her good humor, the trip taxed her. Gillian seethed with restless, physical energy that cried out for relief. Fortunately, Elizabeth had hit on the notion of teaching her how to play cards. It had never occurred to Charles that she wouldn't know how to play. Every day, it became clearer just how socially isolated Gillian had been in her former life. Her family had loved and protected her, but had done little to prepare her for anything approaching a normal life among the aristocracy. He suspected it was her grandfather, Lord Marbury, who'd been mostly at fault.

Regardless, it was now up to Charles to correct the situation.

"You've had a lengthy break from your lessons, Miss Dryden," he said. "But tomorrow we begin again in earnest."

She rolled her eyes. "Five days in a carriage is hardly what I call a break. Besides I'm not sure there's any point in lessons, given what people are saying about me."

"We agreed that we wouldn't think or talk about that," her mother said.

"I know, Mamma. But there's been nothing else to do these past several days *but* think. I don't see how I can come back from the Savage Sicilian much less—"

"Don't even say it," Charles said in a stern voice.

"Everyone else is," Gillian said defiantly. "And pretending otherwise isn't going to make things better. It seems entirely mad to me to believe we can actually fix this."

When Charles narrowed his gaze in silent warning, Gillian simply crossed her arms over her chest and stared back at him, not the least bit intimidated, as usual.

"Tell me something," he said. "Do you actually wish to

fix this, as you refer to it, or would you rather give up? Because I have a sense that you're quite happy to escape town." He shook his head. "It surprises me that you're so willing to back down without a fight. Your brother certainly wants to give it a go."

In fact, Griffin Steele had all but threatened to shoot anyone who dared to say a cruel word about his sister— starting with Letitia Stratton.

Gillian's dark eyes flashed fire. "Are you calling me a coward?"

"Dear me," Elizabeth said. "I don't think we should discuss this now. It's the end of a long, tiring day, and our nerves are quite frayed. Don't you agree, contessa?"

Gillian shot a guilty glance at her mother. "I don't mean to upset you, Mamma, but it seems silly to tiptoe around what happened. You know that better than anyone."

Much to Charles's surprise, the contessa regarded her daughter with a calm expression. "I do. In your case, however, you have done nothing wrong. I earned my shame. You, my love, did not."

Gillian twisted to face her. "You earned nothing but the right to be happy, Mamma. I'll murder anyone who says otherwise."

"It's very kind of you to say so, my dear. But there are those in the *ton* who disagree, and who also believe that my behavior still reflects on you."

"But it was all so long ago," Gillian replied. "Why does it even matter anymore what you did?"

"Because that's the way people are, unfortunately. And to the gossips, you are both a living reminder and an irresistible temptation." She took her daughter's hand. "I understand there is a certain phrase currently making the rounds in London regarding us. I suspect you know what it is."

Gillian's mouth pulled into an unhappy twist. "Like

mother, like daughter," she finally answered with obvious reluctance.

"Yes, along with 'the apple doesn't fall far from the tree.' Both are exceedingly unimaginative, but in our case they have a certain ring." The contessa's smile was so sad that Charles wanted to pummel every simpering prat who'd dared to spread ugly gossip about Gillian and her mother.

"Ugh," Elizabeth said with a grimace. "I occasionally forget how dreary the *ton* can be."

The contessa shrugged. "It's to be expected. But it's also why it made sense for me to leave town with my daughter. My presence would only have fueled more gossip and attention, whether Gillian was with me or not."

"Leaving *your* mother behind to hold down the fort, as she put it," Charles said. Lady Marbury had been unshakeable. "To stay and push back against the gossip."

"My mother refused to run away again," the contessa said. "She said that this time, she was going to stand her ground and fight—for me and for Gillian."

"What a mess," Elizabeth said, rubbing her forehead.

"But you did wish to leave town, didn't you, Mamma?" Gillian asked, sounding anxious. "I hate to think you were forced out on my account, especially after you had just returned home."

"Of course, darling. As if I wouldn't rather be with my child than anywhere without her."

"Then I'm glad we left," Gillian said. "I have no wish to spend my time with people who can be so dreadful to my mother. In fact, I hope we stay away a good, long time. I quite hate English society, if you must know the truth."

"You hated Sicilian society too, as I recall," her mother said.

Gillian breathed out an aggrieved sigh. "Can you truly blame me?"

"No, dear. The way they treated you was distressing. That

is why I'd like to avoid a repeat of it, if at all possible. We'll stay away as long as His Grace deems necessary, then we will return together to London."

When her daughter started to look mutinous, Contessa di Paterini took an unexpectedly firm line. "In the meantime, you will continue your lessons and do exactly as the duke says."

"But, Mamma, as I said," Gillian argued, "I don't really see the point. My reputation is—"

Her mother put up a hand to interrupt. "Your reputation is not ruined. Gillian, I simply refuse to see you labeled as notorious, when you are no such thing. In every way that matters, you are entirely innocent." She looked at Charles, her gaze clear and steady. "This is merely a strategic retreat, is it not, my dear sir?"

He was surprised by her display of maternal fortitude, but it could only help. "That is an excellent way of putting it. Nevertheless, it's best not to underestimate the challenge."

Like mother, like daughter.

To have Gillian already placed in the same category as her mother was more of a setback than he'd envisioned—especially after what Stratton had told him. That was information, however, that he intended to keep to himself.

"What aren't you telling us, Charles?" Elizabeth asked in a suspicious voice.

His sister had always been too damned perceptive for her own good. "Nothing you need concern yourself about."

Gillian's gaze narrowed, as if she were trying to see into his head. "Your Grace—"

The carriage jolted to a halt, rocking violently on its frame. Gillian grabbed onto her mother, while Charles reached out to support Elizabeth before she slid to the floor.

"What the devil?" He heard a muffled shout and the neighing protest of the horses, and then nothing.

He reached for the door, but it swung open before he

could grasp the handle. The barrel of a pistol stared him right in the face.

"Confound it," Gillian muttered. All they needed after another long, dreary day on the road was bandits. She was so bloody sick of bandits.

Come to think of it, she was sick of most everything English, with the possible exception of the people in the carriage. And if the English bastard holding a gun on them dared to lay a hand on her mother or anyone else, she would throttle him.

Leverton shot her a sharp glance. "Let me handle this."

She widened her eyes, as if to suggest that she wouldn't *dream* of causing trouble. He snorted and went back to eyeing the pistol with disdain.

"You, Mr. Fancy. Get out of the bloody carriage," barked the man with the pistol.

"If you will cease waving that weapon in my face, I will be happy to comply," Leverton said coldly. The duke was managing to convey a perfect mix of contempt and irritation. It would take more than highwaymen to rattle His Grace, the Duke of Leverton.

Her mother, however, was trembling like a leaf in the wind. Gillian wanted to hug her, but needed her hands free in case the situation spun out of control. Stealthily, she reached for her reticule.

Leverton uncurled his big body and moved to the carriage door. The brute with the pistol—an exceedingly large fellow, sporting a battered felt cap and a dirty kerchief over his mouth and nose—retreated to let the duke disembark.

"Just be quiet and stay still," the duke said over his shoulder.

Lady Filby looked almost as calm as her brother, although

she'd gone a bit green around the gills. "I will be as quiet as a mouse, I assure you."

"I wasn't talking to you." He flicked Gillian a warning glance.

She scowled, but Leverton had already stepped down to the road. "Who's in charge here?" he said in his haughtiest voice, before stalking out of her line of sight.

By the sound of the answering voices, there were at least two other men besides their guard, who stood a few feet away with his weapon still pointed in their direction.

Her reticule in hand, Gillian leaned in to her mother. "Change places with me, Mamma."

Her mother jerked, her eyes wide and frightened. Gillian's anger flared into a cold, steady flame. This incident would be a terrifying reminder of everything Mamma had lost, and of how helpless they'd all been to prevent it.

"What are you going to do?" Mamma whispered.

"I just want to see what's going on," Gillian said soothingly.

Her mother reluctantly nodded. As they switched places, Elizabeth shot Gillian a sharp glance, but didn't object.

"Oy, you two settle down in there," ordered their guard.

Leverton, now back in her sights, sent her a hard look.

"I had to get my mother out of the draft," Gillian said in a meek voice. "She's quite prone to taking a chill."

"Well, just sit yer arse down and be still," the man said. "Or I'll give you what for." He waggled the pistol for emphasis.

"There's no need for threats," Leverton said. "Especially not to three defenseless women."

"I'll be the judge of that," snapped one of the other bandits.

"No, I will," Leverton replied. "Or there will be hell to pay, on my word as Duke of Leverton."

His words silenced their captors for several long seconds.

Even the pugnacious guard seemed taken aback. Gillian was quite sure that everyone in the county knew how powerful the duke was, including the bandits.

She craned out a bit, trying to see around the edge of the doorframe. Leverton fell back into discussion with a tall, spare man in a long, dark coat, a slouchy hat, and a kerchief that effectively obscured his features in the fading light. She could make out four other armed men, scattered behind the fellow who she guessed was their leader.

In front of the duke's carriage, two carts hooked up to ponies blocked the road. The carts were stacked with small barrels and square bundles bound up in some sort of cloth. Oddly, the wheels of the carts were wrapped with straw. A boy stood at the head of one of the ponies, holding the bridle.

Leverton's coachman and groom were nowhere in sight.

"Can you see anything?" Elizabeth whispered.

Gillian nodded. "Two carts are blocking the road, as if they were crossing from the field on the other side. And there's straw tied to the wheels."

"Drat," muttered Lady Filby. "They're smugglers, probably carrying gin and tobacco. It's quite common in these parts."

"Smugglers? Oh, no," moaned Mamma. She slumped against the squabs, as if on the edge of a swoon.

Gillian mentally cursed as she supported her mother. Smugglers could be exceedingly dangerous if they perceived their run to be jeopardized.

Their guard jabbed the pistol through the door of the carriage. "Keep that ninny quiet, or you'll be sorry. We don't need no wailin' and carryin' on. You'll bring the law down on us."

"Come now, sir," Lady Filby said in a credibly calm voice. "There isn't a soul around for miles. I'm sure you're quite safe."

The brute moved in closer to peer at the countess, or more specifically, at her generous bosom.

I think not. Gillian leaned forward to draw his attention. "You're making more noise than we are. If anyone is calling attention to this lovely little gathering, it's you."

Her gambit worked, since his focus swung round to her. "I said stow it, you silly bitch."

Leverton whipped around, the tails of his driving coat whirling about his legs. "You, there. You will leave the ladies alone. Now."

Their guard straightened. "Or you'll do what, Mr. Fancy? Beat me to a bloody pulp?"

The duke didn't move a muscle, but the look on his face caused the man to take a step back. Gillian couldn't blame the lout. In the flickering light of the carriage lamps, Leverton's eyes and expression conveyed a cold, dangerous fury.

"For Christ's sake," growled the apparent leader of the gang, "the last thing we need is the bleedin' Duke of Leverton up our arses. Just keep watch on them women and keep *your* bleedin' mouth shut, you stupid yob."

The guard reluctantly retreated a few paces, muttering under his breath.

Gillian went back to watching Leverton. "It sounds like the duke is trying to negotiate our way out of this," she murmured.

"We've obviously stumbled into the middle of a run," Lady Filby answered in a low voice. "Although I'm surprised they'd take such a risk before nightfall. But with any luck, we should be on our way in a few minutes."

Gillian blinked. "Just like that?"

"Smuggling has been going on in this part of England for decades. Most landowners find it easier to turn a blind eye than to fight it."

Everything in Gillian automatically rebelled at the notion.

In her experience, nothing good came from ignoring acts committed by ruthless thugs.

The countess obviously deduced her thoughts. "It's the safest thing to do, truly," she murmured.

Perhaps, but Gillian had no intention of sitting there like hapless prey, hoping for the best. Keeping the movement as small as possible, she slipped her hand inside her reticule.

A moment later, their guard reappeared in the door of the carriage, waving his pistol at Gillian. "Wot's that you got around your neck?"

Gillian sucked in a breath. *Hell and damnation.*

At some point, the gold chain around her neck had slipped out from under her collar. That meant that the gold St. Michael medallion embedded with tiny rubies was clearly visible against the dark green of her spencer. While Gillian didn't give a hang about jewels or other fripperies, her stepfather had given her the necklace shortly before he was murdered. It was meant to place her under the protection of the most powerful of archangels and to keep her safe when Step-papa wasn't there to watch over her. Gillian never took it off.

"Just a paste necklace," she said, slipping it back under her collar. Impatiently, she glanced over at Leverton. What in heaven's name was taking so long?

"It don't look like paste to me," the guard said. "Hand it over."

"Here, take this instead." Lady Filby rummaged in her reticule and pulled out a wad of pound notes.

The man plucked the notes from her hand and shoved them in his pocket. "And I'll take the pretty gel's necklace as well. Got to get somethin' more for all the trouble yer causin' us."

"No, you won't," Gillian said in a pleasant voice.

"Feisty, are you? I like 'em that way. If you don't wants

to give me your bauble, how about you give me something else?"

It would be a miracle if she didn't end up killing the swine. "Really? What do you have in mind?"

"Gillian, don't," her mother whispered.

The man leaned in and rested a huge, gloved hand on Gillian's thigh. "How's about you and me get behind one of these trees over there? You give me what I want, and you gets to keep yer bauble."

"Unhand her instantly," Lady Filby said, "or the duke will have your head."

"Shut your gob or you'll be next," the man snarled. "Maybe you'll be next, anyway. I've a fancy to see what's under all that fine frippery."

The countess went pale.

"I think not," Gillian scoffed.

"You ain't givin' the orders." The brute squeezed her thigh hard, then reached for the chain.

He froze when Gillian pressed the barrel of her small pistol under his jaw. "Do not touch my necklace."

He snatched his hand back.

"Now, I would hate to make a mess of this lovely upholstery by blowing out your brains," she said. "Please back away before I am forced to do just that." When he hesitated, she parted her lips in her most vicious smile. "I *will* blow your brains out, without hesitation."

"You're barking mad," he rasped out.

"Then I suggest you do as I say, since you have no idea what I might do next."

He started a slow retreat. Gillian followed, keeping her pistol under his chin. He was poised awkwardly on the steps when he slipped and pitched forward, practically into her lap. His weight threw her off balance, jogging her pistol and causing it to discharge.

"Bloody hell, you shot me!" he yelped, clutching his shoulder.

"So it would seem," she muttered, annoyed that she'd lost control of the situation.

He stared at her, clearly in shock. Then a large, gloved hand clamped on to his shoulder and flung him backwards out of the carriage. The duke loomed in the doorway.

"What the devil is going on here?" he said over the uproar going on outside the coach.

His eyes widened as he took in the pistol in Gillian's hand. He glanced behind him, then back at Gillian.

"Did you just shoot that man?" He plucked the weapon from her hand.

She shrugged.

"Charles, he was robbing us," Lady Filby said in a shaky voice. "And he was threatening to do much worse. What else was Gillian to do?"

"Not start a riot," he said as he shoved the pistol into his coat pocket. "You have just made our lives infinitely more complicated, Miss Dryden."

"I didn't plan it, I assure you. Besides, what else was I to do? You were otherwise engaged," Gillian said with heavy sarcasm.

He was clearly about to retort when somebody shoved him from behind. Cursing, Leverton glared over his shoulder. "What now?"

"Get 'em all out of the carriage," someone growled from behind him.

"Your man attacked one of my companions," the duke said in a cold voice. "She was simply defending herself."

"She bloody well shot my brother. Get 'em out, or I'll drag 'em out myself."

Leverton started to protest, but a moment later a man, presumably the one who'd just spoken, appeared behind the duke and jabbed a pistol against his skull.

Gillian's heart lurched. "All right, we're coming."

The man with the gun retreated, allowing the three women to alight with the duke's assistance. They lined up along the side of the carriage. In the fading dusk, Gillian could make out six men, including the idiot she'd shot and one attending to his wound. One man held a gun on the coachman and the groom, who were sitting on the ground by the carriage, while the others leveled their weapons at the women. Their leader squared off with Leverton.

A quick glance around showed Gillian only one dim light on the other side of the field flanking the road, presumably from a farmhouse or cottage in the distance. The road itself was deserted.

"How is he?" the gang leader asked the man who was tending to his brother.

"Just hit his upper arm. Bullet went clean through."

"Which one shot you?" the leader growled to his brother.

"The skinny gel," the smuggler said in a whining voice.

The leader kicked him in the leg. "Lettin' a girl shoot you—yer a disgrace to the family, you are," he said, ignoring his brother's offended yowl.

"Just tell me how much, and we'll be on our way," Leverton said in an impatient voice.

"We'll be wantin' more than just a few pound notes, Yer Grace. You've caused me a great deal of trouble tonight."

The leader's gaze moved to Gillian, interest flickering in his expression. Fortunately, she had a small but very sharp knife in her boot if she needed to defend herself. Unfortunately, that meant there would still be four armed, angry men to deal with.

When the man made a move in her direction, Leverton stepped between them. "Don't even think about it." His tone held a deadly threat that only a fool would ignore.

The leader was no fool because he put up a placating hand. "I won't touch a hair on her precious head. But I want to see what's so important she was willin' to shoot somebody."

"It's a bleedin' necklace," his brother said. "With rubies."

Gillian stiffened, mentally cursing.

"I reckon that'll even the score a bit," the leader said. He let out a laugh as he looked down at his brother. "Not sure you'll get any, though. Not for lettin' a pampered miss get the best of you."

His men guffawed. When the laughter died away, the gang leader jerked a head in her direction, and one of his men stalked over to Gillian.

She bared her lips in a snarl. "Don't touch me."

"For Christ's sake," Leverton sighed. "Give him the necklace."

"No." It felt like she'd be losing her stepfather for a second time. "They can have anything else, but not that."

The gang leader once more pressed his gun to the back of Leverton's skull. Gillian couldn't help flinching, and Lady Filby sucked in a horrified gasp.

The duke displayed no fear. In fact, he looked ready to kill someone. Probably Gillian.

"My love, please give them the necklace," her mother said in a quiet voice. "It's not worth it."

Gillian stared at the duke, who gazed back at her with an ironic lift to his brows. She was quite sure the gang leader wouldn't shoot Leverton. After all, no one in his right mind would shoot a duke.

But they shot my stepfather, didn't they? She reached up and yanked the chain, not even bothering to undo the clasp. "Here," she said, flinging it at the gang leader. It felt like her heart went with it.

The gang leader caught the necklace and held it up to the light of the carriage lamp. His scarf muffled his satisfied grunt. "Aye, that'll do." He waved a gun at Gillian's mother. "Now give me yer purse."

When Mamma whimpered, Gillian had to swallow a curse. When they traveled, her mother carried a few of her most precious jewels in her reticule, reluctant to consign them even to Maria's care.

Her mother handed over her reticule. Gillian could do nothing but squeeze her hand in sympathy, while rage burned through her brain like a firestorm.

When the bandit moved down to Lady Filby, she bridled. "Your man already cleaned me out."

"Give me that bauble on your wrist," the leader ordered.

Muttering, the countess flung her gold bracelet into the mud at the gang leader's feet. While Leverton scowled at his sister, Gillian had nothing but admiration for her. She understood the urge to cling to the shreds of one's dignity even when a situation was hopeless.

With a shrug, the gang leader retrieved the bracelet. "A little dirt never hurt no one."

"At least he's a practical villain," Gillian muttered. She heard Lady Filby choke back a laugh.

"I trust that now concludes our business," Leverton said, "given the very substantial haul you made with only a trifling inconvenience."

The gang leader gave him a mocking bow. "Aye, Yer Grace, it does. But don't forget what I told you. Talk about this little encounter, and trouble will surely come yer way."

"Your words of warning are engraved on my brain," the duke said. His tone was as dry as the dirt beneath their feet.

The smugglers hoisted the injured man into one of the carts, and they soon melted into the marshes and the encroaching night. Soon, even the rumble of the muffled wheels faded into silence. They were alone, as if the episode had never happened.

Leverton crouched behind the coachman, struggling with the rope around the man's wrists. "John, do you have a knife? This rope is wet."

Gillian pulled up her skirt and slipped the knife from her boot. "Take mine."

The duke shook his head. "Unbelievable."

She repressed a sigh as she handed the blade to him. Clearly, whatever good will she'd built up with Leverton had died an ignominious death. Gillian told herself she didn't care.

The duke swiftly freed his men, but cut off their apologies. "There will be ample opportunity to discuss our mutual failings at a later time. For now, I'd like to get the ladies to Fenfield Manor as quickly as possible. Especially since those damned smugglers took your weapons."

"You still have my pistol," Gillian said. "I have extra shot and powder with my nightgear, but it's tied up in the boot."

"How inconvenient," Leverton snapped.

She struggled to hold on to her rising temper. "It probably wouldn't do much good anyway. It's a woman's pistol, only good for close quarters."

"Unbelievable," he said again, rather unnecessarily, Gillian thought.

"For God's sake, Charles," Lady Filby said, "may we please get back in this confounded coach and be on our way? I'm sure the contessa is chilled to the bone. I certainly am."

Wincing with guilt, Gillian turned to her mother. "Yes, Mamma, let's get you inside."

"I beg your pardon," Leverton said. "Please, madam, take my hand."

Gillian glared at him. "We don't need your help."

As she assisted her mother into the carriage, she swore he was grinding his teeth. Gillian was tempted to snipe at him, but the sadness on her mother's face held her back. She hadn't seen such a haunted look in Mamma's eyes for a long time. "There, darling," she murmured, as she tucked a thick woolen shawl about her mother's legs. "Before you know it, we'll be there, and you can have a nice cup of tea and go to bed."

"Thank you, my dear," her mother said in a voice devoid of emotion. Gillian's heart seemed to drop into a pit.

A moment later, the carriage lurched forward. Gillian fussed over her mother, doing her best to ignore the chilly silence and the duke.

His sister was the first to speak. "Well, that was a first."

Gillian lifted an enquiring eyebrow.

"My first robbery," Lady Filby said with a rueful smile. "And I do hope it's my last."

"I'm truly sorry, Elizabeth," Leverton said in a somber tone. He looked at Gillian's mother. "Madam, I hope you can forgive me for allowing this to happen."

"Please, Your Grace," Mamma said with a wan smile, "this is simply an unfortunate circumstance of life. There is no need to apologize."

"I wouldn't say that," Gillian couldn't help muttering.

The duke's expression went from concerned to aggravated in one second flat. "Do you have something you'd like to say, Miss Dryden?"

"Charles, don't start," his sister warned.

He ignored her. "Go ahead, Miss Dryden. Get it off your chest."

"Very well," Gillian said. "This could have been avoided if we'd been properly escorted and armed."

Something flickered in his gaze. "It's never been necessary before. These roads have always been safe."

"Not according to your sister." Gillian let out a disgusted snort. "And people say Sicily is dangerous."

Leverton shot an irate glance at Lady Filby, who held up her hands. "I didn't say it was dangerous," she protested. "Just that smugglers frequently travel in these parts."

"That sounds dangerous to me," Gillian added triumphantly.

"You are wrong, Miss Dryden," the duke said. "Smugglers generally wish to avoid drawing the attention of the authorities. Tonight's encounter was simply a combination of bad luck and bad timing."

Bad luck? Anger burned at the thought of what she and her mother had lost tonight. "You should have stood up to them," she said.

"Apparently I didn't need to, given your bloodthirsty tendencies. Savage, indeed."

Gillian flinched as if he'd just slapped her. Actually, she'd have preferred a slap. Leverton had a way with words, both for good and ill.

"That's quite enough, Charles," Lady Filby exclaimed.

"My daughter doesn't deserve that, sir," Mamma added in a tone of wounded dignity. "She was very upset by what happened tonight, as were we all."

Gillian squeezed her mother's hand.

Leverton closed his eyes for a few moments. When he opened them, he'd regained some of his control. "I apologize, Miss Dryden." He leaned forward. "But was that blasted necklace worth risking our lives? Hell, I would have bought you another one myself for all the trouble it caused us."

He clearly didn't understand why this situation was so upsetting, both to Gillian and to her mother. Sadly, it appeared that Leverton was not that different from most of the men she'd known, ones who simply expected the women in their lives to fall obediently into line. To not actually fight for what they believed in. Only men, it appeared, were allowed to do that.

"Since you are so utterly devoid of feeling, Your Grace, I will not even try to explain," she said.

And then Gillian clamped her lips shut and refused to say another word.

Chapter Thirteen

Charles stretched his feet out to the fire, letting the peace of the old manor finally settle around him. Fenfield Manor might not be the most modern of houses, but its sturdy tranquility appealed to him. He didn't spend nearly as much time here as he should, since his larger estates—especially his principle seat—demanded more of his attention. Perhaps it was time to redress that situation, though. He had an unsettling notion that the gang they'd stumbled across was conducting runs across his lands. The entire affair seemed too well organized to be coincidental.

He could and did turn a blind eye to various petty offenses committed by locals, who often struggled to make ends meet. But full-scale runs across estate lands by clearly dangerous gangs? That he was not prepared to accept. Thinking about how things might have gone worse in their ugly encounter today raised the hairs on the back of his neck. What might have happened to Gillian—what might *still* happen to her, given her reckless ways—made his blood run as cold as the North Atlantic in winter.

In a matching armchair next to him, Elizabeth let out a weary sigh as she swirled her brandy in an old, cut-crystal goblet. She'd retreated to the library with him after Gillian and her mother had gone off to bed.

To say that their good nights had been frosty was laughably understated. Gillian had refused to even look at him. She'd simply snatched her candle from his hand and stalked off after the housekeeper. Outrage had been plain in every slender line of her body.

Not that she had good reason to be outraged. Not like he did. After all, it wasn't every day that a duke was told to sod off by a young lady who was a guest under his roof. That had been a first, one so surprising that he'd almost burst into laughter. He was restrained only by the horrified gasps from his butler, housekeeper, and especially the contessa, clearly appalled by her daughter's behavior.

His sister, however, had made little effort to hold back her snicker.

Gillian seemed incapable of self-restraint, particularly in situations where it counted most—when their lives were in danger or, possibly even more alarming, when out in polite company. The girl was more adept at dealing with thieves and murderers than she was with oafish aristocrats.

"Honestly, Charles, I don't know what you're going to do with her," Elizabeth said, echoing his thoughts. "Gillian is a darling girl, but she's reckless and outspoken in the extreme. I'm not sure she can ever be brought up to scratch, at least not by *ton* standards."

He put his empty glass on the occasional table between them. "I'm beginning to think it's a hopeless cause. It's a miracle she didn't get us all killed today."

"I'd say it's a miracle that *she* didn't kill someone. To be fair to her, the man was an utter beast. He threatened to take her out behind a tree and . . ." She waved her arm, obviously not wanting to say the word.

The idea of such violence befalling Gillian made him

ill. His worst fear today had been that the women would suffer the basest kind of assault. It was why he'd been so willing to settle with the gang leader, even though Gillian had clearly thought him a coward for doing so. But he couldn't risk a confrontation when they'd been outgunned, outmanned, and stuck in the middle of nowhere.

Fortunately, once the smugglers had realized they'd held up the Duke of Leverton, negotiations had proceeded fairly smoothly. Charles had handed over the fifty pounds in his wallet in exchange for the leader's promise that he and his men would fade away in the evening mists. Just as Charles had been issuing an additional warning that he would pursue justice if the gang ever conducted subsequent runs across Leverton estate lands, all hell had broken loose in the carriage.

"Gillian should have handed over the necklace immediately," he said.

Elizabeth grimaced. "I agree, but it clearly held great sentimental value, as did her mother's jewelry."

"Contessa di Paterini has more sense than her daughter. She didn't kick up a fuss at all." He narrowed his gaze on his sister. "Unlike you."

"The poltroon had already cleaned me out," she protested. "As far as I was concerned, I'd contributed more than enough to the evening's haul."

"We all did. Our combined contributions were substantially more valuable than the proceeds of that run, I'd wager."

"I don't know if you got a good look at Gillian's necklace. She claimed the jewels were paste, but I suspect they were genuine rubies."

"No piece of jewelry is worth one's life."

Elizabeth expelled an exasperated breath. "No, but it wasn't the monetary value that made it precious to Gillian.

And you insulted the poor girl when you suggested as much. Really, Charles, it's not like you to be so clumsy."

"I will admit that it was not my finest moment." There was no doubt that Gillian had a knack for making him lose his temper. But how could one waifish girl be so bloody difficult to handle? He was Leverton, for God's sake. Usually, a simple look would correct even the most obstinate person.

"Offering to replace their stolen jewelry was quite stupid," she said. "They're not poor, and you offended their dignity."

"I was trying to make things better," he said, feeling a tad defensive.

"Gillian and her mother were upset because the items obviously had emotional value that far exceeded their monetary worth. To suggest otherwise was vulgar."

"It amazes me that people think *I'm* a snob. You're much worse."

She laughed. "What utter rot. Everyone knows I'm the nicest person in the family. And you're not a snob, Charles. You never were."

He flashed her a wry smile. Their father had been a snob par excellence, and Charles had always hated the idea that he might be seen as one too. Having standards was one thing. Looking down on people was another.

"And you're only occasionally patronizing," Elizabeth added.

He had to laugh.

His sister's smile faded as she went back to swirling her brandy and staring into the fire. "You do have your work cut out for you with Gillian. She clearly finds you heavy-handed."

"Perhaps, but there was no earthly way I could agree to her mad scheme."

When they'd arrived at Fenfield Manor after a fraught forty-five minutes of silence, Gillian had demanded that he organize a search party to apprehend the smugglers. When he'd tried to explain how fruitless a search would be, especially after nightfall, she'd insisted that he give her a horse and a servant to accompany her. Gillian had made it abundantly clear that she had no intention of sitting idly by while criminals roamed at large with her belongings.

Charles had shut that idea down, ultimately threatening to send her back to her grandmother in London if she didn't comply. By continuing to argue, she'd forced him into a terse and perhaps too harsh assessment of her behavior. That's when she'd told him to sod off. She hadn't been one whit disturbed by the fact that they were yelling like fishwives in front of half the household.

"I understand," Elizabeth said. "But to suggest that she was suffering from hysterics was rather like waving a large red flag in front of a bull."

"I suppose it would have been more accurate to say she was on the verge of murdering someone. But I never like to point out the obvious."

"If she were going to murder anyone, I would think it would be you."

"Don't I know it," he said in a gloomy voice.

The Gillian project had turned into a disaster. His social capital was strong enough to allow the girl to recover from her London escapades, but not if she was going to fight him every damn step of the way. She had no more desire to become a proper lady than he had to join a troupe of jugglers.

What the girl truly wanted was to return to Sicily, the one place that felt like home. Knowing Gillian, she'd fight for the only life that made sense to her and eventually batter her resistant family into submission. True, there were issues regarding her safety if she returned, but Charles felt sure that Griffin Steele could manage them effectively. The former crime lord was powerful, dangerous, and, as her brother, the man best positioned to ensure her welfare.

That being the case, it was probably time for Charles to give up—even if he did have the most annoying feeling that he would miss the blasted girl a great deal more than he should.

"Lizzie, do you ever get bored?" he asked abruptly.

She twisted in her chair to peer at him, her brows winging up in surprise. "Heavens, Charles, where did that question come from?"

"From curiosity, I suppose."

She studied him with a shrewdness he found rather disconcerting.

"I do not," she finally said. "I have two small children and a husband who, as lovely as he is, needs a great deal of managing. Add in our mother and our sister—both quite demanding, as you know—along with two estates and a townhouse to look after. No, Charles, I don't have time to be bored." She cocked her head. "Do you?"

"Sometimes." He went back to studying the fire. "I suppose that makes me sound like a coxcomb."

"You are the farthest thing from a coxcomb. But I believe I know what your problem is."

"Do tell, sister dear," he said, casting her a wry smile.

"It's because you're so powerful, so . . . imposing. Everyone bows and scrapes and instantly agrees with you. No one ever dares stand up to you, except me, of course. I believe you are quite in need of someone to disagree with you. To challenge you." She gave him what could only be described as an evil grin. "And I fancy I know just the person to fit the bill."

"Perhaps I should simply hire a few toddlers to keep around the house instead. Or borrow yours whenever I feel a brown study coming on."

"Perhaps you should get married and have some of your own."

"And on that note," he said, rising from his chair, "I'm going to bed."

"Coward," she murmured, also getting to her feet.

"Elizabeth, I have no intention of having this particular discussion again."

The subject of marriage never failed to put him in a bad mood. He'd already had one near disaster, and had yet to find the woman who would tempt him to make another attempt.

"You're not getting any younger, Charles. Sooner than you think, you'll be drooling into your soup and tottering about in your decrepitude."

"Thank you for that lovely image."

A quiet knock interrupted them. "Now what?" Elizabeth sighed.

"One hopes Gillian isn't raising a commotion. I think I'd rather be robbed again than have further dealings with her tonight. Enter," he said, raising his voice.

The door opened, and the Contessa di Paterini peeked her head inside. "May I come in?" she asked in a hesitant voice.

"Of course." Charles took her hand and led her to the chair he'd just vacated. She settled into it with a sigh, looking pale and wan, although still neatly coiffed and dressed in her dinner clothes. He exchanged a glance with his sister, because the contessa should have been abed an hour ago.

"Would you like something to drink, madam? Perhaps a brandy or a sherry?" he asked.

"No, thank you. I'll try not to keep you any longer than necessary, but I do need to speak with you tonight, Your Grace." She smiled, and for a moment looked almost as young and as pretty as her daughter. The contessa was still a lovely woman, with an appealing, feminine charm. Gillian greatly resembled her, at least physically.

"I'm sure you wish to speak privately with my brother," Elizabeth said. "I'll wish you both good night."

The contessa held up a hand. "No, please stay, Lady Filby. You have been so kind to lend us your countenance, and I have no wish to keep secrets from you. Besides, you were also affected by Gillian's behavior tonight. I'd like to explain why she acted as she did."

"You certainly do not owe me any explanations," Elizabeth said with a kind smile.

Still she sat down, as Charles had known she would. His sister loved nothing more than a good gossip. But he also knew she had Gillian's best interests at heart.

The contessa smoothed her cambric skirts, perhaps taking a moment to order her thoughts. "It's hard to know where to start."

Charles propped a shoulder against the mantelpiece. "Why not start with her reaction to the robbery? She seems singularly focused on recovering what was taken, even though she must know how unlikely that is."

"There are two reasons Gillian behaved the way she did," her mother said. "The first is that her stepfather was killed by bandits."

"I'm so sorry," Elizabeth said. "How dreadful for both of you."

"Gillian's emotions regarding my husband's death are quite complicated," the contessa replied. "She has what one might call an exaggerated sense of justice."

"I don't understand," Elizabeth said.

"The men who killed my husband were never brought to justice. My daughter has not been able to forget that."

Charles raised his eyebrows. "Did Gillian not redress that situation, herself?"

"Goodness, Charles," his sister exclaimed. "Don't be ridiculous. How could a young girl bring a band of murderers to justice?"

"After the local authorities gave up on finding my husband's killers, Gillian spent several years hunting them down," the contessa said.

Elizabeth's mouth gaped open. "Ah, what did she do once she found them?"

"She killed them," the contessa replied.

The color drained from Elizabeth's face. "Now you know why I didn't tell you details of her past," Charles said dryly.

"Indeed," said the contessa. "We have kept it as quiet as we could. But what Gillian did was exact revenge, not justice. And although she did eliminate the men directly responsible for my husband's death, bandits still freely roam the Sicilian countryside, exacting tribute from the local nobility and terrorizing the peasants."

The contessa leaned forward, pinning Charles with an intent gaze. "To remain in Sicily would have meant certain death for Gillian. Eventually, those evil men would have come after her, to exact *their* revenge on her. They would not rest until they did, no matter how long it took. Their honor and reputation would demand it."

"Good God," Elizabeth said in a faint voice.

Christ. Charles had known the situation was tricky, but even Griffin Steele couldn't protect her from that—not for years on end. "So, there is no going back for Gillian. I understand."

"But she doesn't," her mother said softly. "Not yet. I hope *you* might be able to convince her, since her grandmother and I have failed. It might not seem so right now, but she does respect you."

Charles doubted that, but what choice did he have but to try? "Gillian's disgust toward the men who stopped us tonight is certainly understandable, given her history. But I still don't understand why she's so set on recovering the stolen goods. She must know it's an all-but-impossible quest."

"Her stepfather gave her that necklace on her birthday, shortly before he was killed. It was the last gift he ever gave her."

"The poor child," Elizabeth said. "But she seems even more adamant about retrieving your jewelry, does she not?"

The contessa nodded. "I had a similar pendant from my husband, along with a few other valuable pieces. I am unhappy to lose them, but naturally would not expect anyone to risk his life to retrieve them. I do not need jewelry to remind me of my husband or of what I've lost."

"Have you explained that to your daughter?" Charles asked.

"I just spent the last hour attempting to do so," she said. "My darling daughter, however, does not believe me."

"Whyever not?" Elizabeth asked.

"Because she feels she owes me a great debt. Among other things, Gillian blames herself for my husband's tragic demise."

Charles frowned. "But she was little more than a child at the time."

"One already much older than her years," her mother said. "Gillian was raised on my husband's estates. While we were often at court in Palermo, she stayed behind. She preferred to be in the country, as there she was less likely to be a target of gossip." The contessa grimaced. "And she could avoid my father, who was not as kind to her as he should have been. My husband and I thought it best that Gillian spend most of her time where she felt happy and secure."

And where she'd clearly been allowed to run wild. Charles knew, however, that it was pointless to raise that issue. "I still don't understand why she feels responsible for your husband's murder."

"Gillian insisted that he do something about the bandits," she explained. "The Sicilian gangs are ruthless and dangerous. They bedeviled the countryside and made life miserable for the local peasants. Because Gillian saw those poor common folk every day, she had great sympathy for them. She wanted to help."

"Goodness, what an extraordinary girl she is," Elizabeth said.

"My daughter has a generous spirit," the contessa said with pride. "My husband always encouraged her natural sense of compassion and kindness. It was partly for Gillian's sake that he took on the task of ridding the countryside of the bandit scourge. Like her, my husband believed it was the right thing to do."

"And he was killed in the process," Charles said with sympathy.

"Yes, he and his bodyguards were ambushed one evening while returning from visiting a neighboring landowner. My husband and all his men were murdered."

"How utterly tragic," Elizabeth murmured.

The contessa nodded. "Naturally, Gillian was devastated and guilt-ridden. She believed that if she'd left well enough alone, her stepfather would never have been in danger. But it wasn't true, because my Mario was a noble and just man. He did what he thought he must."

"Surely you explained that to your daughter?" Charles asked.

"I certainly should have, but I was unable to at the time. On learning of my husband's death, I collapsed. My mother was primarily taken up with my care, which left Gillian mostly on her own during a very fraught period. And at the mercy of my father, who was not, as I mentioned, patient with her."

Charles had to tamp down a flare of anger. "I trust, however, that he did not abuse her in any way."

The contessa looked startled. "Oh, no. He never lifted a hand to her. But he was not an affectionate or particularly kind man, and he resented the embarrassment her birth caused our family." She sighed. "As if that was her fault, not mine. Unfortunately, I lacked the strength to stand up to my father. I'm ashamed I was such a coward."

"Nonsense," Charles said. "You defied him by choosing to keep Gillian with you. That in itself was a tremendous act of courage."

"Oh, well done, brother," murmured Elizabeth.

He shrugged. They both knew the damage fathers could do.

The contessa gave him a grateful smile. "I was fortunate that my mother supported my wishes. But Gillian has always been painfully aware of the sacrifices I made to keep her, as she puts it. As I said, my daughter is convinced she owes me a great debt for not putting her aside. I wonder sometimes if I made a tremendous mistake by keeping her with me. I suspect she would have been happier being raised by a loving family in the country, leading a simpler life. Instead, she's been forced to move between two worlds, never fully accepted in either one."

"It's pointless to think that way," Charles said. "Gillian is where she deserves to be, and where she belongs."

With me. He mentally blinked, startled by how easily the thought had slipped into his mind. He forced himself to shrug it off and focus on the immediate problem of how to help Gillian.

"I for one think you've done a bang-up job with your daughter," Elizabeth said in a stout voice. "She's a splendid girl."

The older woman beamed at her. "Thank you, my dear. I think she's a splendid girl, too. I simply wish more people would take the time to see that."

"Which brings us to the point of this conversation," Charles said. "What, exactly, do you want me to do?"

Gillian's mother looked him steadfastly in the eye. Despite her frail temperament and health, he was beginning to realize that she could be something of a tiger when it came to protecting her daughter. "Please don't give up on her," she said. "Gillian deserves to be happy."

How could he give up now, after all he'd heard? "I won't, madam. You have my word."

Chapter Fourteen

Gillian put down her knife and flashed a smile at Fenfield Manor's cook. "Thank you, Mrs. Peck. Those were absolutely delicious biscuits. I don't know when I've ever had any so good." Not that she'd ever had walnut and cheese biscuits before, but these tasted like ambrosia. Of course, skipping several meals in a row did tend to whet one's appetite. But it was a sacrifice she'd had to make in order to avoid encountering Leverton.

"Now, miss, I was worried since you've hardly touched your victuals since arriving here. But I'm that glad to see you get an appetite back." The cook beamed as she plopped another plate of biscuits on the kitchen table. "And there's plum bread if you fancy it, too. Just fresh out of the oven."

"Truly, I'm stuffed," Gillian said. "If I eat anything else, I won't have room for dinner."

Mrs. Peck lacked the sophistication of the great French chefs who cooked for the London aristocracy, and she certainly didn't look the part of a grand kitchen master. Tall, spare, and hatchet-faced, she appeared as if she ate hardly anything at all, much less sampled her own cooking. But like all the staff Gillian had met at the manor, she was efficient, kind, and welcoming

For some odd reason, the servants had taken a shine to Gillian. That was a bit of a miracle, considering how badly she'd behaved on the night of their arrival. She'd thoroughly lost her temper with His High and Mighty Grace, embarrassing herself in front of at least half the household staff. And the ones that hadn't been in the hall had probably heard her, since she'd made no effort to lower her voice. She still cringed just thinking about the mortifying scene, and about how she'd stormed at Leverton like an awful shrew.

But instead of being offended by her behavior, the staff had gone out of their way to pamper and fuss over her. Gillian suspected they were trying to prop up her spirits after the incident with the smugglers, which was terribly sweet of them. Was it any wonder that she'd been spending as much time belowstairs as possible since her arrival? At least with the servants, she didn't have to worry about receiving a scolding or another lecture on proper conduct from the man who seemed to have written the book on the subject—a man who clearly considered her an utter failure when it came to following the precepts of that dreariest of tomes.

She'd half expected Leverton to ring a peal over her for spending a good deal of her time in the kitchen and stables, or roaming about the estates. Such, however, had not been the case. Since their arrival three days ago, he'd barely seemed to notice either her presence or her absence. He'd been locked up in his library or out on horseback with his estate manager. On the few occasions when he and Gillian had run into each other, Leverton had been perfectly polite, but made no attempt to speak with her beyond a cursory word of greeting.

Unfortunately, his cool behavior seemed to have a strangely lowering effect on her spirits.

She was also disturbed that, apparently, little effort was

being made to track down the villains who'd robbed them. Then again, the duke didn't seem like the kind of man who could be bothered to hunt down a band of nefarious smugglers over a few pieces of stolen jewelry. He'd clearly found the entire episode regrettable and distasteful—and probably *her* behavior the most distasteful element of all. Gillian had little doubt that for him the incident was over and done with.

For her, such was not the case.

"Well, all right," Mrs. Peck said, clearing her plate away. "But I'll be expecting a good report from the footman tonight after dinner. I'll not be having you send back a full plate. I'll be thinking you don't like my cooking."

"Nothing could be further from the truth, Mrs. Peck," Gillian said.

"Then I expect you to be more than a mite *peckish*, since you've only had a little snack this afternoon," the cook said with a sly grin.

"Mrs. Peck, that is an exceedingly bad pun," Gillian said. Still, she couldn't help chuckling. It felt good to laugh again, even over such a silly joke.

"I'll have what Miss don't finish," Teddy Bell piped up from the other side of the huge oak table that spanned half the length of the kitchen. He stuffed another walnut and cheese biscuit into his mouth, his eyes practically rolling with bliss. "I always has me a good appetite, Mrs. Peck."

Between his broad Lincolnshire accent and his full mouth, Gillian could hardly understand the lad. But the stable boy was clearly enjoying his afternoon tea, and even more clearly enjoying that he was allowed to share it with Gillian. The child had become her shadow, attaching himself to her whenever he wasn't busy in the stables or doing errands for Mrs. Peck.

Teddy was also a fount of information about the residents of Fenfield Manor and the local parish, including the smugglers. According to the lad, free trading was worse and closer to home than perhaps the duke realized.

"As if I would waste His Grace's dinner on a young rascal like you," Mrs. Peck retorted as she handed the dishes off to the scullery girl. "Now enough sitting around and jawing with Miss Gillian. Get yourself back to the stables and to work. Reid will be looking for you."

The boy pushed back his chair, stuffing another biscuit into his mouth for good measure. He gave Gillian a wave, his mouth obviously too crammed to speak, and scampered for the door.

"I'll be sending a package home to your ma, Teddy," Mrs. Peck called after him. "Don't forget to pick it up before you leave." The cook sighed when the boy let the kitchen door slam behind him. "Forgive his lack of manners, Miss Gillian. He's a good lad, but a little rough, even though his ma tries to smooth him out."

"She's a widow, is she not?" Gillian asked.

"That she is." Mrs. Peck retrieved a cloth-covered bowl from one of the shelves built into the old masonry walls of the kitchen. She carefully removed a large mound of risen dough and placed it on the table, then began to knead it with a swift, expert touch. Gillian relaxed even more, lulled by the warmth of the kitchen fire, the smell of roasting meat from the brick oven, and the cheerful order that made the low-ceilinged room a welcome retreat.

"Things haven't been easy for Sarah since her husband passed on a few years ago," Mrs. Peck said. "She takes in washing and does some baking, but there's not much work to be had in a village as small as ours. That's why Mr. Hewitt took little Teddy on to help in the stables and in the house."

"That was very kind of him," Gillian said. Hewitt, the butler at Fenfield Manor, was a quiet, unassuming man who ran a well-ordered household. He didn't lord it over the other servants or go out of his way to make life more difficult than it needed to be. The staff seemed almost like a family.

The only exception was Mr. Scunthorpe, the estate manager. Gillian had only met him once. A well-dressed, good-looking man in his late thirties, he obviously had quite a fine opinion of himself. That had only been her general impression, since she'd not spent much time talking to him. But Gillian fancied that he'd looked down his nose when introduced to her, as if slightly offended by her presence.

But it was more than that. Instinctively, she didn't trust him, but she couldn't quite determine why.

"He's a good man, is our Mr. Hewitt," Mrs. Peck said. "We don't really have need for a stable boy, because Fenfield is so quiet. Why, we barely see His Grace from one year to the next, and he never tarries for more than a few weeks. But young Teddy needed a job, and a job he got. Mr. Hewitt is right loyal to the boy, no matter what that Scunthorpe has to say about it."

That last bit was muttered, but it certainly confirmed what Gillian already sensed. Scunthorpe might be a competent manager, but he was not well liked by the rest of the staff.

"Is Mr. Scunthorpe from around these parts, Mrs. Peck?"

"That he is not. He's from up north. Yorkshire way." From the way Mrs. Peck pounded her dough, she obviously didn't have much love for either Scunthorpe or Yorkshire.

"And why does Mr. Scunthorpe—"

Gillian broke off when she heard the kitchen door swing open behind her. Mrs. Peck's flour-covered hands stilled, and her eyes went wide. Gillian twisted around, half expecting to see the estate manager, annoyed that they'd been gossiping about him.

She almost fell out of her chair when she saw Leverton at the top of the short flight of steps that led down to the stone floor. He regarded her with an ironic lift to his brows.

"Hewitt told me I would find you here or in the stables," he said. "The stables I can understand, but I never took you to be the domestic sort, Miss Dryden."

He flashed her a warm smile, as if to take the sting from his words, and it sent her heart thudding like the hooves on a galloping horse. The man was impossibly handsome, even dressed more casually than his usual wont. Attired in buckskin breeches, tall boots, and a riding jacket, he looked like masculine perfection coming down from Mount Olympus to join the mere mortals. The simpler country garb suited him, showcasing his broad chest and shoulders and his long, muscled legs. His Grace might be the most sophisticated, urbane man she'd ever met, but no one could accuse him of being soft.

When amusement crept into his eyes, she realized she was staring at him. With her mouth open. *Idiot.*

Gillian clamped her mouth shut and settled a scowl in place to compensate for her momentary lapse. She'd been laid low before by a handsome face and a nice set of shoulders, and that experience had taught her a lot about rich, arrogant men like the Duke of Leverton.

"Ah, what a shame," he murmured. "For a moment, I thought we were friends again."

"Um, what?" Then she winced. What was it about a handsome face that so often reduced her to sounding like a foolish schoolgirl?

"Goodness me, Your Grace, I never thought to see you in the kitchen," Mrs. Peck said, bobbing a curtsey. "Everything's a right mess, too."

"Nothing of the sort, Mrs. Peck. Everything looks trim and tidy, as always. I wish that all my houses were as comfortable and well run as Fenfield Manor."

Mrs. Peck actually blushed. "Thank you, sir. We all love Fenfield, and consider ourselves right blessed to work here."

"The blessings accrue to me, I assure you."

Gillian had to admit that although Leverton might have a habit of ordering people around, he certainly wasn't a snob. He was comfortable conversing with his cook, and seemed not at all nonplussed by spending a little time belowstairs.

He glanced down and caught Gillian's gaze. For several long seconds, they sized each other up.

"You're going to get a crick in your neck if you keep staring up like that," he said.

"I wouldn't, if you would sit down," she said, just as affably.

His lips twitched.

"As if His Grace would ever be doing that down here," Mrs. Peck exclaimed, clearly appalled. "If you can be telling me exactly what you need, sir, I'll have it brought up to you in a trice."

"That won't be necessary, Mrs. Peck. I was simply looking for Miss Dryden."

"Well, you found me," Gillian said.

"Indeed. And if you're finished hiding away belowstairs, I wonder if you'd like to come for a walk with me."

She stiffened. "I am not hiding."

"Then how clumsy of me to make such an assumption. I am, however, simply repeating the term your mother used."

Blast.

Mamma had given her quite the lecture this morning about *moping about* and avoiding everyone. There was more to it than that, of course—not that Gillian could tell anyone what she'd been doing these last few days. Her mother would go into hysterics, and Leverton would probably have her locked in her room. And although her bedroom was both comfortable and pretty, it was on an upper floor. Whenever possible, Gillian made a point of not climbing down trellises or hanging off downspouts to reach the ground, since they were notoriously unstable and likely to break at the most inconvenient moments.

She made a show of peering out the high window of the half-cellared kitchen. "The weather doesn't look very conducive to a walk."

It had been another wet morning. Gillian had always known that England had a damp climate, but she was beginning to worry she might sprout moss around the edges. The dreary weather made her long even more for Sicily, with its dry sunny days.

Mrs. Peck peered out the window too. "It was a cold mizzle just a bit ago, and that snithe wind could freeze a body to the bone."

"What's a snithe wind?" Gillian asked.

"It means bitter, in the local parlance," Leverton replied.

The cook gave him an approving smile. "Aye, sir. You'll be talking like a native before you know it."

Gillian laughed. "I'd like to see that."

"You might be surprised," he said. "I spent quite a bit of time at Fenfield Manor when I was a boy. I have very fond memories of the place."

"And it's grand to have you back with us," the cook said, bobbing him another quick curtsey. "We all hope you stay with us a good while."

"Thank you, Mrs. Peck." The duke stretched out a hand to Gillian. "Come for a walk, Miss Dryden. I promise I won't bite."

She stared at his hand, as if it would do exactly that. But it wasn't him she didn't trust. It was herself. "Thank you, but I think I'd better go spend some time with Mamma."

"Your mother has just gone upstairs to lie down. She has a touch of a headache and doesn't want to be disturbed."

That announcement promptly sent Mrs. Peck bustling about. "Ah, the poor thing. I'll make up a poultice to put on her forehead. Frim folk like her ladyship often get megrims in this terrible damp weather."

"She means strangers to this part of England," the duke said, answering Gillian's unspoken question. He crooked a finger at her. "Come, Miss Dryden." His tone was warm, gentle, and implacable.

Sighing, she took his hand and rose. "I suppose you want to resume our blast—er, our lessons."

"We'll see," he said, leading her to the kitchen steps.

What did that mean? Gillian wasn't sure she wanted to know. She waved good-bye to Mrs. Peck and followed Leverton upstairs to the main entrance hall. Maria, her mother's maid, awaited them with Gillian's pelisse, bonnet, and gloves.

"You really weren't going to take no for an answer, were you?" Gillian asked in a wry tone.

"It never even occurred to me that you would say no, Miss Dryden."

She rolled her eyes. "Your Grace, do you realize that you're sometimes a tad arrogant?"

"Surely you jest," he replied with a smile that would have made her toes curl had she not been wearing such sturdy boots. It was annoying how bloody charming the man could be. Gillian had no doubt that a crook of the finger after one look from him would bring every woman in London scurrying to his side.

After all, it had worked on her.

As they walked down the steps to the circular sweep in front of the house, Mr. Scunthorpe appeared from the direction of the stables. The estate manager took off his hat. "Good afternoon, Your Grace." He paused a moment. "Miss Dryden."

Gillian frowned at the way the man's gaze flickered over her with a cool regard.

"Scunthorpe," the duke replied with a nod. "Just back from Skegness?"

"Yes, sir. I delivered all your letters and met with your banker, as instructed."

"Good man. We can discuss it after my walk with Miss Dryden."

The estate manager directed another wary glance at Gillian, one that goaded her into speech. "The duke is showing me around the grounds," she said with an entirely artificial smile. "I'm quite looking forward to it."

"Indeed. You've already seen a good deal of it on your own, as far as I can tell," Scunthorpe said in a polite tone.

The man *had* been watching her, but whatever for?

Leverton frowned. "You're not suggesting there's a problem with Miss Dryden's walking about the grounds by herself, are you?"

"Of course not, Your Grace," Scunthorpe quickly replied. "In fact, I would be happy to escort her at any time, if she should so desire. The grounds are extensive as you know, and it would be my pleasure to serve as her guide."

"Thank you," Gillian said, "but I quite prefer to roam on my own. Except for today," she hastily added when she took in the sardonic expression on Leverton's face.

"As you wish, Miss Dryden." After a few more words with his employer, the estate manager excused himself and hurried into the house.

Gillian started walking, but stopped when Leverton didn't follow. She turned to find him studying her with a thoughtful air. "What?"

"Are you having a problem with Scunthorpe?" he asked.

"Not that I know of." He was a disapproving snob, but that was hardly a rarity in her world. As for her sense that the man wasn't entirely trustworthy, he was the duke's employee and not her concern.

Leverton nodded and took her elbow, steering her along the gravel sweep.

"Where are we going?" she asked.

"There's an interesting chapel not far from here, built during the seventeenth century. I thought you might like to see it."

"How nice."

Though she tried not to sound utterly bored by the prospect, she'd obviously failed, since the duke let out a derisive snort. "You might attempt a little more excitement, you know." He drew her closer, tucking her against his side. "Monkton Chapel is considered to be both an architectural and historical gem."

Unlike the proposed outing, his touch *was* exciting. Whenever she got this close to Leverton, Gillian's nerves tended to jump. He was a physically imposing man at the best of times, but with virtually no distance between them, he was almost overpowering.

He glanced down at her with some amusement. "I understood that you were quite fond of history."

"I am. It's just that anything less than four hundred years old doesn't seem worth the trouble. After all, I grew up with Roman ruins in the bottom of our garden." She waved an airy hand. "If you wish to impress me, Your Grace, you'll have to do better than a paltry two or three hundred years."

"Miss Dryden, in the spirit of continuing with your lessons, may I point out that a young lady doesn't generally wish to offend by suggesting that an outing organized for her pleasure is a dead bore."

She widened her eyes at him. "But what if it is a dead bore?"

He smiled. "Such a challenging pupil. I think you already know the answer to that question."

"Unfortunately, I do. I'm to simper and smile and pretend everything is lovely, especially the gentleman who is, in fact, as tedious as one can imagine." Gillian shook her head. "No wonder so many English girls seem wan and listless. They're bored out of their skulls."

"Well, let's hope you acquire a few suitors who can do better than that," he said. "There must be at least one or two who might meet your exacting standards, even if they aren't in the habit of hunting bandits."

So far the only man she'd found at all interesting since coming to England was the duke himself—an alarming notion. Even more alarming was the obvious fact that Leverton was resuming her lessons. That meant her family had not given up on the idea of finding her a suitable husband—a husband who, no doubt, would object to the notion of his wife's spending most of her time in Sicily.

They were quiet for a minute or two as he led her off the drive and down a wide path through the tree-lined gardens. White and pink blossoms littered the path, knocked down by rain that had fallen the previous night. Sparrows flitted from one tree to the next, bravely twitting away despite the cool weather and the occasional gust of wind. It was a bucolic and peaceful scene, and would no doubt be smashingly lovely on a warm and sunny day. At the moment though, Gillian found it rather forlorn and damp, words that perfectly described her mood.

"The trees are very pretty in this part of the garden," she said, trying to rally. "Can you tell me what they are?"

"Wild cherry and crabapple, I believe. I'd have to check with the gardener to be absolutely sure. We could try hunting him down if you'd like. I'm sure Pierce is rolling about here somewhere."

"No, thank you," she said. "I was just trying to make conversation."

He laughed. "You can be a most daunting companion, Miss Dryden, although you did start off well with an unexceptionable topic. But your last comment was not likely to foster subsequent conversation."

"Sorry," she said, wincing. "I'm not very good at that sort of thing, am I? I'm afraid you have your work cut out for you."

"Believe it or not, I generally find you a very interesting person to talk to. You have, shall we say, a unique view of life. But I suspect you have something else on your mind. Perhaps something that is weighing on you and making it difficult to have an easy conversation."

She cut him a sideways glance. He was regarding her with a slight smile that curved up his wickedly attractive mouth. "You know you can speak to me about whatever you wish, Miss Dryden. I promise I won't be shocked."

Gillian could think of a few things that would probably shock him, at least when it came to her past, present, and probably future behavior. But on this particular subject, there wasn't much to be gained by avoiding it.

She stopped in the middle of the path, forcing him to come to a halt. "By your comments, sir, I take it that you do intend to continue with my lessons in etiquette."

"Of course. Why wouldn't I?"

"Because I'm a rather hopeless case?"

"I wouldn't say that by any means. You can be exceedingly charming when you make an attempt at it."

She snorted. "Yes, I'm sure all the men think so. Especially Lord Andover."

"We won't speak of that unfortunate incident, other than to say that his lordship earned exactly what he got." His gaze flicked down over her figure, bringing sudden warmth to her cheeks. "And in case no one has ever told you, Miss Dryden, you are a very attractive young woman."

"Actually, I have heard that before." She turned abruptly and continued along the path, heading for the field beyond the formal gardens.

The duke caught up with her and grasped her hand. "Gently, my girl. There's no need to rush off in a huff."

"I'm not in a rush, and I'm not huffing," she snapped,

trying to yank her hand away. He held on in a gentle but firm clasp. She stared straight ahead, hating that her cheeks must be blazing a furious pink.

"Gillian, I didn't mean to insult you," he said, drawing her around to look at him. "I meant what I said. You are a lovely and intelligent young woman, and any man in his right mind would be happy to spend time in your company."

Her heart thumped as he spoke her name in his deep voice. It thumped even harder at the look in his eyes. She well knew that the Duke of Leverton could charm the birds from the trees, but he didn't seem to be engaging in empty flattery. His gaze was open, admiring, and apparently sincere.

"Thank you," she managed.

He studied her for a few moments. Then he blinked, as if something unpleasant had just occurred to him. "Miss Dryden, has someone insulted you by being overly familiar?"

He was back to being formal. "Not lately," she said.

"What does that mean?"

"Nothing at all. I assure you that no gentleman other than Lord Andover has insulted me or been overly familiar. Although I suppose they wouldn't really be gentlemen if they did."

"You'd be surprised."

"Sadly, I would not, but that is hardly the point."

"Then what is the point, Miss Dryden?" he asked, sounding exasperated.

She tugged her hand away and strode down the path, forcing him to follow. She always found it easier to talk about unpleasant subjects while moving. According to her grandmother, it was more like running away, but Gillian didn't necessarily agree with that view.

"It's just that you've set yourself an impossible task," she said over her shoulder. "Mamma, Grandmamma, and you in particular. Surely my reputation is all but ruined by now. Why even make the effort?"

He caught up and again tucked her against his side. "The effort is entirely worth making. Your reputation is not ruined. Just a little, well, tarnished."

"I fear you're going to need vats of polish to get it shining again."

"I am up to the task." His tone of voice conveyed not one shred of doubt.

Gillian let out a small sigh. "It must be lovely to be so convinced of one's superiority."

The frozen silence that met her remark brought her up short. "Confound it," she muttered. "I did not just say that."

"It would appear that you did." Amazingly, he didn't sound angry. His lips were pressed tight, as if he was trying not to laugh.

"Are you mocking me?" she asked suspiciously.

His grin finally broke free. It dazzled, as if the sunshine had broken through the gray, lowering sky, and surrounded her with light and warmth.

"I wouldn't dream of it," he said. "But may I point out that you just delivered an extremely adroit insult. I would suggest you refrain from that sort of tactic when conversing with gentlemen you actually like."

She had to smile back. "Understood. You, however, are surely impervious to insult."

"Hardly."

"I suspect that very few women—or men, for that matter—would ever mock or laugh at you. After all, you *are* Perfect Penley."

Even though Leverton didn't move or bat an eyelid, she had the sensation that he'd just retreated. "You'd be surprised," he said.

"Blast. I'm sorry. Now you know why I have so few

friends—I inadvertently insult them. Truly, sir, you're wasting your time on me."

"I don't believe that," he said. "And apology accepted."

She crinkled her nose. "Really?"

"Yes, to both. All I ask is that you try your best. Leave everything else up to me."

"Of course." She figuratively crossed her fingers behind her back, hoping he didn't sense her lack of enthusiasm.

They came up to a fence that ran the length of the field in front of them. Gillian let go of his arm and leaned on the top rail, gazing out at the peaceful view. While nothing like the beloved and imposing vistas of Sicily, it was green and fresh, and she caught a hint of a salty tang coming from the fens.

"It's very pretty here," she said. "I like it."

He turned sideways to look at her, leaning an elbow on the fence. "I'm glad, but I know you miss Sicily. In fact, you want to go back, do you not?"

Blast. This was the last topic she wished to discuss with him. "It was my home, after all. And you must admit that the weather in England is simply ghastly," she said, trying to be nonchalant.

"It's clearly more than the weather. You feel like you don't fit in—that England could never be home."

"I didn't really fit in back in Sicily, either." Aghast at the words that had just popped out of her mouth, Gillian gazed blindly out at the field. Somehow, those simple words rang true—too true, now that she thought about it.

His hand came up to her chin, a leather-gloved finger gently turning her face to him. "You would fit in here very well. Even in London, if you gave it half a chance."

Gillian stared up at him, trapped in a gaze as blue and endless as a summer sky. And just as warm. She had to swallow before she could answer. "Why do you even care?"

His gaze moved down to her mouth, then back up. "Because you deserve that people should care about you."

No, no, no.

No matter how handsome or good a man he was, or how sincere, she would not stumble again. He was a duke and she was . . . well, she knew exactly who and what she was.

She slid away from him to the stile that led into the field. "This is a very unusual sort of contraption," she said brightly. "I don't think I've ever seen a stile like this before."

"Yes, it is unusual," he said in a husky voice.

She hadn't heard him move, but he was right behind her, caging her in between the stile and his big body.

"It's called a kissing gate," he murmured in her ear. "Can you guess why?"

Chapter Fifteen

Gillian froze, the elegant line of her back as stiff as the fence post in front of her.

Charles cursed himself. He fully realized the danger she posed to his peace of mind. But this close to her, he could see the flush of emotion color the golden glow of her face, could smell the faint scent of jasmine drifting up from her glossy hair. It was madness, but he couldn't seem to step away. In fact, it took a mighty effort of will not to step closer, to press his inconvenient half erection against the pretty swell of her bottom.

What the hell was wrong with him?

You want to kiss her; that's what's wrong.

Kissing Gillian was the worst idea he'd had in a long time. And now that the thought had taken hold, it seemed to be the *only* thing he wanted, as if every moment with her had been leading inexorably to this very point. But giving in to desire would lead to nothing but trouble for both of them, assuming he could even get that close before she slapped him. Or even stabbed him, knowing her.

He'd just worked up the will to step back when she slowly turned. She looked up at him, her extraordinary eyes as wide and startled as a fawn's. Through her slightly parted lips, he could hear the quick exhalation of her breath. That pink mouth and clear golden skin made him think of strawberries and honey. He wanted to taste her as much as he wanted to breathe. If he didn't move away, or if she didn't shove him away as she should, he would probably do just that.

Being Gillian, she did the opposite of what made sense. She seemed to sway a bit, closing the gap between them to a mere whisper of air.

"What an odd name." Her voice held an exotic, enticing hint of sun-kissed, foreign lands. "Why is it called that?"

Charles propped one hand on the fence, caging her in. Her chest rose on a quick breath, brushing against him as lightly as an angel's touch. What a laughable notion. Gillian might be an innocent in all the ways that mattered, but she was hardly an angel.

His thoughts were certainly anything but high-minded and pure. And his body stirred in ways that had a great deal more to do with fire, brimstone, and sweet, dark sin.

Charles forced himself to answer. "Apparently, it's because only one person can pass through at a time. So if a man is taking a young lady out for a walk—"

"As we are right now," she interrupted in a dreamy voice. Her eyes had gone heavy-lidded, and her mouth soft and tempting.

"Exactly," he said hoarsely. "The gentleman passes through first, so he can hold the gate open. But if he has less than honorable intentions, he will hold the gate shut and demand a kiss before he lets her through."

Her mouth curved up into a lush smile, pulling him in. "How devious of him."

Almost unconsciously, he bent down to meet her. Her mouth grew softer, her eyes starting to drift shut.

Yes . . .

Gillian let out a funny squeak and jerked away from him, bumping into the fence. Charles froze, caught between the desire to take what he wanted and an absolute sense of horror. She slid away from him in a hurry, practically stumbling over her own feet. Gillian was never awkward, at least not physically. He'd clearly rattled her.

"Perhaps it's because the arm automatically kisses the fixed part of the gate when it closes," she said, shoving the gate open and passing through into the field. "What nonsense to develop a silly explanation for something that's perfectly sensible."

Bloody hell.

If Gillian hadn't come to her senses, Charles would have kissed her and kept on kissing her until she melted in his arms. The girl had a great deal more self-control than he had, he was sorry to say.

Or perhaps she simply didn't want him to kiss her, which was a more discouraging thought than it should have been.

"You are no doubt correct," he said in a brisk tone, following her through. She practically leapt away from him, as if to underline the point that she would not be extracting a toll for his passage. "There is no need to indulge in sentimental flights of fancy over a cattle gate."

He had to admit that her eagerness to put distance between them was annoying. And that was demented, since he would no sooner marry a girl like Gillian than cut off his arm.

While her unfortunate parentage was a strike against her, it truly didn't bother him. Nor would it be an insurmountable impediment in a wife, although his mother and older sister would surely go into hysterics at the very idea. No, Gillian was unsuitable not due to her scandalous background but due to her scandalous behavior. She was trouble personified, and Charles had had enough trouble of the female persuasion to last him a lifetime. When he finally decided to relinquish his comfortable bachelor's existence, it would be for marriage to a mature woman who would never give him a moment's worry. Such a marriage would be rather like a well-made and dependable traveling coach, carrying them over the rough roads of life with an elegant and quiet sense of security.

His duchess would be the exact opposite of the girl who was standing before him, glowering at him as if he'd just offered her a carte blanche. Marriage to Gillian would be the equivalent of spending one's life dashing about in the highest of perch phaetons—exciting but dangerous, and ultimately more trouble than it was worth.

And still, he wanted to drag her into his arms and kiss her until she couldn't breathe.

"Are you making fun of me?" she demanded.

He frowned, caught by the suspicious tone in her voice and the wary, almost vulnerable expression on her face. It was the second time she'd asked him a question of that nature, which suggested she had a particular fear of mockery. She'd deny it, and claim that she didn't care one whit for what society thought of her. But Charles suspected that she cared more about the opinion of others than she wanted to admit.

And who could blame her? She'd spent a lifetime dealing with rejection and scorn. He knew how painful that could be, thanks to his father, for starters.

"Of course not," he said gently. "Would you like to take my arm? The ground is rather uneven in this field. I would hate to see you fall and twist your ankle."

She rolled her eyes, although she did lose the rigid set to her shoulders. "As if I would be so clumsy. I'm not one of your simpering girls with die-away airs, Your Grace. I'm more than capable of walking across a field without falling on my a—er, without falling."

"Well done," he said. "Hardly anyone would guess what you were going to say."

Her mouth twitched, and then she burst into laughter, her

suspicious demeanor evaporating like morning mist. No one would ever accuse Gillian Dryden of trying to hide what she was feeling. Her emotional honesty, as blunt as it could sometimes be, was refreshing.

"Except for you, of course," she said.

"Naturally. I am your tutor. I see all; I know all."

"Oh, la," she exclaimed, giving him a flourishing and really quite respectable curtsey. "Like a god, come all the way down to earth to take pity on the masses."

"Now you are the one mocking me, Miss Dryden. But I am magnanimous and will forgive this shocking display of disrespect toward your tutor." He set off toward the stile on the other side of the field.

She fell in beside him, her easy strides well able to keep up with his. "Since you are all-knowing and all-seeing, then I think you must be the perfect person to tell me something I've been wondering about."

"Which is?"

Her brief hesitation alerted him. "I want to know what the *ton* is saying about me," she said. "After the unfortunate incident at the ball, as my grandmother calls it. I especially want to hear any nicknames."

"You mean besides the Pugilistic Princess and the Savage Sicilian?" he asked dryly.

"Yes. I know there's more, and I know you're all keeping it from me."

"Isn't that enough?" he hedged.

Gillian didn't answer, lost in thought as she stripped off a glove and brushed the palm of her hand over the tops of the wild lilacs growing in the field. He'd noticed that—the way she reacted to her surroundings, especially outdoors. More than once when they'd gone for walks in the park, Charles had been forced to remind her to put on her gloves or don her bonnet. Nothing seemed to give her more pleasure than the feel of the sun on her face or the breeze blowing her dark locks into a tangle. Most girls would be horrified to see their complexions darkened to a burnished bronze, or to have their carefully constructed coiffures destroyed by the wind.

Not Gillian. She was a veritable Diana, who clearly loved the natural world.

Even the less attractive parts of the animal kingdom didn't bother her. One afternoon on the trip into Lincolnshire, an enormous spider had crawled through a window gap in the coach. Charles had been about to kill it—after his eardrums had been all but shattered by the shrieks of his sister and the contessa—when Gillian had scooped the creature up in her hand and gently deposited him outside the window. She'd then gone back to reading her book, as if nothing untoward had happened. The average country girl would have grimaced and killed the thing as a pest, while most of the fashionable ladies he knew would have reacted with well-bred hysterics.

He found it interesting that Gillian could be so ruthless yet also so gentle with the weak or vulnerable, whether it was her mother, a shy girl at a ball, or even a hapless spider who'd wandered across her path.

"I know you're all trying to protect me," she finally said, glancing up at him. "But it's not necessary."

"I would disagree. But I must admit to feeling some curiosity about why you don't think you need—or deserve—my protection."

"That's hardly the point."

"Then what is?"

"Your Grace, I can fight my own battles," she said in a tone that clearly labeled him as feeble-minded. "I've been doing so for quite a long time. And very successfully."

"With the exception of that bullet hole in your shoulder."

She batted that away with an insouciant wave. "A mere

technicality. You might also remember that I achieved what I set out to do."

He couldn't repress a flare of anger at her reckless disregard for her own safety, and at the inability of her family to take better care of her.

I would have, and I will. "The consequences were quite severe," he said. "Or have you forgotten that?"

Gillian stopped to glare at him. "Of course I haven't forgotten that. I am, as you point out, the one with the blasted hole in my shoulder, and I had to leave the only home I've ever known because of those consequences. Possibly never to return."

"And was it worth it, then? Achieving what you set out to do?"

She turned and stalked off.

Oddly, her refusal to answer seemed like progress to Charles. If she had to think about the question, then clearly she was starting to ponder the sacrifices her actions had forced upon her.

"You do know that you're not alone anymore," he said when he caught up with her. "You never were. The contessa and Lady Marbury have always been in your corner."

"I know that," she said, sounding less snappish. "But there were some fights they couldn't take on. I had to do it for them."

"Your fighting days are over. I will take on any problems from now on." Or, at least he would until she found a suitable husband.

"Well, that's very kind of you. But, as I said, not necessary."

He tried a different tack. "Let's say I suddenly found myself in a foreign country. Sicily, perhaps. And let's say I inadvertently encountered a bandit problem. Would it not make sense to ask for help from a local person well versed in dealing with that particular situation? Someone with intimate knowledge of the problem and someone who could defend me?"

Her mouth twitched. "That would be sensible."

"Then think of me as your guide and defender in *this* foreign country, Miss Dryden, much as you would be my guide if I appeared on your doorstep in Sicily."

She laughed. "I suppose that means the English *ton* is the equivalent of Sicilian brigands, does it not?"

"You must admit they can be rather terrifying."

"Unfortunately, though, I can't shoot them," she said. "How very inconvenient."

He smiled. "As much as I sometimes share that sentiment, I would beg you to refrain. Instead, seek my help the next time you find yourself in trouble."

"All right, but under one condition," she said.

"Which is?"

"That you answer my question. What is being said about me in London?"

Well, she'd probably hear about it eventually, and better she hear it directly from him. But he hated the idea of hurting her more than she already had been.

"Just tell me," she said in a resigned voice. "I assure you I've heard worse."

"That saddens me, but very well." He had to force himself to say it. "You're being referred to as 'the Doxy Duchess.'"

He thought he detected a flinch. But then she frowned. "I don't quite understand."

"Ah, you do know what a doxy is, don't you?"

She cast him an impatient glance. "Of course. I just don't understand the duchess part."

"It's because you're the daughter of a royal duke. Princess, of course, would make more sense, but accuracy is hardly the point, I suppose, when making up insulting names."

She threw him a wry glance. "I now understand why you sent me back to the house with Griffin and Justine that day in Hyde Park. You must have worried how I'd react. You probably thought I would mill poor Mr. Stratton to the ground for being the bearer of such unfortunate news."

She was taking it better than expected. In fact, she was taking it far better than he had when he'd first heard the ugly name. He'd only managed to contain his rage because he and Stratton had been on a path in Hyde Park, in full view of half the *ton*.

Gillian shook her head. "What a trial I'm turning out to be. At this rate, I'll soon have an entire alphabet of nicknames trailing behind me like a dirty cloak."

"Good God, I hope not. The entire point of our rustication is to put an end to that sort of gossip."

"Yes, of course," she said, now sounding rather distracted.

When they reached the stile, a more conventional configuration of rough steps over a stone fence, Charles extended a hand to help her. Deep in thought, Gillian ignored it, instead laying a hand on top of the wall and launching herself over to land lightly on the other side. Sighing, he followed.

A moment later, she came to an abrupt halt in the laneway beside the wall. "Wait. That doesn't make sense."

Hell and damnation. He had been afraid she'd figure it out.

"What doesn't make sense?" he asked, fully prepared to hedge as long as he could.

She peered up at him. "Why would they call me a doxy? It's not as if I've got any suitors to dally with, married or otherwise. You're the only man I spend time with."

He gestured in the direction of the chapel, further down the lane. "Shall we walk?"

She crossed her arms at her waist, calmly regarding him. "What aren't you telling me, Your Grace?"

"You do know that you don't have to address me so formally. Leverton will do perfectly well."

"If you think that's going to distract me, you're sadly

mistaken. You might as well tell me, since I'll find out sooner or later."

Gillian would have made an excellent spy for Wellington. Still, Charles tried to think of a way around it.

"It's all right," she said in a kind voice. "I won't be angry, I promise."

He took her arm and steered her down the lane. "All right, but let's keep walking, shall we? For some reason it's easier that way."

"Ah, you're embarrassed, so it must be unpleasant. Well, you needn't spare my feelings. I can take it."

She'd had to *take* too much in her life, and that infuriated him. It made him all the more determined to protect her going forward.

"People are making assumptions about your character," he said, "based more on your mother's history, I suspect, than on anything you've done. Your unconventional behavior does complicate the situation, I'm afraid. Those who wish to believe the worst see it as confirmation of what they believe."

"That's as clear as mud," she said dryly.

He was still trying to think of a way to soften the blow, when her eyes lit up with understanding. "I see. People think I'm engaged in an affair. How vulgar and predictable of them." She shook her head with disgust. "And how unfair to Mamma. She made one unfortunate slip when she was very young, and no one will allow her to forget it despite years of fidelity to my stepfather."

"You are rather a vivid reminder, although I would never refer to you as an unfortunate slip."

She flashed him a grin. "How kind of you. And who is my apparent amour, if I may ask?"

No point in putting it off any longer. "Me."

She slid to a halt, her feet kicking up a little puff of dust.

"That's . . . that's ridiculous. Why would anyone make so insane an assumption?"

"It's not very flattering to either of us, I'll grant you that." Charles had to repress the instinct to argue with her. Aside from the fact that he would never take an innocent young woman as his mistress, there were a thousand reasons why he and Gillian would never suit—starting with the fact that they would likely kill each other within a month. Although he had to admit that a month with her in his bed would almost be worth it.

She emphatically shook her head, her cheeks flushing a bright red. "It's the most absurd notion I've ever heard. No one would ever believe that someone like you would wish to . . . you know"—she windmilled her arm—"with someone like me."

He got her walking again. "As I said, I think your mother's history is at the heart of the matter, along with the fact that you and I spend a great deal of time together. If one were inclined to make such a scurrilous assumption, then I am the easiest target."

"The whole thing is ridiculous," she huffed.

He'd never seen her so disconcerted. "I'm sorry, my dear. I would have preferred to spare you this knowledge."

She waved an impatient hand. "I'd like to kill whoever started that rumor, for my mother's sake. And yours. How beastly of anyone to think you would do such a thing. They clearly know nothing about you."

He'd been infuriated about that too. His friends would never believe him capable of such shabby behavior, but he'd been surprised by how many members of the *ton* apparently did. He supposed that was as much a comment on his arrogance as it was a reflection on them.

"I share your sentiment," he said. "Not the murderous intent, though. I hope you won't feel the need to commit mayhem in order to defend our reputations."

"I'd have to kill half the aristocrats in England before it would make a difference, I suspect. But I do want to know who started the rumor. Was it Mr. Stratton?"

"No, surprisingly. He feels genuinely sorry about it, and is remorseful about his own inadvertent part in the affair."

"Then who did?"

"It doesn't really matter, does it?"

"Of course it matters," she snapped. "As does the fact that you're so reluctant to tell me. It leads me to conclude only one thing."

"Which is?"

"That the troublemaker is Lady Letitia."

Charles had to swallow a curse. The confounded girl was too smart by half.

"Ah, ha!" she exclaimed. "I thought so."

He grimaced. "It's most unfair, and I wish I could have sheltered you from such ugliness."

"I cannot say I'm completely surprised. Grandmamma warned me that something like this might surface sooner or later. I suppose that's why she's always harping on about my behavior."

"Indeed. The more circumspect your behavior, the less likely you are to be a target. And even if rumors do circulate, people with good sense will ignore them—if, that is, you can manage not to give them additional fodder."

She shook her head. "I could go around dressed in a nun's habit, spending all my time giving alms to the poor, and I suspect many would still believe the worst. In the eyes of the polite world, I'm a child born of sin. That's what I'm supposed to be. That's what I'm supposed to *do*. It's easier for people to be comfortable with their assumptions than it is for them to see the truth."

Her clear-eyed pragmatism in the face of so much ill will made him want to throttle every last person who'd ever injured her.

"You never told me you held a degree in philosophy," Charles said, trying to lighten the mood.

"I'm a practical philosopher, sir. I gain knowledge through observation," she said, giving him a quick smile. "Which is why I'm puzzled by something."

"And that is?"

"Why does Lady Letitia hate me enough to start such base rumors? I barely know the woman."

"It's not you she hates," he said in a grim tone. "It's me."

Chapter Sixteen

Gillian's narrow, straight brows pulled together in a skeptical frown. "It seemed the opposite was true. In fact, I can't understand why she didn't marry you all those years ago instead of Mr. Stratton. She clearly prefers you."

"Not the case," Charles said.

"At the Barrington ball, Lady Letitia attached herself to you like a leech."

He could feel heat creep up his neck. "That is a remarkably inelegant way to put it. And inaccurate, I might add."

She shot him an incredulous look. "If you say so. But there is clearly some degree of intimacy between you."

"There is no intimacy between us, I assure you," he said in a stern tone.

"It's such a mystery why people think her so wonderful. If you ask me, she's positively horrid. Why is she being so beastly to you?"

"Because I refused to agree with something she wished me to do."

Gillian seemed to puzzle over his vague statement for several seconds before clarity dawned. "Oh! The flirtatious Lady Letitia wanted to have an affair with you."

"Ah . . ."

"But if you said no—"

"Of course I said no." What a wildly inappropriate discussion to have with an innocent maiden, even if that maiden was Gillian.

"Of course you did," she said in a soothing tone, as if he were a fractious child. "But if that's the case, then why did she go after me? It's laughable to think that I pose any kind of threat to her."

It wasn't laughable, though. Letitia knew him better than he liked to admit, and she'd clearly picked up on the fact that he had feelings for Gillian—feelings he must keep to himself.

"Revenge is the simplest answer," Charles said. "Letitia is angry with me, so she did the most effective thing she could think of, which was to attack someone under my protection."

"What a hypocrite," Gillian said. "You turned her down, so she accused me of the behavior she wished to engage in herself. But she's the one who broke off your engagement years ago and married someone else. Why is she still trying to hurt you?"

"It doesn't matter."

"Of course it matters. She's trying to smear both our reputations." Gillian poked him on the bicep. "You owe me an explanation, Leverton. After all, I'm the one labeled as the Doxy Duchess. Perfect Penley can't even begin to compare."

He sighed. "You're not going to let this drop, are you?"

"I'll pester you until you run shrieking through the fields to get away from me," she said. "And just think of the gossip that will cause."

"You really are the most annoying girl."

"I know I'm a trial. But at least I'm not falling into hysterics over the whole thing, so you've got to give me credit for that."

He let out a reluctant laugh. "Very well. Do you know how I got my ridiculous nickname?"

She let her gaze trail over him. "It seems quite obvious."

He couldn't fail to hear the admiring note to her voice or see the warmth in her eyes. The girl was a menace to his sanity, and she probably didn't even know it. "Perfect Penley was the name bestowed upon me by Lady Letitia after I refused to marry her."

Gillian jerked to a halt again and gaped up at him. "*You* broke it off? I thought a man never broke off a betrothal, at least not honorably. And you would *never* act dishonorably."

"I appreciate the vote of confidence," he said, giving her a slight bow.

"It's the truth. Anyone who knows you would agree."

Her simple, heartfelt assertion meant more to him than the most fulsome compliments. Charles was beginning to discover that Gillian Dryden's plainly stated admiration held a powerful allure, one much too disturbing to his peace of mind. "I'm honored by your trust and confidence, Miss Dryden."

"Now that we've engaged in an exchange of compliments, perhaps we can return to the subject at hand—why you broke it off. What went wrong?"

"It was wrong from the beginning. Letitia never truly wanted to marry me. She wanted to be a duchess and a leader of the *ton*, and she saw me as a means to that end."

Gillian pursed her lips and let out a long, low whistle. "And you fell for that old gambit? You don't seem the type."

"Thank you for that," he said sarcastically. "But you might be a tad more charitable if you knew that I was barely twenty years old. Letitia was two years older and already an experienced young woman." Very experienced, as he was to find out. "And may I point out that young ladies do not whistle."

"Duly noted, sir. So, Lady Letitia got her hooks into

you, which is unfortunate. But why would that even matter? Aristocrats often marry for reasons of status and fortune. Love doesn't seem to enter into it, more often than not. After all, you're all trying to marry me off, regardless of whether I'm in love with the poor fellow."

"No one would force you to marry anyone you didn't care for." Charles wouldn't stand for it. In fact, he was beginning to think that he wouldn't stand for her marrying anyone.

Get a grip, old man.

She grimaced in sympathy. "Ah, you were in love with her. Sorry. Did she tell you she loved you back?"

"May I just say that this is one of the most embarrassing conversations I've ever had?" he said.

"You may, but I'd still like you to answer the question."

Charles gazed up at the sky as he wrestled his exasperation under control. "Fine. Yes, she did say she loved me. I was fool enough to believe it, even though I was warned."

"Who warned you?"

"My father." The old fellow had considered Letitia grasping and vulgar. He had been correct, of course, but Charles had been too besotted to see it. He and his father had fought mightily over her, with severe consequences for both of them. "Unfortunately, I didn't listen to him."

"Young people rarely listen to their parents, especially when they think they're in love."

He raised his eyebrows. "And you know this how?"

Gillian ducked her head. "Just through general observation."

That was obviously a lie, but he let it pass—even though it just about killed him to do so.

"When did you find out that Lady Letitia didn't love you?" she asked.

He chewed over the gristly memory in silence for a few moments. "When I discovered her in a compromising position with my best friend."

"Hell and damnation," she murmured.

For once, he didn't feel inclined to correct her.

"Mr. Stratton?" she guessed.

He nodded. "Letitia had strong feelings for him."

"I should certainly hope so, since she shagged him."

Charles shot her a frown. "Must I really point out that, although perfectly accurate, your language is inappropriate to a lady of your standing?"

"I apologize. But I'd like to murder them for hurting you like that," she said with a quite adorable growl. "What cads, the pair of them. I only wish I'd punched Stratton instead of Lord Andover."

He couldn't hold back a rueful smile. "Your support overwhelms me. In any event, I made it clear to Lady Letitia that I would not marry her, since her affections lay elsewhere."

"I'll wager she wasn't happy about that," Gillian said.

"She was not."

"How did you get her to agree to break it off? She could have simply refused, and you would have had to ruin her in order to salvage your own reputation." She flicked her hand, as if waving away a noxious insect. "But of course you would never do that, which she must have known."

He found Gillian's unquestioning faith in him humbling. "The details are unimportant. Suffice it to say that the three of us reached an agreement. In order to preserve her reputation, we agreed that she would be the one to formally break the betrothal, citing that she had changed her mind and wished to marry Stratton."

"That was awfully decent of you," Gillian said earnestly, hugging his arm. "After all, it didn't cast you in a very good light."

"It's easier for men to recover from that sort of hit."

She sighed. "Don't I know it. But what does all this have to do with your nickname?"

"That was Letitia's revenge. She told her friends that I

was so perfectly correct and boring that she would have gone mad if she'd married me. She took to calling me Perfect Penley, the man who was going to drive her perfectly insane."

"What a shrew. But you seem to have turned that around. If anything, it now seems to be a compliment."

"In the aftermath, I tried to conduct myself as a gentleman, hoping the poison from the insult would soon drain away. It turned out I was right."

"Hmm, I don't think that'll work with the Doxy Duchess." She didn't sound particularly bothered by the notion.

"You're missing the point. No sensible person responds to deliberate and juvenile attempts to provoke." He raised an eyebrow at her. "A lesson you might try learning."

She scrunched her nose up. "The name suits you. You *are* perfect."

"I wish that were the case."

"Really? I can't imagine why anyone would want to be perfect. It would be too much work."

"I feel relatively confident you needn't worry about that."

Gillian choked out a laugh. "That was a truly splendid insult, Leverton. Well done."

"I try not to make a habit of it, but you seem to bring out the worst in me."

She stopped and gave him an extravagant bow, right in the middle of the dusty country lane. It was absurd and utterly charming. "Then my work here is done."

"You are a ridiculous child," he said, smiling at her. "Come, the chapel is just ahead." He nodded toward a quaint seventeenth-century building a few hundred yards down the lane.

"It looks very pretty," she said politely. "I'm sure I'll enjoy it very much."

"I doubt it, but I will appreciate the effort."

Gillian cast him a sideways glance. "May I ask you another question?"

"That depends on the topic."

"It's about the smugglers. Is there anything afoot to recover our jewels?"

Gillian was dogged, if nothing else. "I rode into Skegness yesterday to discuss with the excise officer what could be done. Unfortunately, there's more than one gang operating in the area, which makes it difficult to identify who attacked us. Although the officer promised to do his best, I think you must resign yourself to the loss."

"But the smugglers must be local. Could we not launch an investigation ourselves? Speak to people in the village and in the closest town? Surely they will know something."

"If they do, they're not going to talk to me about it." A few minutes in the village pub the other day had put the boots to that idea. Everyone had clammed up as soon as he'd walked through the door.

"But—"

"Scunthorpe and I also discussed the issue at some length. He's been managing Fenfield for more than five years and knows the area extremely well. According to him, runs across Penley lands are rare. It was pure bad luck that we happened to stumble across one the other night, and it's unlikely the free traders will make the same mistake again. I suspect it's the end of the matter."

She stalked along beside him, her head tipped down, her face mostly hidden by the brim of her bonnet. Charles had no doubt she was scowling up a storm.

"I understand," she said, "but I simply can't accept that our jewels are forever lost."

He reached down and took her hand. She jerked a bit, but then her fingers closed around his.

"Gillian, I deeply regret that you lost something precious to you," he said quietly. "And I wish I had better news. But I won't lie to you. The jewels are likely already in Lincoln, or even in London, where they will be broken up and pawned. I'm sorry."

She clutched his hand like a child, staring up at him. Her amber-colored eyes glittered with anger, but also a sadness that tugged at his heart.

"They took something that can't be replaced, and they must answer for that," she said in a tight voice. "I must do something about it."

"Not you," he said. "Me. I will do my very best to run those men to ground, but you must promise that you will not do something foolish."

She opened her mouth to object, but he headed her off. "No, Gillian. I will take care of this. You have my word."

Defiance flickered in her gaze, but then she arranged her winsome features into a polite smile. "Of course, sir. Whatever you say. Now, shall we go look at that chapel?"

Her sudden acquiescence was as artificial as the silk flowers on her bonnet. Clearly, she would bear close watching over the next few weeks.

It occurred to him, and with more than a little dismay, that there were worse ways to spend his time than keeping an eye on Gillian Dryden.

"Well done, Miss Dryden," enthused Mr. Hurdly, peering down the range at the target. "It's the first bull's-eye of the afternoon!"

Gillian lowered her bow, critically inspecting her shot. "Thank you, but I just barely nicked the edge."

"Dear me," said Miss Farrow. "You shoot as well as the men, which is certainly unusual. I cannot imagine how you do it, especially with such a big bow." Her tone was not one of admiration.

"It's truly not that difficult," Gillian said. "Would you like me to show you?" When she gave Miss Farrow a toothy smile, the young woman responded with a haughty lift of the brow. Well, at least Miss Farrow wasn't avoiding her.

The other girls attending Leverton's impromptu garden party had all given Gillian a wide berth. Not that they'd been rude. After all, no sensible—or marriage-minded—young lady would wish to offend the extremely eligible Duke of Leverton. If they hadn't figured out that Gillian was under the duke's protection, their parents certainly had, and had no doubt instructed their daughters to act with an appropriate degree of courtesy.

But make friendly overtures? Perish the thought. A sideslip of a royal duke, even one sponsored by Leverton, was hardly the sort of female the local gentry wished their daughters to befriend.

The bachelors attending the party, however, were another story. They clearly thought Gillian bang up to the mark, as one pimply but nice young man said to her. She'd already bested them at archery and rolled them all up at shuttlecock. Clearly, her athletic prowess made her worthy of enthusiastic acceptance among their ranks, and she half expected them to invite her along to a local cockfight, or to the prizefight they'd been discussing with such relish.

What the gentlemen weren't doing, however, was flirting with her like they were with the other girls. She didn't mind, but it did rather defeat the purpose of the occasion, which was to introduce her to the young people of the neighborhood and help her polish her social skills.

"No thank you, Miss Dryden," Miss Farrow said with an equally insincere smile. "Besides, I'm sure David would be happy to help me practice my archery skills, wouldn't you?" She batted her eyelashes at Mr. Hurdly, who grimaced.

"Dash it, Margaret," he exclaimed. "I've tried to show you a thousand times, but you always get bored after five minutes. What's a fellow to do?"

"Not be rude to one of your oldest friends, for one thing,"

the young woman said with a pretty pout. "And for another, you could take me to the refreshment table for a beverage. I'm roasting out here in this sun. I'm sure I'm going to turn as brown as a nut before the day is through."

That last comment was clearly aimed at Gillian, whose complexion had been darkened by years under hot Sicilian skies. And it was anything but roasting, although at least the day was, for once, sunny and almost pleasantly warm. Perhaps for the average English girl that counted as roasting.

Miss Farrow clearly wanted to get Mr. Hurdly away from her. The young lady had marked out her territory some time ago, Gillian suspected, and saw her as competition. It was laughable how many women seemed to view her that way, including the seductive Lady Letitia, who believed that Gillian had somehow destroyed her chances with Leverton.

As if a man like him would ever be remotely interested in Gillian.

Unbidden, the memory of the duke looming over her at the kissing gate, his gaze heavy-lidded and warm, made her neck go prickly. He'd looked awfully interested at that particular moment, which she'd found both terribly exciting and alarming. But it was a momentary lapse, as his subsequent behavior had demonstrated. He'd not shown one iota of amorous interest in the four days since their walk to the chapel. Instead, he'd once more adopted a professorial tone, lecturing her on proper language and decorum, and generally boring her out of her skull with his ever-growing list of social admonitions. If the man hadn't been so bloody lovely to look at, Gillian would have shot herself days ago to put herself out of her misery.

"Truly, David," Miss Farrow added in a plaintive voice, "I'm parched."

"If you insist," Mr. Hurdly said with a dramatic sigh. "Would you like to walk back with us, Miss Dryden? You too must be feeling the heat after all that activity."

Gillian almost laughed when the other girl rolled her eyes. "Thank you, but I'd like to retrieve my arrows first."

"The boy will do that. There's no need for you to get your gloves dirty," Mr. Hurdly said.

"What boy?" she asked.

Miss Farrow nodded in the direction of the target at the other end of the lawn. "Over there. The one staring at you."

Young Teddy was standing just off to the side of the target, looking straight at her. He practically vibrated with excitement, as if he had something to tell her that simply couldn't wait.

"That's Teddy," she said. "He works in the stables."

Mr. Hurdly frowned. "He looks like he has ants in his pants, hopping about like that."

"He's just fidgety, that's all." Gillian smiled at Miss Farrow. "Why don't you two go on without me? I'll catch up."

"There's no need for you to rush," Miss Farrow said as she took Mr. Hurdly's arm. She started to drag him off toward the refreshment table.

Her companion protested the cavalier treatment, but a moment later they were chatting and laughing like the best of friends as they strolled toward the terrace at the back of the manor house, where most of the guests had gathered. Miss Farrow glanced over her shoulder at Gillian and flashed her a quick grin, followed by a roguish wink.

This time Gillian did laugh. Perhaps she and Miss Farrow might become friends after all—as long as Gillian steered clear of Mr. Hurdly. That would be no trouble, since the only man she had any interest in was a certain charming, if sometimes arrogant, duke.

She headed across the lawn to the target where Teddy waited, his skinny body wriggling with excitement.

"Miss, I've been waiting ever so long to get you," he hissed in a dramatic whisper. "But I couldn't sneak away from the stables until this very moment."

"Easy now, Teddy," she said in a quiet voice. "We mustn't let anyone know what we're talking about. We don't want to raise suspicion."

He hugged his arms around his narrow belly, making a visible effort to contain himself. "Yes, miss. I'll try."

"Now, why don't you fetch my arrows? That will give us an excuse to talk."

He scampered over to the target and began pulling the arrows.

Once Gillian and Teddy had struck up their friendship, she'd asked him to keep his ear to the ground for rumors about the local smuggling rings. She'd even offered to compensate him and had been surprised when he'd turned her down flat. Later, she'd learned that his father had been killed by free traders, severely beaten when he'd refused to allow one of the more notorious gangs to use his barn as a hiding place for gin and tobacco brought in from Holland. He'd died of his injuries a few weeks later.

Teddy was as eager to see the smugglers—any smuggler—brought to justice as she was.

"You've heard news?" she asked as she moved to stand beside him.

"Yes, miss, at the Fox and Firkin. I help Mr. Dodd, the publican, when Ma and me need the extra blunt. I hear all sorts of things there. Some men last night was talking about a run."

"No one saw you eavesdropping, did they?" she asked. "I won't have you putting yourself in danger, Teddy. Do you understand?"

He grinned, exposing the gap where one of his front teeth should have been. "Nah. No one pays me any notice, miss. I'm so little, they forgets I'm even there."

Teddy *was* little, too little for a boy his age. Gillian was determined to help both him and his mother, who struggled to support her son and her three-year-old daughter.

"All right, but be careful," Gillian warned. "For your mother's sake, if not your own."

He nodded, handing her the arrows. "Yes, miss."

She glanced over her shoulder toward the house. Most of the guests were availing themselves of a generous nuncheon that had been set up just inside the French doors of the drawing room. But she got a nasty jolt when she spied Leverton watching her. He stood on the terrace steps, ostensibly chatting with a young lady who was fawning all over him. It was clear, however, that his attention was on Gillian, not his officious admirer.

She returned her attention to Teddy, taking the arrows from him. "Quickly now, tell me what you learned."

He filled her in. Gillian thought for a moment and then nodded. "Can you meet me behind the stables at midnight?"

"I can," he said.

"Excellent, and if you can—"

When Teddy's eyes went wide with surprise, Gillian froze for a second before giving the lad a friendly nod. "Thank you, my boy. I would have wrecked my gloves if I'd not had you to help me."

"Well, what do we have here?" drawled that familiar deep voice from behind her. "If I didn't know better, Miss Dryden, I might even think you were up to something."

Repressing a curse, Gillian forced a smile and turned to meet Leverton's suspicious gaze.

Chapter Seventeen

The long-case clock outside his library had sounded on the half hour a few minutes ago, and everyone but Charles was long in bed. The contessa had been the first to go up, shortly after their late supper. Elizabeth was made of sterner stuff, scoffing at the notion that a garden party could wear her out. But she had also retreated a few minutes later, hiding a yawn behind her hand. Gillian had gone up with her, making a great show of fatigue and claiming that she could barely find the will to drag herself up to bed.

That, as Charles knew, was absolute bollocks. The girl had more energy than a platoon of soldiers on leave. The little minx was up to something. He'd known it the minute he cornered her by the archery targets this afternoon.

He'd seen it even from the terrace, where he'd been trapped in conversation with Emily Meadows, who'd done her best to engage him in a genteel flirtation. Emily was wellborn, well mannered, and in possession of a considerable dowry. She was beautiful too, a luscious blonde with big blue eyes. In short, just the sort of woman he should wish to spend time with. If he were in the mood for courtship, Emily would be at the top of the list.

But his focus had been entirely on Gillian, and he'd instantly known that something was wrong. If the tense set to her slim body hadn't tipped him off, then the wary glance she'd thrown his way certainly had. Even from a distance, he'd come to recognize that look. It had raised the hairs on the back of his neck and sent him stalking from the terrace, leaving poor Miss Meadows gaping in dismay at his abrupt departure.

After only a month in Gillian Dryden's company, he'd adopted the manners of an oaf. Instead of his good habits rubbing off on Gillian, her bad habits were rubbing off on him.

Naturally, the blasted girl had tried to throw him off the scent. She'd rounded her pretty eyes in a ridiculous display of innocence, claiming that Teddy was helping her with her arrows. She'd ruffled the lad's hair and turned to Charles with a smile so enticing and unconsciously seductive that he'd almost forgotten his own name.

Gillian had clearly taken on her own search for the smugglers, and apparently had enlisted his stable boy to assist her. Not that Charles truly expected anything to come of it. According to Scunthorpe, most of the free trading happened further up the coast. Smugglers had known for years to steer clear of Leverton lands, since neither Charles nor his father had ever tolerated their nefarious activities. There were some who tended to sentimentalize smugglers and their ilk, turning a blind eye to their violent ways, but Charles wasn't one of them.

When the clock in the hall bonged out the three quarter hour, he waited for the echo to fade. He listened, but heard nothing but the quiet crackle of the dying fire in the grate and the soughing breeze moving through the trees outside the library windows. Everyone in the house was obviously asleep, and it was time he went up, too.

But as he set his half-finished brandy down on the desk, he heard the quiet creak of a protesting floorboard, then something that sounded suspiciously like a closing door.

He got up and hurried out to the back hall. At the end of the corridor, a large sash window overlooked the courtyard and the stables. He cursed when he saw a slender figure, garbed in a black greatcoat and barely visible under a pale, weak moon. The person ghosted around the side of the stables and disappeared.

Christ. Even though she was dressed in a man's coat and wearing breeches and boots, Charles knew exactly who was skulking about his stables. It sent a surge of anger flooding through his veins.

He took the back steps down to the kitchen three at a time and reached the courtyard seconds later. He cut behind the stables, but saw no one. Unfortunately, he thought he heard the cantering of hooves down the lane, although the wind was strong enough in the trees that he couldn't be sure.

In the worst-case scenario, Gillian was heading toward the coast, less than three miles away. But smugglers could land anywhere along the flat stretches of sand from Ingold-mells to Maplethorpe. He couldn't just saddle a horse and set out to look for her, not with all the paths that snaked through the countryside and the marshes. Even having spent much of his childhood here, Charles didn't know a tenth of the routes she might be taking—any one of which could land her directly in the path of men who would think nothing of slitting her throat.

He bolted around the side of the building and up the stairs to the head groom's apartment. He rapped loudly, not caring at this point if he woke up the entire bloody household.

Less than a minute later, Reid yanked open the door. Clothed only in his nightshirt, his sleeping cap askew on his head, the head groom stared at Charles in sleepy bemusement. Then his eyes popped wide. "Your Grace, what's wrong? Is it fire downstairs?"

To any groom, a stable fire was the worst of all possible catastrophes.

"No, nothing like that. But I need to know if one of the horses is missing."

Reid frowned. "Couldn't be. I've got Teddy on watch tonight. He'd come tell me if something was wrong."

Charles let out a low curse. "Where are the other two grooms?"

"Sleeping, I expect. I have Teddy come one night a week to spell the other lads, mostly because the boy and his mother need the extra blunt." Reid's normally placid features pulled tight with consternation. "I hope that doesn't offend you, sir. Seemed the right thing to do."

"Put on some clothes and meet me downstairs. Be prepared to ride."

A few minutes later, Reid joined him in the center row of the modern brick stables that his father had built just a year before his death. Most of the stalls were empty, since Charles hadn't spent much time at Fenfield in the last several years. Reid immediately saw that one of the mares was missing, as was Teddy. Charles could only hope that the lad would be wrong about where local smugglers were likely to come ashore, or what route they would take this night.

Charles had to find Gillian before she got into trouble. And once he had found her, she would be in a different sort of trouble—from him.

"At least the little fool had the brains to put out the lantern," Reid said, shaking his head in disgust. "I'm sorry, sir. I don't know what he's about. Teddy's never done anything like this before."

"I know exactly what he's about," Charles replied grimly. "I need you to tell me if you've heard anything about smuggling gangs on estate lands."

When caution flickered across Reid's face, Charles's heart sank. He didn't know the man well, since Reid had only come to work at the estate a few years ago. Even though he wasn't a local man, he'd been highly recommended by Charles's stable master in London.

"I don't care *how* you know," Charles snapped. "I just want the information."

Reid grimaced. "Sorry, sir. I do my best to steer clear of that sort of thing. It doesn't pay to get mixed up in it. Not in these parts."

"Are you saying there is a smuggling problem on my lands?"

The groom gave an emphatic shake of the head. "Most wouldn't dare. But I've heard tales that some cut close to Leverton lands when the customs officers clamp down on the regular routes. And they have been clamping down of late, from what I hear down in the village."

"Where would they be likely to land if they wished to do a run across the estate?"

Reid frowned, clearly pondering. It taxed Charles's patience, since Gillian and Teddy could be anywhere by now. And in serious trouble.

"Aye," the groom finally said. "I think they would come ashore near the most direct route across your lands up to Lincoln."

Charles strode toward the tack room with Reid in his wake. "I need you to take me there."

"Yes, sir. But I still can't believe young Teddy is mixed up in such doings. If the lad took one of the horses, somebody put him up to it."

Charles grabbed his saddle off one of the blocks. "I know exactly who that somebody is."

"There, miss," whispered Teddy. He pointed across the tidal flats, perhaps two hundred feet from where they crouched behind a small sand dune. "They're pulling the boat in there."

Gillian cautiously raised her head to follow his pointing finger. The moon was close to setting, and she had to strain to see. Fortunately, it meant the smugglers would likely miss them. Still, this stretch of the coast was mostly flat, with nothing but the occasional small dune or clump of marsh grass. Gillian and Teddy had been forced to leave the horse several hundred yards behind them, while they practically crawled to reach a position where they could see in all directions over the flats and out to sea.

She was already regretting their little escapade—not on her own behalf, but because of Teddy. He was quick as anything, but still only a little boy. Back home, Gillian had always had Stefano to watch her back—a seasoned, lethally tough man who knew every inch of the Sicilian countryside. Here, she had only Teddy. And here, while she was fairly adept at navigation, everything was unfamiliar—the sky, the land, even the scent of the ocean. Never in her life had she felt less confident about her ability to handle a situation.

More important, her worries for Teddy had her second-guessing herself, and that was exactly the wrong response when dealing with dangerous men.

"Are you sure?" she whispered. "I don't see anything."

"I can hear 'em."

The boy vibrated with excitement, and that worried her, too. Hunting human prey required calm, cool thinking. Stefano had cuffed her on the back of her head whenever she let her emotions run away with her. It had been harsh medicine, but effective. It hadn't taken long before Gillian had learned to control herself, throttling back anything that might get in the way—nerves, fear, or even elation that her target was within her grasp.

She was feeling anything but in control tonight, a signal that it was time to retreat. She needed time to think and plan, rather than rush off half-cocked. Gillian could only be thankful that Stefano wasn't here to see how she'd bungled the situation.

And Leverton's likely reaction if he ever found out was simply too gruesome to contemplate.

She was just about to pull Teddy away when she saw a

light up the beach. It wavered and feebly danced, as if someone was jogging a small lantern. In the darkest period before the first reaches of dawn, it was impossible to miss.

"There they are," she murmured.

Teddy shook his head. "That's what they want you to think. They ties a lantern to a pony and sends it walking down the beach in the opposite direction. Fools the bleedin' excise officers almost every time."

Gillian didn't miss the contempt in his voice. Clearly, the excise officers would be more effective if they had small boys from local villages to lend them a hand.

"That's a handy trick," she whispered back. "I'll have to remember that one."

Teddy again pointed across the flats, and this time she saw three men dragging a small boat out of the shallows. "Who's meeting—" she started.

Teddy's warning hiss cut her off. To their left, less than a hundred feet away, a group of men emerged from one of the paths coming from the marshes. They were leading several ponies. Gillian flattened herself into the cool sand, holding her breath. Teddy did the same, although he started to rise up a minute later. She reached over and pushed him down flat, keeping a firm hand planted in the center of his back.

Finally, when the faint jingle of the ponies' bridles told her that the men were well past them and down the beach toward the boat, Gillian relaxed. "I told you not to take any risks," she whispered. "You're not to do that again."

Teddy shot her a cheeky grin before stretching up to watch the smugglers. "I knows what I'm doing."

Gillian muttered her disapproval as she inched forward over the small dune for a better view. The smugglers were clustered around the small boat, working swiftly to transfer the cargo to the backs of the ponies.

"Looks like tobacco," Teddy whispered. "Easier to carry,

since you don't need the carts, depending on the size of the load."

In just a few minutes, the smugglers would finish and head back inland. That meant Gillian had a decision to make. Should she follow them, hoping they would lead her to one of their hiding places? According to Teddy, the gangs often hid their contraband for days or even weeks at a time in abandoned barns or sheds, waiting for the right time to move their cargo up to Lincoln. Sometimes, they used farmhouses to store the goods, finding sympathetic farmers or ones they could bully into compliance.

"And you're sure about this?" she asked. "These are the ones who held up the duke's carriage?" There was no point in trying to track them if they weren't.

Teddy gave a vigorous nod. "Aye, miss. No one else has dared come here since the King's men shut down the old Critchfield gang three years ago. These right bastards are new. Only here the last six months or so, according to old Dodd."

Dodd owned the village tavern where Teddy helped out. As far as Gillian could ascertain, the publican was not involved in any smuggling. But some of his customers were, and they'd made it clear to the old fellow that he'd best mind his own business and keep his mouth shut. Dodd had passed that advice on to Teddy as well.

Once again, guilt tugged at her. Now that they were facing real danger, Gillian realized she had no business involving Teddy in her problems. After tonight, she would never do it again.

"Don't swear," she whispered absently.

The boy's quiet snort told her what he thought of that.

Now that the smugglers had their ponies loaded and ready, should she send Teddy back to Fenfield and follow them alone? Even if she could track them, would she be able to find her way back to the manor house? Without the boy, she would likely be stumbling about, as good as blind. Still, it was a golden opportunity, and a chance she had to take.

"Teddy, I want you to take the horse and go back to Fenfield," she murmured. It was only three miles or so to the house, so he should be back well before any of the servants were up. Whether *she* would be was another matter, but she couldn't worry about that now.

"I ain't leaving you," Teddy hissed. "You'd never find your way back."

They spent the next minute or so in heated albeit whispered argumentation, while Gillian kept a wary eye on the smugglers. Perhaps their debate explained why she didn't hear the man creeping up behind her until it was too late. Biting back a curse, she rolled over, pulling her pistol from the back of her breeches. Before she could bring the weapon up, a hard masculine body came down on top of her, crushing her into the sand. A big hand curled around her wrist in a brutal clasp.

"Stop struggling," whispered the Duke of Leverton. "And don't say a word."

Chapter Eighteen

Gillian blinked up into Leverton's face. He wore an odd, soft hat that threw heavy shadows over his features. Still, she could see his eyes blazing with anger. If she were prone to flights of fancy, she could imagine they were fiery beacons lighting up the beach.

Since she was not prone to such fancies, she directed an irate scowl right back at him, furious that she'd allowed him to sneak up on her. She wriggled, trying to ease the pressure of his weight on her ribs and stomach.

He bit back a curse. "Stay still, blast you, or you might get more than you bargained for."

She had no intention of obeying his orders, not with the smugglers still nearby. With every passing second, her chances of following them slipped away. She started squirming once more to make it clear that she wanted him off. Then she froze when she detected something quite unexpected pressing into her belly.

Leverton was decidedly aroused. Since her open greatcoat had belled out around her, she had only her breeches to act as a barrier between his body and hers. And from what she could feel, his breeches weren't up to the job of preserving her modesty either.

"Good God," she breathed.

He leaned down, as if to whisper in her ear. Instead, he seemed to draw in her scent, and his chest expanded against hers. Gillian's body sparked to life with the most bloody inconvenient timing.

"Now you understand," he murmured in her ear. His bristled cheek brushed her face, sending shivers rippling through her body.

"Get off me," she choked out.

"Be still," he murmured. "They're coming up from the beach."

Gillian brought her free hand up to push him off, but froze when she again heard the jingle of pony bridles and the murmur of voices. She held herself motionless, even though every instinct urged her to get out from under Leverton.

Well, that was a lie. Right now her instincts were urging her to wriggle closer to him and his lovely erection. How appalling.

Leverton pressed down on her harder as the smugglers went by, apparently only a few dozen yards away. Gillian had to bite her lip against a whimper—not because he was hurting her, but because it felt so good. Clearly, she was losing what little sanity she had left.

She turned her head, looking for Teddy. The boy hadn't uttered a word since the duke had appeared. He lay still and flat on the sand, a few feet away. Teddy had excellent nerves, but his eyes had gone wide as he stared at them. Clearly, he was as shocked by his employer's appearance as she was, albeit for different reasons.

Thank God it was too dark for the lad to notice the silent, physical drama that was playing out between her body and Leverton's.

The three of them stayed immobile for what seemed an eternity. As the seconds ticked by, Gillian's discomfort grew. Now Leverton didn't feel quite so nice. Rather, his body's hard, muscular planes jabbed into her most sensitive parts, and she was certain a piece of driftwood was digging into the small of her back. Even worse, her nose was starting to itch. Any amorous feelings she had been experiencing were rapidly fading under the discomfort of being trapped between a body that felt like granite and cold, lumpy sand.

Leverton didn't seem to share her discomfort, since his arousal apparently hadn't decreased at all. She had some knowledge of the male physique, from personal experience and observation of ancient statuary. If Leverton was not an anomaly, she was going to have to revise her understanding of the general dimensions of the male appendage.

Finally, he pushed up a bit, which nudged his erection against a certain delicate spot. Gillian couldn't hold back a tiny squeak.

"Sorry," he whispered with a grimace. Then he craned over the dune and breathed a relieved sigh. "I think we're in the clear."

"Then get off me at once," Gillian ordered in a low voice.

"Right." He sounded rather sheepish, as he should. But when he quickly rolled off her, Gillian had to stifle an instinctive sigh of regret.

There was little doubt she was suffering a bizarre form of insanity. Leverton had snuck up on her, squashed her, and generally treated her like a totty-headed female. And yet all she wanted to do was pull him back down, wrap her arms around his broad shoulders, and kiss him senseless.

"Yep, they be gone, Yer Grace," Teddy whispered, going up on his knees. He glanced down the beach. "I don't see the decoy none, either."

The boy's words blasted the remaining sensual lethargy from Gillian's brain. She rolled, moving into a crouch beside Teddy, slipping her pistol into the holstered belt at her back.

"Did you see what path they took?" she murmured. With

any luck, she could pick up the trail and follow the smugglers back to their hiding place.

A hand clamped on to the shoulder of her coat and hauled her up with almost shocking ease. "I fail to see the relevance in that detail, Miss Dryden," Leverton said as he set her on her feet.

She staggered on the uneven sand and had to clutch at his arm. "It's relevant because I'm going to follow them."

His hands slid down to her elbows, steadying her. "I think not. We're going back to Fenfield Manor, where we will have a discussion about tonight's foolish adventure."

She slapped his hands away. "I think not," she retorted, mimicking him. "And every minute we spend arguing means those bloody smugglers are getting farther away."

Gillian tried to brush by him, but he grabbed on to her and hauled her against his body. Cursing under her breath, she drove her heel into his shin.

Leverton barely flinched. "And what do you intend to do once you find them?" he growled. "Face them down with your pathetically inadequate pistol?"

"I'll have you know it's a very good pistol." Then she winced at how inane that sounded.

"It had better be if you intend to take out six smugglers, which I assume is your plan."

"You assume wrong." She was so enraged and embarrassed that she practically choked on it. Unfortunately, Leverton was correct. She didn't really have a plan, although she certainly wasn't stupid enough to confront a group of armed men by herself.

"I simply wanted to track them," she said, "and see where they were holing up."

"And then what?"

She fumed silently, trying to think of something that didn't sound completely ridiculous. Her end game was to recover the jewels, but she'd yet to devise exactly how. Every successful plan was based on knowledge gleaned about one's adversaries. But now, with every passing second, the smugglers were moving out of her reach. Even the chance to acquire the slightest bit of useful information was slipping away.

Sighing, Gillian slumped between his hands. Ever since coming to England, nothing had gone right. She felt out of sorts with everything and everyone, including herself. In Sicily, she'd always known what to do and how to do it. But in England she was full of doubt, no longer even sure what she should care about.

Teddy let out a sigh. "Don't matter much anymore," he said morosely. "They's long gone, but I could try picking up their trail, if you wants me to."

"I do not," Leverton said in a crisp voice as he finally let Gillian go. "Teddy, Mr. Reid is waiting for you where you left the mare tied up. Run along now and join him. I'll speak with you later."

"Yes, Yer Grace," Teddy said, looking stricken.

Gillian reached over and straightened his cap, letting her hand briefly cup the back of his head. "I'll speak to you later too. Get some sleep, my dear, and don't worry about anything. I promise all will be fine."

Teddy eyed Leverton, his pinched-up mouth expressing his doubt. He gave her a nod and then set off through the dune grass.

Gillian scowled at the duke. "You are not to even think of blaming that boy or letting him go. His mother desperately needs the pitiful income he makes in your stables."

Leverton shook his head, clearly disgusted. "Teddy's income is far from pitiful. Reid pays him an ample stipend, with my blessing. I might also add that Mrs. Peck is very generous with kitchen leftovers, which I'm sure you noticed. Finally, he lives in a cottage that *I* own. Since the death of his father, I have not charged Mrs. Bell a shilling of rent.

Do I sound like an ogre to you, ready to throw Teddy into the deepest dungeon?"

Gillian felt her shoulders creep up around her ears. "Well . . . no."

Leverton fisted his hands on his hips. It was too dark to make out the expression on his shadowed face. Still, only an idiot could fail to tell that he was as angry as he'd been when he arrived.

"Thank you for that ringing endorsement," he said sarcastically. "By the way, I do not blame Teddy. I blame you. What were you thinking to drag that boy into such danger? I swear, Gillian, I ought to turn you over my knee and give you a sound whacking for acting in so demented a fashion."

Gillian already felt horribly guilty about Teddy, and Leverton's threat to treat her like a naughty child fired up her temper. "Teddy was quite safe with me."

Leverton slapped a hand to his forehead, accidentally knocking his hat off. "Good God, you are completely insane. Someone should have locked you up in a madhouse long ago."

She'd automatically stooped down to pick up his hat. But instead of handing it to him, she threw it at his chest. "And *you* are nothing but a coward, if you don't mind my saying so, Your Grace. A. Coward," she repeated for emphasis. He wasn't, of course, but at the moment it was the worst thing she could think of to call him.

He stared at her in disbelief. "Because I refused to let a slip of a girl and a small boy hare off after a band of desperate smugglers? You have a very odd notion of what constitutes appropriate behavior, although I shouldn't be surprised since you were allowed to run wild around the Sicilian countryside. Your family has much to answer for, I'm sorry to say."

Gillian leaned forward and jabbed him in the chest. "You leave my family out of it. They did the best they could."

"Nothing can excuse their failure to teach you how a woman of your standing should behave."

"My *standing*? I'm the by-blow of a thoroughly disreputable man who wants nothing to do with me. Which I suppose must be counted as a blessing," she finished with heavy sarcasm.

"That is entirely beside the point," he said in a tight voice.

"It's the entire point, you stupid man. Now, if you don't mind, I'd like to get back to the manor. There is obviously nothing to be gained from continuing this ridiculous conversation."

She tried to stalk past him, but he grabbed her by the arm and reeled her back in.

"I'm warning you, Your Grace," she said.

"Hush. We've got company."

The next thing she knew, he was shoving her down onto the sand. He came down on top of her, mashing her flat.

It took her a moment to catch her breath, since there wasn't a particle of air between them. She was certainly becoming intimately acquainted with various parts of Leverton's impressive anatomy.

"Who is it?" She felt a spurt of hope. Perhaps some of the smugglers had returned. Now that Teddy was safely out of the way, Leverton might even help her track them. They might not see eye to eye on everything, but he would be furious that smugglers were trespassing on his lands.

"Wait," he breathed out.

He cautiously lifted his head to peer over the rise of sand between them and the beach. The sound of a cantering horse, hooves thudding into the hard-packed flats, quickly grew and then faded away down the beach. Leverton still didn't move, his attention focused in the direction of the mysterious rider.

"Could you please get off me," she finally said. "You are completely squashing me."

He looked down at her and frowned, as if surprised to see her there. Gillian raised a sardonic brow.

"I beg your pardon," he murmured, as if they were on the dance floor and he'd simply trod on her foot.

He rolled off, but kept an arm slung across her waist. Gillian tried to push it away, but it felt like a tree trunk was pinning her down. She let out an aggrieved sigh and dropped her head back onto the sand.

"Whoever it was, he's long gone," she said. "Why are we still lying here?"

"I just wanted to make sure," Leverton answered. "I think it's now safe to get up."

"I should hope so. I feel like I've spent half the night lying on this blasted beach." With nothing to show for it but sand in her breeches and an irate duke.

Leverton rolled into a crouch and then smoothly rose. He reached down a hand to pull her up. "And whose fault is that?"

Gillian pulled the tails of her coat back in place and started brushing herself off. "Not mine. If you hadn't shown up, I could have tracked the smugglers back to their lair. That, as you must admit, would have been very helpful."

"Their lair? Good God, you've been reading too many lurid novels. Wait, I forgot," he said, holding up a hand. "You actually believe you're living in one. You fancy yourself some sort of heroine, dashing about, trying to right all the wrongs of the world."

"No, I fancy myself as the hero." She wiggled a leg, hoping to at least shake some of the sand from her backside down to her boot. "The heroines are always moaning and falling down in a faint, waiting for the men to rescue them. I don't have time for that sort of nonsense."

"That is quite obvious to anyone who knows you. Well, I think we've both had enough larking about for one night.

Are you ready to go, Miss Dryden, or shall we wait to see the sunrise?"

"There's no need for sarcasm, Leverton," she said as she bent to retrieve her cap. It had fallen off when he tackled her. "And you still haven't said if you recognized the rider. It wasn't one of the smugglers, was it?"

"No, it was a riding officer, on patrol. He was obviously too late to be of any use."

"Why didn't you flag him down?" she snapped.

"As I just said, there was no point," he replied with exaggerated patience. "The smugglers were long gone."

"No point? He was on a *horse*. He could have easily caught up with them. What were you thinking to just let him go by like that?" Her mother would be horrified at the way Gillian was speaking to him, but she couldn't help it. Leverton had let another opportunity slip away. What was wrong with the blasted man?

"I was thinking I didn't want to expose you to more scurrilous gossip," he said, clearly growing irate again. "I am trying to protect your reputation, Miss Dryden. Explaining your presence here in the middle of the night to a riding officer would hardly assist me in achieving that goal."

"I don't give a hang about my reputation," she shouted. "That was our best chance to find my jewels, and you ruined it."

"It is blindingly obvious that you care not a whit for your reputation. You take every occasion to be outrageous, to behave like a—"

He bit off whatever insult he was going to level. Then he sucked in a deep breath, as if trying to calm himself.

"Gillian," he said.

She waved an impatient hand, ignoring the way her chest seemed to twist and tighten. His tone practically reeked with disdain. "Light-skirt? Doxy? Which is it? Go ahead and say it if it makes you feel better. It won't bother me in the slightest."

It was a lie. She'd spent a lifetime learning to ignore the acidic little jabs and the steady drip of smirking insults, but the pain they'd caused was nothing compared to knowing he felt the same. It seemed to hollow her out, leaving an empty darkness that could never be filled.

"I wasn't going to say any such thing," he said. "I never would." ·

"Well, it doesn't matter. Now, can we please go?" She needed to move, to get away from him. Tears stung her eyes, and she could feel her throat going thick. The notion that she would cry over this—over him—was simply appalling. Gillian hadn't truly cried since the death of her stepfather. That Leverton had the power to call forth such a dreadful sign of weakness infuriated her.

Perversely, that made her want to cry even more. What in God's name was wrong with her?

She tried to shove past him again, but he stepped in front of her and grasped her shoulders.

"Let me go."

"Not until you let me apologize," he said in a gravelly voice.

She tried to wriggle out from under his grip. His gloved fingers held her tight.

"I don't need any apologies from the likes of y-you." Gillian almost fainted in horror to hear the break in her voice. She'd called him a coward, and yet here she was acting like a silly female with the vapors. As if his words truly had the power to harm her.

Sadly, it appeared they did.

She sniffed as she tried to steady herself. Unfortunately, one exceedingly defiant sob seemed intent on forcing itself out.

Damn and blast.

"Are you crying, Gillian?" Leverton asked in a voice of soft amazement.

"Don't be ridiculous. As if I would cry over something as stupid as this." As if she would cry over the mistaken assumption that he liked her, when apparently he did not.

"Then what is this I see on your cheek?" He gently brushed a gloved finger over her face. "Yes, there is a tear, sparkling like a jewel. How extraordinary."

"Don't you dare make fun of me." She glared up at him, rather a tricky feat when one was trying not to bawl.

He barked out a laugh. "Believe me, I find this situation anything but amusing. Painful would be a more apt description."

That dried her tears. "If you don't let me go this instant, I will make you very sorry. And I don't give a damn if you are a bloody duke." He wouldn't be the first man she'd kneed in the bollocks, and she didn't suppose he'd be the last.

"Right now, I don't give a damn either." And with that, Leverton hauled Gillian up on her toes and covered her mouth in a fierce, smoldering kiss.

When he pulled her up, Gillian went stiff as a plank in his arms; her eyes popped wide in shock. Charles knew exactly how she felt. He'd clearly lost his mind, and no amount of effort on his part seemed capable of tracking it down. Not that it would matter. The only thing that mattered was that he'd hurt her. He'd made her cry.

Gillian Dryden, the strongest, most resourceful girl one could ever hope to meet, had shed tears, and it almost killed him. All Charles wanted to do was chase away the pain that had flashed through her beautiful eyes, a pain that told him how many times she'd been insulted by sneering words and casual cruelty. And he wanted to chase away the pain before she recovered enough to knee him in the balls. He suspected she'd been only seconds from doing just that when he slammed his mouth down onto hers.

As his lips moved over hers, he told himself that he was simply trying to disarm her, soothing her until she calmed down enough for them to talk.

Liar.

Soothe her, yes. But talk? What he wanted to do was pull her down to the sand and kiss her into melting submission. He'd wanted to do it from the minute he pushed her under him in a desperate attempt to keep her safe. They'd been inches from danger, and yet he'd been hard-pressed to keep himself from stripping those ridiculous clothes from her body and making love to her.

There was very little doubt that he'd lost his bloody mind when it came to Gillian Dryden.

He slid his tongue just a fraction between her lips, silently urging her to open. Gillian didn't seem inclined to pull away or, thankfully, unman him. If anything, she was swaying closer, eyes now closed and hands pressed flat to his chest as if she needed him to support her. Then she breathed out an endearing little whimper that suggested she didn't know what to do. How to take what he wanted to give her.

And then he was lost in a haze of lust and longing that he'd been trying to deny for what seemed a lifetime. That sweet, vulnerable sound made him shake, as if all the energy he'd put into holding back was straining against an invisible leash. But now that he finally held her in his arms, there wasn't a force on earth that could stop him. Not logic, not reason, not even his vaunted self-control.

He slid a hand up her neck to cup her chin, tipping her face so he could more fully devour her mouth. Her lips quivered and finally parted. He slipped in, teasing her for a brief second, then retreating to nip her lower lip. She moaned and trembled against him, her fingers digging into his coat as she wriggled closer.

Her response flashed fire through his veins, and he slid his other hand inside her coat to cup her delectable bottom. He squeezed, shaping the lovely curve through her breeches—and who had ever thought breeches on a woman could be so seductive. Then he nudged her closer, pressing her against his straining erection. Charles couldn't remember the last time he'd wanted a woman so much. Even Letitia had never kissed him like this, with an open and entirely genuine eagerness.

Gillian was now using her grip on his coat to pull herself up. She clamped one hand around the back of his neck to hold him steady as she kissed him back with an enthusiasm that almost sent his eyes rolling to the back of his head.

Good God.

For a girl who'd been tearing a strip off him just moments ago, she'd certainly gotten into the spirit of things, turning his mind to mush in the process. Her sweet lips wandered over him, teasing and tasting with dainty licks that felt like flickers of fire. When Gillian rubbed her gentle curves against him, Charles felt his knees start to buckle. Every point of contact between them heated to unbearable levels.

Stop. Now.

Charles pulled back from the torrid embrace and tried to put some air between them, desperate to retain a degree of sanity. He felt like he was on the edge of a precipice. Just below, barely hidden from view, were lovely, lush, and dark secrets. All it needed was one little step off the edge to get there.

And he wanted to get *there* more than anything he'd ever imagined.

He needed to think fast and for both of them, since Gillian was resisting any attempt on his part to retreat. In fact, she was practically climbing up his body. She'd hooked one slim leg around the back of his thigh and shimmied up him, placing the sweet notch of her thighs right against him.

The girl was as lithe as an acrobat, and his erection certainly approved. Charles could barely keep himself from ripping open the fall of his breeches—and hers—and plunging into her delicious warmth.

Her virginal warmth, you fool.

He opened his mouth to voice a warning, but Gillian's dainty tongue darted inside, again taking sweet advantage. It took every ounce of strength he possessed not to suck her in deep. Instead, he forced himself to pull back, doing his best to ignore her incoherent protest as he clamped his arms around her waist and eased her a few inches away.

Naturally, being Gillian, she went under protest. She slid her foot down his leg, but still kept it hooked around his calf. Her pelvis remained locked against his groin, even though she leaned back to stare up at him. The woman was a bloody acrobat, all right, twined around him like ivy, all the right parts of her body fitting perfectly with his.

The scowl she directed at him belied a mouth that was lush, wet, and red, and a heavy-lidded, sensual gaze. Gillian looked both thoroughly kissed and thoroughly annoyed that they'd stopped. There wasn't a doubt in heaven that she wanted to keep going as much as he did.

"Why are you stopping?" Her soft, husky voice seemed expressly designed to bleed every particle of common sense from his brain.

"Ah, I want to make sure you know what you're doing," Charles managed. "We need to think about this."

Her straight brows tilted up. "Really? We both seem to know what we're doing quite well."

He choked out a laugh. "That's the problem. It's too damn easy. I can see us getting into a great deal of trouble."

Trouble with Gillian, he was beginning to fear, was exactly what he wanted. All he could think about was her naked and in his bed, with long hours of lovemaking stretching ahead of them. Possibly even days stretching into months and then years.

It was insane.

She unhooked her leg and came down his body in a torturously delicious slide that sent him right to the edge. As if he needed another example of her ability to blow his self-control to smithereens.

She dropped down on her heels and straightened, a frown marking her forehead. "It's supposed to be easy when it's right, isn't it?"

That made perfect sense, but it had to be wrong. He and Gillian didn't belong together, not by any rational argument. Yet it felt right in a way that defied logic and sense, diving deep down into muscle and bone.

Charles stared into her face, taking in the open, vulnerable expression on her elegant features. Gillian rarely looked that unguarded—after all, she'd learned caution in a hard school. But that earth-shattering kiss had stripped her down, revealing a girl so eager for affection that it scared the absolute hell out of him.

He stood there like a great lummox, trying to figure out what to do with her. With them. But the answer hung just beyond his reach.

A change came over her, bitterness shifting within her gaze. "I thought you were different; I truly did." Then she affected a casual shrug. "I suppose I should just let you take what you want, and then we can get back to hating each other."

"What the hell is that supposed to mean?" he bit out.

"Men take what they want, and then cast it aside." She braced her hands on her hips, staring defiantly up at him. In the faint tendrils of light of the approaching dawn, she looked like a fierce pagan goddess. She jabbed him in the chest. "Do you ever think about what I want? Or is it only what you want that matters."

"Of course it matters what you want," he said. "More than what I want, in fact. It means that I will not take advantage of you."

Gillian slid a look down his body, lingering on his groin. She was clearly furious, but there was as much passion in her gaze as there was anger. "And what if I want to take advantage of you? What then?"

He let out a derisive snort. "That's ridiculous. Gillian, you're not thinking clearly. Neither of us is."

She flicked away his comments with a dismissive hand. "It's not about thinking; it's about wanting. And I want you, Leverton, to my utter surprise. And I believe you want me, do you not?" Again, her gaze traveled down to his groin. "Oh, yes, you do," she whispered. "You want me very much, but you hate yourself for it."

How could he not want her? Any man would. "No, that's not it at all."

Like an icy goddess, she sneered at him and turned her back. "Well, you won't have me. I've changed my mind. You're too much trouble for me to waste my time with you."

Her words seemed to set off an explosion in his head. He hardly remembered moving, but a moment later he'd swept her off her feet. She let out a funny little growl and grabbed the collar of his coat.

"What in blazes do you think you're doing?" she snapped.

"I'm apparently losing my mind."

"You don't need me to do that, so please set me down."

"Yes, I'll get to that in a minute." Then he took her mouth in a fierce kiss, invading her when she gasped in surprise. Charles gave her no quarter, holding her tight against him as he devoured her with unforgiving hunger.

For a few long seconds, she seemed too surprised to react. Then she started to squirm in his arms. Finally, he broke away. "Would you please stay the hell still?" he rasped out.

Her mouth—soft and wet from his kiss—hung open in surprise. "Leverton, what are you doing?"

"I'm taking advantage of you, as should be obvious by now." He swooped down to slip his tongue into her mouth for a brief, delicious taste. "And I don't give a damn whether you mind or not."

She blinked up at him, looking rather suprised. "Oh. Well then, carry on."

He narrowed his gaze. "Are you sure?"

"For God's sake," she muttered. "Are all dukes as dense as you are?"

She grabbed him by the ears and pulled his head down, her mouth meeting his in a bold, passionate kiss that staggered him. He stumbled a bit on the uneven sand and then went down to his knees, almost dropping her in the process. She giggled, an endearing sound that vibrated against his mouth.

A moment later he had her safely stretched out beneath him on the soft sand. He nuzzled her mouth as his fingers clumsily groped with the buttons on her greatcoat. Gillian reached up to help him.

"Here, let me do it," she gasped, her voice breathy with amusement.

"Madam, I do believe you are mocking me," Charles answered as he shifted a bit to the side.

"Well, you did almost drop me. You're usually not so clumsy," she said as she opened her coat.

"And you're usually not dressed in men's clothing. It's thrown me off my stride."

She wrinkled her nose in mock dismay. "That sounds rather distressing. What can I do to help?"

He pretended to think about it. "For starters, you could unbutton that absurd waistcoat."

She started on the small buttons. "I'll have you know this

was made by a very fashionable London tailor. As were my breeches and my coat."

He finally took a good look at what she was wearing. Her garments were simple, but obviously well made, hugging her gentle curves with expert precision. On a young man, they would have been unexceptionable. On her, they were devastatingly erotic, a blatant display of the sweet notch between her thighs and her long, slim legs.

Charles could easily imagine those legs wrapped around his hips as he entered her for the first time. Or draped over his shoulders as he took her with his mouth. Gillian might be considered too slender and athletic to be fashionable, but to his mind she had the body of a siren. And he had every intention of seeing it all, naked and spread before him.

Not here, though. This would be just a taste, for both of them.

"How did the tailor get the measurements so exact?" he asked, skimming his hand to her waist. "No, don't tell me. I would have to murder him for touching you."

She rolled her eyes as she finished unbuttoning her waistcoat. "As if I would be so stupid as to go to the tailor myself. That's not . . ."

Her voice died away when he flicked aside the edges of her vest and slid a hand to her breast. He gently squeezed it, then rubbed his palm across her nipple. Through the fine linen of her shirt, he felt her nipple pull into a tight bead.

Gillian sucked in a breath and squirmed. Charles slung a leg over her pelvis, pinning her down.

"I take it you like this," he said as he lazily played with her nipple. He flicked it, then gently pinched it between his fingers.

She let out a moan as her eyes fluttered shut. When he again rubbed the rigid tip, she arched up into his hand.

"That's as good an answer as any," he whispered as he dipped down for a quick kiss.

She reached for him, trying to prolong the kiss, but he pulled away. Her eyes opened. "What are you doing?" she whispered.

He didn't answer right away, instead pulling the fabric of her shirt tightly over her nipple, causing it to stand out in sharp relief. Then he brushed across it with the tip of a finger. "I'm playing with you," he finally said.

"Oh," she managed around a gasp. "Well, that's all right."

When he bent down and sucked her into his mouth, her gasp transformed into a choked cry. Charles circled his hand around her breast, plumping it into a tempting mound as he teased the rigid point with his tongue and teeth. Gillian squirmed in his arms, letting out breathy, enchanting whimpers.

When he finally pulled back, the fabric of her shirt was wet and almost transparent.

"Now, that is truly lovely," he murmured as he palmed her breast. "But I think we can do better."

Gillian peered at him, looking adorably flushed and dazed. "Um, I didn't realize it was a competition."

He grinned at her. "I'm timing myself."

As much as he wanted to linger with her, he wouldn't take any more risks than he already had. Dawn was fast approaching, and he needed to get her back to the house without being seen.

Still, he had no intention of letting her go until she'd climaxed in his arms. Because whatever happened going forward, she was now his. As the night had faded, easing toward the day, the decision had been made. It came to him as quietly as the approaching dawn. Yes, it made no sense, and probably never would. But it felt right. In fact, now it felt remarkably easy. Gillian had said something similar only a few minutes ago, as if it explained everything.

And perhaps it did at that.

"You're timing yourself? What—" She broke off with a laugh. "Good Lord. You mean until I . . . you know."

"Exactly." He pushed her shirt up to expose her breasts. Gillian shivered as the cool morning air washed over her smooth skin.

"That sounds like quite the challenge," she said, her voice breathy. "Would you care to place a wager?"

He'd been about to flick one of her nipples with his tongue, but her comment had him pulling back in surprise. He narrowed his gaze on a sudden, very unpleasant thought. "And what is your basis of comparison?"

She rolled her eyes. "Well, not doing that." She waggled a hand in his face. "Doing this."

He had to laugh. She was the most outrageous woman he'd ever met.

"I don't see why it's so funny," she said. "I know it's not proper, and it's not like I make a habit of it. But one can't help being curious, you know. You can hardly ask someone about it, can you?"

He laughed even harder. It was the most ridiculous conversation he'd ever had. Although, given the circumstances— and given that it was Gillian—he shouldn't be surprised.

"You can ask me next time," he said, once he had his amusement under control.

She looked almost shy. "Well, now that you mention it . . ."

"Next time," he murmured, suddenly impatient. The image of Gillian, naked and with her hand busy between her thighs, had invaded his brain, making his erection strain even harder against the fall of his breeches. He had to touch her or he would lose his mind.

He bent and sucked her back into his mouth, reveling in her startled moan and in the feel of her rigid nipple and velvety skin. For several minutes he tempted them both, sucking and nipping as she writhed beneath him. He clamped both hands on her sweet mounds, gently massaging them while he tortured her nipples—like hard, sweet candies on his tongue.

Suddenly, she moved, twisting sideways. When her breast popped out of his mouth, Charles growled with frustration. But then she flung her leg over his hip, pressing her pelvis tight against him. "If you don't do something soon," she gasped out, "I'm going to shoot you."

His laugh turned into a groan as she undulated her hips against his erection. Only Gillian would threaten a man with murder for not getting on with it. And if she kept rubbing herself against him with such abandon, he would lose the few shreds of control he had left, strip her naked, and take her like a wild animal, right here in the open.

Hardly proper behavior for a duke.

"Hush, Gillian," he murmured, stroking her back. "I'll take care of you."

"That's good," she said in a tight voice, "because I'm feeling rather desperate."

"Lay back, my sweet girl." He eased her down, then swiftly went to work on her breeches, exposing her beautiful body for his caress. He trailed his fingers over the slight curve of her belly, then down to the soft tangle of mink-colored curls between her thighs. She quivered under his touch, and it was all he could do not to push her legs wide and take her with his mouth.

Next time, he promised himself.

"Open, darling," he whispered.

With a whimper, Gillian complied, letting her legs fall open. Charles carefully parted her soft folds, groaning at the slick moisture that covered his fingers. She wriggled her bottom, silently urging him to action. He gave her what she wanted, stroking gently, massaging her. When she arched into his hand and stretched her arms over her head, he couldn't help but glance up.

He was rewarded with the most beautiful sight he'd ever

seen. Gillian, half-naked, her shirt pooled up around her
shoulders as her body arched in a lithe curve, breasts pushed
high, nipples flushed and full. Her eyes were closed, her expression fierce with passion as she approached her climax.
She was so sweet, so bloody natural, hiding nothing of herself and ready to give him everything. Just looking at her
made something inside him explode like a powder keg,
almost knocking him flat. He'd never felt anything like it
before.

Because she's mine.

It was a simple and direct conclusion, and it swept through
him to settle deep in his bones.

Gillian dragged her eyes open, her expression dazed until
it focused on his face. Then her gaze flared with urgent
emotion.

"Charles," she whispered, his name a plea.

"Yes, love," he murmured.

He leaned down to take her lips as his hands moved between her thighs once more. He pressed his tongue into her
mouth, taking her with a kiss that was deeper, more intimate
than any he'd ever known. Gillian's hands came up to his
shoulders, her fingers curling into the fabric of his coat,
holding him tight as she kissed him back with desperate
intensity.

When she pressed her hips up, silently begging, he knew
she was beyond ready. He slicked his fingers over her bud
one more time, then pushed two fingers high into her body.
Her tight flesh cinched around him.

Gillian wrenched her mouth away, letting out a ragged
moan of release as she curled into his body. Charles pressed
his hand firmly on her mound, satisfaction storming through
him as she rode through her climax. His chest rose and fell
like a bellows, as if he'd also had a release. He wished he had,
since he was so damn hard he could barely move.

But it was worth every bit of discomfort to watch Gillian's

face as she came, to feel her body shake and come apart in his arms. As she shuddered through her release, he eased her back down to the sand. He slowly withdrew his fingers and gently cupped her until the trembling fully passed.

Finally, she let out a long sigh and opened her eyes, staring straight up at him. She gave him a misty smile. There was so much emotion in her gaze that his throat went tight.

"Well, that wasn't how I anticipated my evening would conclude," she said in a husky voice. "But it was quite thrilling nonetheless."

It took Charles a good thirty seconds to comprehend that Gillian obviously considered him the consolation prize to a disappointing night.

Chapter Nineteen

Gillian bolted upright from sleep. She darted a glance to her side, half expecting to see Leverton stretched out beside her, his blue gaze heavy-lidded and seductive, his mouth curling up in an enticing smile. Her body seemed to ache with unspent passion, tricked by a dream so real that she swore she could still feel his hands caressing her.

Almost as real as what had happened on the beach only a few hours ago. Then, Leverton had done much more than simply caress. He'd awakened an unexpected passion, catapulting both her mind and her body into the most heavenly state. Oh, Gillian had experienced pleasure before, but nothing like this. Nothing like the joy she'd felt when she fell to pieces in his arms. It was both terrifying and wonderful, and her mind still struggled to comprehend the change in their relationship.

Groaning, she flopped back onto the pillows, rubbing her bleary eyes and trying to sort out the conflicting emotions that were muddling her sleep-deprived brain. Exactly how Leverton felt about her was entirely unclear. First he'd been angry, then passionate, and then simply annoyed. There'd also been that disgraceful display of tears on her part, which still made her cringe. Gillian hated to cry. Tears made her feel stupid, vulnerable, and messy, and they never solved anything.

The effect they'd had on Leverton, however, made her uneasy. Had their lovemaking simply been an attempt on his part to comfort her? Or, even worse, had it sprung from a sense of pity? That would be appalling, but it was something she had to consider given the aftermath of their heated encounter. She'd barely recovered before he was straightening her clothes in a decidedly unromantic fashion, and dragging her off the beach to his horse. When she'd protested his brusque behavior, Leverton had simply hauled her into his arms for a thorough kiss before hoisting her onto his horse. Unfortunately, he'd then spent half the ride back to Fenfield lecturing her about the need to be safely stowed in her bed before anyone discovered she was missing.

Gillian couldn't blame him. After all, her reputation was already in tatters. And ever the paragon of correct conduct, Leverton might even believe he was now obligated to offer his hand in marriage. Men like him didn't dabble with gently bred girls without suffering the consequences. But the idea that she could be his duchess was too absurd to contemplate.

Sighing, she enumerated the reasons why marriage to the Duke of Leverton was the worst idea in the history of mankind. The list started with the fact that he didn't love her and ended with her admission that she was, unfortunately, falling in love with him. But mooning over Perfect Penley wouldn't solve any of her problems, including the still missing jewels and her grandmother's opposition to returning home to Sicily.

As for her disastrous feelings for Leverton, she had every intention of ignoring them until they simply went away.

She threw back the bedclothes, pleased to have everything so neatly—if depressingly—sorted out. Grabbing her wrapper, she glanced at the clock on the mantelpiece. Seeing it was already late, alarm jolted through her at the thought that Leverton might already have spoken to her mother. He wouldn't mention their tryst on the beach, but she wasn't confident he would keep his mouth shut about the smugglers. He was intent on preventing any further action on her part, and he knew Mamma's distress was the one thing that might make Gillian hesitant about continuing her search.

Cursing, she rushed behind the Oriental screen and was dragging her night rail over her head when she heard the door open. Peeking around the edge of the screen, she saw Lady Filby's maid enter the room.

"Good morning, miss," Clara said in a cheerful voice as she went to open the drapes. "Lady Filby and the contessa are waiting for you in the breakfast parlor. I'm to help you dress this morning."

Since breakfast was a rather casual affair at Fenfield Manor with no set time, it boded ill that the others were awaiting her arrival. "Is His Grace also waiting for me?" Gillian asked.

Clara handed her a clean shift. "No, miss. I believe he's in the library with Mr. Scunthorpe."

Gillian's anxiety eased. Likely her mother was simply concerned that she'd slept in so late. "It's very nice of them to wait breakfast for me," she said as she slipped into her stays.

"Yes, miss." The pregnant pause before Clara had answered set off warning bells in Gillian's brain. She glanced over her shoulder, but the girl was intent on her work. "Now, Miss Gillian, don't be twisting around like that. I'll never get you laced up."

"Not too tight, please."

Clara's sigh had Gillian biting back a smile, since she'd had the same discussion with every maid who'd ever waited on her. She preferred not to wear stays at all, but her efforts in that regard always led to bleats of alarm from her mother, and stern orders from her grandmother "to dress like a lady."

It was one of the many reasons Gillian wished she'd been born male instead of female.

Although she certainly hadn't minded being female last night, when Leverton's hands and mouth had roamed her body.

"Stop squirming, Miss Gillian," Clara said. "You're like a worm on a hook."

"Yes, Clara," she said meekly.

Over the maid's protests, Gillian hurried through the rest of her dressing, simply running a brush through her hair and pulling it back into a simple knot. She dashed for the door, throwing Clara a quick word of thanks over her shoulder.

She took the stairs two at a time down to the entrance hall, arriving at the bottom as the butler exited the family dining room. "Good morning, Miss Dryden," Hewitt said. "The contessa and her ladyship are still at table, so I do not believe there is any need to rush."

Gillian grinned at the gentle admonition. "Sorry, but I didn't want to miss any of Mrs. Peck's excellent cheddar biscuits. I'm not usually this late to breakfast."

"I will bring you a fresh plate," he said kindly.

She couldn't help noticing the slight frown on his face or the way he seemed to be studying her. What the devil was going on this morning? Leverton had, in fact, gotten her back to Fenfield before the servants had risen. Only Reid knew about her escapade, and Gillian was quite certain the duke had sworn him to secrecy.

Nodding her thanks to Hewitt, she entered the small but cheerful room with its floral-patterned wallpaper and Chinese-style furniture. The windows faced east, catching the pale sunlight that struggled to dissipate the chilly morning fog that had rolled in from the coast. One advantage of going back to Sicily would be escaping from all the dreary English weather.

But you weren't cold last night, were you? Gillian mentally groaned. She needed to stop thinking of Leverton and what they'd done last night or she would go insane.

"Good morning, Mamma, Lady Filby." She crossed to the table to give her mother a kiss.

Predictably, her mother sat closest to the fire, since she too hated the cold. Mamma would probably be just as glad to return to Sicily as Gillian was. At least Gillian hoped so. Without her mother's support, it would be much harder to convince Grandmamma to go along with the plan. Gillian had the funds to finance her own trip, but the idea of returning to Palermo without the support of her family was daunting.

"Good morning, my love," her mother said. "I was beginning to worry about you, since you never sleep in so late."

"I don't know what came over me." She cast an apologetic smile at Lady Filby. "I'm usually up before anyone."

The countess arched an ironic brow. "Perhaps you were unable to sleep last night. Was that it?"

"Um, not really."

When her mother and Lady Filby exchanged a knowing glance. Gillian's heart took a dive.

"My dear, why don't you get yourself some breakfast," her mother said. "Then we need to have a little chat."

Confound it. "Have you been talking to Leverton?" Gillian demanded.

Her mother smiled and patted the seat beside her. "Get something to eat and then come sit with me."

Gillian stalked to the sideboard and poured herself a cup of coffee from the silver service. Whatever it was they were going to say, she needed coffee to help clear the cobwebs from her brain.

She took a seat at the end of the table so she could face both women. After taking a hefty sip, she sat back in her chair and crossed her arms.

Lady Filby flashed her a quick grin. "No need to look so

put out, my dear. Certainly, we have a lot to discuss, but I do believe most of it falls under the category of good news."

Gillian frowned. "I beg your pardon?"

"Yes, that is true," said Mamma, giving her a surprisingly stern look. "But first we must discuss your exceedingly foolish behavior last night."

Her mother was never stern with her. Nor did she exert much in the way of maternal control. But over the last week or so, Mamma had begun to develop a rather decisive demeanor. Though it was wonderful to see her parent come out of the mopes, Gillian didn't relish the notion of Mamma's suddenly trying to make up for years of benign neglect.

"I'm not really sure what you mean," Gillian said, trying to brazen it out.

"Of course you do. You snuck out last night to track down those awful men who robbed us." Mamma shook her head with disapproval. "I can't even bear to think about what would have happened if they'd discovered you."

Gillian breathed a quiet sigh of relief. She could manage this. "Mamma, I've been doing that sort of thing for years. I'm quite good at it, as you know."

"So good that you ended up with a bullet in your shoulder," her mother said.

"It was just that one time," Gillian protested. "Surely you're not going to hold that against me."

Mamma leaned forward, suddenly looking pale. "You could have been killed, Gillian. I lost your stepfather to violence. I don't want to lose you, too."

Gillian struggled to defend herself against the familiar rush of guilt. "I know, Mamma, and I'm sorry I made you worry. But nobody else was going to avenge Step-papa's death, or even try to bring his killers to justice. It wasn't right."

"I understand, my love. And for too long I was utterly selfish, failing to be there for you when you needed me. If

I'd provided you with comfort and support, you never would have felt the need to embark on so reckless a quest."

"You weren't selfish in the least," Gillian said stoutly. "You were grief-stricken. Besides, Grandmamma was anything but weak, and even she couldn't stop me. It was something that had to be done, and I did it."

Her mother studied her for several long moments, as if seeing her in a new light. It made Gillian shift in her chair. "I have been a terrible mother," Mamma finally said. "I hope someday you can find it in yourself to forgive me."

"That is ridiculous," Gillian exclaimed. "You've loved me more than anyone ever could."

Her mother held up a hand. "No, child. I will no longer excuse the impact my behavior has had on your actions."

"Ah, I'm not sure what that means."

"It means that you are not to continue on this foolish endeavor to recover our jewels. It's not worth it."

Gillian stared at her in disbelief. "How can you say that? Step-papa gave those jewels to you. To us. It's all we have left of him."

Her mother's mouth trembled for a moment, but then she firmed her chin. "I have the memories of our life together, my child. As do you. That must be enough for both of us."

It wasn't enough for Gillian. For her stepfather's last precious gift to be now in the hands of dastardly criminals was too much to bear. And sooner or later, the loss would bedevil her mother, too. Gillian knew that as well as she knew her own name. Right now, Mamma was simply frightened by Leverton's no-doubt exaggerated account of last night.

Gillian would be having a very frank discussion with him about that. He had no business interfering and frightening her mother.

"Darling, you must promise that you will cease this reckless behavior," her mother said. "I could not bear it if anything happened to you."

Since Gillian had no intention of letting anything bad happen to her, she was able to frame an adequate response. "You needn't worry at all," she said, reaching across the table to squeeze her mother's hand. "I promise to be more careful in the future."

Her mother hesitated briefly, then smiled. "Thank you."

"Splendid," Lady Filby piped up cheerfully. "Now we can move on to a much more pleasant topic."

Gillian had almost forgotten that the countess was in the room. But the amused gleam in her ladyship's eyes put her back on guard. "And what topic might that be?" she warily asked.

Lady Filby's eyes went wide. "Why, your impending betrothal to my brother, of course. What else?"

Chapter Twenty

Gillian stalked across the entrance hall, ignoring Hewitt's bleating attempt to precede her. She didn't need anyone opening doors for her, and she certainly didn't need anyone to announce her to the high and mighty Duke of Leverton. Besides, she wanted to take the duke by surprise—or possibly murder him.

When she flung open the library door, it banged against the wall then ricocheted back, forcing her to leap aside to avoid getting smacked in the face. It was certainly a less dignified entrance than she'd hoped for, but at least she didn't fall flat on her backside.

From behind his desk, Leverton rose. "Ah, Miss Dryden. I was expecting to see you at some point this morning, but perhaps not so precipitously."

Blast the man, his lips were twitching with amusement.

Hewitt, still determined to do his duty, sidled in front of her. "Miss Dryden to see you, sir. If that is convenient."

"Thank you, Hewitt." Leverton's voice was as dry as vintage champagne.

The butler stepped aside and gave Gillian a bow that held more than a hint of triumph as he retreated from the room.

"Leverton, what in God's name—" Gillian said.

He interrupted her. "You remember Mr. Scunthorpe, do you not?"

She'd been so focused on the duke that she hadn't even noticed his estate manager, who was standing to the side of the massive desk, a stack of ledgers in front of him. The man seemed to be regarding her with a certain degree of alarm. "Good morning, Mr. Scunthorpe. I apologize for interrupting your meeting in so, er, so precipitous a fashion."

She sounded like an idiot, as Leverton's grin made amply clear. For a man known for his distinguished manners, he could certainly be rude on occasion.

"No apology necessary, Miss Dryden," the estate manager said in a cool tone. "His Grace and I were just finishing up." He cast his employer an apologetic smile and began to organize his books into a neat pile.

"One moment, Scunthorpe," Leverton said before coming around the desk to meet Gillian. He took her hand and, much to her shock, raised it to his mouth. When his lips brushed across her skin, she couldn't repress a shiver. She scowled, irritated at her too-ready response to him.

"Someone woke up on the wrong side of the bed," he murmured. "Perhaps you didn't get enough sleep last night."

"I slept just fine," she replied in a dignified voice. "But I do need to speak to you with some degree of urgency, sir."

He drew her over to one of the leather club chairs. "Of course. But first I would like you to hear what Scunthorpe has to say on an issue of interest to both you and your mother."

Gillian shot the estate manager a sharp glance. "Is it about the smugglers? And about our jewels?"

"Yes," Leverton said, resuming his seat.

Scunthorpe hesitated, his reserved expression replaced by one of consternation. "Forgive me, sir, but is this an appropriate topic of conversation for female ears? I have no wish to cause Miss Dryden or any other lady distress with such unpleasant matters."

Gillian crossed her arms and stared at him. He flushed a bit, but defiantly held her gaze. Clearly, he was loath to discuss the matter with her, which she found rather interesting.

"Don't worry," she said with a smile that perhaps showed more teeth than was necessary. "I promise not to keel over in a dead faint."

"Of that we can be sure," Leverton said. "I assure you, Scunthorpe, that Miss Dryden will not succumb to a bout of hysterics."

"As I mentioned, Your Grace, I have no knowledge of the stolen jewels," Scunthorpe said, looking unhappier by the moment.

"Yes, so you said. I'm referring to your information about the trafficking of smuggled goods across Penley lands, and the continued likelihood of that sort of activity."

"Yes. Of course." Scunthorpe visibly relaxed as he gave Gillian an oily smile. She didn't trust that smile for one second.

Nor did she believe that the estate manager was put off by the notion of having to explain himself to a female. He just didn't want to explain himself to *her*. To a man like Scunthorpe, who was respectable and well educated, but still dependent on his betters for his living, Gillian was an insult or a slap to the face. To him, she was well beneath his notice, likely no better than the unfortunate women forced to make their living on the streets.

"As I was telling the duke," he said in a condescending tone, "having smuggling gangs cross Leverton lands is extremely unusual. The local excise officers have been most efficient in preventing landings along this section of the coastline. I might also add that any local gangs are well aware that His Grace, unlike other landowners, has never condoned free trading. Infractions in the past have always been swiftly dealt with."

"Not very successfully, it would appear," Gillian said. She glanced at Leverton, wondering if he'd told the estate manager about last night's incident.

The duke obviously read her mind. "I have informed Scunthorpe that there was a run across estate lands last night. One that you witnessed," he dryly added.

Gillian felt considerable surprise that Leverton had even discussed the issue with the estate manager, given how obsessive he was about shielding her from gossip. Then again, that obsession hadn't stopped the duke from talking about last night's escapade with her mother and with Lady Filby, as well as his plans to marry her.

She refocused her attention on Scunthorpe. "That being the case, then how do you explain that there were not one, but two runs across estate lands within a two-week period? Just bad luck?"

Scunthorpe's nostrils pinched together, as if a foul odor had just assailed them. "I believe that merely to be an unfortunate coincidence."

"Really? That seems like the beginning of a pattern to me." She glanced at Leverton to gauge his reaction. Aside from a small crease marking his brow, he didn't show any evidence that what he was hearing caused him concern.

"From what His Grace described, last night's incident was markedly different from what occurred on the night of your robbery," Scunthorpe replied in a manner so brittle that Gillian fancied she could take a mallet and start chipping away at him.

"In what way?" she asked.

"You were robbed by a large, well-organized gang of owlers who were making a substantial run. What occurred last night sounds like a much smaller, hastier affair, thrown together without a great degree of planning. Nothing like the well-organized run you stumbled across two weeks ago."

"While I agree that the run was smaller," Gillian said, "it was anything but disorganized. Those men knew what they were doing, and they did it very efficiently."

"Miss Dryden, you were no doubt extremely flustered by what you saw last night. I'm sure in the emotion of the moment those men seemed like the worst sort of criminals. Very frightening, indeed."

"I was not the least bit frightened," she said, letting her irritation show.

His only answer was a treacly smile, a masterpiece of polite disbelief laden with a healthy dash of contempt.

Leverton finally intervened. "Scunthorpe, I would suggest you stick to the facts instead of making assumptions about Miss Dryden's state of mind."

"Of course, Your Grace. I certainly meant no offense."

"Yes, let's stick to the facts," Gillian said, "which seem rather thin on the ground at the moment. Have you actually conducted an investigation into these smuggling runs, Mr. Scunthorpe?"

"I have indeed, Miss Dryden. Well before last night's incident."

She frowned. "If your investigation was conducted before last night's incident, how can you draw such firm conclusions regarding that incident? That makes no sense."

"It makes perfect sense," he replied in a haughty tone. "All the information I was able to acquire reinforces my belief that what you saw last night was a small run by local men that will not be repeated any time soon, especially with His Grace in residence."

"That's the silliest thing I've ever heard," she said in disbelief. "The duke has been in residence these last two weeks, and that didn't bloody well stop them from making a run, now did it?"

Scunthorpe's patronizing smile disappeared. He made no attempt to respond to her accusation, instead glaring at her with poorly concealed fury.

Leverton rose in a leisurely fashion and stood in front of his desk, leaning against it. The faintly exasperated expression on his handsome features suggested he thought Gillian and Scunthorpe little better than quarreling children. "I'm sure our little band of free traders was not expecting to be spied on by guests from the manor. Perhaps that accounts for their reckless behavior last night."

"For God's sake, don't tell me you believe this errant nonsense," she retorted.

Leverton's eyes narrowed to irritated slits. "I believe we have exhausted any useful discussion on this particular topic." He nodded brusquely to his estate manager. "That's all for now, Scunthorpe."

"Yes, Your Grace," the man said with a respectful bow.

As he passed Gillian, he gave her a triumphant little sneer. Naturally, the coward's back was to the duke, or else he wouldn't have had the nerve. All she could do was give him a ferocious smile and silently fume as he slithered his way to the door.

"And Scunthorpe," the duke added.

"Yes, Your Grace?" Scunthorpe asked from the door.

"About those smugglers. I do hope your assessment is correct."

Gillian turned to look and felt a wee bit of satisfaction when she saw Scunthorpe's self-satisfied smile wobble.

"I will keep a close eye on the situation, sir," the estate manager said. "I give you my word."

"See that you do."

Once the door closed, Gillian eyed Leverton, annoyed that he was clearly going to ignore her opinion on the issue.

He crossed his arms and lifted a questioning brow. "You might as well tell me what it is you're fuming about."

"You know very well what I'm fuming about. We've been discussing it for the last fifteen minutes."

"Yes, but I'm not precisely sure what aspect of the situation aggravates you the most," he said.

"Don't pretend to be contrite when you're nothing of the sort."

When he grinned at her, her foolish heart skipped a beat. The man was ridiculously handsome and charming when he wasn't acting so autocratically male.

"Very well, but why are you so put out by Scunthorpe's report?" he asked. "His theories about last night's encounter sound fairly sensible to me."

She crossed her arms, imitating him. "Do you truly believe there are two gangs running your lands, and that it was only by chance they happened to conduct those runs within a two-week period? And, even in the unlikely event that such is the case, do you really think they're not going to do it again?"

"I must defer to your expertise when it comes to the criminal classes, but recall that I made it quite clear to the gang leader who held us up that I would not tolerate any such activities on my lands."

"He no doubt was shaking in his boots the entire time," she answered sarcastically.

Her reply triggered a subtle transformation in his expression, one that did make him look quite intimidating. "Trust me, my dear," he said in a cool tone. "Our nefarious friend amply understood the message I delivered."

Gillian chewed that over for a few moments. "All right, but, by your own admission, you have not spent much time at Fenfield Manor these last several years. How can you be sure that *all* the gangs understand how serious you are about stamping out the trade on your lands?"

"I can't. But Scunthorpe assures me that free-trading activity on manor lands is, for the most part, negligible."

Gillian couldn't help thinking of Teddy's father, who'd been murdered by smugglers. That didn't sound negligible to her. "And you trust Scunthorpe?"

"The man's served me ably for the last five years. The lands are in excellent shape, as are the books. I review them myself, as does my business manager in London."

When she started to argue, he leaned forward and gently interrupted her. "You must trust me, sweetheart. I do know what I'm about."

She blinked up at him, thrown by his affectionate and warm tone. She had to struggle to rally. "Well, it still doesn't add up. It seems like too many coincidences."

"Despite Scunthorpe's assurances, I agree that it makes sense to be cautious. To that end, I directed my business manager to employ a Bow Street runner to look into this matter."

She jerked upright. "You did?"

"I did. If there's anyone who can ferret out information about your stolen jewels, it's a runner. In fact, the man is already in Lincoln. Since most smuggled goods from this part of the coast go there first, it seemed like the appropriate place to start the search. I expect a report from him within the next few days."

She wrinkled her nose at him. "Good Lord. Why didn't you tell me?"

"I didn't want to get your hopes up, only to have them dashed when nothing came of it."

"Believe me, I have never found hope to be a very reliable commodity." Still, she was touched that he'd gone to such trouble. "You employed him after that day we walked to the chapel, didn't you?" she asked in a soft voice.

"Yes. You have a talent for making a man feel guilty. You should employ it more often."

She scoffed. "As if I would ever resort to such shabby

tactics. I would rather take on the task myself then act like a vaporish miss."

"I rather adore that about you. But I must insist that you allow me to handle the problem as I see fit." He reached down and cupped her cheek. "To take care of you, as you deserve."

She stared up at him, trapped in his deep blue gaze. Instinctively, she leaned into his hand, but then she jerked back, horrified by her weakness. "Yes, well," she said, fighting to control her wavering tone. "About that, Your Grace—"

"Charles. Call me Charles."

His deep, seductive tone made her shiver. Gillian swore her brain was turning to sentimental mush.

"You had no trouble calling me Charles last night," he murmured. "Remember?"

She flushed, vividly recalling the moment when she'd come apart in his arms. She was stunned that he would refer to it while sitting here in broad daylight, in his library of all places. Gillian was no prude, but even she had her limits.

Although her behavior last night would probably suggest that those limits were easily breached. Under the circumstances, she supposed she couldn't blame him for launching such a bold flirtation.

"It would hardly be proper for me to address you in so informal a manner," she said, taking refuge in protocol.

He laughed outright at that. "Yes, proper is your middle name."

"That's hardly the point," she said in a lofty tone.

"All right. I concede on that point. In public, call me Leverton. But in private, I want you to call me by my given name." He leaned down, as if he was going to kiss her.

Gillian ducked sideways and slid out of the chair. She retreated a few steps, feeling more in control by putting a little distance between them. Leverton's narrowed gaze signaled his displeasure, but he didn't pursue her. Instead, he lounged on the corner of his desk, looking rather like a large, sleek cat waiting patiently to pounce on a hapless little mouse. Having never been in the position of prey before, she found it extremely disconcerting.

And for some stupid reason, Gillian suddenly became very aware of the state of her dress and coiffure—she, who'd never given a damn about that sort of thing before. Yet now she found herself repressing the urge to smooth her messy curls. If she wasn't careful, she might resort to pinching her cheeks to add color, like some silly schoolgirl.

"Sir, we simply must talk about your conversation with my mother and your sister," she said, trying to sound firm. "There seems to be some sort of misunderstanding about an, er, understanding between us." What was it about the man that tied her tongue in such knots?

"Really? In what way?" he asked politely.

She scowled at him. "You're deliberately trying to irritate me, aren't you?"

"I wouldn't dream of it. You'd probably try to murder me in my sleep." He paused, as if considering. "Although at least I'd then have you in my bed, which would be some compensation for my troubles."

When Gillian started to work up an offended reply, he grinned and held up a hand. "All right, I'll stop teasing. Go ahead and tell me what you're so fussed about."

"Do you really have to ask?" she said, waving her arms. "You had no right to take the decision out of my hands."

"What decision?"

"That I'd agreed to marry you," she said through clenched teeth. Could he truly be that dense? If they did ever marry and have children, she could only hope they'd inherit her brains and not his.

"Sweetheart, I simply indicated to the ladies that I intended to court you. Surely that is entirely appropriate, under the circumstances."

"Then why was your sister going on about our impending betrothal? And why are we even talking about your courting me in the first place?"

"In answer to your first question, my sister is eager for me to marry and settle down, and that eagerness has clearly led her to get a little ahead of herself. As to your second question," he said with an ironic lift of an eyebrow, "I think the answer is obvious."

Gillian propped her hands on her hips. "It's not obvious to me."

Her answer brought him to his feet. She had to resist the impulse to back up—or even flee the room.

"And why is that, Gillian? Are you in the habit of dallying with men simply to amuse yourself?" He didn't raise his voice—he never did—but she could hear the steel behind the soft-spoken words.

"What? Of course not," she exclaimed, outraged. "Not that it's any of your business, I might add."

He studied her for several long seconds, as if she were some sort of puzzle. "I beg your pardon for misinterpreting your answer," he finally said. "Perhaps I was thrown off by your, shall we say, unorthodox response to last night's events."

"Which part?" she asked cautiously. "The smuggling part or the kissing part?"

His laugh sounded more like a groan, and he let his head drop. "What in God's name am I going to do with you?"

Flummoxed, all she could do was shift from one foot to the next. Then the appropriate answer to his no-doubt rhetorical question came to her. *But are you sure that's what you want?*

She squared her shoulders, ignoring the nagging little voice. "You could try to persuade my mother and grandmother to let me return to Sicily."

His head snapped up. "That is out of the question, Gillian. You will remain here in England."

She was startled by his heated response, and even more startled by how relieved his words made her feel. "Well, never mind that for now. I still don't understand why you want to court me. Before last night, you never showed the slightest bit of interest in doing so. In fact, you were training me how to catch a husband. I hardly think you had yourself in mind as a candidate when you embarked on that particular project."

"I was not training you to catch a husband. I was training you to be a proper young Englishwoman."

"The only reason to become a proper Englishwoman is to catch the right sort of husband. They don't call it 'the marriage mart' for nothing, you know."

Leverton shook his head, looking slightly bemused. Gillian had the uncomfortable sense that she was making a fool of herself.

"But I suppose that's hardly the point, is it?" she added.

"Perhaps you could remind me of the original point of this discussion," he said wryly. "I seem to have lost it somewhere."

"Courting me, remember?"

"Ah, yes. How could I forget?" He carefully placed his hands on her shoulders, as if she were potentially dangerous, like an unstable explosive. "Gillian, we engaged in some rather intimate activities last night. Activities that carry a certain set of expectations, at least among respectable people."

"You mean it's now a matter of honor," she said, feeling oddly disappointed. "Since you tampered with me, you now feel duty bound to marry me. But I assure you that's not necessary."

He winced. "Tampered with you? Good Lord. You may find it hard to believe, Gillian, but I do wish to marry you. It's more than a matter of honor. Much more."

She stared up at him, searching for the truth. "You're right; I don't believe it. You couldn't possibly wish to marry me."

His big hands curled around her shoulders. Under that gentle but powerful grip, she felt small and delicate. It was an unaccustomed sensation, to say the least. And it was not an unwelcome one, she was vaguely surprised to note.

"Much to my surprise," he said softly, "I do."

His smile made her heart ache with longing. When she swayed toward him, he came down to meet her. His firm, warm lips brushed across her mouth, barely touching, but promising a sweetness and heat that threatened to melt her into his embrace.

The alarming speed and intensity of her response gave her a good knock to the head.

He's a bloody duke, you nitwit, and a proper one at that. There was simply no way a man like him could truly wish to marry a woman like her. Gillian had learned that lesson years ago, and it had been a painfully instructive one. Leverton was only making an offer because he felt obligated by duty and honor.

She pulled back just as he was about to slip his tongue between her lips, then retreated several steps.

"Good God, now what's wrong?" he growled. "I've all but laid my heart at your feet, and your response is to leap back as if I've grossly insulted your honor."

"Laid your heart at my feet? Hardly. It's *your* sense of honor that is offended, not mine. You believe you have to marry me in order to salvage my reputation and live up to your standards of propriety." She gave a haughty little sniff. "As you know, my reputation is already ruined, so your chivalry is quite unnecessary."

"Of course I want to protect your reputation, and I see nothing wrong in acting with an appropriate degree of honor and respect. But I also happen to like you. Quite a lot." As soon as the words were out of his mouth though, he grimaced. His declaration was so tepid that it simply proved her point.

"Now that's a ringing endorsement. I thank you kindly, Your Grace, but no thank you."

He muttered something quite shocking—even to her— under his breath. Then he took a deep breath and tried again. "Gillian, I have clearly made a hash of this, but I assure you that I do most sincerely wish to marry you."

She eyed him uncertainly. At the moment, he looked anything like a man in love. Annoyed and frustrated was a better description.

"I suspect it's because you're so high in the instep that you've shocked yourself into thinking you have no other choice but to marry me. After all, the Duke of Leverton is not the sort of man to tamper with virginal young ladies. Of course, that is certainly to your credit," she hastily added when she took in his wrathful expression.

"If you employ that unfortunate phrase one more time I will surely do something we both will come to regret," he said through clenched teeth. "Besides, if I were that high in the instep, I wouldn't be proposing marriage to you under any circumstances, and you know it. I'd be setting you up as my mistress."

"Right. This conversation is over." Gillian spun around and marched to the door.

"Come back here this instant," he barked. "We're not finished."

"I'm sorry, I didn't catch that." She swore she could hear him grinding his molars from halfway across the room.

"Gillian Dryden, be very clear on this one fact—we *will* be getting married."

She wrenched the door open, then glared at him over her shoulder. "Your Grace, you will allow me to say that you are the most annoying and stubborn person I have ever met." Then she walked out and slammed the library door behind her.

"That is the blasted pot calling the kettle black," he yelled, his voice filtering through the thick oak.

Gillian ignored a shocked-looking Hewitt, who'd clearly stationed himself to hear the fireworks. But even as she stormed up the stairs to her room, she couldn't hold back a reluctant grin. Perfect Penley's composure was anything but perfect with her, and she was beginning to like that quite a lot.

Chapter Twenty-One

Charles eyed his future wife from across the churchyard, annoyed that she was doing her best to ignore him. There was simply no predicting Gillian. One minute she was shivering with passion in his arms, and the next she seemed to be riven with horror at the notion that they would wed. Most girls would saw off an arm for the privilege of marrying a wealthy duke. Not Gillian. Nothing could ever proceed in the normal manner when it came to her. Then again, perhaps she thought he was a pompous ass. He couldn't entirely blame her.

"Did you hear me, Your Grace?"

The lilting but slightly annoyed voice intruded into his dour thoughts, forcing him to concentrate on the girl standing in front of him. Miss Meadows, a classic English rose, was accomplished, genteel, and very well dowered. In other words, a girl eminently suited by birth and upbringing for life in the *ton*. She would make the perfect sort of wife for a man like him, and Charles had not a shred of doubt that Miss Meadows would leap at the chance to be his duchess.

Unfortunately, he had no interest in being her duke. For some demented reason, he was now fixated on a young hoyden who would surely pitch his well-ordered life into chaos. He'd made a vow long ago to never again let a woman lead him around by the nose, and yet here he was on the verge of such a state.

"Forgive me, Miss Meadows," he said with an apologetic smile. "My wits have gone begging today. I cannot imagine why, given my charming company."

She rewarded him with a flirtatious smile. "Perhaps my new bonnet has dazzled you."

"Ah, yes, that must be it. I believe it's one of the new styles, is it not? Very flattering."

Miss Meadows preened a bit. "How observant, Your Grace. Most men are too dull to notice something like that, much less remark on it."

"Thank you," he said dryly. He could only be thankful that Gillian happened to be on the other side of the small church-yard. If she'd heard that last ridiculous exchange, she'd probably have doubled over with laughter. Or, more likely, rolled her eyes, not making the slightest effort to hide her disdain for foolish small talk.

As if echoing his thoughts, Miss Meadows's gaze wandered across the yard to fasten on Gillian, chatting with two of the guests from the garden party at Fenfield. Miss Farrow and Mr. Hurdly had just become engaged, and Gillian wished to congratulate them. The three of them stood under the towering oak that shaded the old village church, laughing and chattering like the best of friends.

He couldn't help feeling a bit irked. The last few days had been trying, with Gillian doing her best to keep him at arm's length and refusing to acknowledge that they were all but engaged. To see her treating two people she barely knew more warmly was annoying, to say the least.

"Miss Dryden seems to be getting along very well with Margaret and David," Miss Meadows remarked. "I suppose she wanted to offer them congratulations on their betrothal."

Charles could hear the disapproval in her voice. "Is there any reason why she should not?"

His companion's big blue eyes went even bigger in response to his sharp tone, and she hastened to correct herself. "Of course not, sir. If you lend Miss Dryden your countenance, then that must be enough to satisfy even the most punctilious. And it is indeed kind of you to overlook her unfortunate background. It is the height of tolerance and Christian charity."

"I rather imagine she tolerates me," he said, unable to hold back a rueful smile.

A faint wrinkle marked Miss Meadows's pale brow, daring to mar its porcelain perfection. "Surely that cannot be so. You do Miss Dryden a great honor by sponsoring her in so generous a manner. She should be nothing but exceedingly grateful to you."

"I doubt she would agree with you. Now, if you will excuse me, Miss Meadows, I must return to my party."

Giving her a brief nod, he turned on his heel and headed across the lawn. Charles knew he should be sorry for giving the girl so direct a cut, but he wasn't. She was a prig, although the fact that he thought so struck him as ironic. Still, his curt behavior was something of a surprise to him. Gillian's influence, it would appear, was taking a toll on his manners. It would be a miracle if he had any left by the time she was through turning his world inside out.

His sister, who'd been chatting with the contessa and a small gaggle of local matrons, detached herself and intercepted him before he reached his target. Charles breathed out an exasperated sigh. He was still annoyed with Elizabeth for putting such a scare into Gillian before he'd had a chance to speak with the girl about the change in their relationship.

His sister was downright enthusiastic at the idea that he and Gillian marry. That didn't surprise him, since Elizabeth had always been the renegade in the family, and she had a great deal of sympathy for Gillian. Her support would come in handy when Charles introduced his future fiancée to his mother and older sister. It would be helpful to have the entire family on his side to weather the social storm that would inevitably ensue once he announced his betrothal. He had no doubt they could weather it, but he wanted to make things as easy as possible on Gillian and her family.

For now, though, he wished that his sister were slightly less enthusiastic, since any talk of wedding clothes, wedding breakfasts, or wedding trips invariably drove Gillian to make a dash for the nearest exit.

"Charles, a moment if you please," his sister said, darting in front of him. She gave him a smile that he could only describe as fiendish.

"Elizabeth, you are not making life easy for me."

"I know, darling," she replied. "But there is a method to my madness. I'm laying down covering fire. If I prattle on about wedding plans, it draws Gillian's fire away from you."

"That makes absolutely no sense," he said. "Which doesn't surprise me, coming from you."

"It makes perfect sense, Charles Valentine Penley," she said, crossing her arms in a huff. "Gillian needs to get gradually used to the idea of marrying you, and it's much less threatening if I talk about it than if you do."

"That is a ridiculous scheme. Besides, it's not working."

"Well, I don't see you coming up with anything better. You're barely talking to her. Really, Charles, your idea of a proper courtship is sadly lacking."

"I'd like to know how the devil I'm supposed to court my future intended when I'm forbidden from talking about anything to do with courtship," he said. "Not to mention the fact that I can barely get near the blasted girl."

Shortly after their first argument, Gillian had made him promise to refrain from indicating his intentions to anyone outside their immediate family. In return, she had reluctantly agreed to allow him to begin courting her. How he was supposed to do that without signaling his intentions to the outside world was a mystery he had yet to solve.

"Now, isn't that a helpful attitude?" his sister said with heavy sarcasm. "Really, Charles, most men are idiots when it comes to this sort of thing, but I had higher hopes for you. After all, your manners are *so* distinguished." Her tone made it abundantly clear what she truly thought of his manners.

He eyed her with obvious disapproval, which made her burst into laughter.

"Dearest, may I give you a little advice?" she asked.

"I suppose it wouldn't hurt. I seem to need all the help I can get."

"Be gentle with her, Charles," Elizabeth said. "Gillian is feeling very skittish about the whole thing."

"I can see that. I just can't understand why." After all, Gillian obviously liked him rather a lot, if that torrid encounter in the sand dunes had been any indication. Not that he could share that information with his sister.

"Because she's frightened, and unsure of your motivations."

He scoffed. "What nonsense. Gillian isn't frightened of anything."

As if to prove his point, Gillian's laugh rang out as she talked with her new friends. She had a lovely, confident laugh that never failed to lift his spirits. No silly titters or foolish giggles for his Gillian. When something amused or pleased her, she let everyone know it.

He studied her for a few moments. She was obviously telling Miss Farrow and Mr. Hurdly some outrageous story, since they were both in stitches. She acted it out with expansive gestures, clearly enjoying herself and not caring one whit if she was, by society's standards, making a spectacle of herself. Charles found that he didn't care, either. It was a rather shocking discovery, since it was up to him to teach her to avoid that sort of brash display.

"I know," Elizabeth said. "She's a confident, intelligent girl who truly doesn't care what others think of her."

"On that we can agree," he said in a wry tone.

"But she cares what *you* think, dear brother. Very much so. And she certainly knows how high in the instep you are."

"I have it on good opinion that I am, in fact, the soul of tolerance and Christian charity."

His sister let out an unladylike snort. "Has Miss Meadows been making up to you again? I hope you didn't believe her errant nonsense."

Charles couldn't help laughing. "Thank God I have you to pull me down a peg, Lizzie. Or ten."

"You can thank me by realizing that Gillian is more than halfway in love with you."

He practically choked mid-laugh.

"As such," his sister continued, "she's very nervous—and wary of you."

Charles felt like he'd been knocked in the head. "And why is that?"

"Because she cannot believe that a man of your standing, manners, and wealth would have any wish to marry her, especially since your aversion to scandal is so well-known."

"But I assured her that I do genuinely wish to marry her," he protested.

Elizabeth breathed out a dramatic sigh. "You're a proud man, Charles, and a duke. Gillian expects you to marry an equally proud woman of impeccable breeding—someone the opposite of her. Despite your reassurance, she seems to think you're only marrying her out of some exaggerated sense of duty."

He did have an obligation to Gillian, particularly in light of recent events—which he had no intention of discussing with his sister.

As if she'd read his mind, Elizabeth's mouth quirked up in a knowing smile. "I wonder what could prompt her to think that way. Any ideas, dear brother?"

"I haven't a clue," he said in a blighting tone. "And now that you've ripped my character to shreds, how do you suggest I proceed?"

She laughed. "You are the best of brothers, Charles. Do you know that?"

"Of course I do. After all, I've refrained all these years from murdering you."

"How kind. As I said, you need to be gentle with her. More important, you need to show her that you are, in fact, proud to stand with her before the world."

"I would like nothing better, but she's all but forbidden me to do that."

"That is fear holding her back, and it's best ignored at this stage of the game," his sister advised. "In fact, why don't you start by walking her back to the manor. Her mother and I will take the carriage home."

"That is an excellent idea." Not only would that give him the chance to get Gillian all to himself, it would send a very clear signal to the locals, who could be counted on to diligently spread the appropriate sort of gossip.

"I'm full of excellent ideas, if you would only listen now and again. Now, have at it," she said, shooing him away.

When Charles crossed the lawn to join Gillian, she greeted him with a courteous but cautious manner. He did his best to put her at ease by focusing his attention on the happy couple, congratulating them and making inquiries about their plans for the future.

"Well, we must be off," Miss Farrow finally said with a glance out to the lane. "My parents are waiting for us."

"I do hope you will come to our wedding breakfast, Miss Dryden," Hurdly said. He gave Charles a boyishly eager smile. "And you too, Your Grace. It would be great guns if you could. Our relatives would all be thrilled, I assure you."

"Yes. That would be lovely," Miss Farrow enthused.

"Thank you, I would like that very much," Gillian said with shy pleasure. "That is . . ." She cast Charles an uncertain glance.

"If we are still in residence at Fenfield, we would be honored to attend," he said.

With another smile and a quick exchange of good-byes, Miss Farrow dragged her fiancé off to join her family.

"Are you ready to return home?" Charles asked, offering Gillian his arm.

She moved to take it, then froze. "Where is the landau?"

"Elizabeth and your mother took it back to the manor. I thought you might like to walk instead, seeing that we actually have a sunny day, for once."

She eyed him with a skeptical expression. "Walk all the way back to Fenfield, just the two of us?"

"It's only a few miles, Gillian. I wouldn't have thought you would be taxed by so easy a stroll."

"Don't be a nodnock." She gave him a little jab in the ribs. "It's you I'm worried about."

"Whatever for?"

"People will make assumptions. About us." As if to underscore the point, she waved a finger between them.

"I hope they do," he said firmly.

She blinked, then glanced over at the vicar. He was standing on the church steps engrossed in conversation with the local squire and his wife. Charles couldn't help noticing that the squire's lady seemed more interested in eavesdropping on Charles's conversation with Gillian.

"And it truly doesn't bother you?" Gillian sounded so incredulous that he couldn't help feeling a tad annoyed. Did she really believe he would renege on his promise to her? The wary expression in her eyes said that she did. His irritation quickly faded, replaced by the urge to pull her into his arms.

Gillian obviously didn't think she was good enough for a respectable man, much less a duke. And that infuriated him. Like anyone, she had her faults, but she had more character and honor than most of the *ton,* including those with the most sterling of reputations. Charles now knew that she loved deeply, with a fierce loyalty that made a mockery of social niceties and empty courtesies. She was intelligent, brave, and possessed of a passion that could enthrall a man for a lifetime. When compared to all that, neither her impetuous nature nor her unfortunate family history mattered very much.

He placed a hand on her shoulder, letting a thumb stroke along her collarbone. Her dark eyes went wide with surprise. "No," he said, "I truly don't care what anyone thinks about us."

She stared for a few seconds before scrunching up her nose at him. "It's your funeral," she said, affecting a casual tone.

Despite her offhanded response, she looked shyly pleased. Perhaps Elizabeth was correct after all; perhaps Gillian was falling in love with him. It would certainly make life easier. All he then had to do was convince her that his intentions were true and plan from there. If all went well, by this time next week they could be announcing the first set of banns in this very church. It made sense that they marry quietly, before they returned to London. That would certainly be preferable to the sort of extravagant display his mother and sisters would want at Leverton House in London or at the old family pile in Wiltshire.

Charles wanted to spare Gillian the fuss and gossip that would surely attend a more public celebration. Besides, a small, quiet affair meant the two of them could spend more time together, a prospect that grew more appealing to him with every passing day.

Satisfied that he'd got it all sorted, he tucked Gillian's hand through his arm and led her from the churchyard. A quick glance confirmed that the squire's wife was avidly watching them. Soon, the entire village and half the county would realize that the Duke of Leverton was formally courting Miss Gillian Dryden in an exceedingly staid and proper fashion.

Smiling at the few locals who'd lingered to chat in the churchyard, he led Gillian out to the lane. They set out at a brisk pace. Even though the sun was shining, a cool wind blew off the Channel. At this rate, summer would be over before spring had a chance to fully establish itself, which probably meant a poor season for crops. Charles strongly suspected he would have to take steps to alleviate the impact of a bad harvest on his tenants, and he made a mental note to discuss the issue with Scunthorpe.

When Gillian drew her hand away, he realized he'd been letting his mind wander. Elizabeth was right—he was making a sad hash of things, and he needed to do better.

He took her tightly gloved hand and once more placed it on his arm. She glanced up at him, and the look in her eyes suggested she'd been a thousand miles away too. Charles was tempted to laugh at how inept they both were when it came to flirtation and courtship.

"You're looking most fetching today, Gillian," he said. "My compliments on your excellent taste."

In fact, she was positively lovely in her burgundy-red walking gown, with its trim-fitting bodice and gently flared skirts. Her simple straw bonnet framed her face, emphasizing her high cheekbones and amber-colored eyes. He'd come to like her narrow, straight brows very much, because they gave her a serious, almost scholarly aspect, comically at odds with her high-spirited nature. Gillian was a challenge and a mystery wrapped up in a vibrant, beautiful package. Charles found himself looking forward to the day when he could fully begin to solve that mystery, and claim Gillian as his own.

Her brows snapped together in a scowl. "Never mind that nonsense. I'm not Miss Meadows. You don't have to pay me silly compliments or act like a man-milliner, even if you are supposed to be courting me."

Man-milliner? The women in his family were certainly doing a bang-up job of deflating any notions of consequence on his part. Still, he thought he detected a jealous note in her voice, which was encouraging.

"I *am* courting you," he said. "I would also like to note that I was not flirting with Miss Meadows."

"Really? That's certainly how it appeared. If I didn't know better, sir, I would think you are indeed a confirmed flirt."

"You do know me better," he said, pulling her a little closer. Still, he couldn't resist testing the waters a bit. "Besides, I can't help it if women find me moderately attractive."

She let out a hoot. "Attractive? That's a laugh. Women swarm you like flies on a honeypot, and you know it."

"Thank you for placing that remarkably unappealing image in my mind."

"Although I suppose your title and your wealth are probably more of an incentive," she added. "A handsome face and an athletic form are all very well, but most girls on the marriage mart seem willing to forgo those qualities for a title and money." She cast him a critical look. "You could be as ugly as Hades, and I'd wager you'd still get legions of girls hanging all over you."

"Gillian, I do believe you will get along exceedingly well with my mother and my sisters. They, too, like to puncture any sense of self-importance I might be foolish enough to harbor."

She let out a little snicker. A moment later, however, she went back to looking troubled.

He drew her to a halt in the middle of the quiet country

lane, taking both her hands between his. Aside from the birds darting amongst the hedgerows, they were alone. "Sweetheart, I wish you would tell me what worries you," he said in a quiet voice.

Something vulnerable flashed through her gaze, tugging hard on his heart. She looked down at their joined hands, frowning as if their very existence puzzled her.

"You're not afraid to tell me, are you?" he asked. "You have no need to be."

Gillian glanced up. "Don't be silly. You know I'm not afraid of anything." Then she paused, grimacing. "That's not quite true. I'm afraid I'm never going to see home again."

"Ah, Sicily."

"I cannot pretend I don't miss it. I still long to be there again."

"Then you shall, after we're married. We can go on a tour of the Continent."

She let out an exasperated sigh and tried to tug her hands away. He let go of one but held on to the other as he started to walk. She gave another halfhearted tug, but then fell into step beside him, with her hand tucked securely into his. For a minute or so they strolled in silence. Charles let the contentment of the moment settle over him, half amazed at how much he could enjoy so simple a pleasure as walking down a country lane with a pretty girl by his side.

At least when that pretty girl was Gillian.

Still, he could practically feel her seething with questions and worries. "My dear girl, if you are harboring any doubts about my intentions, please share them with me," he finally said. "All of them."

"It's just that I'm afraid I'll never be what you want me to be," she burst out. "No matter how many dancing masters you hire or how many etiquette lessons you give me."

"I thought you weren't afraid of anything?" he teased.

She shot him an irate glare. "I wish you wouldn't be so annoying. It quite makes me want to box your ears."

"Since that is a rather terrifying prospect, I will endeavor to answer your question in a serious fashion."

"That would be helpful, since the only reason I can think of for your wanting to marry me doesn't reflect very well on either of us. It's not necessary for you to salvage my honor, you know."

"Your honor is well worth protecting, I assure you." He cut off her protest. "But that's not the only reason, or even the primary reason."

"I don't follow," she said in a cautious tone. "What other reason could there be?"

"Gillian, do you truly think I would have touched you if I hadn't already made a decision to marry you? What kind of cad do you take me for?"

Her mouth opened, shut, then opened again. Clearly, that notion hadn't even occurred to her. She peered up at him, apparently perplexed. "I suppose I want to believe that, but . . ."

"But you don't?"

Her simple shrug was sufficient response.

Since neither his kindness nor his display of affection was having any impact, it was time to take another tack. "Gillian, you're aware of the kind of man I'm reputed to be."

"Of course. You're a high stickler with an impeccable reputation."

He couldn't help wincing. She made him sound priggish, at best. "I didn't always have such a staid reputation. Not when I was young."

She smiled at that. "Kicked over the traces, did you? I wish I could have seen that."

"By your standards, I was probably a dullard. After all, I was the only son of the highest of sticklers and heir to a dukedom. I was made aware from an early age what I owed the title and my family name. Scandal of any kind was anathema to my father."

"He sounds almost as bad as my grandfather," she said, giving his hand a sympathetic squeeze.

"They were friends and shared a similar world view."

She scrunched up her nose. "How unfortunate for us then. Did you ever stand up to him?"

"Just once—when I asked Lady Letitia to marry me."

"She is very dashing, I'll admit, but she comes from a very respectable family, does she not? You could hardly have known at the time that she would behave so badly toward you."

He nodded. "Letitia's family is distinguished, and her mother was close to mine. Her dowry was good, and she was considered a fine catch on the marriage mart. On the surface, it seemed like a good match."

"So why didn't your father approve of her?"

"He considered her *fast,* and much too unreliable to be the Duchess of Leverton. But while her behavior could occasionally veer toward the outrageous, most people saw her as I did—as a vivacious, beautiful, and accomplished young woman with a great deal of charm."

"Well, she is certainly that."

"You're being very kind," he said.

"Really, I'm just trying to be fair. After all, I do know what it's like to be on the receiving end of scurrilous gossip."

"Yes, but in your case, it's completely unwarranted."

She flinched. He glanced down, surprised to see her mouth pursed tight, as if in pain. "Is this conversation distressing you? Should I stop?"

Gillian flashed him a bright, rather artificial smile. "Not in the slightest. Please continue, sir. I'm all ears."

"Very well. Despite my father's reservations, I was determined to marry Letitia. For once, I did not capitulate to his demands. Since I had always been a very biddable child, he couldn't understand my defiance. Needless to say, he was furious with me."

"You must have loved her very much," Gillian said in a soft voice.

"I thought so at the time, but I realize now that it was simply youthful infatuation. There were dozens of callow youths who were head over heels for Letitia. You could have lined us up and picked us off with buckshot."

"But she chose you."

"As you pointed out, I am a duke."

She gave him an enchanting half smile. "No false modesty, if you please. What happened next?"

"I eventually wore my father down, which surprised both of us. My mother, of course, took my side, as did my older sister."

"Not Lady Filby?"

"No. She never liked Letitia. Sadly, I considered Elizabeth little more than a chit of a girl at the time, whose opinion mattered little."

"I hope you learned your lesson," she said. "I like your sister very much."

"I have learned my lesson. Later, I came to realize that Elizabeth was and is an excellent judge of character. She approves of you, by the way, very much."

Gillian blushed, which Charles also found enchanting. "That's nice of her. So, you wore your father down . . ."

"Yes. He was getting older and was not in the best of health. Now I think he was too sick to carry on fighting with me." Charles had little doubt that the conflict between them had injured his father's already weak heart.

"That's unfortunate," she said. "But he must have been pleased when you broke things off with her."

"He would have been, but for the fact that her lover decided to blackmail my family when I tried to break things off."

She choked out a gasp. "You must be joking. Stratton tried to blackmail you?"

"Stratton *did* blackmail me and my father," Charles said in a grim voice.

"But you didn't do anything wrong," she said, sounding bewildered. "They did."

"Stratton threatened to embellish the details—which were bad enough—and kick up a huge scandal. My father couldn't bear the notion of sordid gossip attached to our name. And Letitia's parents were devastated as well. They begged us not to disgrace her. It was a bloody complicated mess, and as ugly as you can imagine."

Gillian's eyes flashed sparks of fury. "Now I wish I'd punched Stratton instead of that other fellow. I take it your father paid up?"

"He did."

She squeezed his hand. "I'm so, so sorry, Charles, but it wasn't your fault. You mustn't ever think it was. They took advantage of you, the both of them."

His throat went tight, and he took a few seconds before replying. "Thank you. I wish my father had felt the same."

"He blamed you?"

Charles sighed, letting his gaze wander around the bucolic country scene. But he didn't really see it, because all he saw was his past. "Yes, as I blame myself. After all, I killed him."

Chapter Twenty-Two

Gillian plastered her ear to her bedroom door. There was no creak of a floorboard, no murmur of a maid or footman out in the hall attending to late-night duties. Everyone in the household was abed—except its master, she hoped. Charles liked to spend time in the library before retiring, often coming up last. She'd heard his quiet but firm tread almost every night as he passed by her room on the way to the ducal apartments. A few times, those footsteps had paused outside her door.

And more than a few times, she'd been tempted to fling open the door and yank him into her room. That illustrated how weak she'd become when it came to His Grace, the Duke of Leverton.

Gillian looked over her shoulder and eyed one of the windows. She'd thought about opening the casement and climbing down the wall, just to keep in practice. But the brick was in excellent repair, which would mean fewer toe holds, and the ivy twining up the side of the manor house might not be strong enough to hold her weight. The last thing she wished to do was land with a thump on the terrace just outside the library. So precipitous an appearance would hardly put Leverton in good temper.

She opened the door and slipped into the darkened corridor. Since her eyesight was excellent, she had no trouble making her way to the top of the stairs without mishap. A lamp burned on the table in the entrance hall below, and a faint light seeped out from under the library door. She hurried down the stairs and across the hall, but hesitated outside the door. It took her some moments—and a bracing mental lecture—to work up the courage to face the unpleasant task ahead. Finally, she forced herself to open the door and step inside.

Leverton sat at his desk, his head bent over a ledger. He'd taken off his coat and rolled up his sleeves, exposing his muscled forearms. The gentle glow from the lamp at his elbow and the flickering blaze from the fire in the grate sparked gold in his tawny-colored hair and cast shadows under his high cheekbones. He was so handsome it almost hurt to look at him, and Gillian had to resist the urge to rub a sore spot right over her heart.

She closed the door with a decided click. Charles glanced up with a slight frown. He stared blankly for a second, then his expression lit up with a smile that seemed reserved just for her. It held equal parts amusement and desire, and it never failed to bring heat rushing to her cheeks.

He rose and came to meet her. "Gillian, I thought you were abed some time ago."

She dredged up a smile. "I, ah, couldn't sleep, so I thought I'd see if you were still awake."

He tipped her chin up and pressed a soft kiss to her mouth. Gillian had to stifle a moan and the overwhelming urge to lean into him.

"I hope I'm not interrupting you," she said, mentally cursing how breathless she sounded when he released her.

"I'm happy for the interruption." He led her to the low

chaise in front of the fireplace. "I've just been going over the estate ledgers."

She caught a faint note of irritation in his voice. "I hope nothing is wrong."

"Not really. Scunthorpe is an extremely competent manager. That doesn't mean, however, that I agree with all the decisions he's made over the last five years." He ruffled a hand through his hair.

She'd never seen him so casually attired, or with his hair so disordered. He'd even taken off his cravat, exposing the strong muscles of his throat. Leverton could never be anything less than handsome, but his masculine perfection, with never a hair out of place, could be somewhat intimidating. Now rumpled and in his shirtsleeves, he was so appealing that it took her breath away. Even that night on the beach, when she'd come apart in his arms, not even a button on his jacket had been disturbed. Seeing him like this . . . well, Gillian couldn't help wishing to see more, much more.

But she now knew that could never happen.

"I'm forgetting my manners," he said, smiling down at her. "Would you like something to drink? Perhaps a sherry or a ratafia?"

She wrinkled her nose. "Must I?"

He laughed, and the husky sound of it warmed her like summer sunshine. "Of course not. What would you like?"

"Brandy would be nice. Port would be even better."

When he lifted a brow, Gillian couldn't help feeling a tad defensive. "If one is going to drink, one might as well do it properly and not waste it on swill like ratafia."

"That is a sensible though rather shocking philosophy for a young lady."

"I do strive to be sensible at all times, as you know."

He let out a snort, then went off to fetch her a drink from the sideboard between two bookshelves.

"Did you have something specific you wished to talk about?" he asked, glancing over his shoulder. "Or were you simply feeling restless? If it's the latter, I have an excellent remedy."

His wicked grin as he came back told Gillian exactly what he had in mind. And her body's reaction told her that it thoroughly agreed with his suggestion. But there was no point in torturing herself.

"I do wish to speak with you about our current situation, Your Grace," she said. "It's a matter of some urgency."

He set the glasses on a small table, then sat next to her on the chaise, his big body crowding her against the plump cushions. She edged away from him, trying not to make it too obvious.

Predictably, he noticed. Just as predictably, he didn't look happy about it. "Gillian, I thought we agreed we would not address each other formally in private."

She gave him a weak smile. "Sorry. It's a difficult habit to break."

"I have no doubt you will succeed with practice. Now, why don't you tell me what's bothering you?"

"It's what we talked about today. Your betrothal to Lady Letitia."

"I thought we had exhausted that particular topic."

They'd spent the rest of their walk home from church discussing that unfortunate period of his life. Gillian had been mystified and then appalled that Charles had blamed himself for his father's poor health and subsequent death from apoplexy. She'd told him that he was an idiot to think that way, but nothing she'd said had been enough to truly convince him.

"The part about your not being responsible for your father's death?" she asked. "No, I don't think we did reach a satisfactory conclusion on that matter."

"But I am responsible. If I'd listened to my father about Letitia, he might still be alive today."

"Not according to your sister. She said your father's heart had been bad for some years."

"Yes, and my stupidity and stubbornness contributed to that," he said in a grim tone. "He recognized Letitia for what she was. I, however, refused to see it."

"You were young and in love."

"I was an idiot." He stared into the fire, his hands fisted on his thighs.

She forced one of his hands open, wriggling her fingers between his. "Young men generally are, as are young ladies on occasion. But you told me that your mother and older sister approved of Lady Letitia, as did most of your friends and family."

"Yes, only Father and Elizabeth raised the alarm—and Lendale. He saw through Letitia and Stratton from the beginning and tried to warn me about them, but I wouldn't listen."

She smiled. "I knew there was a reason I liked him so much."

He finally looked at her, his gaze narrowed. "Not too much, I hope."

"Please. He *is* only a marquess."

Charles's lips curved up in a reluctant smile. "You are a devil, Miss Gillian Dryden."

"So I've been told. Now, may I make another point?"

"Can I stop you?"

"Don't even try," she said with an answering smile. "Charles, you must know that you are no more responsible for your father's death than I am responsible for the unfortunate circumstances of my birth. It is never wrong to love someone. Ever. If the person takes advantage of that, then the fault lies with him or her."

He played with her fingers as he ruminated over her words. "So young, and yet so wise in matters of the heart. How is that possible?"

"Because it happened to me," she said quietly.

He still fiddled with her hand, as if only half listening. "What do you mean?"

She forced herself to speak calmly. "I mean that I cannot marry you, precisely because I do know what you're talking about. I was betrayed in much the same way as you were."

He sat up straight and turned to face her directly. "What are you talking about?"

She tried to extract her hand from his grip, but he refused to let go. She decided it would be undignified to tussle with him. "When you asked me to marry you, I believed it was because you felt duty bound to do so. Because of what happened on the beach the other night."

"Only in part, which was why I told you about Letitia. Because of that incident, I'm a cautious man, and I would never inadvertently stumble into marriage. From the moment I put my hands on you, my decision was made, and deliberately so."

When hope flared in her heart, she squashed it down. "And that still defies logic. I'm reckless to a fault, and I have a terrible reputation. I'm like a dog with a long, muddy tail, mucking up your pristine floors."

His gaze sparked with quick laughter. "You are decidedly not like Letitia—or a muddy dog."

"Perhaps not, but you need a wife whose character is beyond reproach." She finally wriggled her hand away and stood, putting some distance between them.

"Gillian, in every important way, your character is above reproach," Charles said.

He certainly wasn't making it easy on her. "Are you sure about that?" she hedged, foolishly delaying the inevitable.

"Do you truly need me to reassure you? Very well, then. You must realize that I have made a study of you these last several weeks, and I know you to be a woman of solid character and genuine moral fiber. You have all the qualities a man of sense would seek in a wife."

"Good Lord," she said, startled. "How dreadfully boring. That's not a very compelling recipe for wedded bliss, if you ask me." Then she remembered she was supposed to be rejecting him. "Not that it really matters."

"You did ask, but I suppose I could do better."

"I should think so. Whoever thought I'd be the one to teach *you* proper mating behavior?"

He shook his head as he came to his feet. "My dear girl, the things you say. Then let me try to correct my oafish ways."

He pounced on her, capturing the hands she had clenched against her stomach. He gently pried them apart, first kissing one palm, then the other. The backs of her knees went shivery and weak.

"Gillian Dryden, you are a beautiful, sweet girl. Despite your best efforts to convince me otherwise, you are also utterly charming. More important, you are exceedingly generous of spirit and very loyal, both rare qualities in my estimation."

"I am truly all that?" she whispered, gazing up at him. She knew she must look like a lovestruck fool.

"All that and more. And as for your heart, whatever you might think—and whatever others might think—it is both innocent and true. Given all that, why wouldn't I wish to marry you?"

She could see that he believed everything he said, something she found both wonderful and awful. "But, Charles, that's just it," she said miserably. "I'm not innocent."

He froze for several agonizing moments. "Would you care to explain what you mean by that?" he finally said.

Did she truly have to spell it out for him? "What we did on the beach the other night . . . It wasn't the first time . . ." Her voice died as her nerve reached its breaking point. She swore his eyes had just transformed into shards of blue ice.

"You've been tampered with, to use your unfortunate turn of phrase?"

She nodded, feeling both humiliated and angry. This was exactly why she had no wish to marry and why she avoided men. Women always had to explain themselves to men. It was invariably a tedious and embarrassing exercise, and tonight was certainly no exception.

Except that she did want to marry Leverton.

She repressed the instinct to slink out of the room. Though she was ashamed of that ugly episode in her past, it hadn't entirely been her fault. And she'd be damned if she backed down in front of any man, even Leverton. The past was the past, and she couldn't change it. All she could do was move forward and try not to make the same mistake. Not be dragooned into marriage with a man who would surely come to despise her.

As she stared defiantly back at him, a subtle change came over his features. He still looked disturbed, but his frown now seemed more one of reflection than anger. "Gillian, how old were you when this happened?"

She blinked. "Does it matter?"

"Yes."

There was no reason not to tell him. Perhaps it might convince him that she was past redemption and therefore entirely unsuitable. "I was sixteen."

"Was it shortly after your stepfather's death?"

"Yes, about six weeks later. It . . . it didn't last very long, if that's what you're asking." Despite her determination not to back down, she couldn't hold back a flush of shame. Her family had still been in mourning—she'd still been in mourning—but it hadn't stopped her from acting like a fool.

He closed his eyes and muttered a curse. No doubt he now understood how unsuitable she was to be any respectable man's wife, much less his. If she could persuade him to convince her mother and grandmother that such was the case, she might finally be allowed to return to Sicily. That, of course, made her very happy—or at least it would once she got over the sensation that she'd just ripped her throbbing heart from her chest and flung it at his feet.

"Well, I suppose that's it," she said, desperate now to escape to her room. She had an awful sense that she just might burst into tears at any moment. "I'll explain things to Mamma, of course. I promise that she won't give you any trouble about ending our engagement. After all, it was never really official."

His eyes popped open, then narrowed on her face. A chill slithered down her spine.

"Trust me, sweet, we're barely getting started," he growled.

He wrapped a hand around her wrist and dragged her back to the chaise. When he scooped her up in his arms and plopped her back down on the cushions, she was too stunned to object.

"Do not move," he ordered, pointing a finger at her.

She finally found her voice. "There is no need to manhandle me. All you had to do was ask me to resume my seat."

His only reply was a derisive snort as he retrieved their glasses from the side table. Handing her one, he tossed his own back, as if fortifying himself. Then he sat next to her, once more crowding her against the cushions.

Shrugging, Gillian followed suit with her drink and then gave him the empty glass, refusing to even acknowledge the burn of the alcohol as it seared its way down to her stomach.

He shook his head. "You will be the death of me, do you know that?"

"I know I'm a trial," she said a trifle hoarsely.

"What you are is a menace."

She scowled. "There is no need—" He interrupted her protest by reaching over and dragging her onto his lap. She let out a little yelp and clutched at his shoulders. "What are you doing?"

"Getting comfortable."

"I don't think this is a very good idea, Leverton."

"I disagree." He settled her snugly against him. Then he tipped her chin up and gave her a brief kiss. "Now, I want you to tell me exactly what happened between you and this scoundrel who betrayed you. A cad whom I would like to murder, by the way."

"You'll have to get in line after me. And you've gone mad if you think I'm going to discuss *that* with you in any detail."

"You will, but first things first. What was his name?"

The duke now seemed relatively calm. In fact, he was back to being Perfect Penley, at least in his manner—in control and expecting everything and everyone around him to fall into line.

Gillian let out an aggrieved sigh, knowing she might as well get it over with. At least she had the compensation of sitting on his lap for the duration. "His name was Pietro," she said, trying to sound grumpy instead of happy to be snuggling against him. "He was the younger son of a Sicilian aristocrat."

"How old was he then?"

"Twenty."

Charles made a disgusted noise. "Old enough to know better."

"So was I," she said, trying to be fair.

"Had you known him for a long time?" Leverton asked.

"No, not long at all, actually," she said, wriggling a bit to get comfortable.

He let out a little hiss, then picked her up and resettled her. He was ridiculously strong. Leverton generally preferred to use his brains rather than his brawn, but there was no doubt he was a prime physical specimen.

And he's mine, her foolish brain whispered.

"How did you meet him?" His tone was gentle.

"It was a few weeks after my stepfather's murder. We'd

just moved back to the Marbury villa in Palermo. We'd been living on Step-papa's estates in the country, but his heir wished to take possession of them."

Charles moved one hand to rest low on her spine. She couldn't help leaning into it.

"Did he force you to leave?"

"No, he invited us to stay, but Mamma didn't feel comfortable about it. I didn't want to leave, of course. It was my home." She grimaced, remembering the fights she'd had with her family over that. "But Grandmother was adamant. She told me later that she didn't like the way the count looked at me. Like he somehow had a right to me, as if I were like the rest of the property."

"That's bloody awful," Charles said in a grim tone.

She hated the idea that he might pity her. "My grandmother was overreacting, which is ironic, considering what happened next."

Piece by piece, he gently drew the story out of her. He didn't push her, but it was clear that he wouldn't rest until he knew the entire history of that sad and ultimately sordid affair. Pietro's mother was a cousin of Gillian's stepfather, and a good friend to the family. As such, she and her husband had provided a great deal of comfort and support in the aftermath of the murder.

"Mamma was beside herself, of course," Gillian said. "She took to her bed, almost insensible with grief. That left my grandparents to deal with everything, including fighting with the authorities to bring the murderers to justice."

"Leaving you mostly on your own, I expect," he said.

She nodded. "I was very sad too, of course, and I hated living in Palermo. My grandfather forbade me to go out, even to take rides in the countryside. I thought I would go mad."

"And that's when you met Pietro?"

"Yes. We were thrown together quite a lot, since his

mother spent so much time with Mamma. He was . . . kind to me when I felt so terribly alone."

"You mean he took advantage of you," Charles said in a low, gritty tone.

Gillian grimaced, hating to even think of those dark days. "He did, but I let him. I mistook his kind manner for love, I'm sorry to say."

He tipped her chin up. She gazed into his intent blue eyes.

"It was anything but kind, Gillian," he said. "And you were little more than a child, one who was grieving and vulnerable. The bounder should have been horsewhipped and then shot, as far as I'm concerned. Where the hell was your grandfather while this was occurring? He should have protected you."

"I did my best to stay out of Grandfather's way. I had a knack for annoying him."

He cuddled her even closer. "I'm deeply sorry for that. You deserved better."

"Thank you," she whispered.

"How long did the affair last?"

"Just a few weeks. Pietro quickly tired of me, especially after I told him that I loved him. I was so silly. I truly believed he would marry me." She still remembered every detail of that awful day. How he'd stared at her in genuine shock before bursting into laughter. "He told me that men like him didn't marry a bastard or the daughter of a whore," she added. *Puttana.* He'd tossed out that awful word so casually, with a wry smile that had suggested she should accept his judgment without a fuss.

Charles's voice sounded more like a growl. "If we ever visit Sicily, I will hunt this man down and kill him," he said. "Or beat him within an inch of his life."

"No need. He received his comeuppance."

He leaned back a bit to look at her. "What did you do?"

"I threw a vase at him, then chased him out to the stables. Somewhere along the way I acquired a horsewhip. Unfortunately, I didn't really have the opportunity to do much with it because Stefano pulled me off him."

Charles let out a strangled laugh. "Holy hell. Remind me never to cross you."

"I did it mostly because he insulted my mother," she said. "It was my own fault that I let him take such thorough advantage of me. I had only myself to blame."

"As you said to me only a few minutes ago, you were not to blame." His tone was firm and unequivocal.

"But—"

He pressed a finger to her lips. "I will not debate this with you. I have no doubt you were impetuous, but he was at fault, as was your family for not taking better care of you. Are we clear about that?"

"Yes, Your Grace," she said in a meek voice.

"You mock me at your peril, Miss Dryden. Now, did this poltroon ever bother you again?"

"Indeed not. My grandmother issued a stern warning to his mother about her son's loutish behavior. Stefano also made it clear to Pietro that he would set the bandits on him if he ever besmirched my name. It was an empty threat, but the silly boy believed it." She let out a rueful sigh. "He was rather stupid, I'm sorry to say, which doesn't reflect well on me."

"He sounds like a thoroughly contemptible character. Thank God your taste in men has vastly improved."

She stared at him in wonder. For days, she'd carried an awful weight on her shoulders, dreading the moment she would have to reveal her great shame to him. That Leverton could actually joke about it struck her as a true miracle. Gillian wasn't used to miracles in her life.

Suddenly, she felt light, as if a great rock bearing down

on her had smashed and shivered into dust, blown away on a bracing wind of change. She could hardly keep from laughing. "In my defense, he was very nice looking. Not as handsome as you, of course. That goes without saying."

"Naturally," he said, tucking her back against him. He went silent for several moments.

"Why do I have the feeling there's something else you want to know?" she finally asked.

"That is alarmingly perceptive of you. I do wish to ask you something, but I'm afraid of giving offense. And the vases in this room are shockingly expensive. I would hate to lose them."

She grinned against the silk of his vest. "I promise not to destroy your property."

"Very well, although I suspect I'll regret asking. Did you enjoy it, Gillian?"

She pulled back to look at him, and saw he wore a rather odd expression. "Did I enjoy what?"

"Did you enjoy your physical intimacies with Pietro?"

"Yes, I did, actually. But I gather from the expression on your face that I should not have."

"It's not that," he said, sounding a tad disgruntled.

It dawned on her that he was jealous, and a lovely warmth unfurled inside her. "Well, he was Italian," she said, unable to resist. "They're rather good at that sort of thing."

His gaze narrowed. "Now you're just trying to annoy me."

"Is it working?"

"All too well, but that is more a problem for you than for me."

With that, he tipped her back over his arm and fastened his mouth on hers.

Chapter Twenty-Three

When Charles finally pulled back, Gillian found herself clutching his shoulders, gasping for breath. And that was from one simple kiss. God only knew how she would react when he made love to her.

"Does that answer your question, my dear?" He slid one hand under her skirt, his fingers brushing up to settle on her knee. When he started to play with her garter, she could hardly remember her own name.

"Um, I think I've forgotten the question," she said.

He easily cradled her, one arm around her shoulders as he made little circles on her thigh. The feel of his warm hand on her skin made her weak everywhere, and she had to resist the urge to part her legs, silently begging him to explore.

"It's a national competition, of sorts," he said. "Who is better at making love—an Italian or an Englishman?"

"Well, you're certainly very good at kissing," she said. "But . . ."

He lifted an arrogant brow. "Miss Dryden, are you about to issue another challenge?"

She wanted to make a jest out of it, to show that she could manage their relationship with a light touch, too. But she couldn't. Lovemaking would never be simply a pleasant diversion for her. Not with him. Their encounter on the beach had seared that into her. That night, she'd wanted to take nothing *but* pleasure from him. Instead, she'd discovered herself tumbling headlong into love.

He frowned when she failed to reply. His hand stilled, his fingers holding her thigh in a gentle yet possessive grip. "What is it, sweetheart? Am I rushing you?"

She scrunched her nose. "I don't think so. It's just that I'm not really sure what we're doing. Especially in light of what we just talked about."

His hand started circling again, brushing closer to the curls between her legs with every slow pass. Gillian shivered. Her brain was going fuzzier by the moment, what little focus she had left riveted on the moment when his fingers would finally touch her sex.

"I'd like to make love to my fiancée," he said, "as shocking as that unorthodox request might seem. But I know you're rather a high stickler when it comes to this sort of thing."

She forced herself to pay more attention to his words and less to the sensations he aroused in her. "I'm nothing of the sort. And given our recent conversation that's a beastly thing to say."

He tipped her upright but kept her cradled against his chest, his hand still under her skirt. His erection pressed insistently against her bottom, and it took a mighty effort of will not to wriggle against it.

"I'm sorry, love," he said ruefully. "I couldn't resist. You're remarkably easy to fire up, you know."

"Hmm. I can think of a better way to fire me up than poking fun," she grumbled.

"I agree. Shall we get on with it?"

When he dipped down to kiss her again, she placed a

hand on his lips. He kissed that too, then sucked one of her fingers into his mouth. Gillian gasped, shocked that such a silly gesture could feel so enticing.

"As a matter of fact," she said, struggling to form a coherent train of thought, "I'd like very much to get on with it. But I must ask a question first."

He pressed a kiss to her palm and then placed it on his chest. She could feel the thumping of his heart beneath her fingertips. "You can ask me anything, Gillian. Always."

Curling her hand into the soft linen of his shirt, she gripped it for courage. "Are you sure about this?"

"Sure about making love to you? More so than I've ever been about anything."

"And you truly don't mind that I'm not an innocent?"

He shook his head. "You were vulnerable and in need of comfort. In every way that matters, you did nothing wrong."

"That's very kind of you. But it's a tad hard to believe that you're not bothered by it." She knew what men were like. Charles was certainly better than any she'd ever met, with the exception of her stepfather. But he was a proud man, nonetheless.

He studied her, apparently giving her question some thought. Her heart warmed that he didn't try to kiss her concerns away, or ignore them in a blaze of ephemeral passion.

"It's mostly a relief, now that I think about it," he said. "Bedding a virgin can be a complicated business."

"And have you bedded many before?" she asked tartly.

He leaned down and nipped her lower lip. It stung, but it also made her body clench with longing. "None, which you should understand by now."

"Just checking," she said. "But to be relieved I'm not a virgin seems very odd."

He laughed. "Let's just say it takes the pressure off. I don't have to worry about maidenly swoons or reviving you with smelling salts. Or, worse, that you'll lock yourself in your boudoir and refuse to come out because I've intimidated you with my manly vigor."

When Gillian giggled, she mentally blinked. She never giggled. Then again, she'd never had fun while making love before. How unexpected that it should be that way with Perfect Penley, of all people.

She began to stroke his shoulders. She loved how broad they were, and how strong. "Well, Your Grace, I would say that the pressure is on, rather than off."

"How so?" The hand on her thigh was moving again. This time when his fingers brushed against her curls, she inched her legs open, inviting his touch.

"Unlike a virgin, I'm aware of what will happen next," she said. "And I have high standards, which I expect you to exceed."

Heat sparked in his gaze. "Witch. I'll take that challenge, madam, starting right now."

She stopped him again before he kissed her, her nerves wobbling for a moment. "You're absolutely certain about this. About us?" Gillian had barely any defenses left against him. If she let him make love to her, it would bring the last ones crashing down.

He nuzzled her mouth for a brief, delicious moment before pulling back. "Let me show you just how much I want you, Gillian. How much I will always want you." His deep, serious tone made it sound like a vow. She rested in the moment and let his promise settle deep inside. It slipped into her heart with peaceful joy, as if she were returning home after a very long time away.

Gillian cupped his cheek, relishing the feel of his bristle against her palm. "Yes, please show me," she whispered. She leaned in to kiss him, but he surprised her by picking her up and depositing her on the chaise.

"Oh, Lord. Now what?" she asked, exasperated. Now that

they'd settled on the way forward, she couldn't wait to get there.

"Patience, my love," he said, striding to the door. He turned the key in the lock. "I hardly think Hewitt's coming in to douse the lamps would be a pleasant experience for any of us."

"Oh dear, especially not poor Hewitt."

When he returned, Charles took her hands and pulled her up. "Time to get you out of that dress." He spun her around and swiftly went to work on her buttons and ties. In a trice, he'd whisked the garment over her head.

"You're rather good at this," she said as he started on her stays. "Perhaps you could find extra work as a lady's maid."

"I have every intention of getting you out of your clothes every night for the foreseeable future." His voice was a husky rumble that made her shiver. He leaned forward and pressed a kiss between her shoulder blades, then nibbled up her spine to the base of her neck. When he nuzzled his way over to her shoulder, Gillian had to lock her knees together to keep upright.

"That . . . that sounds nice," she managed.

"Trust me, love, we're just getting to the nice part."

Charles reached around to help her out of her stays, then turned her to face him. Gillian promptly lost her breath when she took in his hungry gaze. It contrasted with the tender smile that touched his mouth as he played with the pink silk ribbons that trimmed the top of her shift.

"Why, Gillian Dryden, I never took you for a lace and ribbons sort of girl."

"Mamma insists that I have nice undergarments. She says that I would go around dressed like a boy if allowed to." The truth was—and Gillian would die before she admitted it—that she liked frilly and feminine undergarments.

"You never look like a boy, Gillian, even when dressed like one."

With a teasing smile, she began to slowly untie the bow on her shift. "So you like the way I look in this?"

"I'd like you even better without it."

Before she could react, he'd fisted the material and swept the shift over her head. Flustered, she let out a little squeak when he tossed it over his shoulder to leave her brazenly clad in her stockings, garters, and slippers.

Heat swept up her neck and onto her face, but she resisted the instinct to cover herself. The look on Charles's face made up for any embarrassment she might be feeling. He was also flushed, and his gaze burned hot with desire.

And there was something else, too. Something that looked like reverence. He hadn't even touched her, and already she felt cherished.

"Bloody hell," he rasped. "You're the most perfect thing I've ever seen."

Oddly, his words made her feel shy. Gillian had always considered herself a bold person, but the present circumstances were a tad intimidating.

As was the bulge in Leverton's breeches.

"Now that's just silly," she said with a sheepish laugh. "I must be the least perfect person you know."

Leverton started to yank at the buttons on his waistcoat. "Never contradict a duke when he's about to make love to you, Miss Dryden."

"Should I be taking notes? I didn't realize we were having another lesson."

He finally got his vest off and flung it onto the growing pile of clothes on the floor. "I have every intention of schooling you, sweetheart. All night."

She was trying to think of an appropriate riposte when he pulled his shirt over his head. Leverton clothed must always impress. Half-naked, he was magnificent. His shoulders were broad, and his arms were corded with muscle. Light brown hair dusted his brawny chest, then arrowed down to darken in a line over his taut stomach.

Gillian had to swallow a few times before she could speak. "Right now, you look more like a pirate than a teacher." A pirate with a massive erection in his breeches. Just looking at it made her go soft and wet.

"And I'm about to do a little marauding right now," he said with a mock growl.

She couldn't help laughing.

Her amusement died a moment later when he snatched her up into his arms and fastened his lips around her nipple. When he sucked on her, she had to bite back a cry. Desperately, she clung to his waist. His body was hot and rock hard under her fingertips.

Charles bent her back over his arm, devouring first one breast, then the other. He licked and sucked, drawing on her nipples until they ached with delicious fire. She squirmed and hooked a heel around his thigh, plastering herself flush against him. Gillian rubbed along his erection, trying to bring him against the peak of her sex. Delicious little contractions began deep inside, sending tingles racing through her body.

With his mouth on her breasts and his cock pressing against her, Gillian gave herself up to the building waves of sensation. She flexed against him, feeling the approach of her climax.

Suddenly, he pulled away, holding her at arm's length. Gillian had to work to get her vision to focus on his somewhat strained-looking features. "Why . . . why did you stop?" she stuttered.

"Because you're too close. It's too soon."

She wrinkled her brow. "One can do it more than once in an evening, can't one?"

He seemed momentarily stunned before he unleashed a

grin. "Yes, and I think that's an eminently desirable goal for both of us."

"And how do we go about achieving such a laudable goal?"

"First, you sit on the chaise," he said, urging her gently down. He loomed over her. Gillian swore his avid gaze felt like a touch, tracing over her sensitized skin. Then he lowered himself to kneel between her legs.

Slowly, gently, as if relishing every second, he pushed her thighs wide. "So beautiful," he whispered.

Gillian blushed to be so utterly exposed. But she did feel beautiful. How could she not, when he gazed at her with so much desire?

He trailed a hand from her throat down over one breast— her nipple damp and flushed from his attentions. "Look at you, love," he said in a raspy voice.

When he brushed his fingers over her stomach, Gillian could barely keep still. And when he finally delved between her thighs, she moaned and let her head fall back against the soft cushions.

Charles was setting her body alight with delicious, consuming fire. He toyed with her stiff little bud, rubbing it with a blunt fingertip. Gillian opened her legs even wider and wiggled her bottom, desperate for more sensation.

"Tell me what you want," he said roughly. When he carefully pressed a finger inside her body, she arched up on a breathy cry.

"I want you," she gasped. "Inside me."

"And you shall have that. Just not quite yet."

When he slipped his hands under her bottom and tilted her up, Gillian blinked. "What—"

She lost the ability to think coherently—much less talk— when he bent and fastened his mouth on her.

Good God. Pietro had never done anything like *that*.

Gillian was still getting over the shock of Charles's head

between her legs when he glanced up to meet her gaze. His eyes gleamed with a decidedly improper combination of lust and amusement.

"Did you like that, sweet?" he murmured.

"Um, I'm not quite sure, yet."

One of his eyebrows shot up. "No? Then I'm sure you'll want me to continue."

"Hmm, yes. It might be useful to be certain about it."

"I'd like to be very certain." In a leisurely fashion, he lifted her legs, one after the other, and rested them on his shoulders. She thought she'd been exposed before, but clearly she'd been wrong. Never in her life had she felt so intensely vulnerable.

And utterly wonderful

"Ready?" he murmured as he bent to her again.

She could barely draw breath, so she simply gave him a tight nod.

And fell to pieces under his skillful mouth. Gillian had no choice but to give herself up to him. She writhed under his tongue, but he clamped firm hands on her thighs, holding her open for the passionate assault.

She could hardly believe it was happening. Leverton was the most disciplined man in the world. A paragon of civility and good taste, a man who made Beau Brummel seem like a failure. And yet here he was, crouched between her thighs like an untamed beast, lavishing her with wild, primitive pleasure. He'd bared her body and soul, and yet never had she felt so safe and cherished.

Gillian was madly in love with him, and it frightened her half to death.

When he pushed two fingers inside her, then flicked his tongue over the tight knot of her sex, Gillian curled forward and grabbed his shoulders. "Charles, stop," she panted. "It's too much. You're driving me insane."

He raised his head. His features were tight with passion,

and his eyes glittered with an intensity that made her heart skip a beat. But he immediately drew his hand from her body and gently lifted her legs down.

"Do you really want me to stop?" he asked in a husky voice.

"Yes . . . no." She huffed out an exasperated breath. "Blast. I sound like an idiot." How could she tell him that it wasn't the physical sensations that overwhelmed her, but what he was doing to her emotions?

Charles leaned forward and gave her a tender kiss that tasted like musk and port. She sighed and kissed him back. It was earthy and honest, and she loved it. He pulled back a bit and then gave her a sly grin. "From your reaction, I'm assuming this isn't a Sicilian custom."

She languidly draped her arms over his shoulders. "Not in my part of Sicily, anyway."

"Then I'm glad I was your first. But you do still seem a bit taken aback, Miss Dryden."

"Stunned, more like it. I never imagined such a thing. It was a bit overwhelming, I admit."

He frowned. "Gillian—"

She ruffled his hair. "I loved it. It just takes some getting used to. It's very . . ."

"Intimate?"

She nodded.

He sat back on his heels and studied her. "Then why don't you show me what you feel comfortable with."

She blinked. "I don't understand."

He waggled a hand. "This, remember? You told me on the beach."

Gillian stared at him and then burst into laughter. "You cannot be serious."

His smile was slow and predatory. "I am. In fact, I've been

thinking about it ever since that night. I'd love to watch you, Gillian. Teach me what gives you pleasure."

While he spoke, he slowly unbuttoned the fall of his breeches. When he freed himself, her mouth went dry. His request was outrageous and exciting —especially coming from him—and she was suddenly wild to do whatever he wanted.

She grabbed a pillow to stuff behind her back, then wriggled closer to the edge of the chaise and tucked her knees snug against his hips. Then, blushing, she reached between her thighs, slipping her hand between her soft, damp folds.

"That's it, sweetheart," Charles growled. "Show me what you like. God, you're so gorgeous."

While she pleasured herself, Charles curled his big hands over her breasts. He stroked and played, then gently dragged his thumbs over her stiff nipples. Gillian moaned and arched into his hands. She increased the pressure between her thighs, rubbing the slick, hard knot. Pleasure radiated from beneath her fingertips, storming through her body, rapidly taking her to the edge.

When Charles leaned in and sucked her breast into his mouth, gently nipping her, she climaxed instantly. Gillian grabbed his shoulders, shuddering as contractions rippled through her body in luxurious waves.

Before the wonderful sensation faded, Charles fitted himself to her body and slowly pushed deep. Gillian tucked her legs around his waist and pressed against him, wrapping her arms around his shoulders. He felt enormous and wonderful inside her, filling her and stealing her breath. She squeezed her eyes shut, hugging the emotion as tightly as she hugged him.

He nudged her chin up with a gentle hand. "Open your eyes, sweetheart."

She sucked in a wavering breath. Charles was smiling

down at her with an expression so tender that her vision went blurry. "Oh, blast," she said in a gruff voice. "You're turning me into an absolute watering pot."

"Is it all right?" His voice rumbled through her.

She let out a happy sigh and rested her cheek on his shoulder. "It feels perfect. Which shouldn't surprise me, I suppose."

"Love, I'm just getting started."

And then he started to move. Slowly at first, letting her ride through the fading echo of her climax. But then he slipped his hands under her bottom and tilted her up to meet him. He pushed harder now, and even deeper. Unbelievably, another climax built inside where he stroked her over and over.

"Oh, Charles," she gasped, clinging to him. She threw back her head, needing to see him, and needing him to see what she felt in her heart. That she loved him, and always would. There would never be anyone but him.

He stared at her, his gaze turbulent with passion. "Yes, love, that's it. Come for me again."

And she did, flying once more. Instinctively, her body curled around him and clung tight, as if only he could keep her tethered to the earth. With a groan, Charles pushed into her one last time and came with a hard shudder. For an endless moment, they seemed to hang suspended, before collapsing in a glorious tangle of limbs.

After a minute or so, Charles gently untangled them and propped her back on the chaise. Then he joined her, easily lifting her to rest on top of him.

"All right, love?" he murmured, pressing a kiss on the top of her head.

She nodded, struggling for a moment to wrestle her emotions under control. "I do believe I'm splendid," she said, propping her chin on his chest. "Although I certainly wasn't expecting so torrid an encounter. You are full of surprises, Your Grace, I must say."

His slow answering smile was full of promise. "A lifetime of them with you, I hope."

When it came to love, Gillian had never dared hope before. Perhaps, finally, she could.

Chapter Twenty-Four

Charles frowned at Scunthorpe. "You've heard nothing?"

The estate manager's impassive expression didn't change, but Charles fancied he saw something shift in his gaze. Scunthorpe ducked his head and peered down at the floor, as if inspecting the Oriental pattern on the library carpet. But when he looked up, his gaze conveyed only regret—presumably for disappointing his employer. "I'm sorry, sir. I've heard nothing of any relevance about the smugglers, and certainly nothing about the whereabouts of the missing jewels."

Charles leaned back in his chair, frustration leaching away his good mood. Gillian would be with him momentarily. He wished he had better news to impart.

"Is there anything else, sir?" Scunthorpe gently prompted after a long pause.

Charles's manager's report didn't make sense, especially in light of the letter Charles had received from Andris, the runner from Bow Street. But Scunthorpe was a diligent manager, and he had never had cause to doubt his word. "No, that's all for now. But keep an ear to the ground. I refuse to believe those men have simply disappeared into thin air."

"Of course, Your Grace." Scunthorpe, clearly relieved to be dismissed, hurried toward the door. Perhaps he worried that his failure to make any progress on the robbery would adversely affect his employment. It wouldn't, but Charles paid all his employees more than a fair wage, and he had to admit that he'd expected better. He'd placed a great deal of responsibility in Scunthorpe's hands and had never questioned his judgment before.

But something was off, and it would nag at him until he tracked the feeling to its source. That meant it was time to take a more direct role in the affair. Charles had been reluctant to go poking around, since it was likely the locals wouldn't be willing to share what they knew about the smuggling gangs. Some of them might be involved in the runs themselves. Even if they weren't, the locals had to live with smugglers and owlers in their midst. Yes, they owed their duke a certain degree of loyalty, but he couldn't be there every moment to protect his people from the retribution that could result if they talked.

There was nothing romantic about free trading. Many smugglers would think nothing of killing anyone who endangered their trade.

There was a light tap on the door just as Scunthorpe reached it. He opened it, then stepped back when Gillian entered.

"Excuse me, Your Grace," she said, looking uncertain. "Hewitt said that you wished to see me, but I can come back later."

"That won't be necessary," Scunthorpe said. "I was just leaving."

Charles frowned at the man's attitude. It was just shy of outright disrespect.

"Good morning, Mr. Scunthorpe," Gillian said. "It's a lovely day, is it not?" She gave him a sweet smile, but held her ground, deliberately blocking the doorway.

With obvious reluctance, Scunthorpe finally gave her a

slight bow. "Good morning, Miss Dryden. Yes, it seems a fine day."

She peered at him with affected concern. "Are you well, Mr. Scunthorpe? You seem a tad splenetic this morning. I do hope you're not coming down with something. Or perhaps His Grace is piling on the work. He's such a dreadful taskmaster, don't you think? Quite shocking."

Charles had to repress a grin at her tactics. The look on Scunthorpe's face suggested she'd just poked him in the backside with a sharp implement. "I am very well, thank you," he said in a stiff tone. "Now, if you'll excuse me."

Gillian stepped aside. "Have a good day," she called after the manager as he hurried from the room.

Shaking her head, she shut the door. Charles crossed the room to meet her.

"I do not like that man," she said.

"I can see that, but you handled him very well." He took her hand and brought it to his lips.

She gave him a rather shy smile. "It wouldn't be the first time I've had to manage his sort. They expect to put me in my place and are quite surprised when it doesn't work."

Anger flickered within him. "You shouldn't have to manage it. And you can be sure I'll be speaking to Scunthorpe about his inappropriate demeanor."

"I wish you wouldn't. It tends to make things worse," she replied, wrinkling her nose. "Best to just let me deal with it in my own way."

"Gillian, you're going to be a duchess. You don't have to put up with that sort of nonsense."

She tilted her head. "No, but it shouldn't matter whether I'm a duchess or not, don't you think?"

He winced. "Of course it shouldn't. Forgive me, love. That was rather clumsy of me."

She patted his cheek. "I am rather good at the social niceties, as you know. Perhaps I should be giving you lessons, instead of the other way around."

"Like the lessons you taught me last night?"

Their encounter had certainly been a revelation. Despite her assertion that she wasn't an innocent, it was clear she'd had very little experience when it came to lovemaking. But her enthusiasm and willingness to experiment had leveled him. He suspected he would be on his deathbed before he forgot what they'd done on that chaise, and then later in front of the fire. Charles hoped those memories would soon be replaced with many more created over a lifetime with her.

"None of that nonsense, sir," she said in a stern voice. "You'll make me blush."

He laughed and drew her over to a club chair in front of his desk. He would have preferred the chaise, but that was too tempting. It was hard enough keeping his hands off her, especially since she was looking so lovely in a primrose-colored gown that hugged her gentle curves and made her tanned complexion glow with health.

"You're looking very fetching this morning, sweetheart. I quite like that gown on you."

"I'm sure I look a complete hag, since you kept me up for most of the night. Honestly, I thought you would never let me go to sleep." Then she squeezed her eyes shut. "Oh, God. I can't believe I just said that. How indelicate of me."

"Actually, I believe *you* kept *me* up for most of the night."

Her eyes popped open. "Good heavens, Charles, that's quite a naughty jest. What's come over you?"

"You have. It's the oddest thing, isn't it? Here I am shocking you, instead of the other way around."

"I do hope you're not going to regret what's happened between us," she said. "My throwing you off your feed, I mean."

Throwing him off his feed? She'd turned his life upside down, and it felt splendid, which surprised the hell out of him.

He leaned in to kiss her, and, after a moment of hesitation, she stretched up to meet him, instantly opening her mouth to his questing tongue. It was hard to stop, but

Charles forced himself to. "That's enough of that, or I'll have you right back where we were a few hours ago."

"Yes, we must avoid such things," she said, sounding breathless. "You might become unhinged if we gave in to that sort of temptation in broad daylight."

"I can think of no more delightful way to lose my mind," he said with mock solemnity.

She tried—and failed—to hold back a smile. "You are too kind, Your Grace. Now, did you wish to speak with me about something specific?"

He sat on the edge of his desk, reaching back to grab the letter on his blotter. "We have a great deal to discuss, including plans for our wedding, but there was something else I wanted to show you first."

"Our wedding. Oh, yes, of course. I'd forgotten about that."

He froze for a second. "You'd forgotten about that?"

"Not really, but . . . never mind, I'm just being silly," she said, flapping a hand. "Did you want me to see that letter?"

Gillian was obviously still ruffled at the notion of becoming his duchess. He could think of a number of pleasing ways to soothe her nerves, but this matter, unfortunately, had to come first.

"Yes," he said, handing it to her. "It's a report from Joshua Andris, the runner I hired. As I mentioned to you earlier, he's currently in Lincoln. I'm sorry to say he's not making a great deal of progress in tracking down your jewelry." He crossed his arms over his chest, watching the range of emotions flickering over her expressive face. She'd switched her focus to the letter, apparently reading it through twice before handing it back.

"I'm not entirely sure I understand. Why is he so certain the jewels aren't in Lincoln? Did you not say it was the most likely place to find them?" She grimaced. "I hope they haven't already been taken to London. Surely they would be lost if such were the case."

"Andris is quite certain that such is not the case. He's cultivated some promising leads on identifying the gang who robbed us. It would appear that they operate out of Alford and deal exclusively with pawnbrokers based in Lincoln. There's no evidence to suggest they took the goods to London."

Gillian perked up. "So if our jewels haven't shown up in Lincoln yet, that means the smugglers still have them."

"Likely so."

She leaned forward in her chair. "How far are we from Alford?"

"Seven miles."

She jumped up. "Is there an excise officer there that we can contact? Failing that, we can begin making enquiries ourselves, don't you think?"

Charles stood and rested his hands on her shoulders, gently urging her back down. "Not so fast, my love. I've instructed Andris to do just that. We should have a report from him within a few days."

"But the smugglers could take our jewels to Lincoln in the meantime. They could even start pulling the stones out of the settings, and then we would never recover them."

"I understand your concern, but Andris and I believe this is the best way to proceed."

"I don't agree," she said with an emphatic shake of her head. "I don't see why we can't at least discuss this with the authorities. It's better than sitting around doing nothing."

When he hesitated, she narrowed her eyes at him. "Charles, what aren't you telling me?"

"I can't be entirely sure, but it would appear that the excise officer for that area is not entirely dependable."

"Do you think he might be taking bribes to look the other way?"

"Very possibly."

"How appalling," she said indignantly. "How do you know this? I thought you only spoke to the authorities in Skegness?"

"I also had Scunthorpe follow up with the excise officer in Alford. He thought it suspicious that the officer displayed so little interest in the case."

"Why didn't you tell me?" she asked, scowling at him.

"Because I didn't think it would help. And you were already upset enough as it was."

"That is unacceptable, Charles. We're to be married. You shouldn't be withholding information from me."

"I don't mean to be overly precise," he said in an apologetic tone, "but we were not formally engaged at the time of our initial discussions of this topic, if you recall."

She silently fumed for a few moments. "Very well. I concede the point. But in the future, I expect you to discuss everything with me. Is that clear?"

He placed a hand on his chest. "I will be an open book to you, my love."

Gillian scoffed. "Trying to charm me into compliance? It won't work, Your Grace."

"It was worth a try," he said. "Now, what else would you like to know before we leave this matter in the runner's capable hands."

"I don't agree that we should leave everything up to him. And I want to know why you didn't report your suspicions about the excise officer to his superiors."

Charles throttled back an exasperated sigh. "Gillian, I have absolutely no proof that the officer is taking bribes. I will not ruin a man's career based on my estate manager's vague feelings, which might be entirely wrong." He held up a hand when she started to protest. "And that is exactly why I'm asking Andris to investigate this officer and see what he can uncover."

She mulled that over a bit, then gave him a nod. "Very well, I accept that. But I still don't see why we can't make a little visit to Alford. Poke around, as it were. See what we come up with."

"Ah, yes. The Duke of Leverton and his fiancée poking around the local tavern and shops, making thinly veiled enquiries about smugglers and stolen jewelry. That couldn't possibly get the wind up."

"There's no need to be sarcastic. I wasn't suggesting that we ride into town in the ducal carriage and commence interrogating the locals. We could go in disguise. Just a farmer and his wife, perhaps."

He stared at her in disbelief. "I would be recognized on sight, since I am fairly well-known in these parts. Nor can I imagine myself playing the role of farmer with any degree of credibility."

She rolled her eyes. "Yes, you are a very important man, after all. I'm sure all of England would recognize you on sight. Very well, you stay home, and I will go in disguise. No one will know who I am."

Charles propped his hands on his hips. "That is the most ridiculous thing I've ever heard. It's entirely unacceptable." He knew he had little chance of intimidating Gillian simply by looming over her with a fierce scowl, but he didn't expect her to regard him with something that looked remarkably like indulgence, either.

"On the contrary," she said. "I've done it a thousand times before, and I'm very good at it."

"Your days of playacting are over," he said. "This isn't Sicily, Gillian. It's England, and young ladies don't go running about the countryside in disguise, trying to break up smuggling rings and recover stolen goods."

She crossed her arms over her chest and gave a haughty little sniff. "I wouldn't be forced to resort to such tactics if you would listen to me. But since your staff—and the runner—

are apparently incapable of doing the job, it appears I must do it myself."

"They're entirely capable. And may I remind you that it's my job to take care of problems like this, not yours."

"You're not doing a very good job of it either, Leverton. I simply refuse to sit by and allow those thieves to make off with something that means so very much to me *and* to my mother."

"And I refuse to allow my future bride to make a spectacle of herself." As soon as the words escaped his lips, Charles knew he'd made a colossal blunder. Still, he couldn't back down. He could not allow Gillian to risk both her reputation and her life.

She met him toe-to-toe, her slender figure practically vibrating with outrage. "That's what this is really about—your blasted ducal pride. Let me tell you something, *Your Grace.*" She made the honorific sound like the worst sort of insult. "If you don't want a wife prone to making a spectacle of herself, you shouldn't be marrying me."

"You do have control over your actions, Gillian. You can choose to behave in a more circumspect manner, or allow others to act on your behalf."

She jabbed him in the cravat, demolishing it. "Sometimes the situation demands direct action. I refuse to sit around like some milksop miss and let others do for me what I'm perfectly capable of doing for myself—and better, I might add."

Charles studied her tight, angry expression, his frustration growing. She had to learn to accept his help, and also to recognize that her life was about to change in significant ways. "My dear, you're going to be a duchess. Along with the obvious benefits of that position—"

"You mean marriage to you?" she interrupted, her words dripping with sarcasm.

He ignored the barb. "The benefits are matched by the responsibilities. And a certain, shall we say, code of conduct."

"Like that of my natural father and uncles?" she asked. "Is that how dukes and duchesses should behave?"

"I hope you won't put me in the same category as that lot," he said in a mild voice.

His response brought her up short. She hesitated, then gave him a reluctant nod. "Of course not. And I don't intend to embarrass you, at least not on purpose. But I also won't pretend to be less than who I am."

"I wouldn't want you to, my dear. I have every confidence that you'll grow into the role and learn to conduct yourself with an appropriate degree of decorum." He gave her what he hoped was an encouraging smile. "I'll continue to do my best to guide you, of course."

"How very decent of you. I hardly know how to thank you."

Charles couldn't help mentally wincing. He knew he'd sounded a tad pompous.

"What I truly want from you," she went on, jabbing that lethal finger at him again, "is for you to take me and my concerns seriously. That means helping me recover what was taken from me."

"That's exactly what I'm trying to do. I'm sorry, Gillian, but you'll simply have to be satisfied that I know what's best, and leave this issue to me to manage as I see fit." He dredged up a smile. "Trust me, love, everything will turn out just fine."

She studied him with evident disappointment before giving a grim little shake of the head. Then she spun on her heel and marched toward the door. Halfway there, she stopped and turned back to him. "Do you know how many people have said that to me over the years? 'Trust me. Just do what I say and everything will work out fine.'"

"Gillian—"

"Do you know who I've learned to trust over the years?" She tapped her chest. "Me. That's whom I trust to do what is right for my family. And if you can't accept that I'm more than capable of doing so, then we have a problem. A large one."

Christ. "Could you be more specific?"

"Very well. I'm saying that we probably don't suit." Then she let out a bitter laugh. "Probably? No, of course we don't suit. I was a fool to think we ever did."

Charles was in front of her before he even realized he'd moved. Her eyes widened in dismay, but she held her ground. "Let's be very clear on one thing," he said from between clenched teeth. "We will be getting married."

"Is that so? I take it, then, that you've changed your mind and will go with me to Alford?"

He could barely keep his jaw from dropping open. "Are you really trying to blackmail me by refusing to marry me?"

She shrugged. "I don't see it that way, but I must do as I see fit."

"For Christ's sake, Gillian, you're an extremely intelligent young woman. For once, please put those brains to good use instead of acting like an impetuous chit."

Her gaze flung thunderbolts at him. "Thank you for that piece of advice, sir. I'll commence doing so immediately by telling you that, regretfully, I cannot marry you."

She turned to head for the door, but he clamped a hand on her shoulder and spun her back.

"I do not accept your refusal," he thundered.

"And I do not accept your refusal of my refusal," she shouted.

They'd clearly descended into farce. Charles couldn't remember the last time he'd so thoroughly lost control of his emotions. He made one more effort to throttle back his temper. "I'm sorry, Gillian, but the die is cast in that regard. After what happened between us last night, I should think that would be abundantly clear."

Her defiant little chin ticked up another notch. "I will not be coerced into marriage, Leverton. Not by you or by anyone else. Let go of my arm, you great lout, or I'll be forced to do something dramatic."

He stared at her, dumbfounded for a moment, before his brain lurched back into action. "If we don't get married, then something dramatic *will* happen—the complete ruination of your reputation, which already hangs by a thread. I will not stand accused—even in my own mind—of taking advantage of you."

"I'm not an innocent, you stupid man," she said in a tight voice. "Or have you forgotten that fact?"

"Gillian, I will not allow you to make the same mistake as your mother, or allow you to be labeled a . . ."

"A doxy?"

The ugly word she flung at him brought him up short. He took in her flushed cheeks and glittering eyes, bright with unshed tears.

What the hell was he doing?

"Good God." Charles gently smoothed his hand down her arm. "I'm sorry, Gillian. I should be horsewhipped for talking to you in so callous a manner."

Her gaze darted off to the side. "Yes, you should. I'll be happy to help with that, if you like."

"Perhaps later, after we've had a chance to talk this through."

A few moments later, her gaze returned to him. She'd regained control. "May I ask you something first?"

Her cool manner sent prickles of warning down his spine. "Of course."

"Do you love me?" She used the same tone that one might employ to ask *do you like chess* or *did you eat the last lobster patty?*

"I might ask you the same question," he replied, stalling for time.

"I asked you first."

Damn. He never employed that term anymore, not after

Letitia. He'd been madly in love with the bloody woman, and that reckless emotion had all but ruined his life. That was not what he wanted with Gillian. He wanted something better, but he couldn't seem to find the words to describe it.

He reached up to cup her cheek. "Sweetheart, you know how very fond I am of you. How much I want to be with you. I showed you how much last night."

She calmly removed his hand from her face. "At least Pietro was honest with me. Charles, why the devil do you wish to marry me, anyway?"

"I simply do. Is that not enough?"

She grimaced. "That's the best you can offer?"

Apparently, it was. Gillian was right—he was stupid. He'd just never known it until now.

"When you come up with the answer," she said, as he stood there like a great dolt, "perhaps you'll be good enough to share it with me."

And on that blighting note, she swept from the room.

Chapter Twenty-Five

Gillian sat on her bed, tailor style, ignoring the elegant little tea tray Mrs. Peck had sent up to coax her into eating. Since she was supposed to be ill, the kind woman had prepared some delightful little ginger biscuits and a bland pudding. Unfortunately, an enormous lump had taken up residence in her stomach after her argument with Leverton. Gillian had been so rattled by their verbal brawl that she'd spent the rest of the day in her bedroom, pleading a vague digestive complaint that probably fooled no one, especially her reputed fiancé.

During their epic screaming match, even Charles had lost his famously even temperament. Ordinarily, that might have constituted quite an achievement on her part, but now it felt like a hollow victory. Her dreadful behavior had no doubt made it abundantly clear that she was the last sort of woman he should wish to take as his wife.

"And isn't that what you wanted?" she whispered to herself.

She'd always thought so, especially if it meant she could return to Sicily. No doubt Charles would now be thrilled to put her on the boat, so Gillian simply had to recover the stolen jewels and then she and Mamma could book passage back to Palermo. They could retire to a little villa outside the city. Gillian could take care of her mother, and . . . well, Mamma would find something to do.

There was just one blinding flaw in her plan. She'd discovered that she didn't want to go anywhere, at least not without Charles. The notion of life without him now struck her as so appalling that she could think of nothing better to do than hide out in her room, trying to sort out where everything had gone wrong.

So far, the answer eluded her.

Gillian slid off the bed, thoroughly sick of her own company. Until she could sort out what to do with Charles, she might as well do something about recovering her stolen property. As she'd made clear to him, she had no intention of sitting around while the thieves smuggled her jewels out of Lincolnshire. If nothing else, she could head down to the beach in the faint hope that they might make another run. If they did, she'd follow them. She'd familiarized herself with most of the paths running across the estate and would be back to the manor before anyone knew she was gone.

With a little luck, she might soon have solid evidence to present to Charles about the smuggling activities on his lands. Even better luck would yield information on where her jewels had gone.

As she rummaged in the tall cupboard for her boots, a gentle knock sounded on her bedroom door. Since it was after ten o'clock and she'd already told the maid she was going to bed early, she wondered if it was Charles, coming to apologize. Gillian let out a small snort at the notion. She suspected he was no more inclined to apologize than she was, which meant they'd reached an impasse.

Ignoring the melancholy triggered by that thought, she shoved her boots back into the cupboard and took a flying leap for the bed, scrambling under the covers.

"Come in," she called out in what she hoped was a pathetic voice.

Lady Filby peeked in. "Hello, my dear. May I come in for a minute?"

"Of course," Gillian said, repressing a sigh. She'd managed to fob off Mamma with her Banbury tale of an upset stomach, but the countess would not be as easy to fool.

Lady Filby walked over to the bed with a kind smile on her elegant features. "I saw the light under your door. How are you feeling, my dear?"

"I'm fine," Gillian said, forgetting for a moment that she was supposed to be sick. "I mean . . . a little better."

Her ladyship's brows arched up. Then she glanced at the tea tray. "Have you had nothing to eat? Your mamma said you sent your dinner tray back untouched too." She laid a hand on Gillian's forehead, then her cheek. "You don't feel feverish, but one can't be too cavalier about these sorts of things. It's always so damp along the coast."

Gillian smiled, warmed by her concern. "I'm sure I'll be fine in the morning. I just . . ."

"Wanted to avoid my brother?" Lady Filby responded with a knowing grin.

"I suppose you heard us this morning. Things did get a bit loud."

"Rather. I expect they heard you in the stables."

Gillian flopped back on the mattress and dragged a pillow over her face. "How embarrassing," she said, her voice muffled. "You must think me a terrible shrew."

"Nonsense. I entirely sympathize with you. Charles has driven me absolutely demented on more than one occasion. I have learned, however, that retreat is generally not the best option when dealing with a man, and certainly not with my dear brother. You must stand your ground."

Gillian edged the pillow aside. "I thought I did that."

"Yes, for a time, but then you sounded a rather early

retreat. That was a tactical mistake." The countess regarded her with an understanding smile.

Gillian let out a heavy sigh as she sat up. "It's such a mess, and I'm not sure what to do. I'm not even sure if Charles and I should marry."

"Of course you should. You're the best thing that's ever happened to him."

"I find that rather hard to believe."

She blinked when Lady Filby kicked off her shoes and climbed up onto the bed. The countess tucked her feet under her gown, settling her silk skirts and getting comfortable. From her manner, no one would ever guess she was a powerful society matron and the sister of a duke. Tonight, she was simply a very nice woman whom Gillian liked very much.

The countess took her hand. "My brother is the best of men, but he likes to get his own way. He can't help it, you know, since almost everyone defers to him. It comes with the territory."

"The territory that includes a shipyard and a trading company, five large estates, and the mansion in London," Gillian said dryly.

Lady Filby laughed. "I see you've been doing your homework. Yes, the title has given Charles considerable power, something he uses judiciously and to good effect. He's a much better duke than our father ever was, although he refuses to believe it. He has, however, got used to thinking that he knows best about everything. That may be true when it comes to managing crops and livestock, or working on Parliamentary concerns, but relationships with one's nearest and dearest do not flourish under such conditions."

"I hardly think Leverton would put me in the category of nearest and dearest. Not after today, anyway."

"I disagree, although I will admit he doesn't quite seem to know what to do with you."

"Nobody ever does," replied Gillian, trying not to sound

gloomy about that fact. "That's why it's probably best for Mamma and me to return to Sicily. We can live quietly there, and no one will think twice about us."

Lady Filby's eyebrows crawled up her forehead. "Really? Including the bandits who tried to kill you?"

"I took care of that problem. No one will be coming after me."

"I don't think your grandmother agrees with that assessment, but let us leave that aside for now. Do you truly think your mother wishes to return to Sicily?"

Gillian thought she knew the answer, but the tone of Lady Filby's question gave her pause. "I don't know why she wouldn't," Gillian finally said. "It's her home. Besides, it's not as if everyone in England has welcomed her with open arms."

"Many have. And don't forget that her family is here. The Marburys are most eager to have your mother and your grandmother back in the fold. Besides," Lady Filby added gently, "you can hardly think your mother will wish to leave *her* mother. After all, Lady Marbury is getting on in years."

Gillian frowned. She hadn't really grappled with the idea of what it would be like to leave Grandmamma behind in England. Along with Mamma, they'd been their own little family for so long, as close as any three women could be.

"I think you would miss Lady Marbury a great deal," the countess said in a quiet voice.

"Yes, I would," Gillian whispered.

"Once you are respectably married, the gossips will lose interest in you and your mother. Truly, Gillian, there is no need for you to run back to Sicily."

"But Sicily is my home. England isn't."

"It could be, if you gave it half a chance. If you gave Charles half a chance."

A funny little ache formed in the center of Gillian's chest. She had to look away from Lady Filby's knowing gaze. "I don't think he truly wants to marry me. He's just doing it because he thinks he has to."

"Are you suggesting that my brother has acted . . . inappropriately?"

Damn, damn, damn. She squeezed her eyes shut, feeling her face go hot.

A gentle hand tapped her cheek. "Look at me, Gillian."

She cracked open an eye. Since Lady Filby seemed amused rather than outraged or horrified, Gillian opened the other one.

"Have you and my brother been intimate?" the countess asked.

"I suppose you could say that."

Lady Filby smiled. "How extraordinary. Well, you have no choice but to marry him now, I'm afraid. And I'm sure he's insisted on it, has he not?"

"He has, but I don't agree that we have no choice. It was only that one time. Well, twice, but the first time we didn't . . . you know." She twirled a hand.

"I see. But the second time, you did. . . ." Lady Filby twirled a hand back.

"Yes." It had been more than once over the course of the night, truth be told, although Gillian would die before she shared that little detail.

"In the most practical sense, once is enough. You might already be with child."

Gillian almost swallowed her tongue. That had never occurred to her, which only showed how bloody stupid she was when it came to Charles. "I forgot about that."

"My dear, are you in love with my brother?"

"What difference does that make?" Gillian had to resist the urge to flee from the embarrassing interrogation. "We all know I'd make a terrible duchess."

"Charles does not agree, or he would not have asked you to marry him."

"But it was all a huge mistake," Gillian said, exasperated.

Lady Filby let out a most unladylike snort. "My brother does not make mistakes like that. He's the most cautious person I know." Then she suddenly laughed. "Bravo for Charles. I must say, I'm quite proud of him."

"What's there to be proud of? I'm a walking scandal, after all."

"You are no such thing. You're a vibrant young woman with a great deal of character. As far as I'm concerned, you are just what Charles needs. You'll shake him up."

"I doubt it. They don't call him Perfect Penley for nothing."

"Exactly my point," the countess said. "I think we can agree that Charles is a most disciplined man with a very even temper, is he not?"

"Well, not lately."

"Again, bang on the mark. He *was* the most even-tempered man in London. An absolute paragon of courtesy until he met you."

"I drive him insane," Gillian said in a morose voice.

"Did he tell you that?"

"Yes."

"Even better. Gillian, he's acting that way because he's developed feelings for you—very strong feelings. You've broken through that hard shell he's built up over the years. No one's been able to do that since Letitia."

"And look how well that turned out."

Lady Filby climbed off the bed and slipped her shoes back on. "You're an altogether different and much better person than that horrible woman. Now, stop fretting. You and Charles will do splendidly together. There is not a shadow of doubt that you're exactly what he needs."

If what he needed was someone to drive him demented, then Gillian supposed she fit the bill.

The clock on the chimney mantel sounded the late hour.

"Goodness, I shouldn't be keeping you up any longer,"

the countess exclaimed. She gave Gillian a quick kiss on the cheek. "We can talk more in the morning, if you like."

"May I ask you a question before you leave?"

"Of course."

"Did Charles ask you to speak with me?"

Lady Filby shook her head. "Charles doesn't need me to fight his battles. I simply wished to explain why he sometimes acts the way he does. And I also wished to tell you that I look forward to calling you sister very soon."

Gillian gave her a half smile, far from convinced that such would ever occur.

The countess was halfway to the door when she turned back. "You never answered my question. Are you, in fact, in love with my brother?"

Gillian winced, embarrassed. But it felt cowardly to avoid the truth any longer. "Unfortunately for both of us, it would appear that I am."

Lady Filby's answering smile was both warm and understanding. "Then everything will turn out fine. I promise."

After the door closed, Gillian flopped back on the pillows and stared at the ceiling. Promises, she'd found out long ago, were made to be broken.

Gillian jolted awake, her brain struggling to identify the sound. When she heard it again, she knew what it was. Slipping out of bed, she snatched up her wrapper and dashed for the window. She started to open the sash, only to pull back when another handful of pebbles rattled against the window.

She cautiously opened it and stuck her head out. "Hush, I hear you," she hissed to Teddy, who stood below. She glanced around the garden at the shrubbery that looked like ill-shapen beasts crouching in the shadows. "Are you alone?"

He nodded, shifting restlessly from one foot to the other.

Even in the dark, she could see the nervous energy vibrating through his small frame.

"Wait there," she said. "I'll be right down."

She glanced at the clock as she hurried to the armoire. It was not yet one o'clock, which meant she'd only dropped off a half hour ago. After her disconcerting chat with Lady Filby, she'd decided against a scouting expedition that night, too tired and rattled to concentrate on tracking down her prey.

But Fate—and Teddy—seemed to have other plans.

It took only a few minutes to dress in breeches and boots and retrieve her brace of pistols from under a pile of shawls. After shrugging into her coat, she returned to the window and climbed out onto the sill.

"Bloody hell, miss," Teddy gasped.

"Hush, I know what I'm doing." She studied the ivy creepers running down the brick facing, then mentally shrugged. They would have to do, since she didn't dare risk creeping through the house and alerting anyone—especially Charles.

Gillian made her way carefully down the side of the house, breathing a sigh of relief when the sturdy creepers supported her weight. She paused several feet from the ground, craning left to catch a glimpse of the French doors that led into the ducal library from the terrace. Unless her fiancé was sitting there in the dark, the library was deserted.

Kicking away from the wall, she dropped down the last few feet into a flowerbed, the soft soil muffling the sound of her landing. She stayed crouched down for several seconds, listening. Then she rose and turned to find Teddy staring at her with eyes as big as Mrs. Peck's cheddar biscuits.

"Coo!" he said softly in a tone of reverence. "I ain't never seen anything like that."

"I'll teach you how to do it, if you like."

"That'll be grand," he whispered. "Miss, I comes to tell you—"

Gillian clamped a hand on his shoulder. "Not here." She

steered him into the shrubbery and pulled him down behind a large hydrangea bush. "Now, what's so important that you're sneaking around in the middle of the night?"

"I found 'em, miss," he replied, excited. "Them smugglers we've been looking for."

Her heart jammed against her ribs. "You found them? Where?"

"At the Fox and Firkin, where I was helping old Dodd tonight. Two of the rum coves came in for a spell. Stayed late, makin' plans about movin' their stuff. Baubles and fripperies, the one called it. Said they was sure to fetch a pretty price in the city."

That squared up with what the Bow Street runner had told Charles about the goods not leaving the county. But Gillian had been correct too, since the thieves were obviously getting ready to move them out.

"Did you get any clues about the whereabouts?" she asked.

Teddy looked perplexed.

"Where they're hiding the, er, fripperies," she clarified.

He nodded. "I followed them when they left the tavern."

She practically toppled over. "Please tell me they didn't see you." Gillian had promised Charles—and herself—that she'd never put Teddy in harm's way again. If anything happened to the boy, she'd never forgive herself.

"Nah, they didn't. Besides, they'd think I was too afraid to follow. After—" He clamped his lips shut, as if annoyed with himself.

Gillian moved closer, squinting to see his face. Fitful moonlight barely illuminated his features, but she could see enough. Fighting a surge of fury, she gently touched his bruised cheek. "Who did this to you?"

He pulled away, clearly embarrassed. "It ain't nothin', miss. The big one—he be their leader, I think—he cuffed me for lurkin' about their table."

Gillian's heart all but stopped. "Did he think you were spying on him?"

"Nah. I burst into tears and said I was just doin' my job, sweepin' up. Old Dodd backed me up. He said I was true blue and would never stain."

"And did they believe him?"

"Aye. The one that hit me even gave me a penny to make up for it," he said. Then he scowled. "Course, old Dodd made me give it to *him* for causin' so much trouble."

Gillian patted Teddy's shoulder. "I'll give you half a crown to make up for it. Tell me what you did next."

"Old Dodd sent me home, but I waited outside until the smugglers left. They was on foot, which I thought was queer as all get-out, so I followed. Turns out they's got a snug little hole in the old gamekeeper's cottage right here on the duke's lands. No one stays there anymore. It's only used to store traps and such."

"How far is it from here?"

"Less than two miles." He huffed out a cynical laugh that was much too old for his years. "Can you believe it? They were right under His Grace's nose. You think old Scunthorpe woulda known about that."

"He probably did," she said, repressing the urge to curse. Scunthorpe was almost certainly in on it and had been from the beginning. No wonder he'd done everything he could to divert the duke's concerns.

"Do you want me to take you there, miss?"

Gillian glanced up at the old house, dark and settled for the night. Part of her wanted to alert Charles, but her instincts told her there wasn't a moment to lose. Besides, the duke would probably wish to question Teddy and no doubt engage in yet another argument with her before taking action. Meanwhile, the villains could be slipping away with the jewelry.

According to the boy, there were only two of the black-guards. Armed as she was, she had little doubt she could handle them, if necessary. "Yes, but you must do everything I say, Teddy. We must be sure not to get caught."

He grinned at her. "No fear, miss. I'll be as silent as the grave."

His choice of words sent a warning shiver dancing across her skin, but Gillian clamped down on it. She'd always trusted her instincts, and those instincts were telling her to act. If the situation looked like something she couldn't manage on her own, she'd send Teddy back to Fenfield to raise the alarm.

Casting one more glance back at the house, she turned and followed the boy, who was already disappearing like a phantom into the woods.

Chapter Twenty-Six

"There, miss." Teddy pointed to the decrepit-looking hut in the small clearing. A fitful light beamed out from behind broken shutters. "What did I tell you?"

"Well done," Gillian whispered. "But I have to get closer. I can't properly see anything from here."

"Let me. I'm quick as anything, and no one will hear me." He started to wriggle through the underbrush, but Gillian quickly clamped a hand on the scruff of his jacket and pulled him back.

"I need you to stay here and keep watch," she hissed in his ear.

Teddy gave his head a stubborn shake. "Spyin' ain't proper business for a lady."

"Do I look like the average lady to you?"

He eyed her. "No, miss, but it's my duty to protect you. His Grace would be right frosted if I let you get hurt."

"His Grace would be right frosted if he had the slightest inkling of our present activities. Now, stay here, and, if you see or hear anything odd, just give me a quiet whistle."

He clutched her sleeve. "It ain't right, miss. If you was to get hurt . . ."

"Did I ever tell you about the time I shot a bandit lord?"

His eyes popped wide. "No. Did you kill him?"

"I did. So you needn't worry that I can't protect myself. I have my pistols, and I have this." She slipped out the blade she always carried in her boot.

"Coo, that looks sharp," Teddy breathed.

"Very sharp. Now, I'm just going for a look. I promise I'll be right back."

When he reluctantly let go of her arm, Gillian went flat on the ground and carefully crawled forward. She'd been hunting for years, both animal and man, and had learned long ago to move in silence. That skill had kept her from discovery on more than one occasion, and she had every confidence it would now.

She slithered her way through the underbrush to the back of the cottage. It took but a few moments to make her way to a window that was missing one shutter, with the other sagging halfway off its hinges. Hunkering down, she listened to the rumble of masculine voices inside and felt a flare of triumph when she identified Scunthorpe's.

"How much longer?" the estate manager said in an impatient tone. "That bloody man of yours should have been here ages ago."

A low voice answered him. "Christ, man, it's the bleedin' middle of the night. No one'll be up in the big house for hours yet. You're safe."

She was fairly certain she recognized that voice, too.

"The longer we wait, the greater the chance of discovery," Scunthorpe whined. "His Grace is getting more and more suspicious. I don't know how much longer I can hold him off."

"That pompous ass? You've got me shiverin' in me boots."

"Leverton is no fool. And if you're not afraid of him, you should at least be afraid of that runner he's hired. God only knows what he'll find out."

"That's why we're moving the loot tonight. Christ, you're

worse than a nagging old tabby. You might try growin' a pair of balls."

"Aren't you the brave one?" Scunthorpe retorted. "But I expect you wouldn't be so bold if your brother knew about this. He promised Leverton there would be no more runs across estate lands."

"My brother's a fool. We've been usin' Fenfield Manor to make our runs for nigh on two years. No need to stop just because that bleedin' nob is hangin' about. He and his kind won't be stickin' around for much longer, I reckon."

"They can't leave soon enough for my taste." Scunthorpe's tone was bitter. "Why Leverton had to take it into his head to remain in residence is beyond me. I've kept the estate in prime order, but now he's camped down here looking over my shoulder. He's ruining everything."

"Shut your gob before I shut it for you. I hear someone."

A moment later, Gillian heard Teddy's soft, trilling whistle, as if a bird had been disturbed from its slumbers. She crouched lower. Since she was at the back of the cottage, she should escape detection.

"Is it your man?" Scunthorpe asked.

Gillian heard shuffling footsteps and then a door creaking open.

"Aye, it's Billy," replied the other man.

Since the voices had moved away from the window toward the front of the cottage, Gillian decided to risk a look. Slowly, she came up and peeked over the windowsill to see a barely furnished room with a few broken-down chairs and some old hunting traps piled in the corner. A single lamp, placed on the roughhewn table near the door, lit the room. Three men clustered about the table, half turned away from the window. With Scunthorpe and the new arrival was the lout she'd shot the night they'd been robbed. It was his voice she'd recognized.

Gillian quietly slid below the window. The gang leader—

the one who'd negotiated with Leverton—had ordered his men to avoid estate lands, and he'd clearly kept his word. Just as clearly, the man's idiot brother had defied him. That Scunthorpe would align himself with so great a fool was rather surprising. The man's disloyalty would be a heavy blow to Charles, and Gillian didn't relish the task of telling him that his lands had been at the center of a smuggling ring for quite some time, thanks to his estate manager.

Well, at least she could help Charles put a stop to it.

The voices inside the cottage had been rising for the last few minutes. Apparently all was not going as planned for the merry little band of thieves.

"What do you mean I have to go with you to fetch the carts?" Scunthorpe angrily asked. "I never get involved in the transport of goods."

"I can't do it meself," said the newcomer. "It ain't my fault that Sam and his mate never showed tonight. You know that, right, Jenkins?"

Jenkins. Now she had a name to go along with the face.

"I know that I'll be beatin' the piss out of Sam next time I see him," said Jenkins. "But we'd best be off. It'll take most the night as it is, with just three of us to haul the load."

"No," Scunthorpe said. "I'll stay here and—"

"You'll do exactly what I say, or I'll beat the livin' piss out of you too, you snivelin' coward," Jenkins snarled. "Do we got that clear?"

Gillian held her breath, praying that Scunthorpe would do as he was told.

"All right," the estate manager finally said. "But after tonight, I'm finished with you lot."

"Suits me," Jenkins said. "You're nothin' but a pain in me arse. Now let's be off before it gets any later."

Gillian heard them shuffling around, then the cottage went dark. She quietly made her way to the corner of the building and peered around just in time to see three men cut across the clearing, quickly disappearing into the night-shrouded forest.

A rustle sounded behind her. She whipped around, pulling her knife from her boot, but relaxed when she saw Teddy scuttle up.

"Do you know where they are going?" he asked.

"To fetch carts to move their contraband. Any idea where they might be hiding them?"

Teddy scrunched up his face. "Sometimes smugglers store their carts 'n stuff in the tenant farmers' barns."

"Oh, God," she sighed. "How many Fenfield tenants are involved in this?"

"Prob'ly only one or two. They threatens them, miss. Don't give them no choice."

Anger made her stomach go tight. "That ends tonight. Any thoughts about which farmer it's likely to be, or how close the carts might be?"

Teddy shrugged. "Could be close as a mile or as far as five."

"Hmm. I think not the former." Jenkins had said it would take several hours to transport the goods, which suggested the carts were not stashed close by. With a wee bit of luck, Charles could rouse his men and get to the cottage before the smugglers returned, trapping them.

"Teddy, listen carefully. I need you to run back to the manor house as fast as you can. First, you must wake Reid. Tell him to saddle the duke's horse right away and also send someone to wake the duke up. Then you tell His Grace what we've found, and tell him that I'm waiting here for him. He'll know what to do."

Teddy's hand stole up to her arm. "Miss, you shouldn't stay here alone. It ain't right."

"I'll be fine. I'm just going to slip in and take a quick look around, and then—"

"No!" he cried, yanking on her sleeve. "It's too dangerous. You have to promise to wait in the woods till the duke comes."

"You needn't worry about me."

"I ain't going, not until you promise you won't go into that bleedin' cottage alone."

Gillian took in the stubborn tilt of his chin. She needed him on his way, and she needed it now. "All right, I promise to wait out here. Can you find your way back while avoiding the smugglers?"

"Lord, miss, I ain't a dummy."

She couldn't help a grin. "You are anything but. Now, go as fast as you can."

He scuttled into the forest, taking the overgrown path that led back to Fenfield. Gillian listened until the sound of his footsteps faded. Then she slipped the knife back into her boot and sat down under the window to wait.

Gillian guessed that at least forty-five minutes had passed, but there was still no sign of Charles. She felt slightly guilty that Teddy had to face Leverton's wrath, but the option of leaving the boy at the cottage had been no option at all. Even though the smugglers would probably take at least a few hours to return, Gillian was taking no chances with Teddy's life.

As for her own safety, she wasn't worried. She had excellent hearing and vision, so there was little chance that Jenkins and his merry band of poltroons would catch her unawares.

When a muscle in her leg started to cramp, Gillian danced a bit to get the blood flowing. Then she slipped around to the front of the cottage, pausing for a good listen. She heard what she expected to hear—nothing. No one was within a mile of the place, she would swear, which made her promise to Teddy even more annoying. By now, she could have already tossed the place at least twice over. It was foolish to sit about doing nothing when she could be searching for the missing jewels. Besides, it would pass the time while she waited for Charles.

Closing her eyes, she took another good listen, identifying all the sounds that drifted out from the surrounding woods. She heard the hoot of a distant owl, the scamper of a small nocturnal animal, and the whisper of a soft wind through the trees. She was convinced there was nothing out there that didn't belong.

Gillian turned and examined the cottage's heavy oak door. Unlike the rest of the exterior of the building, it seemed in fairly good shape. It was also locked. She could climb through a window, but she might as well get the door open for Leverton and his men.

Unearthing her picklocks from an inside pocket, she went to work. Fortunately, the lock was well oiled, and she had the door open only a minute later. It moved silently inward, the hinges clearly oiled, too—another indication the smugglers had been using the cottage as something more than an occasional place to stash their goods. Gillian slipped into the inky-dark room, closing the door behind her. Treading carefully, she crossed to the back window and pushed the shutter fully open to let in what little light was to be had from a half-moon behind broken clouds.

"Better," she whispered, slowly turning to scan the room.

Left of the window, a large, misshapen object caught her eye. It was covered by an oilcloth tarp. She lifted the cover and saw at least twenty small casks stacked up against the wall. The heady scent wafting up told her they contained tobacco.

Repressing a flare of impatience, she pulled the tarp

completely off and wrestled the casks in the back row away from the wall. She took another good look, but saw no small package or box stashed behind them. The casks all seemed to be well sealed, and Gillian didn't relish the task of prying off twenty lids in what would probably be a fruitless search for the jewels.

Allowing herself a muttered curse, she stood and took another slow scan of the room. Unfortunately, there was nothing that would serve as a hiding place for the jewels, or anything else that might be classified as baubles or frippery.

Had Teddy misheard the conversation in the tavern? Was this simply the last of the smuggled goods that had been stowed here after a final run? Perhaps the jewels had never been here at all, or Jenkins had already moved them. The grim reality was that they could be hidden away in any number of places or, even worse, they could already be on their way to Lincoln to be broken up and sold.

Reluctant to give up, she started moving more casks in the faint hope that she might stumble upon a secret cubbyhole in the floor. She'd just pulled another one away from the wall when she heard horses' hooves. She quickly pulled the tarp back over the casks, then slipped out the door and took a position around the side of the cottage, drawing her pistol.

A single rider was coming along the main path through the woods. Gillian cocked her pistol and waited for him to emerge. Though it was most likely the duke, there was no point in taking any chances.

The horse slowed, then stopped. She heard the jingle of a bridle, then nothing. Whoever it was had decided to exercise caution.

Gillian ghosted back underneath the eaves of the cottage, crouching down behind a sad old water barrel half on its side. Straining her ears, she finally heard a soft footfall. Whoever he was, he was bloody good at concealing his movements.

A moment later, a dark form emerged at the edge of the

clearing. A tall man in a greatcoat came to a halt, his head cocked as he listened. Gillian would have recognized those broad shoulders and that confident stance anywhere.

"Charles," she called softly as she stood up.

His head whipped around, and then he stalked across the clearing, swift and silent. His greatcoat swirled around him like an approaching storm.

"Goddammit, Gillian," he growled. He hauled her into a fierce embrace. "Are you all right?"

For a moment, she let herself enjoy the feel of his arms around her. "Yes, except for the fact that you're smothering me and may have just cracked one of my ribs. Other than that, I'm quite fit."

He slid his hands up to her shoulders and gave her a little shake. "I don't know whether to laugh or give you a sound spanking. Probably both."

"Well, you can try. That might be rather fun, now that I think about it."

He did choke out a soft laugh at that. "God, woman, you are incorrigible. What the hell am I going to do with you?"

She wriggled out of his arms, but then took his hand and started toward the cottage door. "For one thing, you can help me search for my jewels. For another, you can tell me where the rest of your men are."

He allowed her to pull him inside. "Christ, it's like a tomb in here. I can't see a blasted thing."

"Your eyes will adjust in a minute. Now, Charles, please tell me you didn't come alone."

"Contrary to what you might think, I'm not an idiot. Two of the grooms are right behind me, at least I hope so."

"Only two?" she asked in some dismay. "What about the footmen?"

"Yes, well, who knew that neither of my footmen could ride?" he said sardonically.

"What about Reid? With him and the two grooms, that would make five of us. That should suffice."

"Unfortunately, in all the commotion, Reid slipped while saddling my horse. It appears he may have broken his ankle."

She winced. "Oh, that's not good."

"No, it's not," he said. "Gillian, I need to get you back to the manor immediately."

She scowled at him. Clearly, his vision had adapted because he scowled right back. "I have no intention of leaving before the smugglers come back," she said.

"My grooms will keep an eye on them until I return here. I promise you I will deal with the smugglers."

"Charles, I'm not leaving."

"Gillian—"

"Please, just look at this." She hurried over to the casks and threw back the tarp.

He crouched down to inspect the goods. "That bastard. I warned him what would happen if he didn't stay off my lands."

"It's not the leader. It's his brother."

He frowned up at her. "How do you know that?"

"What did Teddy tell you?"

"Not much. I didn't give him a chance."

"I do hope you didn't frighten him," she said in a stern tone. "He was very worried about that."

"You're the one who should be worried, especially if our unwelcome visitors return."

When he started to tug her toward the door, she dug in her heels. "They won't be back for at least another hour. They have to fetch their carts."

"Gillian—"

"Charles, please trust me," she said quietly.

He muttered a few oaths under his breath, but then nodded. "All right. Tell me what you know, but quickly."

By the time she finished, he was fuming. "Scunthorpe

certainly played me a merry dance. I'm sorry, Gillian. I should have listened to you."

"Let that be a lesson to you for the future, my dear sir," she said with a cheeky grin. The narrowing of his eyes told her that he wasn't yet ready to joke about the situation. "But never mind that now," she added hastily. "We need to find my jewels. I'm afraid that even when we capture Jenkins, he won't give them up. It's not as if he would receive any clemency for doing so."

She didn't need light from a lamp to see how much he hated that idea. Gently, she laid her hand on his arm. "I need to do this."

He stared down at her for long, agonizing seconds, his handsome features grim. "All right," he finally said. "We'll look for a few minutes, but then we're leaving. Agreed?"

She went on tiptoes and pressed a quick kiss to his cheek. "Thank you."

Quickly, they moved the casks but found nothing underneath. Then Charles peered under the table to make sure that Jenkins hadn't nailed a packet to the underside of the top. But there was no sign of the jewels.

"I don't understand it," she said. "Teddy seemed certain they talked about moving baubles and fripperies tonight."

"They used the word 'baubles'?"

"Apparently."

As he stood in the center of the room and did a slow turn, Gillian tamped down a growing sense of despair. They'd all but ripped the room apart and found nothing. "Confound it, it's hopeless."

"Hmm. Perhaps not." Charles crossed to the fireplace. He ran his fingers around the edges of the fireboard that sealed off the hearth from rodents or birds coming down the chimney. "You wouldn't happen to be carrying a knife, would you?"

She extracted the blade from her boot and handed it to him.

"Of course you would," he said in a tone as dry as the dust on the floor. He slipped the tip of the blade into the seam between the board and the brick surround. After a few sharp tugs, it popped off. He returned her knife, then reached into the empty grate and extracted a cloth pouch.

"I'm an idiot for not thinking of that," Gillian said. "Well done, Charles."

She was reaching for the pouch when she heard the scrape of a boot. Charles slowly came up from his crouch, his face grim.

Blast. She'd been so eager to find the jewels that she'd stupidly dropped her guard. She whipped around, already knowing what she would see in the open doorway.

As one might expect from a ruthless, despicable villain, Jenkins had a pistol aimed right at them.

Chapter Twenty-Seven

The brute hadn't come alone, Sounthorpe and another man crowded in behind Jenkins, both aiming guns, although the estate manager was obviously quaking in his boots. Charles had every intention of murdering the bastard if he and Gillian weren't murdered first.

"Good God," Gillian said, sounding disgusted. "You lot weren't supposed to be back for at least another hour."

"Let me handle this," Charles gritted out.

"Handle it, will you?" Jenkins said in a mocking tone as he set a lamp down on the table. "Try anything and you'll be takin' a dirt nap sooner than later."

"I don't take kindly to threats," Charles said. "Your brother understood that. You, unfortunately, don't appear to be as wise as your brother."

"Wise enough to aim a pistol, you bloody arrogant prick," the man snarled.

"Actually, that would be very unwise," Gillian said. "He's a duke, as you know, and a very powerful one. I imagine the Crown wouldn't be too happy if you murdered him. They might even send troops into Lincolnshire to search for you."

Charles mentally cursed when Jenkins's gaze darted to Gillian. He prayed to God the smuggler wouldn't recognize her as the woman who'd both shot and humiliated him in front of his gang.

"That's true," Scunthorpe piped up. "The government would see us hanged. Let's just tie them up and be on our way."

Jenkins threw him a sneer. "I ain't leavin' without those casks. Nor without them jewels, neither." He waved his gun. "Throw the pouch onto the table."

Charles considered throwing the pouch into the man's face, then making a dive for him. But with the other pistols and Gillian in the mix, he couldn't take the chance.

Gillian hissed out a regrettable oath when he tossed the pouch on the table. Not that he truly blamed her, under the circumstances.

"But we don't have the carts," Scunthorpe said. "How are we to move the casks without them? It was terrible luck to encounter those riding officers on patrol. They've obviously got the wind up."

"We'll just have to wait until the bastards clear out, now won't we?" Jenkins said. "They can't go on hangin' around that old barn forever."

Scunthorpe waggled his gun hand, clearly agitated. "But that could take hours. Or they could start searching again and stumble upon this place. Then what would we do?"

"Happens he's right, Jenkins," the third man said. "Them officers heard us take off into the woods, I reckon, and won't be givin' up so easily. They's between us and Preston's barn for sure."

"We'll wait as long as we have to," Jenkins snapped. "And stop spillin' your guts in front of the likes of them."

"That explains why you returned so early," Gillian said. "You ran into the law. How very unfortunate."

When she gave Jenkins a taunting smile, it was all Charles could do not to groan. What the hell was she trying to do—deliberately provoke him?

Then it clicked. It had to be what she was aiming for, in
the hope that Jenkins would lose his temper and do something
foolish to give them an opening. It was typically reckless—
though brave—of her. All Charles could do now was keep on
his toes and hope he could react quickly enough to protect her.

The smuggler moved closer to Gillian, looming over her
and making her look like a fragile slip of a girl. "Been
spying on us, have you?" Jenkins asked. "Who the hell are
you, anyway?"

She lifted a mocking eyebrow. "Why, I'm your worst nightmare, as you're about to find out."

Jenkins peered at her, as if trying to puzzle something
out. Then he reached out a beefy hand and yanked off her
cap. Her long hair, barely contained by a loose braid, tumbled down to her back. Gillian didn't even flinch, but it was
all Charles could do not to launch himself at the bastard for
touching her, despite the two pistols trained on him.

Jenkins let his gun hand drop to his thigh, and his jaw
sagged open. "Bloody hell, I know who you are. You're the
little bitch who shot me."

"That's right," she said calmly. "Care for a repeat?"

In the uneven light cast by the lamp, Jenkins's expression
looked nearly demonic. And he was much too interested in
the fact that she was a woman, as evidenced by his avid
perusal of Gillian's form in her snug-fitting breeches.

"It might be best at this point to cooperate rather than
provoke," Charles said. Trying to create an opportunity was
one thing, but Gillian might as well be poking a dangerous
animal.

She flashed him a sweet smile. "Thank you for the advice,
sir. But I assure you that I'm quite capable of taking care of
myself."

"She can taunt me as much as she wants," Jenkins said.
"In fact, I hope she don't cooperate. I'd like nothin' better
than to get some payback from what she done to me." He let

out an ugly laugh. "And running around and spyin' on gents in the middle of the night, I'm thinkin' you might enjoy some larks. I'm just the man for a wild filly like you."

"Listen to me, Jenkins," Charles said in a low voice. "If you dare to touch her, I'll kill you with my bare hands." His fingers started to curl, as if already wrapped around the bastard's throat.

"I'll be doin' more than touchin' her," Jenkins said. He used the barrel of his pistol to flick open Gillian's coat. "Fancy running around dressed like a boy, do you? You're obviously a little doxy who won't mind a good shaggin' from a real man."

Charles heard a guttural sound and realized it was coming from him.

"Is she your woman?" Jenkins asked. "Maybe I'll let you watch."

"For God's sake, man," Scunthorpe burst out. "We need to get out of here right now. If the riding officers don't discover us, then surely the duke's men will come looking for him. You'll get us all killed."

Charles turned his coldest smile on his former employee. "In your case, I'll see to it that you're deported—after you spend a year or two on a prison hulk."

Scunthorpe flinched. "This is insane. I'm leaving."

"Suit yourself," Jenkins said, never taking his hungry gaze off Gillian.

She, however, simply regarded the thug with a slight upcurve of her lips. With her arms hung loosely by her sides, Gillian looked as relaxed as if she were at a garden party. Actually, she seemed more at ease now than she had at the *ton* events he'd dragged her to.

"I'll go," Scunthorpe said, "but not until I get what's coming to me." He waved his pistol toward the pouch on the table. "Either give me one of the jewels or pay me what I'm owed from tonight's shipment."

Jenkins turned to scowl at his erstwhile partner in crime. "Piss off, Scunthorpe. Them baubles are mine. I earned them when the bitch shot me. My brother gave them to me by right."

"Your brother is a thief and a smuggler," Gillian said in a crisp voice. "And you're an idiot if you think I'm going to let you keep what belongs to me."

Jenkins spun, turning his attention back on her. His henchman also seemed caught up in the little drama, his gaze drifting away from Charles to settle on Gillian and Jenkins, who were engaging in a ridiculous argument over who rightly owned the jewels. Scunthorpe, the fool, had shoved his pistol into the pocket of his greatcoat and was edging toward the pouch.

While Gillian kept the smugglers occupied, Charles slipped his hand into his pocket. Turning slightly away, he drew out his pistol. Quietly, he cocked it, the click concealed by the raised voices—which included Scunthorpe's increasingly strident demands for payment. If it weren't for the weapons involved, it would have been more farce than drama.

"You need to get it through your incredibly thick skull that you will not be taking my jewels," Gillian said. She gave a haughty little sniff. "I don't think I've ever met anyone as stupid as you. One wonders about your parents, although I suppose your mother took to an early grave over the grief of raising a son like you."

Jenkins's complexion turned purple. "You leave my mother out of it, you silly cow. You don't know nothin' about her. And *you* shot me. You owes me for that, by God."

Gillian scoffed. "No wonder your brother is the leader of the gang. It must be quite a trial for him, having deadweight like you to worry about. He'd probably be happy to give you up to the riding officers."

"Enough," roared Jenkins. When he lunged at her, Gillian

dodged and ducked under his arm. Her hand whipped down to her boot, and Charles saw a flash of steel. The smuggler let out an anguished scream. He crashed to the floor, Gillian's knife stuck in his thigh.

The sight of Jenkins crashing to his knees finally jarred his stunned henchman into action. When he made a move toward Gillian, Charles brought up his pistol and fired. The henchman yelped and stumbled, clutching his shoulder.

When Jenkins fumbled to bring up his weapon, Gillian lashed out a foot and kicked him smartly under the chin. He fell back, his head connecting solidly with the stone surround of the fireplace. From what Charles could tell, he was out cold.

Scunthorpe, with a terrified yelp, bolted for the door and disappeared into the night.

The henchman was down but not out, and he struggled to aim his pistol at Gillian. But just before Charles reached him, she planted her boot on the man's wounded shoulder and shoved him back down. He bleached white as old bones and fainted.

For several long seconds, Charles and Gillian stood frozen in a bizarre tableau, as if waiting for some other villain to burst through the door. Finally, she blew out a long breath and tugged her cuffs back into place. "Well," she said, glancing around. "It looks like that is that, wouldn't you say?"

Charles let out a disbelieving snort. At some point, he would be very angry with her, but right now all he felt was relief—and a degree of awe. Gillian Dryden was the most extraordinary person he'd ever met.

They heard pounding footsteps from outside, and then Teddy calling out. The lad burst through the door, followed by one of the grooms holding a pistol.

Charles eyed his out-of-breath groom. "Thank you, Tom, but as you can see, everything is under control."

"Coo," Teddy said, staring wide-eyed at Gillian. "You were right, miss. You can handle anything."

She waved a self-deprecating hand. "That's nice of you to say, Teddy, but I couldn't have done it without help from His Grace."

Charles shook his head, then set about restoring order to Gillian's mayhem.

Chapter Twenty-Eight

Dawn was approaching by the time Gillian and Charles finally made it back to Fenfield Manor. There had been the local constable to send for and riding officers to track down, and then they had to give them detailed explanations of events. Since the constable was a rather ponderous fellow, it took a considerable time before Jenkins and his henchman were bundled up and dispatched into the tender arms of the law.

As for Scunthorpe, he was in the wind. Gillian could tell that made Charles furious, but she was too tired to give it much thought. In fact, almost as soon as he had pulled her onto the saddle of his horse and settled her in front of him, she'd all but fallen into a doze. That had been as much a self-defense tactic as anything else, since Charles was clearly itching to ring a peal over her head. But he was too much of a gentleman to berate her while she was dead on her feet.

Any hope she had held that she might slip up to bed without speaking to anyone—including her fiancé—died a quick death. The manor house was lit up as if for a party.

"Blast," she muttered.

"What was that?" Charles drew the horse to a halt before the front steps.

"I suppose it's too much to hope that my mother and your sister were not disturbed by the evening's events."

He let out a snort. "The evening's events? Such a dainty way to characterize it, don't you think? An epic disaster would be a more appropriate description."

She did her best to ignore his sarcasm. "Well, it all turned out fine in the end, didn't it? We brought the villains to heel and recovered the jewels. I rather think we may have heard the last of smuggling runs across estate lands as well, so hurrah for us."

When Charles didn't respond, Gillian twisted around in the saddle to look at him. He was staring at her like she'd sprouted wings from her temples.

"You're demented," he said.

That stung, but she made herself shrug it off. "You're not the first to say that, and I expect you won't be the last."

He muttered a few choice words—rather shocking ones, coming from him. When one of the footmen yanked open the door and ran down the steps to grasp the horse's bridle, she took the opportunity to slide to the ground.

"Gillian, wait," Charles called as she dashed into the house.

She ignored him and headed for the central staircase. Unfortunately, she was only halfway there when the door to the library flew open and her mother rushed out, Lady Filby in her wake.

"Gillian, thank God." Mamma pulled her into her arms. "I've been so worried."

Gillian returned the embrace gingerly, not wanting to smear mud all over her mother's wrapper. "I'm fine, Mamma. Just a little dirty."

"Goodness me," said Lady Filby. "You look like a street urchin. Where is my—ah, there you are, Charles. I must say you don't look much better than Gillian. Have you be rolling about in the dirt?"

"Actually, yes," Charles said as he stalked across the hall to join them. "And in a variety of other noxious substances that don't bear thinking about."

"Oh dear," Gillian said as she gave his tall form a quick perusal. "You are rather a mess."

He'd lost his hat somewhere along the way, and his hair was disheveled, flat in some parts and sticking straight up in others. His jaw was rough with stubble, he had a dirt smudge on one cheek, his cravat was askew, and his normally shiny boots were scuffed. He looked rough, dangerous, and as far from Perfect Penley as one could imagine.

But perfectly wonderful for all that, Gillian couldn't help thinking. Unfortunately, his eyes had narrowed to irate slits, and his gaze was fastened right on her.

"Poor Charles," said Lady Filby, trying not to laugh. "I cannot imagine what your valet will say. He might have an apoplectic fit."

"He'll likely quit on the spot as soon as he sees me. Not that I give a tinker's damn, at this point. What I do give a damn about is Gillian's outrageous—"

Fortunately, the long-case clock in the hall interrupted them, conveniently bonging out the hour.

Gillian took quick advantage. "I had no idea it was so late. Really, Mamma, you should not have waited up for me. Come, I'll go up with you right now."

Charles's big hand whipped out and grasped her wrist. "Oh, no you don't." He started to drag her toward the library. "You're not going anywhere until we talk."

"But Mamma is exhausted," she protested.

"Don't think I don't realize you're trying to avoid me. It won't work."

"Are you calling me a coward?" she demanded.

He raised an ironic brow. All she could do was scowl ~k at him because, well, she was being a coward. She wanted to have this conversation as much as she wanted to go to a masquerade ball—which was to say, not at all.

He hauled her to a chair by the fireplace, then waved her mother and Lady Filby onto the settee across from her. He chose to stand in front of the mantel, legs braced, arms crossed over his chest. He radiated rough power and assurance, along with an inferno of masculine ire.

Much to her disgust, Gillian found it wildly attractive. In fact, she almost wished they were alone so she could throw herself into his arms and kiss him out of his bad mood. Really, the man had made her go entirely soft in the head.

"My love," her mother said, "why would you embark on so dangerous an escapade?"

Gillian reached into her inner coat pocket and pulled out the cloth pouch. "I recovered our jewels, Mamma, *and* brought the thieves to justice. I'm sorry you were anxious, but there was never anything to worry about. Leverton and I had everything under control."

"Oh, for the love of God," Charles said, sounding thoroughly disgusted. Gillian decided to take the high road and ignore him.

"See," she said, opening the pouch. "Here's my necklace, and your ring and bracelets. Unfortunately, your gold medallion is still missing. I'm so sorry about that. I know how much it meant to you."

Her mother got up and crossed to her. Barely glancing at the pouch, she took it and placed it on the table by the chair. Then she went down on her knees, taking Gillian's hands. "Darling, you are my most precious jewel. You are what's important to me, not some silly old baubles."

"But my stepfather gave us those necklaces," Gillian sai "You were so upset when that blackguard took it from yo

Mamma let out a sigh laden with regret. "What a te ble mother I've been to allow you to think for a momen a necklace is more important to me than your safety or happiness."

Gillian blinked. "How can you say that? I know how much you love me. You've been a wonderful mother."

Mamma tilted her head to study Gillian. "In what way have I been a wonderful mother?"

"Well, you kept me, for one thing. Most women in your position would not have done so."

"Most women in my position would not have been given the choice. Fortunately, your grandmother lent me her support, even over the objections of your grandfather."

Gillian felt her ears begin to flame. How embarrassing to haul out the family skeletons in front of Charles and his sister. The Penleys were paragons of decorum, while the Marburys were anything but.

She glanced up at Charles with a grimace of apology. He simply regarded her with a thoughtful air, before giving her a slight nod, as if encouraging her.

"I, for one, think it was exceedingly brave of you to keep Gillian," Lady Filby said in a stout tone. "Well done, I say."

Mamma let out a funny little sigh and patted Gillian's hands before rising. "I would like to believe that it took an act of courage to keep Gillian with me, but I'm afraid the opposite was true. I loved her too much to part with her, even though I probably should have. Selfishly, I couldn't bear the thought."

Gillian jumped to her feet. "How can you say that? You suffered so much. You were exiled to Sicily, forced to leave behind everything you loved. *And* you had to put up with Grandfather's being so beastly about it all."

"I won't say it was easy, at least in the beginning," Mamma said. "But then I met your stepfather, and for some reason I could never fathom, he loved me without reserve. So did you, my dear." She flashed Gillian a rueful smile.

"And why not? You were the most engaging little scamp. He adored you from the first."

"Then it worked out for both of us, didn't it?" Gillian said. "Even Grandfather came around before he died. I had a very good life in Sicily, and you have nothing to feel guilty about."

"My sweet child," her mother said. "You've never held a grudge against any of us, have you?"

"She only holds grudges toward dastardly villains," Charles said. "Then she turns into Nemesis."

Gillian shot him a scowl. He gave her a lopsided grin that she found ridiculously endearing.

"Why would I hold a grudge against any of you, Mamma?" Gillian asked, returning her attention to her mother.

"Because we never allowed you to be fully part of our family, or part of the society in which we moved. You lived in the shadows, never truly belonging to any world but the one you created for yourself." Her mother shook her head. "I did you a great wrong, Gillian. I was too selfish to give you up to a family that would have accepted you completely, and I was too cowardly to take on your grandfather and anyone else who pushed you away. I should have taken better care of you. You should have always been the most important thing in my life, and the shame is mine that you were not."

Gillian felt like giant hands were squeezing the breath from her body. "I . . . I don't know what you want from me, Mamma."

Her mother stood straight and tall, looking ready to take on the entire world on her daughter's behalf. "I want you to let me take care of you from now on."

Gillian had no idea what to make of this version of her parent. "Can you give me a hint as to what that actua entails?"

Mamma flicked a glance in Lady Filby's direction the countess rose to stand beside her. The women

Gillian with a feminine determination that she found rather intimidating.

"Your mother and I have been talking," Lady Filby said. "She feels quite strongly that you must give up your goal of returning to Sicily—"

"It wasn't truly a goal. Just idle chat, really," Gillian said, casting a nervous glance at Charles. After all, she was supposed to be engaged to the man. She could hardly expect him to move back to Sicily with her.

He arched a sardonic brow, looking not in the least surprised by Lady Filby's revelation. Meanwhile, the countess carried on as if Gillian hadn't interrupted her. "Your mother and I agree that England is now most certainly your home. There must be no more talk of running away to Sicily."

"Certainly not," said Mamma in a firm voice.

Gillian glanced at Charles. "And were you part of this little cabal deciding my future?"

He raised his hands, palms out. "I had no part in any of it."

That gave her a nasty jolt, although it probably shouldn't have. After tonight's misadventures, he'd probably be happy to put her on the boat himself.

"Gillian, you seem to think we don't have your best interests at heart, but nothing could be further from the truth," her mother said impatiently. "There is nothing left for you in Sicily other than old memories and old enemies. I want more for you than that. I want you to remain in England, with me."

Gillian frowned. "But you only left Sicily because of me. You had a good life there, even after my stepfather died. You were so popular at the Court of Palermo. The queen adored you."

"My darling, Italian aristocrats are just as snobby as their English counterparts," her mother said in a wry tone. "You only weren't as exposed to it, which was perhaps the only benefit of living on the fringes of society. Regardless,

England is my home. This is where I wish to live and, one day, wish to be buried."

"That's a rather morbid way to put it," Gillian said.

"You know I do tend to run to the grand gesture," Mamma said. "How else am I to manage such a strong-willed family?"

Gillian stared at her for a moment, then they both started to laugh. It was certainly the strangest conversation she'd ever had with her mother, and the most honest. It actually felt quite wonderful.

"Besides," Mamma said, "I don't wish to leave your grandmother. She's not getting any younger, and she has no intention of returning to Italy. She will need both of us in the coming years."

"No, of course we can't leave her." Still, Gillian couldn't help feeling a degree of skepticism. "And you truly don't mind all the gossip about us? The nasty names and rumors?"

"Those will fade in time." Her mother pointed a finger at her. "If you stop fueling them."

"I don't do it on purpose," Gillian protested.

"Ha," Charles said.

She'd almost forgotten about him, which was rather amazing. Then again, it wasn't every day that one's ideas about one's mother were turned upside down.

"Very well," Gillian said. "I'll stay. If Charles doesn't have a problem with it, that is."

"I do have a problem," he said in a clipped tone. "A very big one."

Well, that did not sound good.

"I believe this is our cue to leave," Lady Filby said. S'
stopped to pat her brother on the cheek. "Don't be a co
plete ogre, or Gillian will be forced to stab you."

"An outcome I will do my best to avoid," he said c
cally.

Mamma gave Gillian a brief, fierce hug, then '

the countess from the room. Suddenly, Gillian was left to face the wrath of Perfect Penley on her own.

"Cowards," she couldn't help muttering under her breath.

"What was that, my dear?" Charles said in a low voice that sounded rather like a purr. He stalked her like a big cat, all golden and ruffled, crowding her against an inconveniently placed bookshelf. She let her gaze roam about the room, looking for the best avenue of escape.

"Don't even think about it," Charles said. He braced one hand beside her shoulder, caging her in.

"I have no idea what you're talking about," she replied in a lofty tone. She simply refused to be intimidated—or seduced—by his ducal magnificence.

But when he loomed over her like that, his tempting mouth moving ever closer, her resolve started to waver.

She sniffed the air. "What is that awful smell?"

With an exasperated sigh, he straightened and cautiously sniffed his sleeve. "Me, unfortunately. It certainly isn't you."

"Yes, I smell like good, clean dirt. You, however . . ."

"The jewels apparently weren't the only things in that fireplace. I believe birds were in residence as well."

"Ah, that explains it. Well, then," she said in a brisk tone, "you'll be wanting a bath and a change immediately. I know how particular you are about your clothes."

"I don't give a damn about my clothes. And you're not going anywhere, smell or no smell. We're going to talk this out, and we're going to do it now."

She couldn't help chewing on her bottom lip. There was ‚ trace of humor in his expression.

She braced herself for the worst. "Very well. What do you ⹁ to say to me, sir?"

ᵂ wish to say that I'm done with this, Gillian."

ᵘld you be a trifle more specific?"

ᵃ᷈ved a sweeping arm that seemed to take in the

whole library. Gillian felt certain, however, that his irritation did not stem from philological concerns.

"I'm done with this mad dance you've led us on, and the danger and the risk you tumble into," he said. "I won't have it anymore, do you hear me? It ends now."

Gillian swore her heart shriveled several sizes in an instant, but she'd be damned if she let him see how much he was killing her. And while it was true that she was more than willing to modify her behavior for his sake, she couldn't change her essence or what she believed in. Not even for him.

"I understand perfectly, sir," she said, forcing a calm smile. "And of course I release you from your promise to me. That goes without saying."

He shook his head in disgust. "You clearly don't understand a bloody thing, you goose."

Gillian's temper flared. "There is no need for name-calling, you brute. And if that's the way you're going to act—"

He hauled her up onto her toes and into a crushing embrace, smothering her protests with a kiss that sent fire through her veins. He devoured her mouth with such passion that Gillian could do little more than feebly clutch his shoulders.

Escape, naturally, was impossible.

Finally, he let her breathe, and Gillian tried to force her brain into some working order. "So I take it you're not breaking our engagement?"

"Why would I do that?" His gaze smoldered with an unspent passion that put ideas into her head—ones that contained large copper baths, two naked bodies, and a great deal of slippery soap.

"Because I'm always getting into trouble?"

He gently grasped her chin, making her look straight his eyes. "The only trouble you will get into from now on be with me—in our bedroom."

"That sounds nice," she said, patting his shoulders. "But it's not as if I go looking for trouble, not really."

"Trouble is your middle name. Trouble follows you like a puppy follows its mother. Trouble moves right in and—"

"All right, I take your point," she said with a scowl. "One would think you didn't realize that I'm perfectly capable of taking care of myself."

He dropped a kiss on the tip of her nose. "How selfish of me to object to allowing the woman I love to deliberately put herself in harm's way."

"You love me?" Her voice came out in a squeak.

"I'm as astounded by that development as you are."

She pinched his arm. "I'm serious, Charles."

"I am, too." His expression was both tender and amused. "Listen, my darling, because I mean every word. I know that I'm a terribly boring, overly correct person who isn't nearly dashing enough for a magnificent creature like you. Nonetheless, I cannot give you up. I thought my life before you was nearly perfect. I controlled everything and everyone around me, and I had everything I wanted. At least I thought I did, until you blasted into my life and turned the world upside-down."

"That doesn't sound very pleasant. Are you quite sure you love me?"

"You have disconcerted me on more than one occasion, I will admit. But it's good for me to be knocked off my pedestal. Elizabeth would certainly agree with that, and I suspect my mother and my older sister will as well."

"And you're sure you love me?" Gillian asked again. It seemed impossible—glorious, but still impossible—and she needed to hear it again.

He cupped her chin. "I love you, Gillian Dryden, and I promise to love you for the rest of my life. I can pull out the family Bible and swear on it, if you like."

She found herself actually blinking back tears. "That

won't be necessary," she whispered. "I know you to be a man of your word."

"Good." He slipped his hands down, settling them lightly at her waist. "Now, I have a question for you."

She found it a tad difficult to speak, so she simply gave him a nod of encouragement.

"Do you love me?" he asked, deadly serious.

"Good God, you mean you can't tell?"

"I'm a rather unimaginative fellow, if you haven't noticed. I would never assume that a glorious creature such as yourself would deign to love me."

"Idiot. Of course I love you. I never would have let you do all those scandalous things to me if I didn't."

"Naturally, I am very relieved to hear that."

Gillian couldn't quite believe it, but he did look relieved, as if he'd been expecting a different answer. She gently rested her palms on his cheeks. "Charles Valentine Penley, I love you with all my heart. I have for some time. I simply found it impossible to believe that you could ever love me."

"It would appear that we were both laboring under hideous misapprehensions."

"Well, as for me, it is rather hard to believe that Perfect Penley would fall in love with such a hoyden."

"Then it's time to disabuse you of that notion once and for all." With that, he swept her up into his arms and headed for the door.

"What are you doing?" she asked with a startled laugh.

"I'm taking you upstairs, where I'm going to make mad passionate love to you. When I'm through, there will be n doubt in your mind as to my feelings for you."

"You'll do no such thing," she said, scandalized. " mother is sleeping right down the hall."

He juggled her a bit when he opened the door to th "I promise I'll be quiet."

"It's not you I'm worried about. Besides, I'm a wreck, and I'm covered in dirt."

"Good, clean dirt, as you pointed out. Ah, Hewitt, there you are," he said as the butler appeared from the back of the hall. "Bring a sufficient quantity of hot water up to Miss Dryden's room. She needs a bath."

"Yes, Your Grace." Hewitt's poker face was excellent. Gillian couldn't detect even a hint of surprise.

"Charles, it's the middle of the night," she said. "Surely we can make do with a splash of cold water."

"As you so trenchantly pointed out, we smell. It's going to take more than a splash to fix that."

"No, you smell," she said. "And it's a great deal of fuss and bother for the servants."

"I'm sure they won't mind, especially since you have them all wrapped around your little finger," he said as he carried her up the central staircase. "And all they need do is bring up the water. I'll be helping you bathe."

"Good Lord," she exclaimed, affecting a shocked demeanor. "Are you sure you are quite yourself? This is hardly proper behavior for a man of your stature and reputation. What would the *ton* think about this?"

"I don't give a damn about the *ton*, because apparently I've turned into a reckless adventurer who chases bandits, smashes heads, and makes love to his fiancée on the beach. Does that sound like a pattern card of decorum to you?"

"Indeed not."

He stopped at the top of the stairs. His smile faded, replaced by an intensity that made her heart pound. "Gillian, despite that ridiculous nickname of mine, I don't pretend to perfect. But I do know one thing beyond a shadow of a bt."

 What's that?"

 at I love you with all my heart. I know how much iving up for me by remaining here in England. I hope my love will compensate for that sacrifice. Because, my darling, I cannot bear to live without you."

Gillian shook her head, knowing she was giving up nothing and gaining everything. "You silly man," she whispered. "Everything's perfect."

He rested his forehead against hers. "Thank you."

"You're welcome. Now, Your Grace, I do believe you owe me a bath." She grabbed at his shoulders, laughing as he set off at a jog toward her room.

Epilogue

London
July 1816

"Would you like another glass of champagne, Your Grace?"

It took Gillian a moment to register that Griffin was speaking to her. After all, she'd only been the Duchess of Leverton for a few weeks—barely enough time to become used to her new title. "Mock me at your peril, dear brother," she said in a lofty tone. "The duke will be most displeased if you fail to treat me with the respect due my elevated status."

Griffin clapped a dramatic hand to his chest. "Do you mean to say he'll read me a stern lecture, or deliver a devastating setdown? The mind reels with horror."

Justine poked her husband in the arm. "Behave yourself, ﬀin Steele. This is Gillian's big night, and you shouldn't ﬀasing her."

ﬀ flashed his wife a grin. "I can't seem to help it. Who ﬀave foretold my rapscallion little sister's marriage to ﬀenley, the most proper man in all of England?"

ﬀothing of the sort," Gillian said, leaping to her

husband's defense. "Well, at least not when it matters most."
Like when they were alone, in her bedroom. Charles was
anything but proper in that setting, which the last several
weeks had made abundantly clear. He'd snuck into her room
almost every night before their marriage.

Not that she'd done anything to stop him, aside from a
tepid and completely insincere protest on her part. Still, it
was much easier now that she and Charles were married.
They could make love whenever they wanted—which so far
had been quite a lot.

"Not to belabor the pun, but I knew Gillian and Charles
were perfect for each other almost from the beginning,"
Justine said, "As usual, I was right."

"You were, my sweet," Griffin said. "And much to my
surprise, I find myself agreeing with you." He glanced
around Lady Minchester's ballroom, which was bursting at
the seams even though the Season was all but over. "Thanks
to Leverton's influence, my sister is well on her way to
becoming the most popular woman in London."

"Hardly," Gillian said. "Although I must say it's rather
nice not to have everyone in the room waiting with bated
breath for me to cause a scene."

"No, only half of them," her brother teased.

Gillian rolled her eyes, and Justine gave her husband
another poke in the arm. But Griffin wasn't entirely wrong.
Despite Charles's success in reforming Gillian in the eyes of
the *ton,* she would always have her detractors. And Gillian
cared not one whit. She had the love and respect of the best
man she'd ever met—a man who accepted her for who she
was, and who asked for nothing in return but her love.

"The contessa is looking wonderful, Gillian," Justine
said, once she'd finished reprimanding her husband. "It's so
nice to see her out and about, and in such good spirits."

Gillian cast a glance at her mother, who was sitting
against the wall and chatting in an animated fashion with a

group of matrons. "Yes, she's happy to be back in town with her friends, and to see Grandmamma again. It was lovely at Fenfield Manor, but a bit isolating for her."

"She's happy that you're happy," Justine said. "That's what's truly most important to her."

"And seeing all your enemies—and hers—get their comeuppance," Griffin said. "There's nothing more satisfying than a nice bit of social revenge."

"No one understands that better than I do," Gillian said, "but don't tell my husband I said so. He would be appalled at my sad lack of character."

"Leverton would be happy to exact revenge if anyone dared to insult his wife," Griffin said. "He's quite a changed man, thanks to you."

"Yes, isn't it lovely?" Gillian said cheerfully.

"What an exceedingly bloodthirsty family I've married into," Justine said with a dramatic sigh. "Speaking of your husband, where is he? I haven't seen him for at least a half hour. He usually sticks to your side like glue."

"He was out in the hall talking to Dominic Hunter, last time I saw him," Griffin said. "Dominic was no doubt congratulating himself on your successful marriage to Leverton."

Gillian frowned. "What does Sir Dominic have to do with my marriage?"

"He's the one who suggested I look you up when we traveled to the Continent," Griffin said. He gently tugged one of her curls. "I would have done it anyway, pet. I'd been thinking about doing so for a long time."

Justine nodded. "That's very true. Griffin had been planning a trip to Sicily for ages."

"Then why did Sir Dominic wish you to look me up?" Gillian asked.

"Because he's an old busybody," Griffin said. "I'll tell you about it another time. Besides, I do believe I see your husband forging his way through the mob."

"He's hard to miss," Justine said. "He's taller than almost everyone in the room."

"And handsomer," Gillian said. As she did every time she saw Charles, she went a little weak in the knees. It was almost embarrassing the effect he had upon her.

"While we're waiting for the Duke of Leverton to grace us with his august presence," Griffin said, "shall I fetch you ladies another goblet of champagne?"

"None for me," Gillian said. "Charles wants me to dance the waltz with him. If I drink too much, I'll be sure to make a complete fool of myself. I'm not the most graceful of dancers, sorry to say."

"As if he would care," said Griffin. "The man is ridiculously besotted with you."

"And is there anything wrong with that?" his wife asked with some asperity.

Gillian listened to their playful argument with half an ear as she watched her husband make his way over to join them. When their eyes met, a slow, seductive smile curled up the edges of his mouth.

"Hello, my love," he said when he finally reached them. He took her hand and twined his fingers through hers. "I hope your rogue of a brother has been taking proper care of you in my absence."

Gillian scoffed. "As if I need anyone taking care of me, especially in a silly old ballroom." When Charles raised a brow, she gave him a sheepish smile. "Except for you, of course. That goes without saying."

"Naturally," her husband said wryly. "Now, I believe the orchestra is about to strike up a waltz, and I would very much like to claim my bride for this dance."

Gillian took a deep breath and nodded. "Lead on, Your Grace." In truth, she *was* a bit nervous. This was her first waltz in public, and she wanted Charles to be proud of her.

Clearly reading her mind, he leaned down to murmur in

her ear. "Don't worry, sweetheart. I'll always be there to catch you—whether you need me to or not."

"I know," she whispered back. "And I'll always be there for you, too. I promise."

He swept her into the waltz, spinning her in a joyful whirl. Gillian only stepped on his toes once.

Books by Bestselling Author
Fern Michaels

___The Jury	0-8217-7878-1	$6.99US/$9.99CAN
___Sweet Revenge	0-8217-7879-X	$6.99US/$9.99CAN
___Lethal Justice	0-8217-7880-3	$6.99US/$9.99CAN
___Free Fall	0-8217-7881-1	$6.99US/$9.99CAN
___Fool Me Once	0-8217-8071-9	$7.99US/$10.99CAN
___Vegas Rich	0-8217-8112-X	$7.99US/$10.99CAN
___Hide and Seek	1-4201-0184-6	$6.99US/$9.99CAN
___Hokus Pokus	1-4201-0185-4	$6.99US/$9.99CAN
___Fast Track	1-4201-0186-2	$6.99US/$9.99CAN
___Collateral Damage	1-4201-0187-0	$6.99US/$9.99CAN
___Final Justice	1-4201-0188-9	$6.99US/$9.99CAN
___Up Close and Personal	0-8217-7956-7	$7.99US/$9.99CAN
___Under the Radar	1-4201-0683-X	$6.99US/$9.99CAN
___Razor Sharp	1-4201-0684-8	$7.99US/$10.99CAN
___Yesterday	1-4201-1494-8	$5.99US/$6.99CAN
___Vanishing Act	1-4201-0685-6	$7.99US/$10.99CAN
___Sara's Song	1-4201-1493-X	$5.99US/$6.99CAN
___Deadly Deals	1-4201-0686-4	$7.99US/$10.99CAN
___Game Over	1-4201-0687-2	$7.99US/$10.99CAN
___Sins of Omission	1-4201-1153-1	$7.99US/$10.99CAN
___Sins of the Flesh	1-4201-1154-X	$7.99US/$10.99CAN
___Cross Roads	1-4201-1192-2	$7.99US/$10.99CAN

Available Wherever Books Are Sold!
Check out our website at www.kensingtonbooks.com